CASEBOUND: 978-1-937356-31-6
TRADE: 978-1-937356-32-3
EBOOK: 978-1-937356-33-0

Library of Congress Control Number: 2013900113

Publisher's Cataloging-in-Publication Data

Collins, Theresa.
NOTOWN / Tess Collins.
p. cm.
ISBN: 978-1-937356-31-6
1. Murder–Fiction. 2. Family violence–Fiction. 3. Missing children–Fiction. 4. Angels–Fiction. 5. Kentucky–Fiction. 6. Appalachian Region–Fiction. I. Title.
PS3603.O4559 N68 2013
813–dc22

2013900113

Published by BearCat Press: www.BearCatPress.com/
BearCatPress logo by Golden Sage Creative
Front Cover Photograph by Paula Melton
Book design by Frogtown Bookmaker

NOTOWN

D1519631

OTHER BOOKS BY TESS COLLINS

FICTION

The Law of Revenge
The Law of the Dead
The Law of Betrayal
Helen of Troy

NON-FICTION

How Theater Managers Manage

NOTOWN
Tess Collins

BearCat
PRESS

San Francisco

Acknowledgements

Just as Notown is part of Randi Jo's physical, mental and emotional landscape, the neighborhood where I grew up, in Middlesboro, Kentucky, is part of mine. When I lived there, Noetown had the reputation of being the rough part of town. My grandparents moved there in 1942, even though Granny had tried to talk Granddad into moving into town onto the fashionable Cumberland Avenue. But Granddad had to have his hunting dogs, so we became Noetowners. When I was a teenager, and many years after Granddad's passing, I lived with Granny and found out firsthand about the dangers of Noetown when late one night a drunken man swaggered into our yard. That was also the night I learned Granny slept with a loaded .38 caliber Smith and Wesson under her pillow. Whatever the man had in mind, he skedaddled at her yelling that she would cap his ass.

We had great neighbors there, Bill and Paralee Webb, and Jim and Myrtle Walters. We looked out for each other, and there were many good people living in Noetown who did the same. So while my fictional Notown is inspired by the place I grew up, for purposes of this story I've drawn its darker aspects. Had I not grown up a Noetown girl, I could never have written this book, and so, to that community I owe much of my fictional roots.

I also want to thank my mother, Anna Ruth Cosby Alwood, for remembering details of growing up in Noetown in the 40s and 50s; my sister and Doctor extraordinaire Cindy Collins Code for helping with the medical aspects of this story; Helen Latiff Coleman, Joddy Collins and Jessie Collins for the million little details I always email them and ask if they remember, and they usually do; and finally, my late father, Joseph S. Collins, who left me a wealth of memories on a cassette tape in hope that they might help me with my storytelling. They did so much more than that, Daddy.

My sincere appreciation to Waimea Williams, who has been a great supporter of this book from the very beginning; James N. Frey, who never hesitates to remind me: "it's about the conflict, stupid"; and Beth Tashery Shannon, whose eagle eye is measured with a mystical understanding of character.

Dedicated to my Aunts, most of whom are also Noetown girls:

Aunt Nancy Sullivan Cosby
Aunt Sandy Holder Cosby
Aunt Sue Richardson Cosby
Aunt Thelma Cosby Marsee

And in memory of:

Aunt Delores Cosby Frohwerk
Aunt Dorothy Finch Collins
Aunt Helen Knowles Collins
Aunt Juanita Collins Latiff
Aunt Maude Fletcher Collins
Aunt Patsy Cosby Love

1

That Day . . . June 30, 1987

For as long as Randi Jo Gaylor could remember, fear had been her guiding angel. She even knew what the seraph looked like: broad wings laced with chain, rope-tight muscles flinching at nocturnal sounds, surly eyes squinting in the dark, spread talons anticipating attack. And yet, It knew how to mimic defeat–a pleading, pitiful gaze that begged for mercy, baring purplish gums and jagged teeth. At times, the hollow sound of submission had been Its survival. Maybe if life had been kinder to Randi Jo, she might now be holding a wedding corsage instead of a gasoline can ready to torch a man she'd once loved.

He stared at her with eyes of fear. Licorice-colored irises followed her as she paced in front of him. His pasty forehead sweated raindrops and she wished she could

1

see his mouth–that know-it-all grin had once made her tingle like a teenager meeting a movie star. She peeled a side of gray duct tape from his cheek. Fear-latticed eyes glared at her on the edge of panic. She paused, thinking, *there's that word again.*

Fear.

She pressed down the tape and gave his jaw a smack. His wrists twisted against nylon cord trapping them tightly to the chair arms. He'd given up kicking out his spread-eagled legs, also tied firmly. Her humble grandfather had built this oak chair, infused it with his valorous mettle. Strong wood. Strong chair. Holding her worst enemy.

"Ship to China's already sailed, sweetness," Randi Jo mocked words he'd once said to her. "So drop the crabby act." She set the gasoline can aside and stared past the man tied to the chair, out a window she used to call the Daydream Portal. Her gaze traveled down the wrinkled hillside, across rusted railroad tracks scorched from overloaded L&M trains hauling coal from the mines. In her memory the haunted wail of a train whistle rumbled on a cold fall day, mixing with the crunch of her feet kicking dead leaves along the track. Running parallel to them was a weathered two-lane road, over-paved until it protruded from the ground like a swollen tongue. Wink's Market clung to an older chunk of Laynchark Avenue. The store remained one of her favorite childhood haunts and stirred memories of candy melting in her mouth as she watched a lanky teenage boy sprawled on the steps licking an ice cream cone into a swirl. Hunger pinched her gut.

Randi Jo knew to wait until dark before igniting the blaze, or the Quinntown Fire Department might make it up the hill before the deed was done. At night they wouldn't come as quickly as for a fire in a more prosperous neighborhood. Townfolk thought Notown was the home of nogoods, good-for-nothings, and the poorest white trash in Crimson Country. Three streets, half a dozen hills, two thousand residents, and if half of it burned down, Quinntown would consider that a favor from the good Lord.

Crimson County anchored the southeast portion of Kentucky, deep in Appalachia's Cumberland Mountains. The big show was Contrary, a place everybody aspired to go, where there were beauty shops and banks, restaurants and jewelry stores. Flowers grew in planters lining the main street and creek banks were, for the most part, clean and free of yesterday's trash and discarded washing machines. To the east sat Quinntown, a white-trash cousin that acted better than it was, and Notown, its retarded little brother, the secret both communities tried to hide in case the outside might be looking in.

Notown led up to the mines. Its roads had crumbled from oversized coal trucks, the air was dusty with soot, the ground water poisoned, and every other hillside sodden with cancer-ridden old folk who refused to give up their unfiltered Camel cigarettes. Meanness ran in people's veins. Gangs of boys would throw rocks through your windows and knock down your mailbox as a rite of manhood. Most had been or would be in jail before their sixteenth birthday. As they got older they'd find a girlfriend, slap her into submission, and then pop

3

out babies for welfare money. The women were more likely to buy Maybelline makeup than food for their babies, dyed their mousy locks ice-blond, and ordered sluttish clothes from Fredericks of Hollywood. From girlhood they knew how to hold onto a man even if he occasionally strayed with a sister, cousin or best friend. After a hair-pulling knockdown, life eventually got back to normal. There wasn't nothing good about Notown that Randi Jo had ever known.

Her stomach growled. She looked over at him, still as a tree stump probably for the first time in his sorry life. He wasn't going anywhere and there were a few more items she had to buy. He grunted as she opened the door. "I'll be back," she said and blew him a kiss. "Promise."

Outside, June smelled like strawberries. Cautiously Randi Jo ambled down the forty-five-degree slope. Houses dotted the steep hillside like mountain climbers hanging on for dear life. Somehow the feeble pole porches held them up against wind, rain, flood and the carnage of man, almost as if they had sprouted from a fallow earth. Not one building had changed since she'd been a child growing up here. The Dunway house that kids thought was haunted because it looked like a vacant-eyed skull. A clutch of four-room cabins lined the railroad track, yards were littered with rusted-out washtubs and disabled cars and furniture whose stuffing had seen better days. From one house radio gospel tunes rang out, from another rock-and-roll.

Quickly Randi Jo looked up and back at her mother's house. Chalkboard walls. Tin roof. The concrete porch was all that would stand if a strong wind shifted direction. This house defined her. Perched crooked on the hill, not facing the sunrise or the sunset, it seemed like an out-of-season fowl with no sense of direction, but to Randi Jo it was the one place she could breathe. *Randi Jo Gaylor, the nobody from Notown,* the downtown kids used to tease her, elongating *no* and *No* into a little song.

She crossed the railroad track and cut through a backyard to the main road. Mrs. Cooley weighed three hundred pounds now and couldn't twist her neck to see who might be on her property. Ever since her only son died in Vietnam she'd sit in her porch rocker every afternoon, rain, shine or snow, counting the school kids who walked by as if waiting for a ghost to pass or for Armageddon to arrive. Farther on, Connie Phillips parked a green van painted with American eagles behind her house but didn't notice the petite woman looking both directions before crossing Laynchark Avenue. Nor did Nora Pryor as she hung white sheets on a clothesline. On husband number six with thirteen kids, two of the girls pregnant and none of the boys living at home, Nora positioned the sheets to hide her current husband's personal patch of marijuana.

Wink's Market had been Randi Jo's hangout as a young girl and she wondered if that family still owned it. The boy who had been eating ice cream was long gone when she arrived. The building's off-white paint had dulled with the thickness of several coats. Redbrick planters lined one side where pansies caught the late afternoon sun. The rusted red-and-gold weighing machine was gone and Randi Jo felt a sad pang of what used to be. She swung open the door and a chime wrinkled the air.

A blond-haired girl of about eighteen perched on a counter stool, reading *Glamor* magazine. She glanced up, studied Randi Jo, then went back to flipping pages. The smell of cooking wafted past, a meaty stew and dinner rolls. Pretty much the same, Randi Jo thought, as she looked around the one-room store that would have been the living room of a house. The Winks had lived in the back, a door to their quarters covered by two chenille blankets hung like drapes. A wooden beaded curtain had replaced those and a black terrier nosed its way through it to see who had entered.

Randi Jo leaned down and scratched the pooch behind the ears and the girl glanced over. "Mighty pretty dog," Randi Jo said.

"Sylvester's my Momma's." The girl went back to her magazine. "I prefer cats."

Randi Jo bought chips and soda, a bottle of Mr. Clean cleanser, a sponge, plastic gloves, pack of Marlboros, and a lighter. As she dropped them on the counter she noticed a rack filled with pink and white Sno Balls. The memory of marshmallowy sugar spread through her mouth. She chose a package of white, holding it in both hands like the tiniest of infants. Maybe if they'd had white Sno Balls all those years ago, she would never have fallen in love with Connor Herne.

2

When I was nine . . .

Pink Sno Balls were on the top shelf and I couldn't reach them. Chocolate cupcakes were on a bottom ledge but they lacked the coconut taste I craved. I was only fifty inches tall, small for my age. When my teacher, Miss Singer, acted concerned about my size, Momma told her my daddy was a little man, so not much else was ever said.

Old Mr. Wink sat on a stool behind a crumbly Masonite counter reading *The Crimson County Sun* and smoking a pipe that sent a whiff of nutty-flavored tobacco into the air. I kept an eye on his reflection as I studied soda bottles and picked out an Orange Crush and Lays potato chips. I only had fifteen cents and didn't want to spend it all. If he would turn around I might be able to shake a pink Sno Ball off that top shelf. I wished even more that they had the white ones. I loved white Sno Balls. They reminded me of the first winter snow, when the air vibrated crystal and the world was clean.

Good thing Mr. Wink's wife ain't working now, I thought. Can't steal a thing under with her beady hawk eyes. She could grab a pack of Winston cigarettes stacked behind her, bag it with the other groceries, ring up the cash register, and still keep count of what boy was reading which Tarzan comic book in the far aisle. Mr. Wink, on the other hand, often fell asleep listening to his radio or he'd open his newspaper so you could pocket candy without him noticing. With him, it was all in picking your moment.

I waited. He opened the news page wide. The headlines were bold and announced something about people arguing over whether to make Israel a new state. I'd learned in school that we had forty-eight, so, you know, what's one more? I crept up beside the shelf, stood on my toes and, using the Orange Crush to give me a few more inches of height, popped the soda bottle through the wire stand and sent a Sno Ball up into the air. Catching it with my free hand, I slipped it under my skirt and into my panties.

Mr. Wink put down his newspaper and stared at me over thick glasses that made his amber eyes look like huge ladybugs. "Ready, little sweetie-pie?"

"Just this Orange Crush and chips." I slid a dime across the counter.

"Let me open that for you." He held the pop bottle against the backside of the counter and tore off the lid.

The aroma of orange sent sparks through my mouth. "There you go, little sweetie-pie."

"Thank you, Mr. Wink." I pushed open the front door and a shopkeeper's bell dinged. The hot August sun brought out a slew of kids playing around the railroad tracks. The Barton brothers were fighting and a crowd had gathered round them. Good. Nobody would notice me. I traipsed up the hill toward our house behind the high weeds overgrowing the banks of a dry gully. I could hardly wait to get the first bite of the Sno Ball. The best place to eat was in Daddy's fishing boat locked in the garage. If there was sugar around, my twin sisters would smell it and come running. Hiding my food was something I'd learned to do a long time ago.

The busted lock on a high window of the garage dangled by a screw. I pulled a ladder leaned against the coal shed over to where I could climb up and poked my head through the window. An oily, dank smell filled the dark room but strips of sunlight through the flat-board walls cast enough light for me to see. I pulled myself inside. It was a short drop onto a rusted icebox that we didn't use anymore since getting electricity. From there I stepped into Daddy's silver canoe. I liked sitting in the tip. It was small, pointy, and just my size.

Trying to sip the Orange Crush to make it last and tearing open the packaging of the Sno Ball was like a blur. I gulped more than sipped then pressed my whole mouth into that chewy marshmallow with chocolate blended in. For sheer joy I couldn't see as the flavors exploded in my throat.

"Who's in here?" my older brother called from the high window.

"Me," I told him sternly. "Go away, Pug!" I don't know why I said it 'cause I knew he wouldn't, and within seconds his head leaned in the window as far as his shoulders.

"What'cho you doing in here?"

"None of your beeswax. I said go away!"

He crawled the rest of the way in, landed on the icebox, and stepped into the boat. "You steal that?" He pointed at my Orange Crush, chips and Sno Ball.

"Did not. Bought it with my fifteen cents Daddy gave me last week."

Pug squatted, causing the canoe to shift. He was a fat little boy even though he wasn't all that much taller than me. He reached to take my Sno Ball and I kicked at him. He smacked me across the mouth and took it anyway.

"Mmmm," he moaned, staring down at me, chocolate and pink coconut on both cheeks as he bit into it.

"You're a snotty, fat pig." Tears welled up in my eyes and he made a face at me and took the Orange Crush and chips, too. Without so much as a word, he and my food were crawling out the high window. I sat on the edge of the boat looking after them, knowing there wasn't much I could do. "Fat pig!" I screamed after him. I heard him laughing as he climbed down the ladder. I kicked the other side of the boat, trying not to cry. I only had a nickel left. I picked at chocolate crumbs on the boat seat and licked them off my thumb, then crawled out the window and went to the house.

Mayonnaise and white bread, along with some powered milk, were in the refrigerator but other than that and two sweet pickles there wasn't much else to eat.

Unless you considered beans. Pinto beans simmered in a big tin pot on the coal stove. Momma boiled them up on Monday and that crusty soup pan sat there until Thursday, giving the house a salty aroma. I hated beans but ate a lot of them.

I crawled up on a chair and dipped in a spoon, dry and mushy from two days of being re-heated. I didn't want beans. I wanted a Sno Ball.

My sister Kim stood at a cracked mirror nailed over the sink, applying eye makeup.

"Pug took my Orange Crush and Sno Ball."

She spit on the tip of an eyeliner brush and began lining her eyes. "Pug's a pig."

"That's what I told him." My nose burned and I still felt like crying.

She looked over at me. "How much money you got?"

"A nickel."

She lined her other eye then cast a glance toward the living room. "Momma, me and Randi Jo are going out walking."

I could see the back of Momma's head as she sat beside the radio, leaning her ear toward it to make out the sound through crumbly static. "Hush up," she yelled back. "My story's on."

Kim motioned for me to come with her and we pranced down the hill to walk the railroad tracks and crossed to the paved road. We slowed down as we passed Wink's and looked inside. "Shoot," Kim said. "Ole lady Wink is perched at the register."

"Well, scrap that," I said and pointed to the street. "Let's go over to Notown Road. Least three stores there."

"Read my mind." Kim petted the top of my head and we walked on. "Wait," she said and jerked my arm hard.

"What?" Suddenly I saw why she'd pulled me back. Two colored men were crossing Gray's Pin, a hairpin curve that divided white Notown Road from the Negro section of Divergence. Gray's Pin was the only place where both races could go and so that area was called Gray. The coloreds would no more come onto Notown Road than a white would venture up into Divergence. Gray's Pin was shared, usually when a white was there the coloreds held back, and if a Negro was winding around the bend then the white people waited for him to finish crossing. If ever a white and a colored ended up on the same patch of land at the same time, there was always talk that somebody would get killed. But I'd never known that to happen. Maybe we were lucky or just had more common sense than outsiders supposed. It was like this–they have their road and we have ours, and all of us understood that.

I backed up against Kim and waited. Both roads curved onto Laynchark Avenue where our house sat high on the mountainside. Either white or colored could go on Laynchark, which led through Quinntown and over into Contrary, Kentucky, one long, snaky road growing out of Notown's rotting roots and ending up in Contrary's fine redbrick houses. Everybody in Notown wanted to live in Quinntown, and everybody there wanted to live in Contrary. Folks who lived in town were different. Somehow, they smelled better. I'm not sure why but we all acted like we'd been brought up by the Queen of Sheba when we went to town. Except for Pug, who always acted like a fool.

Kim held my hand as the two colored men crossed. One of them glanced at Kim. He looked away real fast and her hand tightened on mine. She tapped her foot impatiently as if they were taking too long. The two men continued up the road toward Divergence. Kim tugged me and we crossed onto Notown Road.

"New place at Stony Fork creek," she said. "Herne's Market and Barbershop."

"Sounds fine," I answered, but knew she wanted to loll around the bridge at the creek. That's where boys hung out.

I looked back at Gray's Pin. The two men had disappeared. I thought they might have followed us although it would have been crazy for a colored man to come on Notown Road. It was hard being around colored people. I was not supposed to talk to them or I'd get whipped.

3

I liked Kim. She was my older sister by six years but she treated me fine. There were nine of us in all, but half the time I couldn't remember the little ones' names. They were always screaming for something or other and I just yelled, "Shut up!" Let's see, there was Gene, Melvin, and Casper, the three boys younger than me, Kim, and Pug, there was the twins Patsy and Rhoda, also known as the three-year-old terrors, who did most of the screaming, and there was baby Gregory, who for a infant was pretty good and didn't cry much even though he did stink up the house. Pug's real name was Burl but he always got into fights, and once it took three deacons from the Holiness Church to carry him down the aisle and throw him out the door. The preacher banned him from services for "pugnacious behavior." Since then we'd called him Pug.

I was named after my father, Randy Joseph Gaylor. He worked in the coal mines, leaving the house around four a.m. and was usually asleep by the time I got home from school, so we didn't see him all that much unless it was summer. Daddy's foreman at the mines called him a squirrelly man who was part gnome because he could fit into the smallest places and still bring out a brimming bucket of coal. He was proud of that and usually at the end of the week had loaded more coal than any man on his shift. Momma was Malva. She traded paperback romances with her friend Brenda Cooley and smoked Camel cigarettes. She hollered a lot and after a while we tuned her out unless she was about to whip one of us. Mostly she listened to her stories on the radio. *The Guiding Light* was her favorite. She worried about those people on the radio and whether they'd be able to work out their problems. Momma is a worried kind of person. Kim and me kept the house. My job was sweeping and that was okay with me.

When Kim and me got to the bridge, Bo Raynes was smoking with some of his buddies so I figured it'd be a while before we went into the store. Kim sauntered past them and leaned against the concrete railing. Her body was long and curvy like Momma's and she practiced a half-tilt Veronica Lake pose. It worked 'cause Bo, who was a few years older than her, left his friends and lit her a cigarette from his own. I went to the other side of the bridge 'cause I got all choky when smoke was blown in my face. Down by the gurgling water, a blond-haired boy about my age played at the edge of the creek. He had built a dam from creek rock, pooling the water into a circular pond. Beside him lay a toy boat made of twigs, peeled coffee tree bark and grape vines.

"Hey, Randi Jo," Kim called out. "Bo wants to talk to you."

I skipped across the road quick as I could. Any time Bo noticed me, giggly swirls boogied all through my stomach. Bo's blond sideburns grew down his cheeks and he flipped his bangs back from his forehead with a short black comb. He flashed that kind of grin that made you want to do anything for him and I stared up at him like a puppy eager to please.

"Wanna make a dime?" he asked.

"What do I have to do?"

He pointed at a house on the opposite side of the creek. "Run 'round to the rear and tell me how many windows are on the back wall."

It sounded easy enough and, for a dime, it was a solid job, but to tell you the truth, I'd have done anything for Bo.

"Don't let anybody see you."

Kim smiled, loopy from the cigarette smoke, and one of her hands rubbed Bo's back. I re-crossed the road and crawled through a barbed wire fence, running the length of the yard. The house was set back a ways from the road. Brown creek rock formed its base and white tile sides set off the sparkling black tarpaper roof, partially shaded by a giant beech tree. Yellow husks covered the ground around the tree and purple irises grew alongside a concrete porch. I squatted, ducked under a window, and flattened myself against the wall. I counted four windows, two on each side of a back door. Around back a stone well built beside a smokehouse stood opposite a barn and chicken coop. Looked like some grapevines

16

covered part of a dog lot and out near the creek three white bee hives lined up beside an outhouse.

From inside the house, a woman's voice carried wavy as water and her song described the banks of the River Jordan. Peeking in the back door, I saw a brown-headed woman, her back toward me as she ironed. Don't think I'd ever seen a cleaner house. Bedroom with pink bedspreads and lace doilies on the pillows. This room seemed to be a catch-all space filled with a foot-peddled sewing machine, a brand new radio with a Victrola underneath it, and assorted canned foods lining several shelves. Peaches. Okra. Tomatoes. Green beans. Russet-colored honey still on the comb.

"What's workin' you?" a boy's voice asked.

I spun around fast as a dog chasing its tail. The boy from the creek stood a short distance away staring at me. He held his boat against his hip and scratched his head. My face heated up and my knees trembled. The awful feeling of being caught replaced the giddiness of Bo's favor. "Heard pretty singing," I lied. "Thought I'd listen a spell."

The woman's voice gently lifted out the open door. He glanced at the house and I turned and ran. At the road, I looked back, grateful he hadn't chased me off.

"Took longer than piss," Bo said, impatiently

"No windows," I lied again. I couldn't tell them about being caught looking inside the house by the boy. "Just a locked door."

"Dern it," he said and glanced at his friends.

"Let's haul over to Quinntown," a snaggle-toothed boy said. "Fancier houses over yonder." Bo got up to leave.

"What about my dime?"

"That ain't worth a dime." Bo wagged a finger at me.

"Kim!" I looked at my sister and pouted. She flashed a big smile for Bo and pinched his arm.

"She did as you asked. You owe her the dime."

He dug into his pocket and flipped the coin to me. I caught it and held it in my fist tight as I could. After Bo and his friends left, I sat on the bridge with Kim while she finished the cigarette. "They gonna rob that house?"

She didn't answer. Instead, she grabbed my hand and pulled me to the store as she flicked the cigarette into the creek. "Mr. Herne's in the barber shop so grab a Sno Ball faster than spit."

His door had a bell too, and he smiled as we came in and said, "Howdy-do." A mint-green wall split the store from the barbershop. Two barber chairs with lion paw arms sat opposite mirrors that reflected each other in eternity. The room smelled of lacquer, and mounds of hair were piled around one chair. Mr. Herne was cutting Vincent Maroney's hair and he had a lot of it. Some people said he was so hairy his momma must've been a bear. Kim gave me a nudge and I went to the store while she looked at barrettes clipped to a cardboard cutout of a smiling woman who favored Lana Turner.

The Sno Balls were on a shelf I could reach. Even though Kim said there was nobody else in the store, I liked to check it out myself and looked down the length of the room. I reached for the white Sno Ball, holding the edge of my dress so I could quickly scoop it into my bloomers.

"Little girl?"

My heart jumped like a spooked rabbit. Behind me, a teenage girl perched cross-legged on a counter like a cat hanging on a tree limb. I must've walked right past her and not seen. Either that or she had a way of making herself invisible. She wore thin wire-framed glasses that made her eyes seem big and bulged out like Mr. Wink's, and her dirt-colored hair was twisted into a topknot. I dropped the Sno Ball back on the shelf. "I'm looking while I wait on my sis." I pointed at Kim.

The girl closed the book open on her lap and hopped off the counter. She was taller than Kim and probably a few years older. "Think I can't see what you got up your sleeves?"

"I don't have any sleeves." My face warmed up but I looked into her eyes just as mean as I could. Kim could probably stomp her and I had half a mind to yell out.

Just then the door slammed so hard it covered the sound of the dinging bell. The girl and I looked in that direction. The woman from the house stood just inside the door, frowning like a frog and holding the boy by the arm.

"No, Momma!" the boy cried, his face twisted in a scowl.

She jerked him forward and lifted him into the barber chair. The girl went to the front and I followed her. Kim gave me a nod like this was the perfect time to get the Sno Ball but I couldn't help wanting to see what was happening.

"Everything all right, Mom?" the girl asked.

"Your brother has lice." The woman struggled to hold the boy in the second barber chair.

"Do I have to pick it out?" the girl complained.

"Leave me alone." The boy twisted but his mother held him firm. "Ain't got no lice!"

"Tempy," the woman said firmly to the girl, "mind the store." She nodded toward Kim and me, and suddenly Tempy turned toward us like a hawk on rats.

"Connor, hold still." The boy slipped out of the barber chair but his mother grabbed him by the scruff of the neck.

"Here, son." Mr. Herne stepped away from Mr. Maroney. "I'll take care of that lice." With a few strokes of the shaver Connor's blond hair fell from his head in cake-like strips. His hands gripped onto the lion's paws as if pain seared through him and his lower lip trembled. His cheeks warmed pink and finally, big puppy tears escaped his squinted eyes. With the last swipe of hair gone, he bolted out of the chair and whizzed passed me. The door banged in its frame and the bell swayed wildly.

"You got the money for that?" Tempy asked Kim.

Kim had been watching as well and took advantage of the haircut episode to slip a barrette into her bra. I could tell she wanted the other one too but now that Tempy was on us, she couldn't take the chance. I came up next to my sister and offered her my dime. After all, she was the one who got it for me so I guess I could do without a Sno Ball. While Kim paid for the second barrette, I went outside and waited for her.

Peering over the bridge, I saw Connor throwing rocks hard as he could into the creek. "Hey," I yelled down at him.

"Leave me alone!" he yelled. The peaks of his face were pink as cherries.

"You can get a cap to cover your head and it won't look so bad," I said.

He hurled the rocks, splashing water high as possible.

"They have 'em at John's Store for a nickel." I waited silently. "I'll loan you my nickel." I held out the shiny coin that I had left. He picked up a rock and threw it at me. It missed by a mile but I figured right now I wouldn't look over the bridge rail again. I felt sorry for that boy–Connor Herne. Until that time I'd always had a crush on Bo even though I knew he liked Kim.

Connor had pluck, challenging his mother like that, then taking his medicine. He reminded me of the wounded hero in Daddy's Jack-tales, and even though Connor had thrown a rock at me I had a feeling we could be friends.

Friday was the day we got meat. Momma beat it with a hammer, salted it and dropped the pieces in sizzling lard as all nine of us sat at the table squirming like bugs as we waited to suck in the salty, juicy taste. Momma always put some aside for Daddy. One time Pug sneaked a piece from his plate and she blistered his backside with a hickory switch. The big, oval platter painted with red roses floated out of the kitchen like a cherub from heaven; steaming and fragrant. Yes, Momma held it but all I saw was crusty, chopped steak. Me and Kim reached first, beating Pug to the plate because he had such short arms.

"Don't act like heathens," Momma yelled, picking up a slice for herself and retreating to the living room to listen to the radio.

This was probably the only time of the week one of us wasn't fighting with another. The room filled with slurps, grunts and gnawing as our teeth tore into the tender beef. I stopped only once, to help Casper cut up his meat 'cause he was only four and couldn't use a knife. Kim helped the twins do the same thing, but we kept our eyes on the older boys, making sure they didn't take more than their share. After that, the world ceased to exist except in our mouths and the occasional loud burp of static from the radio. Half the time I didn't know what kind of meat it was and I didn't much care. When I finished off my fourth piece, I leaned back in the chair, stuffed like an overfed puppy. Kim and the twins did the same. Their mouths hung open, eyes glassy and lids heavy. The four boys worked on the base of the mound of meat, and Melvin dipped his forefinger into the salty grease at the bottom and licked it. Wasn't long before even the boys dropped away from the table.

"Gonna pop," I said.

"Me, too." Kim closed her eyes and leaned back in the chair.

Our Friday ritual started in anticipation and ended in gluttony. Preacher Hicks said gluttony was one of the seven deadly sins but I thought that if people were really hungry, why would God care if they ate their fill? The boys went to the bedroom and passed out on their mattress. The twins curled up around Momma, still on the couch with her ear cranked toward the radio. Kim yawned, pushed her plate aside and rested her head on her arms. My vision blurred on our feast of the fifth day as my eyelids blinked, once, twice, then a swell of watery sensation covered me and I dreamed cornstalks towered over me. Dirt crumbled under my feet. Sun, hot on my face like looking into the coal stove. June bugs buzzed overhead. My feet were rooted into the ground with potato bugs gnawing on my toes and somehow it seemed okay. I woke up abruptly when it started . . . banging on the wall . . . every night for the last week, right after dinner. Kim popped up too, and we both stared at the wall, afraid to look away, afraid to acknowledge what we weren't supposed to talk about.

"Randi Jo," Mamma hollered out. "You know what to do."

"Why do I always have to do it?" I complained as I slipped off the chair and stretched.

"Don't sass me," Momma yelled back.

In the kitchen waited two plates of cooked meat and a brown bag also filled with meat, the grease soaking through the bottom. I took one plate and balanced it carefully so no juice would run off and hit the floor, 'cause if it did I'd get smacked. Momma snuggled with the twins in the corner of the couch, their brown heads curled in the crook of their arms and eyes half-closed. Then Momma sat up, took a drag from her cigarette, and nodded toward the door.

"Go on," she motioned with the cigarette, a line of silvery smoke curling up like cursive writing.

I balanced the plate in front of me and pushed open the bedroom door with my shoulder. Quietly, I passed through Momma and Daddy's room where the boys were laid out on their mattress. In the next room Pug was spread across mine and Kim's bed. Now we'll have to smell his stink all night, I thought.

No door between our rooms, only a sheet hung between two nails. But there was a door to a back room opposite our bed. Until last week it was where my brothers slept, but now they were on mattresses all around Momma and Daddy's bed while the twins slept on a foldout couch in the living room. The door to the backroom had an eyehole cut in the center about as big as my fist.

A big blue eye stared through it at me. No matter how many times I saw that eye, it sent shivers to my stomach and churned up the meat. I knelt and put the plate on the floor, never taking my eyes off the wide blue pupil watching me. The door opened just enough for a slender-fingered hand to reach out and pull it inside. A few seconds later, the same paw pushed out a dirty dish; grits still on it from breakfast. A sour whiff of stuffy air rushed past me, and the door shut just as quickly. I guessed that as usual Uncle Luther had smelled the meat and didn't want to wait for Momma to bring it to him so he'd banged on the wall.

The pounding irritated Momma to no end but she put up with it 'cause Uncle Luther was Daddy's brother. He was wanted by the law. I wasn't sure why, but he hadn't left the house since he came last week. I only saw a flash of him as he passed by my bed in the middle of the night. Pug wasn't too happy getting thrown out of his room but he was too afraid of a whipping from Daddy to complain. One night, I heard Momma and Daddy talking and something was said about a girl named Bette. I couldn't hear most of it, but since then Uncle Luther had lived in the backroom. If he ever came out, it would have been when we were outside playing. I wished he'd take a bath 'cause his room sure stunk. We kids were told never to tell anybody he was here or we'd be whipped. I knew what a whipping felt like so I never did. Nobody could ever find out that Uncle Luther stayed in our house. It was my Daddy's secret.

Out in the living room, I propped my back against the cold pot-bellied coal stove and listened to the Cas Walker Show on the radio. The twins were still sacked out on the couch and Momma was in the kitchen. Kim applied her makeup and changed into a crisp white blouse. Momma came out with the bag of meat, now bagged a second time to absorb the grease, and handed it to Kim.

"Can I go with her?" I asked.

Momma dropped onto the couch, scooting the twins toward her feet so she could stretch out. She looked over at me and winked. "Come straight home afterwards."

That meant Kim had a date. I followed my sister down the hill, glad to be out of the stuffy house and into some fresh air. At the road, we looked both ways. I knew what Kim had to do and I always thought I was kinda her look out. We waited until we were sure there were no cars in sight. Then, sure no one saw us, we crossed into Gray's Pin.

"Wait here." Kim pointed to the side of the road beside a patch of blue chicory dotted with honeybees that kept me on what was considered the white side.

Again she looked both ways and then hurried up to a clapboard shack that sat back from the curve of the Pin. The porch boards were jagged on the ends as if someone had gnawed on them through the years. She balanced the bag against her hip and knocked, glancing back at me and again down Laynchark and Notown. The door opened quarter way to reveal a tall colored man. He nodded to Kim, swung the door wide, and took the bag from her. Kim turned without speaking to run back across the road toward me. The tall man usually stepped out onto the porch, always giving me a good look at him. He had Momma's nose, or I guessed it was more right to say Momma had his. His hair was straight black, cut just above his collar. Gray bug eyes and wide mouth that was a mite big for his face, just like Momma, too. Only difference was his skin, tan like milky coffee.

Kim took my hand and we walked down Notown Road. We never spoke of the colored man though I guess we both must've known he was related to us. In our minds we held him at a distance, a mean distance, a kind of pout-out-my-lower-lip-and-dare-you distance. I didn't give any thought to what might have happened if he'd come out and started talking to us. This was just the way it was. He stayed on his side of the road and Kim brought him meat every Friday. That was the deal. I looked back once. He stood on the porch and watched after us. We were never supposed to tell anybody about him or we'd get a whipping. I didn't know his name and he'd never called out to me. He was Momma's secret just like Uncle Luther was Daddy's. I guessed if these were their secrets then they were mine, too.

Sooner or later, I'd look back and he'd be gone inside his house. Every now and then he'd sit outside on the porch in a chair made of vine-binded tree limbs and wolf down the meat. Reckon that was the only day he got meat, too.

"You can only walk halfway," Kim said. "I'm meeting Bo at the bridge."

"Thought you weren't supposed to be seeing him," I said. "Momma thinks you're dating the preacher's boy." Kim didn't answer me and I gave in first. "Can't I walk to the bridge?" I pleaded.

Kim didn't answer again. She seemed to have a lot on her mind and we were almost at the bridge before she told me to hurry home, with a warning not to tell Momma that she'd let me walk this far. I would never have told on Kim. She was my best friend, even better than Sissy Renner. I watched as she sashayed up to the bridge and sat on the concrete banister, smoothing her skirt like she was ironing it with her hand. Bo smoked at the other end, talking to two of his friends, then he broke from the pack, came over and put his arm around Kim. He was a lot older than her but Kim had him twisted around her little finger, as I heard said on one of Momma's stories. She looked in my direction and waved her hand for me to trot along.

It was okay that I couldn't stay. What I'd really come for was to walk past Herne's Market so I might run into Connor. I peeked in the door as I passed. Mr. Herne was behind the counter reading a newspaper. The headline read something about people still fussing about this Israel. I learned in school that we had forty-eight states and today I wondered why we needed another. Connor's house was set back from the road on the other side of the store and his momma sat on the porch shucking corn. I started to say hello, but her stern face was as strict as when she'd dragged Connor into the store. She looked up at me once and her expression wasn't any friendlier.

I smiled but she didn't smile back and I walked on. Then I saw him. In his backyard Connor swung on a tire that had been tied to the branch of an apple tree. Chickens pecked in the dirt around him and he'd swing in their directions to see if he could scatter the birds. Once or twice he did. I reckon his momma must have loved him some 'cause he wore a gray cap, the same kind they had at John's Store. I didn't feel brave enough to call out to him. Not with his momma on the porch like that. But there was always next Friday.

5

When I got home Daddy was hunched over the table eating his plate of meat. Momma sat with him smoking a cigarette and I noticed a hint of *Evening in Paris* that she always dabbed behind her ears before he came home. His skin was black as motor oil from coal dust and the chalky whites of his eyes were like fried eggs with green yolks. The twins peeked in the dining room door and made fun of him. He snarled and played back. "I'm Bloody-Bones, gonna eat me some children," he growled out. They screamed and giggled and ran to hide behind the couch. "You kids be good in there and I'll tell you about how Jack stumped a troll that lives under the bridge down by the railroad tracks."

"They'll have nightmares," Momma scolded him.

"Well, then how about how Jack climbed a beanstalk?"

"With a sore foot," I said to the twins to peak their excitement. "And even with his big toe throbbing with pain, ole Jack rescued the princess from a blue-skinned ogre and beat him to death with a magic drumstick that he'd borrowed from a traveling musician." I told it just like Daddy had told it to me when I was a little girl. The twins squealed and clapped their hands. I doubted they understood a word either of us said, but they enjoyed our acting out.

"Randi Jo, start boiling water for Daddy's bath," Momma ordered just as I had slipped into the chair beside him.

"You load more coal than Cecil Johnston today, Daddy?"

"More'n him and Bill Fitzhugh put together."

"Water," Momma reminded me.

I went outside and topped off the coal bucket from our coal shed, picking up medium-size wedges with my fingertips so I wouldn't get all sooty. It only took two big chunks of coal to fire up our stove but I didn't want to have to go back outside a second time if somebody else decided to bathe. At the sink I pumped water into a pail. After empting three buckets into a washtub, I filled every pot on our coal stove to heat the bathwater. Momma and Daddy talked in whispers. I leaned toward the door and listened.

"Law was snoopin' around today," Momma said.

"You let 'em in?" Daddy asked.

"Practiced my soap opera acting skills." Momma sighed a deep breath and I could hear her foot tapping on the floor. "He can't stay here much longer."

"He didn't do nothing, honey."

"And neither did the other two thousand Notown residents but that don't mean a hog's hoot."

"They'll railroad him."

"We don't need trouble with the Stark family."

Daddy didn't answer her, and Momma again let out a long breath.

A pot of water boiled over, hissing as it struck the stove. Some of it landed on the floor with a slapping thud.

"Randi Jo! I swear to God!" Momma rounded the corner and smacked me on the side of the head. "Can't you do a'thing right?"

"Momma, no!" My head stung and I held back tears as I crunched against the wall, holding in my hurt. She raised her hand to hit me again when Daddy stepped in front of her and picked up a pot of water, throwing it into the washtub.

"I got it, honey," he said.

"Don't you start bawling!" Momma tried to move around Daddy to get at me but he grabbed another pot and poured it into the tub, splashing some of it Momma's way.

"Malva, honey," he said, winking toward me. "I got to clean this soot off while the water's hot." Then, Daddy coughed. It was a deep, congested cough followed by a wheeze that shook his whole body. Momma handed him a towel and patted his back as he doubled over. He spit up black mucus and I held my breath waiting for the fit to pass.

In my mind, I prayed for God to heal my father. Just one divine act like the dozens I'd heard about in Sunday school. If all those ancient people could have miracles as great as the parting of the Red Sea, then why couldn't we have just a little one? Daddy didn't deserve that cough, hard as he worked. That strangling sickness inside of him was our fault . . . all of us kids. We were greedy little hogs consuming every piece of food he brought into the house and the price was his breath.

I took the towel from him and put it in the sink, trying not to look back. His reflection in the cracked mirror over the sink made my heart break.

He slowly straightened up, arms crossed over his chest to sooth the burn. His eyes closed and mouth strained as he slowly took in air, waiting for normal breath to come back to him. "Sure hope none of my kids ever work in the mines."

"I'm gonna be a movie star, Daddy."

Momma huffed, "Wipe up that spilt water, Tallulah Bankhead." She dumped the last pan of hot water into the tub. Daddy looked at me on my hands and knees, drying up the mess, and grinned. His white teeth glistened against his stained skin and the dank odor of the mines wafted off of him. "Get ready for bed, Pollywog."

"Daddy, I'm not sleepy."

"Look out of your daydream portal 'til the stars open their eyes and dance like Valkyries. They're good friends of mine and they'll sing you to sleep."

Daddy was always in a good mood. My eyes were green like his, a shade between moss and clover. And I was glad of that. I liked being the same as my father.

၅

Momma calmed down after awhile. Friday was her night to go dancing at the Quinntown Pool Hall with Daddy. With Kim out on her date, that left Pug in charge. Ick. He was mad 'cause he had to stay inside and we were all told to go to bed right after listening to Danny Thomas on the radio. The little ones usually fell asleep during the show and I carried them to their mattresses 'cause Pug was too lazy to help. The baby was with Mrs. Cooley and the twins slept in Momma and Daddy's bed until they got home. Pug stayed by the radio listening to *The Thin Man* and *Amos 'n' Andy* and sometimes singing with the commercials. I liked listening to those shows too but tonight, with the room to myself, I could get a little quiet.

In the bedroom, I counted out my dresses. This was the last Friday before school started and I wanted to make sure my clothes were mended and pressed. Three of my dresses were made from flour sacks, cream-white with blue flowers, another with pink and one yellow. Each had frayed-edge collars that looked like fine crochet. Kim had helped me sew them over the summer. They smelled slightly floury but everybody else wore them too, so nobody ever made fun. My other dresses were Kim's hand-me-downs, a green checked shift that hung a little long on me, and Momma's brown factory dress that she'd worn when she worked at the tannery during the war. It had been given to Kim but she hated that dress so much she deliberately hemmed it too short so that it would only fit me. Kim didn't think she looked good in brown. She liked bright colors. So did I, but I wasn't willing to take another smack on the head for not wearing it.

A crisp breeze blew through the window, lending a slight smell of autumn headed our way. I leaned on the sill and looked up at the September stars. In those specks Daddy had shown me dragons and princesses. Monsters that terrified armies and brave princes mounted on white steeds racing to the rescue. And Valkyries, hot-blooded fairies, dancing on the sky. Now and then one would shoot across the heavens like it'd been propelled from a cannon. Daddy called the window my Daydream Portal, and I called it that, too. Down the hill, twilight fuzzed the houses so that they looked like children tumbling down the hill. I liked the way I saw the evening world in my head. It seemed like a painting I'd seen in a book, like a dream I never wanted to forget.

But that night I had my first nightmare. That night, I dreamed the Fear Angel into existence and she became a constant companion for all of my days. After the radio was turned off and everyone in the house slept, I slept, too. It did start as a dream—marshmallow and floral, a taste in my mouth and a sweet odor in my nostrils. Too wonderful a place to exist even in my mind 'cause all at once a wild dog jumped at me, foaming at the mouth. It twisted into a female creature that crawled out of the muck like a horny toad out of pond scum. She shivered in her nakedness, her wings filthy with mud and manure. Unhealed scars marked her arms and she licked blood from a busted lip. She pierced me with ancient eyes, a hungry look that sent shivers up my back.

I jerked awake, realizing that Pug's hand was across my mouth. I could smell meat on his palm and I kicked out at him. He threw his legs over mine, holding me down. "Pug, stop it!"

He smacked my mouth and shook a finger. "Say a word and I'll punch you sideways." He grabbed my hand and held it between his legs.

"Stop it," I gurgled between his fingers, now over my mouth again. My hand was on something and he rubbed it up and down. I bucked against him but he was too big and his palm smothered me. Over his shoulder I saw it– The Eye. The blue Eye was watching.

Uncle Luther kicked on the door, causing Pug to bolt straight up. I scrambled to the corner of the bed, taking the covers with me and held them tight around my neck. Pug looked back and forth from me to the Eye. In the next room one of the twins called out, then the other one laughed as if they had dreamt the same dream. Pug froze and again pointed at me. I knew it was a warning to stay quiet. I clenched up like a fist in the corner, both walls against my back. Somehow I knew my safety was in stillness, waiting to see what would happen next.

Pug stood and adjusted his pants. He walked over to the door and kicked it, challenging the Eye. "I know what you did, old man. You spill a word and I'll tell the law where your carcass is stashed." Then Pug turned to me. "You keep your yap-trap shut too." He made his thumb and finger into a gun shaped and pointed at me.

My every muscle trembled from inside out. I wasn't entirely sure what had happened. I wiped my hand on the outside of the covers. Touching Pug where he went to the bathroom made me want to throw up. I'd tell Momma in the morning. No, I wouldn't. She'd probably whip both of us for what we'd done. I couldn't tell anybody. How could I? Pug would make fun of me and nobody would want to touch my hand. I didn't want anybody to ever know. Even if Pug had made me do it, I could never tell, never let them see it in my face. What would my Daddy think of me?

Some of the meat I'd eaten that night came up in my throat and I swallowed it back down, holding my clean hand over my mouth and wiping my nose. If I had wanted to cry, tears were hidden too deep inside to show themselves. Jittery knots tied in my belly and part of me felt like I wasn't in my body. I held this frozen position, hoping not to have to fend off another attack, wondering if Uncle Luther would come to my rescue a second time. We didn't have a clock with a second hand, but I'd seen one in the dime store in Quinntown. I put it in my head and imagined the seconds ticking by. How long? This couldn't last forever.

Across the room Pug bounced on his bed atop the covers. I watched him from my corner, afraid to move. My stomach pumped full of shame. The Eye stared and I held myself like an owl gripped on the highest barn rafters until Kim got home. Only then could I sleep.

6

School opened with a Labor Day parade and picnic even though it wasn't the official holiday. I wore my pink flour bag dress 'cause its wide hem would let me run full-steam in the three-legged sack race. Me and Sissy Renner had come in second last year and this year we planned to win. I had two holes in the bottom of my right shoe and a crack in the left sole, so Daddy helped me cut new cardboard inserts for both shoes. Now this pair would last at least another year. We used soft cardboard so I'd have plenty of "spring in my sprint" as Daddy said.

Schools from Contrary and Quinntown gathered by age groups at Copperhead Field in the park centered between the two towns. As we ambled past, the Contrary people sang, "Watch your toes, pinch your nose, here comes the nobodies from Notown!" Some of our boys waved their middle fingers and Sissy stuck out her tongue more than once. The Quinntown students didn't fare much better as the Contrary kids turned around, grabbed their ankles, and wiggled their backsides. One Quinntown girl yelled "Up your nose with a rubber hose!" Our teachers shushed us and a couple of boys got swatted on the noggin. After a speech from Mayor Floyd Stark, we marched by grade to Laynchark Avenue in Quinntown and lined the street to watch the parade.

The mayors of Quinntown and Contrary rode down Laynchark in Cadillac convertibles waving at people. Most of us just stared at the cars, long and black, with shiny red interiors that had automatic ignitions. People ooo'd and ahhh'd 'cause most Notown folk, if they owned cars, still had hand-cranked models. The politicians were followed by several coal mine owners: Lucius Carmack, Thomas Colson, Bobby Sevier, and the Contrary Junior High marching band. That included some Quinntown kids who they let play with them since their own school didn't have enough for a complete troop. Crimson County High had a whole group complete with majorettes. Finally came the miners, usually just a representative group of about fifty straggling in the rear, their carbide lamps on their heads and some carrying tin lunch pails. They were clean-faced and dressed in dungarees and work shirts. Daddy marched with them, his pickax over his shoulder. I hollered out at him and he waved, grinning so wide that you could tell his far-side teeth were missing. But still he looked like a shining prince to me.

The funny thing was, on the real Labor Day date the same parade would be held in Contrary, minus all the

Quinntown people. This parade was kinda like a present they gave us each year, maybe to keep us from complaining that their streets were better taken care of than ours. I heard some men talking about exactly that.

After the parade Sissy and I walked toward Copperhead Fields, where the games were held. I toddled along and motioned for her to slow down so several kids passed us 'cause Connor Herne and his buddies, Rusty Haskew and Herman Cahill, swaggered around at the rear. Sissy figured out what I was doing but didn't complain since she had a crush on Herman.

"Yonder it sits, the snot-colored one," Rusty said as me and Sissy came up beside them. He pointed down Marcescent Street at a green building called the Regal Hotel. "Let's sneak over and take a peek. We'll circle the block, walk the canal, and come in behind our class. Teacher'll never know."

"Get our backsides tanned if'n we're caught." Connor looked at Miss Singer marching like a soldier two classes ahead.

"Where ya going?" Sissy asked.

Rusty whipped his head around like a snake. "Hey! Who said your mouse-face could come back here and listen!"

"She only asked a question," I said, just as surly.

"Get your hindends back with the little kids or you might end up like Bette Moss."

I glanced at Connor, his cap worn sideways on his head, eyes expressionless like he didn't give a hoot one way or the other if I was there.

Sissy's lower lip trembled and Herman patted her shoulder. "Go on," he said to her. "Girls don't need to be around Marcescent Street."

"Follow me," Rusty motioned and the three boys trotted off.

"What's on Marcescent Street?" I asked Sissy.

She bit her lower lip, Rusty's scolding still bothering her. "It's where they do it."

"Do what?"

"You know . . . men and women . . . that hotel . . ." She cupped her hand around my ear and whispered, "It's a whorehouse."

"Oh," I said, not sure what that was. "Bette Moss must live there."

"She got her head sawed off."

"What?"

"Heard my daddy say the law is keeping it quiet. They only found her body. Even the police chief's hunting dogs couldn't track down her head."

"Lord Almighty! And now Connor, Herman and Rusty are off looking for the head?"

"It's said bloody sheets were thrown over on the canal bank. Probably went to look at that."

We continued walking silently, me thinking about Bette Moss's head and wondering about men and women and whorehouses. "Sissy," I decided to ask, "just what do men and women do at whorehouses?"

She rolled her eyes and cupped a hand at my ear again. "They touch each other between the legs and then the women make babies."

"Oh, yeah, now I remember." My cheeks warmed as we turned the corner toward Copperhead Fields and I saw my reflection in a car window. My eyes seemed droopy and sad, lips pressed in a flat line, jaws red like radishes. All I could think was touching between the legs and babies. Pug had made me touch him. I touched Pug between the legs. Was I going to have a baby?

7

Sissy and I came in second again in the three-legged race. She said it was because I still hadn't grown enough, but my mind was mountains away and my stomach flip-flopped like a frog trying to escape a container. How could I tell Momma about the baby? I sweated shame and prayed repentance to make it not be so. If I dropped dead where I stood, that would be easier.

Up on the hillside I hid underneath a willow tree and watched while Herman won the fifty-yard dash and Rusty came in second on the long jump. Connor missed his spot in the rope-climbing contest and Rusty took it, but only won second place again.

When I looked around for Connor I didn't see him even though his family sat just a couple tables away from mine. His mother busily set out baloney and biscuits. An old granny rested in the grass nearby, swatting flies from her swollen legs. His father talked to a group of men.

43

Over at my family's table Momma smacked at the twins to keep them from eating the pinch cake she'd made. Daddy tossed a giggling baby Gregory into the air. My gaze swept over the dozens of picnic settings and bunches of kids on the playing field. No Connor.

I walked to the edge of the woods where the canal emptied into a shallow lake. Rusty and Herman had returned from Marcescent Street. Where was Connor? They would have followed the canal to the lake, then run back over the hill and joined our class. That was the best way not to get caught by the teacher.

Tempy Herne paced on the far side of the canal where the forest met the water. She cupped her hands around her mouth and called out, "Connor!" I hurried over to that side. By the time I arrived she was twisting her hands in front of her like a cook worried that a cake would fall. Strands of hair had fallen out of her topknot but she didn't notice. "Brother!" she yelled at the woods.

"I'll help," I said.

She turned briskly and eyed me up and down. "Get away from me. Don't need your help."

"Two people looking are better than–"

"Scram, stupid girl!"

I slumped back, my shoulders scrunched up to my ears. She pushed past me and headed toward a cove with park benches and picnic tables. Her tone shivered to the bottom of my toes and I stood there praying that I didn't fall down. In the time it took me to breathe regular again, I'd dropped to my knees. Echoes of Tempy's shrill words still cut through me. Except for my mother, no adult had ever spoken so harshly to me. Minnows darted around a small pool, and I concentrated on them, trying to rid myself of the terror the sound of that voice had sewn into my muscles. As I stared, a boy's features reflected in the water. I whipped around.

Connor stood there, his face sagging like a wilted petal. He moved his lips but words did not form. I stepped closer and touched his arm. "Rivers of blood," he said. He stared like he was seeing another world, somehow caught in a place he struggled to escape.

A picture of a head dripping blood came into my mind and I swallowed hard, thinking Connor might have found it. His skin felt cold as creek water and he didn't appear to see me. "Your sis's hunting you," I said, shaking his shoulder. "I'll lead you back."

Suddenly, he let out a puff of air as if he'd been holding his breath. He recognized me and seemed embarrassed. Before I could say anything, he darted off and ran around the lake toward his family. I started to follow him but he plopped down beside his grandmother. I wondered what had happened to him out in the woods. Preacher Hicks sometimes said people go through a dark night of the soul when they get lost. They need to believe in Jesus to bring them to the light. Connor found his way out so I guessed he must've prayed the right way. Tempy was still on the far side of the lake calling for her brother. After she'd been mean to me, I decided to leave her out there.

The final event of the day was the tug of war. The Quinntown students defeated Contrary pretty easily so now they went up against Notown. Pug anchored the end of the rope for our side. The Contrary people drifted away, no longer interested since they had no stake in the matter. Behind us a man sipping corn liquor slurred, "Too bad them kids from Lincoln School ain't here. We'd win, then."

Momma's back stiffened and she stared straight ahead. Daddy looked over at her and she forced a slight smile. The Lincoln kids were Negroes. They never came to the Labor Day picnic. I wasn't sure why, their parents worked in the mines alongside Daddy and he never had a bad word to say about them. I had a feeling Momma was just as glad they weren't here. She didn't like being around colored people. And if any of us ever talked to one, we'd get a whipping. Mostly, I just didn't think about it. I snuck a peak at Connor, but he never glanced my way. Next time I looked, his family had left.

A starter pistol popped. Both sides stretched the rope taunt. Pug leaned his weight into a rear loop and that brought the battle to a stalemate. I could hardly look at him, and when I did I wanted to throw up. Quinntown had won last year, and wouldn't it be something if my piggy brother ended up being the hero of the day? Lester Corn, known for his spitting, turned the tide when he let loose a wad right into Jason Sevier's face on our opponent's front line. Jason lost his grip and Notown pulled the Quinntowners straight through a mud puddle. He jumped up ready to fight and may have even landed a punch or two, but Mayor Stark and several of his policemen walked among the boys congratulating all of them. Jason was pulled back, still cussing for everybody to hear.

"Momma," I asked. "What if we had another baby in the family?"

"Don't even think it." She half spit the words. "Your Daddy's promised me this 'un's the last. Barely got eats for the ones we got."

"Momma, what do the women on Marcescent Street do with their babies?"

"Marcescent Street?"

My cheeks grew hot and I stared at the ground. Her olive complexion had pinked up as well.

"You're never to set a toe on Marcescent Street. Hear me?" She pinched my arm tight and shook me like a wet towel, with baby Gregory balanced on her hip. "Don't let me hear a blather about Marcescent Street ever again."

"Don't you know a girl named Bette Moss got her head sawed off?"

"Shhhh!" she said in a firm whisper. Her eyes blazed and she glanced around to see if anyone had heard. "Say her name again and I'll knock your silly head into tomorrow."

"Malva," Daddy called out from down the hill. "Car's packed, let's get the young'ins and get home." He looked at me, realizing something had just happened.

Momma corralled Gene, Melvin and Casper, and nudged the twins with her leg. They headed toward the car, leaving me standing. For the second time today I'd been hollered at for no reason and my insides trembled like I stood wet and naked. Daddy knelt down in front of me. "What is it, Pollywog?"

"Daddy . . ." I looked into his green eyes, starburst wrinkles shot out from the side and long lines embedded across his forehead. "Daddy, I . . ." I sniffed and looked away.

"You want to ride on my back?"

I nodded and he turned around and let me climb on. The steady gait of his walk was like an old plow mule we'd once owned. It was comfortable and safe. A stiff breeze had come up so his shoulders braced against the wind and as I looked above his head, suddenly the world couldn't touch me. I loved my Daddy. He made even the deepest hurt better.

At the entrance of the field a man distributing leaflets gave away groceries from the bed of a black truck. "Come on, folks," he called out. "Don't swallow the government's combustible vitriol that sits ready to explode in your belly. Here's real food for hungry babies."

Daddy gave them a wide berth and sat me on the hood of our car.

"They're handing out food, Daddy. Shouldn't we get some?"

"No!" Momma and Daddy answered in unison.

"We don't take charity," he said.

"Especially from them," she echoed.

Daddy jacked his foot up on the car bumper and cranked the starter round and round. I looked over at the man wearing the derby hat and bow tie. A black-haired, skinny woman in pants joined him and took over giving out the leaflets. I didn't notice anything wrong with them but just about all the Quinntown and Notown people walked by without taking anything–leaflet or groceries.

I didn't know if it was pride or pressure from neighbors that no one else had grabbed a bag. I was sorry 'cause there were sacks of flour and I could have made me a few pair of bloomers. "But if the food don't cost nothing?"

"In the car," Momma snapped.

Daddy pulled me down off the hood. I figured Momma would have smacked me if I had gone over to her. Inside our Ford, the twins were yakking in their own special language and Casper and Melvin pinched each other. Gene napped while Pug admired his blue ribbon. I slid in front to sit between Momma and Daddy.

"Why don't you get back here?" Pug asked.

"Cause I'd have to smell you," I said.

"When I move to the big city," he sneered, "you're not invited, Randi Jo."

"Sooner you're out of the house, the better."

That shut him up.

Momma and Daddy exchanged a few words I couldn't hear but when they got in the car, everybody except the twins and Casper quieted down.

"Randi Jo, boys, Pug," Daddy said in a serious voice. "Your Momma and me want you to hear something. See those people standing yonder?" He pointed at the man and the woman in pants giving out papers and free food. "They're Communists. You're never to take anything from them, ever. Hear?" He waited until each of us, except the twins and Gregory, said *Yes*, and then we drove home.

The sky turned red in the mountain crest, making the land look like it was on fire. As our car chugged along, I went over in my head everything that I needed to know about my life. No talking to colored people. No talking to Communists. Never go to Marcescent Street. Never tell about Uncle Luther. Never tell about the man who lived at Gray's Pin. Never mention Bette Moss.

I thought I had it all down. I just didn't know what I was going to do about this baby.

When we got home Kim lay across the bed crying. Momma came into the room right behind me and Kim sat up and looked away. At first I thought my sister might be sick. "Feeling poorly, Kim?"

She glanced up, not at me but at Momma, and looked away again just as quickly. Momma froze but only for a few seconds. She shuffled past me and pinched Kim's chin between her thumb and forefinger, twisting her face toward her. Kim stared into Momma's eyes, then looked down. Momma yelled up at the ceiling, "Lord God Almighty, no!" She slapped Kim hard across the cheek, knocking her back onto the bed.

"Momma!" I ran to Kim's side and jumped up on the bed, thinking I'd take the whipping for her even if I didn't know what she'd done. Kim sobbed into her hands. Momma stomped from the room.

I patted Kim on the back but she couldn't stop crying. Just as fast as Momma left, Daddy came in, his footsteps hard thumps on the raw board floor. He yanked Kim up by the shoulders. "Who is it?" he asked in a gruff voice I'd never heard from him. "Randi Jo, get in the other room," he ordered.

"I'm sorry, Daddy, I'm sorry," was all Kim whimpered.

I slipped toward the foot of the bed.

Momma returned with a hickory switch and laid into Kim before I knew what was happening. I fell back on Pug's mattress, frozen at what I was seeing. Daddy kept shaking Kim, demanding to know who, and Momma switched every square inch of my sister's bare skin. Her cries were pitiful and every thrash made ripping sounds so I thought she might get cut to pieces. I put my hands over my ears and buried my face in Pug's pillow. Then Daddy left the room and seconds later the front door slammed.

I raised my head to see Momma hit Kim with the switch a few more times, then she also left the room. I heard her ordering the boys and the twins to go out on the porch. Scooting beside my sister, I touched her shoulder in the only place that looked like it wouldn't hurt. Her arms were covered with red welts and slices on her cheek were dotted with blood. "Kim, what's happened?"

She stared at the wall. When she tried to speak her voice hiccupped and moaned. Momma appeared at the door again. She carried a tin washtub and dropped it on the floor. Something in her hand gleamed. She pulled Kim's best blue dress off its hook and threw it in the empty tub. Then she tore her white blouse into pieces and continued to fill the tub with Kim's clothes. I saw the gleam again and knew what it was–gold foil on the cover of the pool hall's matchbooks. Momma struck a match.

I'd seen plenty of lit matches but somehow this one set my blood ablaze. It tumbled through the air like a dancing Valkyrie. I could hardly believe what I was seeing. Momma grabbed Kim's pink linen party dress and threw it on top of the smoldering clothes. I'd been with her when she stole that frock off the rack of Colson's Dress Barn. I'd been Kim's lookout, so the dress had a special meaning to me, too. Kim watched, unable to move.

"There!" Momma screeched. "All your little whore clothes, now you can't run after every tomcat prowling the road." Her eyes were stern and she bared her teeth like she might growl. "It's that Raynes boy, ain't it? Wait 'til your Daddy gets hold of him."

Finally I realized what this was all about. A flurry of thoughts scrambled through my head, dazed as the smoky haze rose and drifted out the window. A boy had touched Kim between the legs and now she was going to have a baby. "Momma," I said, daring to touch her arm. "Maybe it wasn't her fault."

For the first time Momma looked at me. "I said outside! You need a switching, too?"

I looked at Kim, not wanting to leave her. My sister motioned with a nod for me to go. The dissipating smoke filled my lungs and made me dizzy. Behind the wall Uncle Luther coughed and part of me wondered why he didn't kick the door and help out Kim the way he'd helped me with Pug. My insides twisted like gnarly rope.

Outside, I ran around the house to the barn, climbed the ladder and fell over onto the icebox. Curling up in the tip of the boat, every muscle trembling like I was freezing. But I wasn't cold, I was afraid. Terror slipped down my throat like oil, filling me with a combustible vitriol that I wasn't sure I could keep down. The wings of the Fear Angel closed around me and hid me from the sight of humankind. I knew then I belonged to her.

9

I was lost at school without Kim. Momma had been keeping her home and she stayed in our room, hardly a sound ever coming from her. Even though Kim went to the county high school, she had always walked a quarter mile out of her way to meet me and Gene at Montgomery's Market at Notown Road and Wilson Lane. Even in two feet of snow or if the sun was blistering, she'd be there. We'd play word games and practice my spelling until we got to Laynchark, then cross somebody's backyard to the railroad tracks. They paralleled Laynchark until the mountains closed in around our pack of houses hanging on the hillside like lanterns on a tree.

At recess I didn't hear Miss Singer ring the cowbell and sat outside staring at the creek. When I realized that only the first grade students were left on the playground, I hid behind the coal shed and waited for school to finish.

September had turned chilly and I huddled against the wall with my flour bag dress pulled over my knees. Once I peeked around the corner at the two-story redbrick building. Smoke puffed from two chimneys and I could see students standing to recite or answer a question. I thought maybe I could sneak in and sit behind the coal stove where it was warm. Maybe the teacher wouldn't notice . . . but if she did, I'd get whipped. Connor was in the upstairs classroom and though I rarely saw those kids except at recess and lunch, I was still afraid he might hear about me getting the ash switch. No, better stay here.

Miss Singer never noticed I was missing and when school let out I waited until Gene came from first grade, then we fell in behind the rest of the kids like nothing had ever happened.

"Where's Kim today?" Sissy asked.

"She's sick," I lied. My younger brother glanced at me but didn't say anything.

"She was sick yesterday, too."

"Tummy miseries," I lied again.

Sissy must have realized it was a fib 'cause I dawdled at the intersection of Notown Road and Wilson Lane. I kept thinking maybe what had happened to Kim wasn't so bad and that she'd be there and life would go on the same as always.

Nearby the Communists had set up a truck with their bags of food. I guess they'd figured that what they couldn't give away to adults they could convince children to take. Sammy Jenkins and Lottie Crandall were at the back of the truck, eyeing the cans of Spam, corn, peas, bags of rice, and loaves of white bread.

"Reckon they'll take it?" I asked.

"They better," Rusty said behind me as he plopped down on a log bench. "The Jenkins have two new babies, they'll need the food."

"What do you think the women on Marcescent Street do with their babies?" I asked before realizing the words were out of my mouth.

Sissy snickered. "Why would you wonder such a thing?"

Rusty ignored the question and waved to Herman and Connor as they came out of the schoolhouse together. Herman had some licorice and sat beside Rusty to share. I chewed on the piece Herman handed me, closing my eyes as the peppery taste exploded in my mouth, but still I wondered where Marcescent Street babies went. Remembering Gene, I gave him half my licorice.

"Probably give them away," Sissy said matter-of-factly as if she'd thought on the question before.

"How could anybody ever give away a baby?" I was horrified by the idea, thinking, what if I'd been that baby? Rusty covered his mouth and whispered to Herman and Connor about what I'd asked in the first place.

"I've known people to drown a sack of puppies if they couldn't afford to feed 'em," Connor said.

Lonnie Phelps leaned into the Communist truck and a woman dressed in a blue fitted suit handed him a sack of food. I saw Raisin Bran and Sunbeam Bread brimming the top of the bag and couldn't help thinking how good it would taste. Billy Proctor took a sack, too.

Sissy stood, smoothed her skirt and glanced at Herman. "Got to get home." Herman bounced off the log like a grasshopper to follow her. Rusty gave Connor a poke in the arm and pointed at the two of them, hiding a snicker with a dirty hand across his mouth, then he pushed himself up, got a sack of food for himself and followed Herman at a distance so his friend could talk to his sweetheart. I should have gone with them, but I stayed seated. Not because of Connor or because I was waiting on Kim. I knew she wouldn't come. But I was thinking.

"You okay?" I asked Connor.

"What'd ya mean?"

"When you came back from looking for Bette Moss's bloody sheets you seemed real upset."

Connor rested his chin on his fist. "Ever wonder why she lost her head?"

"Seems the law would know."

"Daddy says it had to be done by somebody who knows how to hide in the light of day."

I swallowed hard, thinking about Uncle Luther in the room next to me. I'd overheard Momma and Daddy talking about him and somebody named Bette. Could Uncle Luther be hiding in the light of day? He seemed a nice enough fella when I scooted his food to him and he'd scared Pug away from me.

"Or it could be somebody she knew," I said. "Somebody who got mad at her."

"Hecka thing to do cause you're mad."

"Must've hurt." I wondered if Bette Moss saw the Fear Angel when she died, the way I saw that terrifying

58

image when I was afraid. And I wondered if I'd see the Fear Angel when I died. My hand went to my throat. "She must've been really scared."

"Anybody would be." Connor stared at the ground between his feet. "Didn't see the head or the bloody sheets, if that's what you're wondering."

"Reckon I was. You seemed kinda in another world."

He stood up. "If you don't mind, I'd rather not talk about it."

"I don't mind. There's things I don't like talking about either." I stood up, too, and looked down the road toward his house. He only had a little ways to walk and I had what seemed like at least a quarter mile. His hair had started to grow back but he still wore his John's Store cap, tilting it back on his forehead. I could tell then that his eyes were brown, not an autumn leaf brown but more a russet brown with flecks of gold.

A few more kids had taken food from the Communists and a couple of them walked past us. "Reckon them kids'll get whipped when they get home?"

Connor stared after Agnes Littleton, balancing a food bag as if it were a boulder, the load almost as big as she was. "Pop said the Communists saved lots of people from starving during the Depression."

I didn't know what a depression was and felt too silly to ask, but Connor seemed to be saying he didn't have a problem with people taking free food if they really needed it. And when I thought about it, some of the better-off students often gave me or the other kids without, their pencil stubs or broken crayons or even the last few sheets of paper if they had a new notebook.

Nobody ever said that was wrong. "Momma holds that gravy has saved my people many a time . . . and beans too, but I don't like them so much."

"See you on the flip side of night." Connor hopped off the hillside onto Notown Road and skipped along. I watched until he disappeared at the curve of the road, then I took Gene's hand, went over and got a bag of Communist food.

~

"Take it back." Momma pointed at the door. "This family does not take charity, young lady."

I set the bag of food on the table and started unpacking it. Flour, rice, celery, lettuce, bread, lima beans, sweet corn. This was good. It'd feed us a few days and the flour would last several weeks for biscuits and gravy if we could get some milk.

"I said, take it back," Momma repeated.

She wore her brown town dress and had her makeup done. After I pulled out the Gerber baby food from the bottom, I turned squarely toward her. I remembered how Connor had stood up to his own momma and drew in a breath. "I ain't taking it back," I said firmly, arms crossed over my chest. "We got babies in this house and we need all the food we can get, so we're taking Communists' food or Baptist food or Guiding Light food, I don't care. This week we're eating more than beans."

Momma bent over me but straightened up in a huffy stance. She stared down at the floor, then to the side, then back at me, though she didn't look me in the eye. "Well, we'll just let your Daddy talk to you, Miss Uppity." She grabbed her purse and brown cloth coat. "I'm going to Mrs. Cooley's house for a haircut. You wash the dishes while I'm gone and there's . . . beans warming on the stove." She looked at the floor again and then at me. I halfway expected her to take the food, but she didn't. When the door closed, my lips broke into a big grin. It was silly, really, 'cause I was lucky not to have had my face smacked.

I put the groceries away and left out a side of pinch cake on the table. The twins and Casper lay in front of the radio listening to *Hopalong Cassidy*. Outside I heard Gene and Melvin playing cowboys. I went to the bedroom to see Kim. She was packing what clothes she had left.

"Kim?"

"Sit down, Randi Jo."

"You can't leave, Kim."

She stared out the window, refusing to look at me. I moved into her line of sight. She picked up a pillowcase and folded it. "Bo's coming for me and we're going to Indiana."

"Where's Indiana?" I wondered if it was as far away as Israel.

"Up north. I'll try and visit after the baby's born."

"When?"

"After Christmas. Maybe in the spring."

"Kim, you're the only one who's always on my side." Crying welled in my chest and when tears spilled down my cheeks she touched them and looked at her fingers as if she held diamonds. Her forehead was lined and her eyes were red from her own weeping. "Let me come with you."

Kim sat on the bed, still unable to look at me. "You'll understand when you're older."

"I understand now, Kim. You have to let me come with you. I'm going to have a baby, too."

"What?" She turned toward me, squinting, her brow furrowed. "What are you talking about?"

A swell of embarrassment heated my cheeks until they felt tomato red. I looked away this time. "I can't tell."

Kim moved beside me and put her arm around my shoulder. "You can tell me, Pollywog."

I looked up into her eyes, green as Daddy's. She wiped my cheek with the hem of her dress and leaned her forehead to touch mine. "It's Pug," I said through trembling lips, my voice shaky. "He made me touch him between the legs and now I'm going to have a baby, too. So see, I can go with you. I won't be any trouble. I don't take up much room or eat too much and I don't mind taking food from the Communists."

Kim's gaze focused on Pug's mattress and something in her eyes hardened. I stared down at the floor, unable to look up. She put a hand under my chin and raised my face to hers. "You're not going to have a baby," she said. "And I promise you that will never happen again." Kim opened a cigar box and took out the barrette she'd bought from Herne's store. She pulled back my hair and snapped the barrette in place on the left side of my head. "You keep this hair clip for me."

"But what about Momma and Daddy? What'll I say?"

"Momma knows," Kim said matter-of-factly. She looked over at me, taking in the full measure of my body.

"But don't tell, Daddy, okay? Let Momma take care of that."

I nodded.

"Now sit there, and don't cry, and I'll tell you how babies are really made." Kim stared out the window and I wondered if she was daydreaming the way I often did. "To make a baby, a man gets on top of a woman and puts himself inside of her."

"They do not," I said, crossing my arms. "That can't be done."

"Their clothes are off, Randi Jo, and it's the most private part of a man opening to the most delicate part of a woman."

"I don't know why a girl would ever want to do that," I said.

"When you're joined that way and you look into a man's eyes and him into yours, you see his soul . . . and a little bit of that soul comes into you and makes a baby."

"Sounds nasty."

She smiled, then she stood up and kissed me on the forehead. I watched as she balanced a box of clothes on one hip and shimmied down the hill, across the railroad tracks to the main road where she got into a maroon car. It drove down Laynchark and curved off around the mountain.

I watched the car until it disappeared, then I watched the road. I guess I thought she'd change her mind. How could she leave? I mean, how could she really leave? Kim was gone. The room felt hollow and the air around me vibrated with the worst emptiness I'd ever known in my life. I wanted to cry, knew I should cry, but every thought

63

in my mind crumbled into the next, as unreal as a dream, until I couldn't focus on my own name. My tummy twisted and trembled like I was cold, but my eyes burned, unblinking, still watching the road. Still watching the road. Still watching the road.

❧

Pug came home by dinnertime with two black eyes and a knot on his head. He crawled into his chair and stared at his plate as he waited for some of the Communist food Momma was cooking up. He wouldn't look in my direction even though I was across from him and that was okay with me. Before the food came I got up and sat in Kim's chair so I didn't have to look at him and his beady eyes. He whispered to Gene about running away to the big city but I doubt Gene even knew what a city was. Couldn't help but snicker to myself, and every time somebody made a joke I laughed extra loud, knowing those bruises on Pug's face must hurt him awful. No one mentioned Kim.

❧

Without Kim, I stayed awake every night. The twins slept in her old side of the bed. I curled my knees into my chest, wrapped my arms around my legs and hunched up in the corner of the bed with the covers pulled close around my neck. The Blue Eye at the hole in the door watched every night as Pug entered, puttered around the room, and finally lay on top of his covers. I wore Kim's barrette to bed after figuring out that the wire part of it was sharp as a needle. If Pug came near me again, I'd stick him. Guess that's why Kim gave it to me.

Usually my head shifted, finally coming to rest against the wall, and I dozed until a sound jerked me awake. Most nights it was a burp or grunt from someone sleeping. Uncle Luther must also have slept at some point because late at night he wasn't watching. His room still smelled bad but I had come not to mind. Sometimes Pug sat up looking at me. I stuck out my tongue at him once and he rolled his eyes and faced the wall. Then, I went back to staring out the window at the coal-sky with its blinking stars saying hello to me and I wondered if Kim was watching them, too.

10

Harry Truman beat Thomas Dewey for president and Daddy bought a bunch of newspapers with a picture showing Truman holding up the headline announcing that Dewey had defeated him. Momma got mad at his spending that money because she had to do without cigarettes. People in Notown were excited about the election because Mr. Truman's vice-president was Senator Barkley from Kentucky. I didn't much care. Politicians seemed old, gray, and faceless, except Mr. Truman did have a nice smile and it was funny to watch little boys imitate the local men by slugging their fists in the air and yelling, "Give 'em hell, Harry!" Yet it all seemed far away to me, and I was still mad about my sister being gone.

Christmas came and went and no one heard from Kim or Bo. I looked up Indiana on the map and picked out several cities where I thought she might be. Someday

66

I'd go there and find her. She would have her baby by now and I bet she was sitting on a porch rocking it the way I had been told she used to do with me after I was born. Daddy never said anything about me taking food from the Communists and Momma never talked about Kim. Sometimes it seemed my sister had never been born. I noticed some of Momma's best white sheets were missing, so I figured that Kim had told me the truth when she said Momma already knew she was leaving. Kim's voice came in my head as she said, *"Momma knows."* I wondered if Momma knew where Kim was now. If she did, she never let on.

My birthday was coming up on April first and I looked forward to being ten. On Saint Patrick's Day the teachers gave a party for all the kids born in spring. That was when I found out Connor had been born on the same day as me. Sissy and I got cake and braced our plates on the windowsill as vanilla icing melted in our mouths. On the pane above us the teacher had hung a paper with the date April first and listing my name and Connor's.

Connor came over and inspected the lettering.

"How 'bout that," Rusty teased, pointing at me and Connor. "Couple of April Fools."

"When's your birthday, Mr. Rusty-behind-the-ears." I frowned at him.

Rusty's face darkened and I thought he might hit me. Herman jostled his friend's shoulders and they went to see if any cake was left over.

"Shouldn't say that to him," Sissy whispered. "Remember, he lives with Mr. Rounder."

At the orphan house. I realized that Rusty didn't know what day he had been born. Mr. Rounder took in boys and raised them until they were eighteen, though some had run away long before that. Stories were told about how they'd barely had enough to eat, and a man from the state went in to investigate. He cleared Mr. Rounder of any wrongdoing but it always seemed his boys were mangy as feral cats. For a minute I felt sorry for Rusty, but then he was back over, fluffing the back of my hair and calling me an April Fool.

The day finally ended and I sent Gene home with Emma Cleveland, who lived on the same hill as us, so that I could walk the same way as Connor. He ignored me most of the way, then I hollowed after him, "Be glad to be ten, won't you?"

"Don't think about things like that."

"What do you think about?"

He turned and looked at me like I was a rock. "Things," he said.

"Bet I can beat you to the bridge." I took off running and I guess he didn't want to get beat by a girl so he ran after me but I'd gotten too much of a head start for him to catch me. We ran right past his house, and I figured he was getting mad cause I was winning. I slowed down and let him pass.

"Won," he yelled, huffing for breath.

"Ready to tell me the things you think about?" When he didn't, I stepped closer to him and called up my best storytelling voice. "I think about what lives in the woods behind my house, fairies, gnomes and Valkyries dancing in the stars."

He hesitated and looked up at the sky. "I think about the stars sometimes."

Before I knew it we'd reached the end of Notown Road and he looked ready to turn back. "See that's more than just things." I hadn't noticed that the colored man sat on his porch just at the curve of Gray's Pin. He was so still he nearly blended with the wall of his house. When I saw him, he stood and waved at me. "Just walk away," I said to Connor, "pretend you don't see him."

"Hey, little bitsy girl, come over here," the man called out.

"Seems like he knows you," Connor said. "Let's see what he wants."

Before I could stop him Connor darted across the road to the head of the hairpin curve. I looked around and nobody was watching, so I followed him. The man towered over us from his porch perch. The closer I got to him, the more I saw his gray eyes against his chocolate skin appeared like stars on a moonless night. "Tell yer Mammy I h'ain't had no meat in a month of Sundee's."

I glanced at Connor to see if he reacted to the colored man. He stood politely beside me looking up at the man as if waiting for me to finish a conversation with King Solomon. My mouth wouldn't form words. I couldn't act like I knew him. Not in front of Connor. All my momma's warnings played in my head.

"You'll tell her, won't ye?" the man hollered at me.

I turned and dashed down Laynchark fast as I could, not stopping until I got to our turnout. My insides filled with scarlet shame at the idea of Connor knowing that I knew a colored man, and I felt sure he wouldn't like me any more. I sat on a rock at the side of the road and thought about how Connor had gone right up to the man, didn't seem scared or put off by him speaking to us. I started to wonder . . . what if the rest of the world was like that, and we only excluded people here in our little patch 'cause we didn't know any better? After I did my chores tonight I decided to think on it some more.

When I got to the railroad track I saw something going on at my house. Five black cars were parked all around the house, angled like fences to block us in. Kim, I thought, Kim's come home!

I ran up the craggy hill quick as my feet would carry me. When I got halfway up the hill I realized men with rifles stood on the front porch. My heart pounded. Daddy was hunched over in the back of one of the black cars. Its door was open and his hands were tied behind his back. A man on the other side guarded him but the lawman's gaze was focused on the house. Momma and the twins were huddled on the porch swing. Casper, Melvin and Gene curled at her feet like pups. Pug was nowhere in sight.

I crawled along the side of the car until I got to Daddy and whispered his name. He saw me and motioned me away. "I'll untie you," I whispered.

"No, Pollywog. It's the law. You go hide 'til this is over."

"They here for Uncle Luther?"

Daddy nodded.

I figured Uncle Luther was hiding under the house, opening the loose floorboard that Pug used to sneak out at night, back when it had been his room. If Uncle Luther barricaded his door from the inside, the lawmen would try to break it down. I looked up at Daddy. "I know what to do."

"Randi Jo," he ordered, a guttered whisper as loud as he dared. "Go hide."

But I was off . . . crawling around the back of the car, and when no one looked, I raced to the side of the house. I heard banging, so they were probably trying to break down the door. I raised my head to peek through my bedroom window. Two men were hammering on the door while a third stood back with a pointed rifle. The eyehole was blocked so I guessed that Uncle Luther had pushed a chifforobe against it. I crept around to the rear of the house.

At a back corner I twisted a loose nail holding in a baseboard. The wood slat came apart easily and a little door leading under our house opened up. I peered into the darkness and saw Uncle Luther cowered on the far side, digging in the dirt. "Over here," I called out.

He scurried toward me and thrust a canvas bag into my hands. "Take it," he said. "Hide it. Hide where they can't find it."

I looked at the sack, unsure what he meant. "Uncle Luther, run to the woods."

He shook his head. "Naw, I'm giving myself up, but you have to hide it, little girl. Promise me."

Before I could stop him he darted across the dirt, went back up into the house through the hole in the floor, and snapped the floorboards shut. I heard him yell out, "Stand back from the door and I'll come out unarmed!"

I could hardly think. I looked at the canvas bag in my hand. Sounds of the door breaking open and Uncle Luther's yells that he was an innocent man paralyzed me. Where to go? Men with guns were everywhere I looked. I ducked behind the garage and considered going into Daddy's boat. A lawman came out the front door and I pressed myself against the wall and held my breath, hoping he'd not see me. The shed behind the barn was full of coal and I'd barely fit in there. About forty yards away was our outhouse. I dashed toward it, splashing through mud puddles and hopping a shallow lake where the ditch had overflowed. Once inside I stared through cracks in the door, holding my nose at the same time.

Then I realized what I smelled that was so horrible didn't come from the outhouse. It was the bag. What in the world had Uncle Luther handed to me? I clutched the opening so tight that my knuckles turned white. Slowly, I pulled apart the mushy cloth and peered inside. Two eye sockets stared up at me through a wisp of red hair. I flung the bag away, horrified, and it landed on the edge of the toilet seat. My back smashed against a side wall. I wiped my hand on my dress as if it was soiled and birthday cake came up my throat. Without thinking, I used one foot to kick the bag into the toilet hole. It landed six feet down with a spongy thud and I threw up.

The sweetly sour smell of rot filled my nose and mouth. I squeezed my eyes shut and wiped my lips. The odor from Uncle Luther's room that I'd noticed all these months hadn't come from him not washing but from that poor thing with red hair. It was all I could do not to bolt for the woods myself.

It seemed like forever until the cars finally left. I raced to the house. All the children cried for Daddy. Momma wrung her hands and hollered, but I couldn't make out much of what she said. At last I learned that the law had arrested Uncle Luther for armed robbery and they'd also taken Daddy to jail for hiding him.

11

Uncle Luther got ten years in the state penitentiary and Daddy got six months in the county jail. They tried to break Luther about Bette Moss's murder. Daddy told Momma that they beat his brother with a belt and barely gave him food, but Uncle Luther denied ever knowing her until they showed him a picture. Her delicate pale hair and milk white skin had tugged a tear from his eye, and he said he was sorry to hear she was dead. But he never admitted to anything else.

With Uncle Luther gone, Pug and the boys moved into his room, giving the twins and me some privacy. I put them up at the head of the bed and slept at the bottom where I could look out at the stars through my daydream portal.

Without Daddy, the Communist food became all the more necessary and Momma even sent Pug with me to help carry it home. I walked on the opposite side of the

74

road and if he spoke to me I'd answer straight ahead like I was talking to the air. Mostly he just complained and bragged about going to the big city. Momma took in washing from some of the coal miners but even with that we didn't have enough to buy meat. I missed meat and the crusty brown flavor sometimes sprang up on my tongue if I thought about it long enough. I stayed up nights helping Momma wring out the black sooty clothes that took several washings to run clean. Working that late made it hard to stay awake in school, and Miss Singer rapped my knuckles several times a day until she finally gave up and just let me sleep.

I never told Momma about the man at Gray Pin wanting his meat. After school I came home by way of Wilson Lane so I wouldn't have to pass his house. I felt bad about him. He must've been hungry and I had nothing to give him. No way I could look him in the eyes. For a while after Uncle Luther's trial Connor's sister or his momma met him after school. I think that was so they could make sure he didn't walk with me. He avoided me anyway. Well, if that's the way his family was going to be, then that was fine with me.

&

On April first, my tenth birthday, I went to Herne's Market to see if I could trade one of my extra barrettes for some food. When I peeked through the window I saw Mr. Herne slumped in his barber chair reading the newspaper. Israel wasn't on the front page so I figured maybe they had stopped fighting about it.

The shopkeeper bell dinged when I entered and he got up and followed me to the store side. I stopped at a shelf stacked with honey jars. The amber gel was so clear I could see through it and my mouth watered.

"What can I do ya for?" Mr. Herne asked.

"Wanna see if I can trade this barrette for some potatoes." I said the word right, just like Miss Singer corrected anytime one of us said 'taters. I stared right up in his eyes. They were amber brown and his eyelashes curled a little on the ends. If he was going to tell me I wasn't good enough to trade in his store, I'd just as soon hear it now. The honey jars were stacked behind the counter as well and he noticed me looking at them. Our Communist food had run out a day ago and my stomach pinched me from inside. The honey would taste sweet as water on a scorching summer day. I thought for a minute that if he turned his back, I could slip one in my pocket on the way out.

"Figure I could see my way to that trade," he said, and clipped my blue barrette to the cardboard sheet with the Lana Turner look-alike smiling at him. He scooped six potatoes from a basket behind him and balanced them on my arm.

"Here," he added, pulling a honey jar off a shelf. "We're giving this away to some of our best customers to celebrate our moving sale." He put the jar in my other hand and came around the counter to hold open the door.

"Where're you all going?" I asked.

"Contrary. Bought a place on Laynchark Avenue right in the middle of town, got a store street level and apartment on top."

"All that way . . ." My thoughts ran to Connor. He'd no longer be going to school with me. I might not see him until high school, and only if he went to the county school. If he went to Contrary High, I might never see him again. "Always heard it's a good place to live." My voice trembled and caught in my throat. Mr. Herne's eyes studied me as I turned to leave.

"Take two jars," he said. "Foolish to move all this glass." He stuffed a second jar in my pocket and helped me re-balance the potatoes in my arms.

"You sure?" I asked as I stepped outside.

"Sure as creeks run," he said and winked at me.

I strolled on down Notown Road, my load cumbersome but not as heavy as my heart. Connor. Connor. Connor. His name played like a song stuck in my head. I would have to get used to him being gone... just like I'd had to with Kim.

As I arrived at Gray's Pin, the gray clapboard house was dark and I couldn't tell if anybody was home. I looked both ways and crossed over. The porch was rotting away and the door had no knob. I rapped on it and held my breath. Someone scooted around inside, and for a minute I was about to run. The door scraped open in a worn groove on the floorboards and a warm scent of burnt wood sailed past me.

The colored man was even taller now that I stood opposite him and his gray eyes shaded toward the color of ashes. He grinned when he saw me, his teeth wide and white, a space between the front two.

"Ain't brought no meat," I said.

He hesitated and looked behind me, I guess to make sure nobody saw us. "Sit a spell?"

I shook my head no. "You take the paper?"

He shook his head that he did not.

"Well, Daddy's in jail and we have to take Communist food. It's barely enough for the eight of us and runs out before the end of the week, so we won't be bringing you meat for awhile."

He nodded as I explained, his lips pressed flat and his brow curved. "Church takes care of me so you'ins just take care of yourselves, okay?"

I nodded that we would, and stepped back.

"Just a minute." He walked back into his house and I heard him fumbling through drawers, then he came out on the porch and knelt down next to me. "Give your momma this." In his fingers was a gold band with diamonds inlaid in the center. "She knows all about it," he said. "If it'll feed you kids, then it'll have done good."

I took the ring and put it in my pocket. It clinked against a honey jar. I pulled a jar out and handed it to him. He took it and nodded in thanks but didn't say anything else.

When I got home, Momma was leaned over a steaming tub of black wash water, rubbing a work shirt against a scrub board. I draped my coat on a chair, dropped the potatoes and the other honey jar on the kitchen table, rolled up my sleeves, then took the shirt from her. She tilted back in a chair and let her arms hang to the side. "We got some mayonnaise and cornbread for supper."

"Momma, look in my pocket. That man said give it to you."

She held up my coat and searched the pockets. The ring gleamed like someone had polished it every chance he got. She recognized it at once and her eyes softened in a way I'd never seen before. She pulled me to her and hugged me tight as she ever had, not seeming to care that my arms were wet and dripping soap on the floor.

It was a while before she let me go, pushing back and wiping her nose with the back of her hand. "I'd only heard stories of this ring, Randi Jo. Wasn't even sure it was real." She held it between us like a lost treasure now found. "I'm gonna sell it and we'll have food 'til your Daddy gets out of jail." She wiped more tears, pressed her fingers to her cheeks and gently rocked back and forth. "Never tell about this ring. Ever. Swear to me you'll never speak of it."

I promised and she sat me down beside her and smoothed back my hair. "You're old enough to hear this now, old enough to know a piece of what you are. This ring, it's justice handed down, a stolen righteousness that made the world a little bit fair again." The ring rested between us in the palm of her hand and we both stared at it like it was a promise and a curse combined.

"Stolen from the man who owned my kind," Momma said. "He had my great-grandmother anytime it pleased him and she bore his children with no complaint. He never said a kind word or gave a nickel to one of them. She died in a smokehouse shack and he buried her in a trench, no service for their kids, no headstone for them to visit. Her eldest ran, finally, but before he did he took

79

this ring. I don't know what he was thinking. Maybe that his momma was that man's wife in a way, and that he owed her more respect than throwing her body in a ditch. Maybe he thought it was his due. If anybody had caught him, they'd have hung him on the spot."

Momma gazed at the ring, her eyes fixed on the stones. "He didn't dare sell it. Could only pass it down and tell the tale. Your grandfather repeated the story to me time and time again, saying one day that jewel would redeem the crime that birthed us. We owe our lives to our ancestor's pain." Momma inhaled several deep breaths through her mouth and the tip of her nose pinked up like she might cry again. "Reckon this day is good as any for deliverance. So many generations has passed no one could ever trace it. Surely, no one could ever find out. It belongs to us now as a promise of our birthright. Bless Daddy's heart. Bless his heart. Bless his heart." She closed her eyes and swayed to and fro as if memories were raining down on her.

Whatever they were, she didn't tell me, but when she had finished the story I accepted the promise and understood the curse.

꩜

I washed the rest of the miner's clothes and hung them on the back porch to drip dry. Some time later everybody was in bed except Momma. She stayed up listening to the radio and smoking her one cigarette of the week. She had almost finished the pack and when it was gone, she swore there'd be no more. She nodded to me as I went to bed.

The sky outside my daydream portal was shadowy with clouds. The stars peeked through now and then, blinking like they longed for sleep. At the edge of the woods I saw her: the Fear Angel dancing jagged through high weeds and tree limbs like a demon scouring for souls. Her ragged and broken wings dragged the ground. She cooed and lashed her tongue, daring me to join her. Somehow I knew she'd been beaten back a step today. And what had tamed her was knowledge.

I thought about all the things that I knew. I knew where babies come from. I knew Connor Herne had been born the same day as me and that Rusty Haskew was an orphan. I knew Communist food tasted just as good as regular. I knew the kindness of a storeowner who saw a need, and a grandfather I could never acknowledge. I knew Momma was not as mean as she acted. All this knowledge had meaning and connected me to this small world I lived in. It might have been a step beyond my true understanding and was more a feeling than a fact. But there was other knowledge that was dangerous, and for now needed to stay hidden. I also knew that I . . . was the only person in the world who could find Bette Moss's head.

12

That Day . . . June 30, 1987

Randi Jo sprays Mr. Clean cleanser on the doorknob and wipes it with a paper towel. "Hungry?" She glances at the bound man, whose eyes follow her. "You ever been hungry, really hungry?"

He holds her gaze with a mixed expression of plea and demand. She answers for him, "Naw, your belly's always been full as a rabbit in the garden patch." She remembers the day they were married. She'd believed she was wedding up, into a society that would give her a solid place in the world. Now, she knows hiding in a dark patch is her lot in life.

Carefully she sprays the door molding and the wall around the light switch, anywhere she might have touched. Ripping off another paper towel, she douses it with more cleanser and wipes the flat surfaces of the bed's headboard. She doesn't remember touching it, but better to take no chances. The white chenille bedspread she'd pulled snuggly around her neck as a child still has a faint smell of bleach. The familiar odor comforts her. This piece of material is now over forty years old. Absently she asks, "Wonder what it's going to smell like in here once you're a crispy critter?"

Randi Jo smoothes the bedspread but its soft texture arouses too much nostalgia. She closes her eyes, willing herself not to fall into the past.

He grunts to get her attention. She ignores him. If he's afraid, she muses, he's not showing it. His fiery glare says he'll kill her in an instant if he gets free.

"Probably like pickled pig's feet," she says. She saunters around to the back of the chair and leans down next to his ear. "Or sour kraut." She flicks his ear with a finger.

He moans, trying to speak. She anchors the Mr. Clean bottle against one hip. "In case you've not figured it out, I've no interest in anything you've got to say." He twists toward her. She stays behind him so she won't have to see his face, and on impulse she sprays the cleanser over the top of his head. Some of the droplets get into his eyes and he jerks to and fro, cursing as best he can.

She stands in front of him holding the bottle like a gun. "Shut up or I'll spray you head on and blind you like a coal mule!"

He holds still, one eye squinted closed, the other glowering at her.

"Got to learn to listen better, darlin'," she says in the singsong tone he'd always used with her. She bends down, eye level with him, and strokes his cheek. "And if you can't listen, then just do what I say. Better it hurts a little now than a lot later."

With all his might he lunges at her, toppling the chair sideways and pulling the bed away from the wall. Randi Jo falls back, catching her ankle on one of the ropes. She barely feels the hard crash to the floor, thinking only, *Don't let him get you.*

His legs now have room to maneuver and he kicks out, catching her on the shin. She scrambles away as fast as she can. He bucks and strains against the ropes, struggling to free himself.

"Stop!" she yells. She grabs the gas can, holds it out and flicks on a lighter. The golden flame shoots high.

He laughs in snorty cackles as he pushes out the tape with his tongue. From one corner of his mouth he spits a question, "Why the hell you cleaning a house you're gonna burn down, stupid?"

She stares at him through the flame, biting back humiliation that only he can make her feel. How many times had he called her stupid, ignorant, a stinkin' rube? Extinguishing the lighter, she tucks it into her pocket. "This is my Momma's house, my Daddy died on the other side of that wall in a bed that to me . . . is holy. No matter what comes of it, this place deserves respect." She drops the gas can with a thud. "Respect."

"Our marriage that much of a bad trip?"

His voice sends waves of spiky spasms through her chest. She clasps her hands behind her back.

"Come on," he cajoles. "Let's hash this out."

"Don't move. And don't try nothing. I'm going to stand your chair upright."

"You . . . you ain't got the strength of a piss ant." He twists his head toward her. "Come on, untie me. We'll fix this and go back to the good times."

Randi Jo laughs. "What would you call the highlight of our relationship, when you kicked the crap out of me, or when I sent your carcass to jail?"

"Still got a mouth on you, girl." He manages a sideways smile, the loose tape exposing his right cheek. "No wonder I fell in love."

Randi Jo circles around him and tugs on the chair until the leg ropes are taut and he can't kick out at her. She braces her back against the chair, grabs the arms and lifts with the strength of her legs, but can only manage a tilt. She drops the chair and stands straight, looking down at him.

"Come on, RJ." His eyebrows rise to a peak. "You know it's not me you're mad at."

"Shut up."

"I ain't worth killing, 'specially when the husband you really hate is alive and kicking."

Randi Jo balls her right hand into a fist and punches him in the face with all the power of her gut.

13

When I was seventeen . . .

Momma had three more babies after Kim left: Hector, Butch and Cane. By then most of us were in school so it was almost like she was raising a second family. I helped out when I could, but like my sister before me, I sought the excitement of staying out of the house.

Pug lived with one of the Rickett girls and had a couple floozies on the side. I figured it was only a matter of time before somebody shot him. He'd been picked up half a dozen times for public drunkenness and spent a six-month stretch in the county jail for shoplifting. Pug never had a lick of common sense. Casper, Gene, and Melvin often stayed with him, and even though Momma and Daddy fussed, they couldn't force my brothers to stay home if they wanted to leave.

Nobody ever heard from Kim or Bo. Not a letter, not a call, not even a Christmas card. For a long time part of me was mad, thinking she'd put me aside like a worn-out dress. But I knew deep inside that wasn't it. She'd never forget about me, and someday she'd come home and tell stories of her wondrous journey to Indiana.

My life felt stuck in Notown, where the future was clear as looking through a rain-spotted window, and yet, as I sat in history class my daydreams drifted to a world where I was the special one, somebody who'd conquered her world. Crimson County high school, built on the backside of Quinntown's retail section, made my senior year a parade of window-shopping and ten-cent chilidogs at Curley's Café. I hung out with Holly Waller, Lynn Moore, and Sissy Renner, who was marrying Herman Cahill soon as she graduated. He worked at his dad's gas station and in a few years would take it over.

With graduation a couple months off, I had my heart set on secretarial school. I was the fastest typist in my class and Mrs. Fuson said I already took shorthand like a professional. Rusty Haskew joined the army and Connor was one of three in his class to go to college: Duke University in North Carolina. This weekend he was coming home, and he didn't know it yet but he was coming home to see me. I'd worked it all out with Holly and her rich boyfriend. They invited Connor to a cookout at Copperhead Fields and just as soon as history class was over, we'll change our clothes and go–

"Miss Gaylor!"

A voice like cracked ice jiggling in a cup interrupted my daydream. I sat up straight and looked at Mrs. Swets standing beside a map of the United States. "I didn't hear the question," I said timidly. There were a few giggles.

She rolled her eyes and tapped the map with a pointer. "What territory is anticipated to be our forty-ninth state?"

Her pointer continued tapping and the paper rustled each time she hit it. My mind was as blank as an undeveloped picture. "Israel," I ventured. The class erupted in laughter. My cheeks burned as if a match had fired beneath my skin.

"If you paid more attention in class and less to dime store lipstick, you'd go a lot farther in life, Miss Gaylor."

Every part of me tingled and sweat beaded my upper lip. A few girls looked over with smart-alecky smirks. I didn't know why it was so hard for me to pay attention in class. I'd look to my left and see a crystal castle high on a hill and me as the princess. Switch to my right and there'd stand Connor, holding flowers and reaching for my hand. Then, I'd look up at the teacher, but instead of the Constitution and the Revolutionary War, I'd hear her describe the vibrating legs of Elvis Presley and how his gyrations would change the world. For the next half hour I twisted in my seat until the bell rang.

"Randi Jo Gaylor," Barbara Dunaway sneered, her sweater pulled tight around a bullet bra. "A nobody from Notown. Doing a swell job living up to your reputation."

Holly put herself between us. "Least it's not your reputation, Barbara." Holly's bosom was twice the size of Barbara's and her sweater tighter.

Barbara swished her books off the desk and sashayed away.

"You shouldn't've done that," I said. "You know she's after Willie."

"Honey, she stands about as much chance with Willie as Mrs. Swets."

By Notown standards Holly was a success story. Her house on the creek bank between Laynchark and Notown Road was a shack even compared to ours, but she'd snagged Willie Carmack when we were in junior high and he didn't have eyes for anybody except blond-haired, blue eyed, busty Holly. The son of a coal mine operator, he was rich, good-looking, and had a future. Out of a class of thirty-two, only fifteen of us Notown kids made it to senior year.

We zigzagged through the rows of desks, Mrs. Swets giving us both a once-over through horn-rimmed glasses. Holly ignored her but I swelled with embarrassment like my skin might crisp from the inside out.

Holly leaned toward me and whispered, "Whatever our future, I don't want to spend fifty years talking about the same ole wars and watch my skin wrinkle like a rotten tomato." We giggled and hurried down the hall.

In the bathroom Holly fixed my lipstick and added mascara around my eyes. "You've got eyes just like Ava Gardner." She spit in the Maybelline and rubbed the brush over the black makeup, applying it skillfully to my top lashes. "Connor's mouth is gonna hang when he gets a load of you."

"Holly, you reckon we're nobodies from Notown?"

"Don't pay any mind to that witch."

"If Willie's family doesn't let him marry you and Connor never looks my way, it'll be because we're from Notown, don't you think?"

Holly inhaled deeply and dropped the makeup in her purse. "Honeychild, there's something beyond Notown and it's a thing these downtown girls ain't putting out."

"Holly!"

"You can be shocked if you want, but believe me, Willie ain't looking at bony Barbara with her bra stuffed full of tissues."

"She packs her bra?"

"Seen her go from B cup to C between English class in the morning and math after lunch."

We howled, and Holly made a back-and-forth measurement chest-level that made us cackle like geese. "Neither of us wants in that department. You're little as a mite and you're still stacked."

We trotted down the steps, our heels clicking on the concrete. Holly waved at Willie and I headed toward the school bus. She called back to me. "Pick you up 'round seven at Gray's Pin."

I nodded and headed toward the school bus. I needed to shake off my nerves and get ready to conquer Connor's heart. I'd rather do it without dropping my drawers but I didn't blame Holly. Willie was the kind of boy that was used to getting what he wanted, and if she hadn't put out, he'd have found somebody who would. She made holding on to a man look so easy as she slipped into the '57 Chevy and gave Willie a peck on the cheek.

I got in the bus line with the Notown kids and watched as they pulled away. The other kids watched, too–boys envious of Willie's car and girls coveting Holly's boyfriend. The Quinntown bus followed the Chevy, and Leonard Horn yelled out the back window, "Is Israel a street in Notown where the nobodies live?"

14

The house was quiet as night when I got home. Hector and Cane snuggled on the couch napping and Butch was in the corner playing with blocks. I paused when he knocked himself on the head with one then stuck a finger in his own eye.

Kneeling down, I took the block and pulled his hand away from his face. He didn't stop me or cry but made his sound. That's what we called it, Butch's sound. It was an *"Aaaaaaa"* wail, and depending on the tone we could tell what he wanted. He reached toward the TV set so I turned it on, keeping the sound off. He scooted forward on one haunch until I picked him up and moved him. His little face pressed against the set and his hand gently smacked the screen. Butch was now four years old. Doctors said he was sixty-percent blind. His withered legs would never grow. Nor would he talk beyond his sound or understand anything we said to him. But I

91

thought we all had a way of being with Butch that made him know us, and he must have felt we were taking care of him. Sometimes I even thought he had it lucky. He'd be a baby all his life while we had to go battle the world.

Momma sat at the table, arms curled around her head, dozing. She woke up when I passed through to the kitchen.

"Sorry, Momma."

She pushed herself up and rubbed her eyes. "I sent the twins and Gregory to eat at Mrs. Cooley's. I don't know where the boys went."

"Probably with Pug. I see him at lunchtime hustling spending money at the pool hall."

"I don't have time to hear about it, Randi Jo."

It bothered her how Pug had turned out but his pool hall winnings usually fed Gene, Casper, and Melvin. In the kitchen I pumped a pan of water to wash up. "I'm going out with Sissy and Holly tonight."

Momma followed me in and stood in front of a week-old pot of soup beans. "Good." She shifted from foot to foot and hummed as she stirred.

"Need me to wash up the babies or change Butch's diaper before I leave?"

"You'll be a good mother someday, Randi Jo."

I watched Momma's reflection in a cracked mirror over the sink as I rubbed a washcloth around my face, careful not to mess up any of the eye makeup Holly had done. "You doing okay, Momma?"

"Daddy missed a second day of work."

"He's probably dead tired, Momma."

"Doctor says he's starting to get that miner's consumption."

The word *consumption* sent fire through my veins.

"Daddy's not sick, is he?" I turned and leaned back against the sink. Momma only stirred the beans and dipped out a slice of pork fat. "I can stay home if you want, Momma." I didn't know what I thought that would do, but somehow Daddy being ill seemed to require the family being home.

She eyed me. "I don't worry about the boys as much. Always thought if I sent you kids to church, made you finish school, you'd do better than Notown."

"We're fine, Momma. I still go to church and the boys ain't dropped out yet."

"That Connor Herne still walking you home?"

"He's in college now, Momma. I only see him every other weekend. Should see him tonight."

"His family's got money."

"Guess so."

"Daddy owns a grocery store in the big town." Momma clasped her hands, paced the short length of the kitchen, and looked into the living room as if to make sure no one was listening. "In the back of my top dresser drawer is a purse full of makeup, some blue eye shadow, peach lipstick. A little apple-red rouge'll look good on you. Side shelf is a quarter bottle of Evening in Paris perfume. You take what you need."

"Momma, something you should know. So far, Connor ain't walked me home. He walks home with a bunch of us, as far as Herman's house, then catches the bus back to Contrary. His daddy won't let him drive his car over here. Afraid some hooligan'll siphon the gas."

"Plenty of churches on that side of the hill. To come over here and pray you either sin more than people know, or something's caught your eye."

"Momma, what are you saying?"

"You need to think on your future."

"I have. I'm going to secretarial school after I graduate. Mrs. Fuson says I'm the best typist in her class, almost fifty-five words a minute."

"There's no money for secretarial school."

"But Daddy said–"

Momma held my shoulders and stared directly in my eyes. "I don't know how long your Daddy has. Eugene Cupp only lasted two years after they told him."

"Momma, no! Mr. McKinnon has lived ten years yet and he's going strong, even still working in the mines."

"You need to take care of yourself, however you have to make that happen." She shot a quick glance at my tummy.

I turned away, staring out the window at a patch of grass that looked like a waterfall flowing down the hill. Part of me was embarrassed and part of me mad, but still I chuckled, realizing exactly what Momma was telling me to do. "You 'bout beat Kim to death for getting pregnant."

"Kim didn't have the sense of a turnip. Bo Raynes? Could she have picked trashier trash?"

"He loved her, Momma."

"No reason Connor Herne can't love you. No reason at all. You're pretty, will have a high school diploma, and

come from good people even if we do live in Notown."
She looked down at the scuffed linoleum. Her cheeks
pinked up and she bit her lip. "I made a mistake with
Kim."

I held a hand to my forehead, half disbelieving what
I heard. "A mistake? That's what you call it?"

Momma stamped a foot. "Okay, I run her off. That
what you want to hear, I said it. I didn't know any better.
Your Daddy didn't either. It was what was done to us,
and it's what we did to Kim. It was wrong but she's gone
and I can't do nothing about it. I got three babies in there
to worry about."

"Do you even know where Kim is, Momma?"

She shook her head and stroked my hair. Then
without another word she went into the living room,
turned up the sound on the black-and-white TV, and sat
next to Butch to watch *I Love Lucy.*

My stomach flip-flopped. I exhaled shivery breaths
that tingled all the way to my toes. What had we come
to? No better than a pack of vermin living in a flooded
rat hole and looking to survive by hitching our tails to
somebody with a better boat. Poor Kim hadn't stood a
chance and she'd known it. Kim had played her cards as
best she knew how, and now I had to play mine. There
really wasn't any choice in the matter. But I had
something different than Kim or Momma. I'd known it
the first time Connor Herne threw that rock at me. I had
faith. He'd thrown a stone, but I knew that act had meant
something else. It meant he hadn't wanted me to see his
pain, but I had seen it. I knew that part of him and never
used it against him or made fun of him or acted like his

tears made him weak. And Connor knew that, too. That's why he came to Notown to go to church. He was more comfortable here. Momma and Kim didn't trust the world, thought they had to trick it into giving them a life. Connor was honorable and so was I. How could he not fall in love with me?

I tiptoed through Momma and Daddy's room toward my own. The shades were pulled down, giving the room a yellow glow from the late afternoon sun. Daddy shifted, turning toward the wall and for a second I stood in place until I was sure I hadn't wakened him.

In my room I opened a cigar box and checked myself in a compact mirror. I looked okay, didn't need more makeup. More would make me seem . . . well, like I was looking for something. I picked up the barrette Kim had left me, pulled back the right side of my hair and clipped it up.

Daddy moaned from the next room. I froze. Waiting. Holding my breath. When no more sound came, I stood in the doorway and looked at him. His reflection in Momma's vanity showed him curled into himself with one hand held against his chest. His breathing scraped against his insides, and his lips, slightly parted, sucked in air with a wheeze. In a way he didn't seem like my father. For several seconds I got lost in a memory of him tossing me up in the air. It was Christmas Eve. He'd dragged in a Scotch pine growing on the mountain up above our house. It was only me, Kim and Pug in those days and I didn't remember much, but I remembered that.

Now, watching this same man bent in pain and grunting out his hurt made me want to turn away. I wasn't used to seeing him like this and part of me couldn't believe this bundle of flesh was my father. But there he was. My father, lying on a bed, dying. I realized then that just because I thought I knew the world, didn't mean that I was right about anything.

Audience laughter from the Lucy show interrupted my thoughts and Butch made an *"aaaaaaah"* sound along with it. The family needed Daddy. Butch would always need him. And I was in the way. Except for the babies, we all were a burden. Momma didn't mean it as a spiteful thing, but I knew she was speaking the truth.

From her vanity drawer I took out the makeup bag, then knelt beside the bed. Daddy's mouth was slightly open, showing the gap between his front teeth. "Please God," I whispered, "let my Daddy be okay. Let him live to see grandbabies and Christmases and let him kiss and make up with Kim and see me graduate secretarial school. I'll type like the wind and I'll be the best there is."

I leaned over and kissed his forehead. He murmured but didn't wake up. I just hoped that God heard me.

When I stepped into the front room Momma looked at the bag in my hand, nodded, and went back to watching Lucy. I stood at the kitchen mirror where the light was good and blended a fresh layer of scarlet rouge to my cheekbones. I touched ruby red to my lips and applied another layer of Maybelline mascara, then dabbed Evening in Paris behind my ears and on my wrists. No reason not to smell good, I told myself. Tonight, I had to make dreams a reality.

15

I read in one of my movie star magazines that Ava Gardner caught the eye of Mickey Rooney by ignoring him. I figured if that strategy had worked for her it was good enough for me. I made Ava my gut goddess, a queen I imagined myself to be. That's who I concentrated on when I slipped on my yellow dress that was tight across my rear end and brushed back my black hair the way she had worn hers in *The Outlaw*. The yellow dress was Momma's suggestion. Sometimes I wondered how she'd gotten so good at that kind of thinking.

On weekends when Connor came home he'd been flirty enough over the last months, walking me home from church, sitting beside me when the girls and me went to Pinkie's Drive-In for a Sunday afternoon hamburger. But there were always other people with us. These times couldn't be called a date proper. I would graduate high school in three months, so I had very little

98

time to move us through dating and courtship to marriage.

On the way to Gray's Pin I stopped at Wink's Market. A red-and-gold weight and fortune scale leaned against the side of the building. Crab grass grew as high as the foot scale, and a missing mirror in the top had rusted through. I stepped up and dropped in a penny. The needle bounced around then settled on one hundred pounds. My fortune clicked up beneath it. *Expect a bountiful surprise in the next month.* I'd gotten that one before but somehow today it seemed like a good omen.

Holly and Willie were necking in the front seat of the Chevy when I came upon them around the curve of Gray's Pin. Behind them the pole shack sat dark. I couldn't tell if the colored man was in there or not. Usually Patsy or Rhoda took him his meat these days, and since Daddy had worked steady we usually sent some store-bought candy along.

"Save it for the honeymoon, children," I announced. Pulling open the car door, I slid into the backseat as they broke apart.

"Good Lord, you look just like Ava Gardner." Holly twisted around to look at me and even Willie shot me a glance.

"Momma loaned me her Evening in Paris. Here, smell." I held up my wrist for Holly to take a whiff.

"One stop before the party, ladies." Willie gunned the gas, and gravel spit on all sides of us as he made a U-turn and sped down Laynchark.

Holly handed me a scarf and both of us tied up our hair as Willie zoomed into Quinntown, then pulled into the alley behind the Stark's Bar and Grill. A large pink neon stork hung off the side of the building and a smaller stork hung off the back wall. When the rear door bird was lit up that meant the bar was open. A scruffy, middle-aged man sat in a chair tilted against the wall, a wide-brimmed hat shading his eyes. He stood up as Willie stopped.

"You know who I always vote for, Buddy," Willie called out to him.

"You ain't old enough to vote." Buddy Stark's brother, Alvey, was the mayor of Quinntown and his cousin Floyd was Contrary's mayor. Mean as a wounded snake, Buddy had stabbed a couple of men in his bar and was pretty well known to cheat at poker and pull a gun to back up his winnings. Rarely did anybody ever challenge him, being the mayor's brother and all. The mayor owned the business but let Buddy run it, I guess to keep him busy and minimize the damage his brother might do if left on his own. Growing up with Pug, I sorta understood.

Teenagers could always get liquor at the back door. Willie gave him some money and Buddy got a case of beer. Since Willie's daddy was a Stark supporter, Buddy threw in a bottle of whiskey, slapped him on the back, and they both laughed.

In the car Holly breathlessly told me about Willie taking her to Knoxville next weekend to an Everly Brothers concert. With her jabbering I barely managed to slip in a question. "Reckon Connor got in this weekend?"

"Rusty's home on leave. Lynn'll be glad." Holly glanced away, distracted, her lips seamed together, then she looked back at me. "I'll let Willie dance with you if it comes to that."

Somehow, I didn't think that was the secret she held behind her pressed lips. Something was wrong. Something she wasn't telling me.

Willie set a case of Schlitz and a bottle of Old Crow in the backseat with me, then we were off to the picnic area at Copperhead Fields. Holly had to be hiding something she couldn't talk about in front of Willie.

When we arrived, Herman and Sissy were roasting weenies over a crackling fire. Rusty had wired a record player into a car battery and Elvis Presley sang "Don't Be Cruel." Herman mouthed the words and snapped his fingers to the beat. I scanned the dozen or so picnic tables and saw Connor a short distance away sitting alongside Lynn, who watched Rusty like he was a Greek warrior walking.

"Randi Jo," Holly whispered toward me. She touched my arm then hurried after Willie. "Just keep your head high."

I headed toward Sissy, calling out "Hey, Rusty, hi Lynn," not including Connor. There was no one here that I didn't know, so what in the world did Holly mean?

"Hey," all three of them said as I walked up to their table.

Connor was busy explaining something to Rusty about rocket propulsion. Sissy gave me an insistent look, dipped her head and whispered, "Did Holly tell you?"

With sudden enthusiasm Connor stood on the picnic table and pointed at the sky. "I'm telling you the Russians are up there right now, and President Eisenhower has got to make it so we're up there, too!"

Rusty waved him down. "We can take the Russians on land, air and sea. Why do we need to take 'em in space?"

I nodded to Sissy and we went over by the record player. "Tell me what?" I asked.

She looked back at the boys, who were opening beer bottles. The record clicked over and "The Wayward Wind" dropped in its place. Sissy bit her lower lip as if she didn't want to speak. "Connor invited a college girl home."

"A college girl," I repeated. My heart raced as I struggled to keep my face from reacting. "That's all?" I said as if it didn't matter. "Why, we're just friends, I don't care if he brings a date." I picked up a few 45s and shuffled through Elvis, Frankie Lymon and Paul Anka. "Let's play 'Allegheny Moon' next." I added it to the stack of records on the player.

Sissy glanced back at the boys. "I put you a weenie in the fire," she said. "It's almost done."

"Be there in a sec." She walked away, to my intense relief, and I bit my lower lip, breathing back hurt I was determined not to show. All those walks home from church, the milkshake he'd bought me, the hamburger he'd paid for when I was ten cents short. Then it struck me like a torn off tree limb had hit me on the head.

He was in college. He had a life there and knew plenty of smart gals who could talk to him about rocket propulsion and such stuff. I was just the dumb Notown girl who didn't even know the forty-eighth state, much less the territory for the forty-ninth. Coming home on weekends, the things he did with me were no more to him than buying a new pair of shoes . . . just something he did . . . nothing else. But to me, those minutes had been the sun and the moon. I knew what shirt he'd worn that first time he walked into my church. He had a scuff on the toe of his left shoe, and every third week, he came home with a store-bought haircut. I'd made a joke about him not caring for the homegrown variety and he had laughed about getting his head shaved years ago. But it was a joke to him, only a funny thing someone said about his childhood . . . to me it had been a connection. How could I have been so wrong?

Vaughn Monroe's "Red Roses For A Blue Lady" dropped onto the turntable and I thought of Kim. That was one of her favorite songs. I hadn't thought of her in a long time. What would Kim do now, I wondered. Could almost see her shaking a finger in my face to the beat of the music. Then it occurred to me . . . Kim would fight. I sucked in my hurt and turned around, my arms spread wide.

"Who wants to dance?" I called out, jiggling my hips as I jostled around the fire.

None of the boys moved, even though Sissy poked Herman in the back. Finally, Lynn came over.

"I need the exercise," she said, shimming up beside me. Rusty, Connor, Willie and Holly came over to join in but we danced as a group, not couples, and for the life of me I couldn't make myself catch Connor's gaze.

I sipped my beer and ate two hotdogs. My stomach flip-flopped but I made a show and talked non-stop about secretarial school. The girls gravitated to one end of the table and the boys argued about the civil rights goings-on in Arkansas.

"The Jenkins family lived over the hill from me my whole life," Herman said. "I played with Mo and Clyde, even got in rock fights with them, next day none of it mattered. We were boys again." He stood and jacked one foot up on the picnic bench.

Rusty got up to throw another piece of wood on the fire. "I played with some of 'em, too. Don't mean I want to go to school with 'em."

"What's it matter?" Holly yelled out, interrupting our conversation about Ingrid Bergman's return to Hollywood. "My great-uncle Harold is octoroon, so don't you be bad-mouthin' my kin, Rusty, or I'll take you out." Holly hopped up and circled her arms around Willie's waist.

She didn't care who knew about a black great-uncle, and that made her one of the bravest people I'd ever known.

"What do you think, Randi Jo?" Connor asked.

I was just finishing the last of my beer and had to spit some of it back in the bottle. "I was listening to the music."

"Schools in Arkansas," Connor said. "By the end of the next decade I'll bet all these places will be integrated."

"Asking for trouble," Rusty said, shaking his head. "Over the summer cooler heads better take charge or there'll be a knock-down-drag-out come September if those kids try to invade that white school."

"Well," I hesitated, wanting to say something intelligent for once in my life even if I hadn't thought it through. "We don't seem to have any trouble getting along here in Midnight Valley, not like up the road in

Coalfire. I mean, most of our stores and restaurants already serve anybody with money."

"Geeezzz," Connor said and slapped his head.

At first I thought I might faint. I must have said something awful.

"Randi Jo is exactly right," Connor said. "You won't find a Negro person in Coalfire. They've run them all off and you know what? They're the weaker for it." He moved toward me and put his hands on my shoulders. "You take us. We've immigrated the Irish, the Scots, the Italians, the Lebanese. Look at the businesses these peoples have started. Stores, restaurants. Most our Negros came to work the mines back in the 20s and they stayed and prospered into communities. Coalfire, on the other hand, is still a hole in the ground."

That town up the road from Midnight Valley was located in a neighboring county. There'd been a federal investigation last year when twenty-five of their Negro residents were found murdered, leaving no black people in Coalfire and only a shantytown at its outskirts called Spit. I knew this because rumors had run through the school that the folks from the black high school were going to come over and beat us up. It never happened, of course, and I think most of us knew it wouldn't. For some reason the boundaries of Divergence and Notown had blurred since I was a little girl. Now, we were all just poor people.

"What about the Negro teachers?" I asked. There was quiet. Only the popping wood in the fire. "If they bring students over to our school, what's going to happen to the Negro teachers?"

"See?" Rusty spit out a laugh. "Knew there was something bad to come of it." He roared a bigger belly laugh and got another beer.

Connor was looking at me like I'd said something he had never considered before. I only hoped it wasn't too ignorant of me.

The sun burned red and disappeared behind the mountains. The air cooled and I put on my sweater. Sissy set "Young Love" spinning on the record player, and she and Herman danced, soon joined in by Willie and Holly. I glanced at Connor staring into the fire and sipping his beer. He looked up at me. "That was an interesting insight you had about the Negro teachers," he said.

"Just popped in my head." The music pulsed as smoke drifted around us and the burnt odor mixed with the sharpness of beer. He smiled slightly, just one corner of his lips, and I knew he was about to take me in his arms. There was no date. I was the only girl he had eyes for.

"Come September we'll know if those Negro kids are brave enough to walk into that white school."

I leaned closer to him, closing the distance. "I admire bravery. I wish I were a brave person. I get scared a lot." I touched his cheek and his eyes rested on my face like it was the easiest thing in the world.

One of his hands rose to my shoulder. "Hey, you're going to have a birthday in a few weeks. Wonder how I know?"

"Hello, there," a woman's voice called out.

From down hill, a white shape emerged from the dark. Connor left the fire's golden circle and went to meet her. She wore a crisp white blouse and white quarter-length pants with flat tan shoes. A short red scarf about her neck was the only bright color. Her hair was black like mine, and a white headband held it back from her face.

"Everybody," Connor called out, "meet my friend Rory Parker."

She approached us with a smile and we all said hello. The boys stepped forward, leaving the girls in a semi-circle around the campfire. It was like they'd never seen a college girl before. Herman offered her a beer, which she declined, and Rusty held up an uncooked marshmallow on a stick.

"I'd love one," Rory said with a deep southern drawl.

The girls and me watched and smiled politely, but I saw the worry in Lynn's and Holly's eyes. They looked at me as if I might crumble like an ant hill. Sissy stayed beside me and rubbed my arm, making a point of telling me how pretty I looked in my yellow dress.

Connor took the marshmallow stick from Rusty and held it in the fire for Rory. "Toasty or slightly brown?"

"Oooo, toasty," she said, "slightly burnt."

He chuckled as if she'd said the funniest thing in the world. I walked away from the fire, stopping at the other end of the picnic table. Rusty had opened Willie's bottle of whiskey and poured himself a cup. I took the bottle from him and drank directly from it. He watched, eyebrows raised, but didn't say anything as I took another long hard swig and then coughed through the burn in my throat. "What do you think he sees in her?" I asked.

Rusty looked over his shoulder then back at me. He took in my yellow dress, seeing it in a new way as if he now understood a river's undertow. "Not a thing," he said. "Something like you walked my way, I'd barely notice some scrawny college girl."

I watched them. Sissy asked Rory where she was from.

"Grew up in Durham," she said, "but my Aunt Edna lives in Contrary, so when I found out Connor lived there, I decided to come visit."

"So Connor drove you up from Duke?" Lynn asked.

"Only got carsick once." They all chuckled, the girls crisp and polite, the boys hearty like it was the most hilarious thing since Jack Benny. "Been wonderful visiting Aunt Edna but she doesn't own a TV yet. Claims radio gospel is enough for her."

Connor offered Rory a crisp marshmallow, cupping his palm underneath it in case it dropped. They linked hands as she took it from him, blinking her blueberry eyes and whispering a soft, "Thank you."

I saw her soft gaze focus on Connor, open and in awe, like the surprise of discovering a baby fawn in spring. She was falling in love with him. The knowledge felt like boulders rolling down the mountains and burying me. Straining to keep my feet planted, my skin iced up as though I might break if anybody gave me a hard look. My thoughts burned with fear that everyone was staring at me as I struggled to act like none of this bothered me.

"Got you a hot dog roasting too," Connor said.

"My hips don't need that," Rory cooed.

He laughed as if she'd said another clever thing. "Got a long way to go before you favor Aunt Edna."

I took another drink of whiskey, now hardly feeling the burn down my throat. Rusty sauntered behind me, the heat of him surrounding me like a vibration.

"Dance?" he asked.

I set down the liquor bottle with a sharp clunk, walked over to the record player, and put on "In the Still of the Night" by The Five Satins. I swiveled my hips to the throbbing beat and my arms waved through the air. Talk faded. I faced them on one side of the fire and they were on the other, looking at me.

Flames leaped like sensuous Valkyries and the group froze into a blurred picture. I stepped into the golden circle created by the flickering light, hands resting on my thighs, swaying to the music, my hair swishing back and forth against my back. I held out my arms, rocking suggestively until a pair of hands rested on my hips, moving in rhythm with my dance. I glanced back and saw Rusty. Knowing those were his hands made me freeze, then I decided to do as Holly had said–take advantage of my assets. I twirled around to put distance between Rusty and me and catch sight of Connor. He sat atop a picnic table with Rory. Her back was toward me as he listened to her, but his eyes were on me.

Rusty grabbed the whiskey bottle as his gyrations mimicked mine. I took it from him and drank deep, the liquid numbing my throat as I gulped. Soon as I finished, I wanted to spit it out, but I swallowed and let my eyes take in the flames like I was possessed

A glimpse of Lynn shook me to reality. She squatted like a squirrel on a fallen log, arms clasped over her stomach, shivering. Her stringy brown hair hung into her eyes and tears brimmed the rims. I knew Rusty was all she had. What had this liquor awakened in me? A surge of nausea crested in my throat. I stopped dancing, held still to find my footing but bumped the record player, causing the needle to skid across the disk in a wobbly slur. The ground spun under me. I lurched, hand over my mouth, and darted into the woods.

Don't know how far I got before the retching started. Part of me prayed the other kids didn't hear and another side of me didn't care, long as I got this poison out of my body. The toxic soup fused my muscles and wrapped around my bones as dry heaves took over. Footsteps crunched off to the left as I held to a hemlock tree. Please, I thought, don't let it be Connor.

But it was. "You okay?" he asked.

"Shouldn't have drunk that," I moaned.

He chuckled, and embarrassment could have drowned me then and there. "Those guys . . . We have just as good a time without the alcohol. Don't know why they bring it, other than to prove they can get it."

I leaned against the tree and hoped the smell was not awful. I inhaled. It was . . . it was terrible. "Let's walk," I said, meaning to get him away from all this mess that made me look so bad.

"Got a better idea. How 'bout I drive you home?"

"What about Rory?"

"She has her aunt's car."

"I mean, won't she . . . care that you're with me?"

"Rory? She's just a friend."

I realized then that Connor didn't know much about girls. Rory was as in love with him as a woman could be, but that was all right because if he thought of her as a friend then I had to make sure she never got her foot an inch further in the door to his heart.

⁓

Connor drove a '55 Dodge his father had given him. I slipped into the passenger seat, popped gum in my mouth and rolled down the window to take in the breeze as we drove. Feeling better, I made a plan and worried that if I didn't carry it out, Rory would.

"Let's stop at the graveyard and get some air." I smiled at him. "Like to clear my head before facing the folks."

He pulled into a gravel parking lot of the Notown Holiness Church and we got out. I steadied myself against the side of the car, looking up into the cemetery. Rounded grave markers poked out of the ground like rabbits hiding in the tall grass and the glimmer from a neon cross burning in the church window lit the surrounding grounds with an amber glow. Connor got a RC Cola from the back seat, opened it on the door handle and handed it to me. I took a swig and then spit it out to clean my mouth. He patted my back and rubbed up and down.

"I'm feeling better now," I said.

"Pop'll settle your stomach." He chuckled.

"You think I'm funny," I said, half a tease.

"Naw, same thing'd happen to me if I drank beer with a whiskey chaser."

"Only thing I'll be chasing is the path to the outhouse."

Notown

He laughed hysterically, slapping his thigh and smiling wide. "Randi Jo, I swear, you remind me so much of what it is to be home."

I pushed my bangs back from my face and anchored the RC cola on the windshield wiper. "You miss us? Off at big-time college, why would you even think of anything back here?"

"I remember running to our Notown outhouse in the middle of winter. I tell that to some of my friends at school and they don't believe me." He looked up at the stars, his face pensive as if remembering last night's dream. "I never realized what I had around here. What a good place this is to grow up. Not perfect, but good."

"Bet you didn't tell about the coffee cans under the bed."

"Chamber pots," he chuckled again, recalling the old days. "No need to scare 'em to death."

"Most kids that get as far as college stay gone."

"Easy to think that until you're away from home and everybody makes fun of the way you talk. A mountain accent among southern ones is like a mangy dog in a poodle pack."

"Is that what it's like at Duke?" I stepped closer to look up into his eyes but he didn't answer. I put a hand on his shoulder and leaned my head on his chest. "I'm sorry. I hoped it would be perfect for you."

His arms embraced my back and we held each other, the silence around us marred only by a trill of a night bird. I closed my eyes, thinking about how Kim had explained sex to me. I knew the mechanics but I needed to make this so much more. I matched my breath to his, then raised my chin and kissed him. As I did, I let one hand slip down over his trousers and between his legs. My insides trembled until he moaned and kissed me back.

He lifted me onto the hood of the Dodge. My legs dangled and I wrapped one around him and pulled him close. "Randi Jo," he said between hungry kisses, "what are you doing?"

"This," I interrupted and kissed him. "And this and this and this," I repeated with each kiss.

"Are you sure? I . . . didn't expect–"

I kissed him again. His hand drifted down my chest and stopped on my breast as his lips found my neck. I let him touch me, hoping he didn't know my frightened heart raced like the spin of a wheel, hoping he didn't feel the tremble in my muscles, fear spreading through my mind like a flooding pond. I lay back on the car's hood and he was atop me, pushing up my dress. I heard the metallic run of his trouser zipper and closed my eyes, praying that I'd do this right. *Remember what Kim said*, I thought. *Remember how she said it was done.* I stared up at the stars wondering if they looked down on my triumph or my sin. But it really didn't matter. Connor would be back to visit in two weeks and I'd be here for him . . . always. Within seconds, the push and delightful rip inside of me. We held still, mouths pressed tight, slow rhythmic movement, better than dance. I looked into his eyes that seemed to catch a sparkle of every star. I guess you could say I saw his soul and with every kiss I begged a small part of it to come inside of me.

Afterward, a hollow void grew around us. He handed me the RC cola then turned toward the graveyard where the moon crested the hill. Raising his arms above his head, he stretched. "Guess that didn't stop the world turning like the teachers and preachers always said it would."

A spark shot through me. "World don't need anybody to look out for it."

He looked back at me and grinned. "But you do, don't you." He stepped toward me and ran his fingers through my hair. "I'll always look out for you, Randi Jo. You're one of the sweetest girls I know. Not conceited or stuck-up, not a selfish bone in your body."

"I can be selfish about some things." I tugged his belt and pulled him toward me.

He kissed me. "I'll let you be selfish on that." Then he kissed me again and rested his forehead on mine. "Wish I didn't have to go back so soon. Lot of work being the boy genius."

I laced my fingers into his. For now, that was about as good of a promise as I was going to get and I knew I had to make wanting me be his idea. "Whatever face you put on for the world is okay with me, Connor. Always know that right here with me, you'll find a safe place where you can be yourself."

He looked toward the stars. "World has a way of beating you to dust. Sometimes even the ground I walk on don't seem firm."

"I know you down to the bone, Connor Herne. Any time you need a nickel, I'll loan you mine."

He hugged me and drew in a deep breath. I wasn't sure where we stood. The coming months would open doors or close them. But I sensed Connor stood on a threshold of choosing between his old world or a new one. I could only hope what I gave him tonight tipped the balance.

I looked up at the waning moon and struggled to feel if any part of me had changed. I'd always wanted to be a good girl, for him as much as for me, but tonight I'd seen a prime example of what a good girl really was. What made Rory fit that image was where she came from and how she dressed. As a Notown girl I knew what people thought of me before I even walked into a room. I didn't have crisp white blouses or beauty shop-styled hair and never would. I didn't know much about segregation or going to the moon. I had changed, though. I knew what I was capable of doing for a better life, and I couldn't say it was a proud thing. *A good girl*, I thought, that was something I'd never have a chance to be.

16

Connor dropped me off at the railroad track just shy of eleven. He'd wanted to walk me home but I said I'd be okay. Most people around here left their porch lights on and I had just enough to see my way up the hill. A growling nausea still knotted my tummy. I walked halfway to the old outhouse before remembering that the new one Daddy and Pug had dug was twenty yards farther on. A mound of dirt covered that first tainted hole. A wave of wind seemed to flap around the dirt as if demons guarded this unholy patch of land where a woman's head lay buried in the unconsecrated ground of our poop hole. I felt bad, giggly, and queasy at the same time. Sweat beaded my skin and I could've sworn I heard the flap of wings hovering above.

I let the wind cool me down, held out my arms, head flung back, and stared up at the stars. The sweat dried as I gulped in air like water. I wondered if I looked any different, or if what I'd done would show on my face. I stared at the charcoal mound of dirt where I'd dropped a woman's head. No suspicion about that had ever followed me. I reckon if that awful deed didn't show on my face after all these years, then what had happened tonight wouldn't either.

Following the worn dirt path home, I promised myself to fix things nice for Bette Moss, make the ground look like a resting place for her. That was the least I could do.

The kitchen light was on as I slipped in the back door. Daddy stood at the sink shaving. "What are you doing up so late?" I asked.

"Got to go to work, young'in. Speaking of late . . ." He tapped his wrist as if he wore a watch.

"But you're sick." I touched his arm and leaned around to look at his face. His eyes were ringed with dark circles like a man who hadn't slept in days and his cheeks were as gaunt as a starved cat's.

"Feeling fine," he said, "and I'll be on time for the midnight shift."

"Daddy, I wish you wouldn't go."

"Hey, who's gonna pay for that secretarial school? I'm up to twenty dollars a day and for eleven kids that ain't much."

"I can get a job without it. Already type faster than everybody in class." I opened his lunch pail and added another slice of cornbread to the half he'd already packed.

"Honey, a job's hard to come by, best you be as educated as you can get." He kissed me on the forehead and grabbed his lunch pail, pick and carbide miner's hat.

"Let your momma sleep. She cut her hand tonight slicing cabbage for sauerkraut."

"She's gonna be mad when she hears you're gone."

A sly grin enlivened his face. "Making up is the best part of being mad. You'll understand when you're older."

"I think I understand now, Daddy."

"Hey, stop that growing up, there." He patted my head as he shifted a pick ax, shovel, and lunch bucket onto every part of him as if he were an old tree.

I watched out the window as he started his Chrysler, remembering when he used to put a foot on the Ford's front bumper and crank it. He could do anything, I'd always thought, and seeing him now hunched over the steering wheel in the middle of the night made my heart ache. I was afraid for him, afraid of his dying and no longer being among us. How could we go on without him? I inhaled a shivery breath and smelled the bubbling dread of an old acquaintance–self-doubt, shaky anxiety and hollow fear blew through the room.

Times had changed and so had I. In the cracked mirror over the sink I saw my flushed face, hair windblown and tangled. Could others see I was a woman full of secrets she could never tell? These eyes had witnessed a future I had tried to change tonight. These lips had told lies that would break another woman's heart.

Nagging scratchy thoughts. What if I was dead wrong and Connor had used me? After all, I'd thrown myself at him, given it away like a common whore. What if I got pregnant and Connor wouldn't marry me? What if Momma's big plan was all for nothing? What could I say to Daddy? How would I ever face him? And then a faint image over my shoulder gave off a malicious chuckle. She'd returned, expectant and haughty. Fear Angel licked her scabbed lips as if to say she'd been away too long. I whirled around to strike her but there was no one there.

Shadows from a passing train flickered on all sides of me. The rumble against the rails vibrated the house and my heart raced as if I was running in front of it. The shrill whistle pierced the walls, challenging the darkness, then the sound faded, leaving only the faint creaking of the cracked chalk walls. It all made me too jumpy to sleep and I picked up a tin can. From the refrigerator I took a head of cabbage, tore it apart, spread the leaves on the table and chopped it with the can's razor edge, but I cut myself too, just as Momma had. That's what happens when you use sharp things.

A memory of Kim swept through me. Only fifteen, she must have been terrified to find out she was pregnant, and agonized over what would become of her, but she'd really loved Bo. Had he loved her back? Maybe it didn't matter because it was all old history. Silently I thanked Kim Gaylor for letting me know what to do tonight. I guess I'd done as well as could be expected. Connor would be home again soon and I'd find out if he loved me. Until then I had to crush out the gargled hiss in my ear. The triumphant return of the Fear Angel.

17

Two months later Momma had me making sauerkraut again. I knew what that meant. At the sink she braced her hands on the rim, took deep breaths, and vomited twice. At the kitchen table I held my breath, stamping the tin can through a head of cabbage. She pumped water to wash out her mouth, then fetched what little sauerkraut was left in the icebox, brought the bowl to the table and sat across from me.

"I can never get enough of this, dang it."

"Momma, that vinegar's gonna eat a hole in your belly."

"Brenda Cooley used to crave sweet, I crave salty."

"Umm," I nodded, wondering why my tummy was as tame as a house cat and yet I'd missed my period this month. "You want a boy or a girl this time, Momma?"

"A girl if the Lord is good. I can't raise any more like Pug and Casper." She wiped vinegar dripping down her chin and finished the last of the sauerkraut, then drank the juice. "What's happening with the Herne feller?"

I squirmed uncomfortably and stared down at the cabbage. "Got a letter from him yesterday."

"You'll need more than letters when some college girl turns his eye and he has to make a choice."

Picturing Rory made me fearful that the college girl might have more sway over Connor than I did. I concentrated on the cabbage, keeping the sharp edge of the can away from my fingers. Didn't dare look up at Momma. She'd see right through me and I wasn't ready to let my secret out. I guess in the back of my mind, I was a little afraid what I'd done might be turn against me even if it had been Momma's idea. I hated not trusting Momma but Kim's screams still echoed in my dreams.

"It's a college girl he'll want to marry, lessen you take things into your own hands."

"Stop it!" I banged the can down repeatedly, shredding like a demon. "Why do I have to trick somebody into loving me?"

"Love is the least of what we're talking about."

I stopped cutting and Momma stared at me like she was looking in a mirror. A dinosaur could have stuck its head through the window and neither of us would've moved. Her eyes bored into mine but I held steady, not wanting her to see the truth. In that knowing way of hers, she leaned back in the chair and crossed her arms. She knew, dang it, she knew.

"Is that all I'll ever be? A silly girl who can't live without a man?"

"It's not like you have choices, baby." Her voice softened and she looked out the window. "If you don't get pregnant and become his wife, there's only one way he'll ever see you. Just somebody who give it to him easy, somebody he'll think about in years to come and laugh at, if he even remembers your name." She took the can out of my hand and ran it faster than I ever could across the crispy leafs. "Now you go get ready. Holly'll pick you up soon. I put some change on your bed pillow."

"Don't need any money, Momma." Stunned, I barely heard my own voice. "Saved my lunch money this week." As I turned to go she hummed "Barbara Allen," a tune she'd sung when I was a little girl about a love that destroyed everyone it touched.

I'd used almost all the Maybelline mascara but still had a quarter bottle of Evening in Paris. When I dabbed it behind my ears the odor seemed rank and I closed the cap. I brushed my hair, pulling it back with a white headband. Momma words rattled around in my head. Out the window I saw the patch of dirt that hid Bette Moss's head and wondered if she had faced my predicament. Maybe through some hateful turn of fate she'd never gotten pregnant. Then her lover left her, and what else could she do except find her way to Marcescent Street? And somehow, ultimately, to Uncle Luther. For the first time I realized that her destiny could be mine. The idea was so horrifying I pressed my fingers to my temples to erase thoughts of people I couldn't do nothing for. Momma was right. I had to think of myself.

Zipping up my white pedal pants, they were snugger than usual. My breasts were tender against my bra. I held still, curious. I didn't feel any different and would have to wait and see. Wait and hope. On the way out the door I picked up Butch and swung him around. He

Aaaaaa'd and smiled and reached out when I put him in his playpen. I rubbed his head. "Gotta go." Whatever your dreams are, brother, I thought, dream a good one for me.

At Wink's Market I put a penny in the gold-and-red weight and fortune machine. The arm bounced around and landed on a hundred and two. Two pounds heavier than the last time. My heartbeat galloped. My fortune said, *Expect a blessing around the holidays.* I'd gotten that one before and shrugged. Behind me a horn tooted. Holly pulled in driving Willie's convertible. Lynn scooted over and I jumped in.

"He's letting you drive?" I'd never seen Holly in this car without Willie. She shook her left hand at me and mugged.

"You're married!" I screamed, examining a large cut stone in her ring.

By the time we got to Pinkie's Drive-in and ordered milkshakes and hamburgers, Holly had recounted going to the Claiborne County courthouse with Willie's cousin as a witness and some poor old farmer they'd pulled off the street.

Our chatter layered over each other's, then Lynn raised both hands to quiet us. "You have to promise not to tell," she said. Lynn took a breath. "I'm pregnant."

We all screamed and the waitress bringing our food nearly dropped the tray. "Sorry," I said, handing off the milkshakes and fries. She took our money and skated to another car.

"Everybody's taken care of except you, Randi Jo." Holly cocked an eyebrow and smirked.

"Working on it," I said, and quickly sipped my milkshake so I'd not have to talk about sex with Connor but nothing to show for it. Not a proposal or a baby, things my friends seemed to have accomplished with hardly a care. I got a weekly letter full of information about his classes and pranks in his dorm and saw him every other weekend, but truth was, I didn't know where I stood on that line that my friends had now crossed. A short distance away Tempy Herne got out of a car with Iona Stark. They saw me watching and sat at a table at the furthest end of the drive-in.

"That's the part about being married to Connor that might make me change my mind," Holly said sarcastically. "Miss Temperance Herne, high priestess of clean and fussy living."

"I'd worry more about his mother," Lynn piped in. "She'll stare you down until you wished you were invisible. My little brother got caught stealing a candy bar at their store and she blistered his back with a switch."

"Gotta find a way to get along with them," I said.

Holly pointed at Tempy and smirked. "I think she likes girls."

We all giggled and tried not to stare, but the two women stood out by the way they cut off all contact with any other people. They went to the movies together, attended church, ate, shopped, and if they had a free Sunday afternoon they'd go out to Indian Creek for a private picnic. Not a friend or family member with them. People thought it was peculiar. Me, Holly, Lynn and Sissy did things together but somehow it was different with those two girls. Like they shared a bond that excluded the rest of the world.

124

"Stop gossiping," I said, putting a hand over my mouth to stifle more giggles. "Just 'cause she never married doesn't mean she don't like boys." I watched Tempy and Iona as they delicately picked French fries from a paper plate between them, their knuckles touching when they dipped into the catsup.

"I'm gonna say hello." I jumped out, smoothed my shirt and handed my milkshake to Holly.

"Yell if you need the cavalry," Lynn called after me.

Tempy and Iona glanced up as I approached. Tempy quickly looked down at her food and I knew I'd made a mistake. "Want to join us, Tempy?" I pointed back at the car. "I'm here with some girlfriends."

Tempy shot me a spiteful expression. "Could that Holly look any trashier?" she said to Iona.

"Connor coming in today?" I asked, pretending I didn't hear the insult to my friend. "Usually meet up Saturday evenings."

Tempy yawned and removed her wire-frame glasses, cleaning them with the hem of her skirt. "Spring Cotillion. Doubt he'll come in."

"What's a cotillion?"

"Dance," she said like I was stupidest girl in the world. "His dear friend Rory is nominated for May Queen. Can't imagine he'll miss it."

I froze, feeling like I'd been hit with a stick. Blood rushed to my head and I imagined my sad clown face. That's what I am, I thought, a pathetic jester playing to canned laughter and Temperance Herne demanding I two-step for the crowd.

Timidly I backed away. Tempy bit into a hamburger, still eyeing me, but Iona never spoke.

Lynn and Holly had moved to the table nearest the car. "Well?" Lynn asked, handing me my chocolate milkshake.

I sucked in the rich creamy ice cream. My two friends waited and it seemed the world whipped around without gravity. I stood stiffly so I wouldn't fall, walked in circles so I wouldn't end up in traffic. Found myself at the side of the car holding the door handle. Lynn and Holly followed me. Faces spun around and mouths moved but I couldn't make out a word. All I could think of was Connor and his May Queen. His good girl would be wearing a crown and his ring. He would marry her, not me. Everything I had trusted about the world collapsed. I didn't trust that my mother wouldn't throw me out of my home. I didn't trust that my father would live. I didn't trust that Connor would marry me. My stomach lurched and the icy cup slipped out of my hand, splattering the ground as Holly and Lynn jumped back. I made it as far as the car's trunk then bent over and retched.

Lynn patted my back and pushed back my bangs as I heaved again. Finally I straightened up, holding to the Chevy. Holly forced a cup of ice water to my lips and dabbed a wet handkerchief on my forehead. She grinned and, for the life of me, I couldn't figure out what was so funny.

"Well," she said, "reckon we don't have to worry about you after all."

My hand went to my stomach. I didn't know if there was a baby growing inside me, but I did know there was doubt, suspicion and fear.

18

That afternoon I sat on a rock by myself staring into the pond that our gang called Lake Fortunato after a character in an Edgar Allan Poe story the seniors had to read. A green slime edged up on the shore like lace on a prom dress. Holly's nasal soprano sang "Long Tall Sally" along with Little Richard on the car radio. Lynn and Sissy sat quietly watching her as if she were a movie star while Willie and Hermann stood back smoking cigarettes and talking about whether Iron Liege would win the Kentucky Derby this year. Willie's uncle owned a horse farm in Lexington so he knew all the horses' names and spoke about them like they were politicians after his vote. He'd promised to take Holly to a race for their honeymoon.

I closed my eyes but the persistent worry of all that could go wrong held me in its fist. With Momma expecting, there was no way I could stay home. High school graduation behind me, and secretarial school was out the window. Maybe a job . . . maybe . . . No, I couldn't even think it, but there it was: *what if I ended up on Marcescent Street*? Why hadn't I thought of all this before? Why hadn't Momma warned me the way she always did Kim? Why didn't I believe this would happen to me? Momma's big ideas, my big plans. What if this didn't work out the way we'd hoped? I'd end up paying the rent by selling my favors to strangers or worse yet–men I knew in this town.

A hand touched my shoulder and I looked up at Sissy. She knelt down beside me and folded her hands under her chin. "Holly told me," she said. "Are you positive?"

"I missed a period and I got sick today." A swell of tears came up in my eyes and she wrapped an arm around me. "He's gonna marry that Rory. She's respectable and beautiful and won't embarrass him." The words clogged my throat like I'd swallowed too much food.

"Shhh," Sissy said. "You know no such thing. Tell him, then see what happens."

"His sister couldn't wait to blab about him escorting Princess Rory to the Spring Cotillion."

"Randi Jo," she said more firmly. "Rory may not be sitting as pretty as you think." She pointed behind me.

I twisted around to see Connor with Willie and Herman, turning down a cigarette and opening a beer. My heart kicked like dozens of fishes leaping from the water, and at the same time I trembled and clasped my arms around my knees. "He's not with her."

"Looks like Rory will have to be crowned without him."

He looked in my direction and caught my gaze, lips curving into a smile. Sissy made her way back to the girls and Connor came over.

"What'd ya doing over here all by yourself?" He dropped beside me and stretched out his legs.

"Cotillion. Tempy said . . . I figured you'd be with–"

"My sister rarely gets to approve my whereabouts. Since Thursday I've been painting Pop's storage room. Here I am in college and Tempy still thinks she calls my shots." He rolled his eyes and smirked the way I remembered him doing as a boy when someone tried to tell him what to do. "Besides, Cotillion's not 'til Sunday. I get to escort one of the princesses at a presentation dinner, but I'm not sure it'll be Rory. Wish you could come down and see me."

"I thought . . ."

He leaned over and kissed me, soft, nuzzling his nose in my hair. "Ummm, nice perfume."

My breath caught in my chest. I pushed back from him and looked into his eyes. I thought about Momma having to give birth at her age, having no choices for her life. Lynn . . . using her pregnancy to get Rusty out of the army. Holly . . . who held Willie so tight in her hand she didn't need pregnancy to help her along. And Sissy, who shared a bond with Herman that went back to their childhood. What did I have with this man sitting next to me? Was it possible that he could take me on love? Could our shared history hold us together? Could he see me as permanent in his life? I wanted that, wanted it like a

Christmas present I'd prayed for, but God didn't grant wishes and no magic genie would come to my aid. I knew I couldn't take the chance.

I swallowed and cleared my throat. "Connor, I missed my period."

He understood right away and stood up. "You're sure?" His voice wavered and broke, a higher pitch than usual. I feared he was about to say something mean but his slumped shoulders showed only sadness. He turned away, hands on his hips. "You're sure?" he asked again, staring at the ground. I was so scared I didn't reply. He focused on a dandelion as if it were as huge as the sun. "I mean, we only done it a few times." He huffed out a breath like the last of him was draining into the dirt at his feet. "Everything's ruined."

He walked away, waving off the guys when they called out to him. Everyone seemed to freeze in a sorrowful tunnel of time . . . all of them looking at me.

એ

Later that afternoon Holly dropped me off at Curley's Café in Quinntown while she and Lynn went to look at baby clothes. Connor walking away from me earlier left me feeling wrung out like a rag and I wasn't sure what would happen to us or me. I bought a five-cent soda and window-shopped. Near the intersection of Marcescent and Laynchark, the Saturday afternoon crowd meandered like ducks in an overcrowded pond. Quinntown amounted to three blocks of retail stores and a bus stop to catch a ride to Contrary. Marcescent Street clung to the farthest side. No way to tell it was the most notorious street in the county, with a hardware store on one corner and a swampy field on the other. Nobody was watching me. Slowly, I walked down the street I'd heard about since I was a girl yet had never set foot on.

Elf's Shoe Repair was on the backside of the hardware store. Dozens of battered soles cluttered the window, a sewing machine whined, and the smell of leather and shoe polish wafted out. A stand filled with mesh sacks of daffodil bulbs propped open the door. A cardboard flyer showed a dazzling array of yellow flowers covering a field. Each sack cost thirty-five cents. If I spent that I'd have to miss two days of lunch next week. I had to eat for two, not just myself.

Next door were restaurants with blacked-out windows that meant drinking and gambling went on inside. A man in a dark suit walked out of Hobo's Alley, bringing a whiff of alcohol and the ring of slot machines mixed with a jukebox playing "Sixteen Tons." A woman wearing a crumpled red dress stumbled out after him. Heavyset with stringy coffee-colored hair, she was downright homely and her feet wobbled as if drunk or maybe she couldn't manage her high heels. She caught up with the man at the corner and grabbed onto his arm. They headed for the Regal Hotel, six floors anchored like a stubborn mule pulling against its reins. Painted a muted green with black window frames, it looked haunted. A billboard for Jumpin' Jonas's Mobile Homes and Used Cars hung on one side.

I walked past the hotel, not brave enough to look inside. Rows of daffodils grew in a planter box lining the front. I dawdled, pretending to read an Old Spice advertisement on an adjacent office building and peered through the window. Several battered and stained red velvet couches had seen better days. Somebody manned a desk against the back wall but I could only see the top of a brown head.

I passed the hotel, intending to study it from a distance. At the cobbler's shop no one was looking so I stuffed a bag of dandelion bulbs in my jacket pocket, then crossed kitty-corner to Lester Street and rested on a bridge rail as I looked back at the Regal.

The woman in the red dress walked out, followed shortly by the man in the suit, who went a different direction. She returned to Hobo's Alley as casually as if doing her daily shopping. Could I get comfortable on this street? My sweater was wet with sweat just from having walked down it. I could sense the Fear Angel rattling her wings in broad daylight. Marcescent wasn't really a street, it was only the last part of the block that good people despised and bad people craved. And here I was thinking of becoming part of it. My head swam with conflicting feelings, coming to one conclusion. An unmarried pregnant girl . . . people in town would class me as one of the bad people, even worse than being from Notown.

A short way down Lester Street Holly came out of a seamstress shop. Our eyes met. She seemed to read my mind and came over to sit beside me on the bridge railing and looked at the hotel and honkytonks.

"This is where trash ends up, Holly." I wrapped my arms around my stomach, hating what I said but knew it was true. "When I think back to how Contrary kids

132

treated us like we weren't good enough . . . well, they've never seen what people do to survive." The woman with the red dress came out of Hobo's with another man and they crossed the street and entered the Regal. "Nobody could want to end up here. All these people must have had awful things happen to them."

"You can't come down here again," Holly said. "Not good for your head, believe me, I know."

"I don't know where else to go."

"Think I didn't consider this my first time?" Holly scooted closer and pressed her lips together. Below us muddy canal water flowed with the stink of sulfur. "Twice actually. Once when I was twelve and again about a year ago." She looked directly at me to gauge my reaction.

"I don't understand," I said, looking at her tummy. "You never went away."

She twisted around and spit into the creek. "I ain't no Abigail Nelson who pops out a kid every year since she was fourteen and takes a trip every summer to give the baby up for adoption."

"What did you do?"

Holly looked up at the sky, a sad look in her eyes spreading to her face, then her lips tightened like reality had set in. "At first, I thought I'd end up here on Marcescent Street, thought that was gonna be my life. Then I found Dr. Huber. He gave me a second chance, and a third."

"You?" My face scrunched up but I was in no position to throw stones.

"I got an abortion," she whispered, blinking several times. "You know what that is?"

I nodded. A few years ago I'd read about it in one of Pug's girly magazines that he hid under his mattress. The idea didn't faze me as much as what I'd have to say to Connor. How would I explain–tell him I'd made a mistake, that I'd only thought I was pregnant? No matter what I told him, I still had ruined everything between us.

"Holly." My voice quivered. "Afterwards . . . how did you feel?"

She stared into the brown water, the stinkish sulfur nauseating. "Can't think about that, and do yourself a favor, don't." She leaned over bridge's edge. "It was what had to be."

"What did Willie say?"

"My second was Willie's but it was too soon. I couldn't tell him. There would have been no way we could have gotten married a year ago. I had to work on that father of his and I got a lucky break when his mother passed away. Tell you something, Sis. All those years with Willie, I never slept with him 'til last year. Got pregnant my first time."

"You been with Willie since junior high so I thought–"

"Everybody in this town did." She laughed. "That's what they always think of Notown girls. But I was smart, gave him a feel and a kiss, but never crossed that line and I'm tellin' you, it was the way I kept him." She laughed again. "Being a man, he just let people think he was getting it." She bit her lip as if contemplating her strategy. "You have to make a man think you belong to him, and he's not going to want anybody else messing with what's his."

"Holly, you're the smartest person I know."

"Me with my C+ average." She held the bridge rail and swayed on her heels. "That first time . . ." She looked directly at me, her blue eyes with a soft seriousness that asked for trust. "That first time was a boy from Divergence."

"Divergence!"

"Dallas Shepard . . . lives over the hill from me, back in the hollow."

"I know the Shepards. He goes to the colored school."

"Ah, he's long gone now. Last I talked to him he was headed to Missouri, had a job as a auto mechanic."

"But you liked him at twelve?"

"Honey, twelve for me was like twenty-two for most girls." She swished back her blond hair and her bosom heaved with each breath. "Him and me, I don't know, we just understood each other. We could lay out under a willow tree deep in the woods and nothing else mattered. Just goes to show, even the most brilliant can't outguess love."

"I fell in love with Connor when I was nine," I said, shaking my head.

"Now see, how was I so smart, falling in love with somebody from Divergence? But love has its way with you sometimes, and now I'm determined to stay out of its clutches. I got a rich man with a richer daddy, and both at my beck and call."

A quiet settled over us. If we'd shared some dark secrets, both of us understood that they were safe: two girls from Notown just trying to make do.

"Plenty of Notown girls have babies and live there just fine," Holly said, "No reason you can't."

"I'd be so ashamed. How could I look my daddy in

the eye? How could I stand all the whispers?"

"Over there, back of the Regal Hotel." She pointed at the office building on Lester. "Second floor, room 203, Dr. Clive Huber. Tell the nurse you have a stomach ache. She'll know what to do." Holly leaned down to a pipe on the bridge that spurted water from an artesian well, took a short drink, then she kissed my forehead and went back to shopping.

At the Regal the red dressed-woman came out for the third time. I wondered how many men she'd been with today . . . how many days, weeks and years she'd keep doing it. Somehow I'd thought these women only worked at night, and just did it with one man at best. Reckon I was wrong.

A mother mallard swam down the canal with a flock of ducklings behind her. They flapped up onto the bank and waddled in the grass. I realized that Bette Moss had lost her life around here. Bloody sheets. A missing head. Had she realized what was happening to her as she died? How many times had she gone in and out of the Regal Hotel?

19

In fourth grade I got shots at the county health department, and the building on Lester Avenue smelled the same way–an alcohol-iodine odor that put you on edge. The doors on the first floor were all closed. I heard typing in an insurance office and female laughter like somebody had told a joke. Maple-brown floor tiles shone with a high gloss and the walls were a sickly mint green but dirty, like someone had rubbed sweaty hands across them. At the end of the hall was an Otis elevator, the levered gate half-closed, and a Negro attendant sat on a stool inside reading a newspaper.

I slipped up the staircase on the left without the attendant seeing me. By the time I reached the second floor I trembled like a solitary leaf trying to hold onto a branch in a snowstorm.

Huber Clinic was the first door at the top of the steps. Inside, a closed window with a note: Ring For Service. I dinged the bell, holding my breath, and sat in an undersized straight-back chair beside a rail-thin woman who kept her hands in prayer position across her knees. A nurse poked her head out and said, "Miss Ryan, you can come in." She looked over at me. "Be right with you." Miss Ryan popped up out of her chair like a grasshopper and disappeared behind the burl door.

I exhaled shivery breaths and covered my face with icy hands. Maybe Connor would change his mind, maybe he'd see all our friends getting married and he'd want to as well. Maybe he'd remember the bond of making love to me. The lost expression on his face when I'd told him haunted me. How could being with me compare to all I would cost him: his future, his schooling, Rory . . . Now I was about to add a baby to my mother's household. What would keep her from tossing me out as quick as she did Kim? And Marcescent Street . . . could I do for money what I'd done for love?

I jerked upright when the door opened and the nurse waved me in with a quick clip of her hand. She ushered me into a much smaller room with an examining table.

My mouth dried up and tongue swelled. "I . . . I have a stomach ache."

"I see." Her eyebrows peaked and she didn't look me in the eye for the rest of the time she was there. Part of me wanted to run out but my muscles stiffened. She placed a sheet of paper on a clipboard. "Let's call you..." She glanced over at a Screenland movie magazine. Tallulah Bankhead's photo was on the cover. "You look

like a Tallulah. Banks can be your last name. Okay, when was your last menstruation?"

My cheeks felt fiery and my nose burned. A breeze drifted through the window blinds and caked my sweat. "A month, halfway through my second."

She took my blood pressure and temperature, still never looking me in the eye. "Dr. Huber will be right in. Now remember whenever you come here, give the name Tallulah Banks."

I nodded like it was the most natural thing in the world but when she shut the door my held breath came rushing out. I considered walking out, and wiped sweat from my upper lip. But what would I do? Where would I go?

A tall man with black hair graying at the temples entered. He adjusted his stethoscope and picked up the clipboard. He looked vaguely familiar as he read all about me. Then, he looked up, and I burst out crying.

"I'm sorry," I kept repeating like a fool as he patted me on the back and handed me a tissue.

"What's your name, sweetheart?"

"Tallulah Banks," I said between hiccups.

"No, your real name."

I swallowed hard. "Randi Jo Gaylor." I inhaled and added, "Out of Notown."

"Well, Randi Jo Gaylor from Notown, I'm here to help you, no matter what."

Something about the movement of his lips as he spoke made me realize that I knew him. "Didn't you used to be a Communist?" I asked between sobs.

He coughed, a slight chuckle to the side, and nodded. "When I was much younger and more idealistic." His smile favored movie stars I'd seen in magazines. "Do I know you?"

"You gave me bags of food when I was a little girl, and it fed my family many a hard day. I didn't mind that it was Communist food. It tasted just fine."

He smiled as if remembering good times then tapped the clipboard with a pen. "Now, what's this trouble you've gotten yourself into?"

Another tear slid down my cheek and my nose burned. I looked at my hands, pressed together in my lap as if I were praying. "Don't think I can talk."

"Won't the boy marry you?"

I shook my head. "Don't think so."

"But you're not sure."

"He's lives in Contrary," I said, not sure somebody like a doctor understood the difference. "His momma would pitch a fit before she'd let him marry a Notown girl." That was probably true even if Connor hadn't told his family. I couldn't bring myself to say Connor wanted to marry a girl named Rory and that the Notown girl he'd had sex with didn't matter none at all. "I'm not sure how I'll pay."

"We have a special fund for cases like yours. Pay what you can, when you can." He made some notes on my chart. "You're sure you don't want to carry to term? Adoption is always a possibility."

I looked out the window, my thoughts swimming like goldfish bouncing against glass. "I don't know what I want."

"Let's do this. I'll take some blood and do an exam to confirm your condition. Let me know by next week if nothing has changed with your young man, then . . ." He took my hand and petted it like it was a small kitten. "Then I'll see to it you get a fresh start."

After the exam, he said I was in the early stages. The nurse gave me an envelope of vitamins to take just in case, but I couldn't look at her and she didn't look at me, and I focused on the linoleum floor.

"Thank you, Dr. Huber," I said on my way out. "This is the second time you've saved my life."

20

Slipping out of the building was a mite easier and once on the street I started feeling like myself again. I even stopped to look at the daffodils in front of the Regal Hotel. They grew in terracotta planters shaped like seashells. Someone had watered them recently and their color glistened bright as butter. I clutched the bag of bulbs in my pocket and knew where I would plant them . . . over Bette Moss's head.

My reflection in the Regal Hotel's front window showed a slip of a girl and I wondered if my features showed my worries to the world. Through gold lettering, a balding, gray-suited man seated inside lowered his newspaper and grinned, showing horsy teeth, then he winked. The implication made me sick to my stomach. He must've had kids my age.

A sharp jerk on my arm startled me and I was pulled into the side alley.

I bounced against the building, ready to holler, then realized who had hold of me. The black man from Gray's Pin. My grandfather towered over me, scowling like a badger.

"The hell you doing on this street?" he demanded, glancing around to make sure no one noticed us. He squeezed my arms and shook me. "Your momma would die to know you was here."

"I, I was on Lester," I stammered, "at, at the doctor's."

"There's three other streets you can walk on to get back to Laynchark. Only the sinful come here."

His glare and firm tenor voice held me still like a captive parishioner in front of a fire-and-brimstone preacher. I looked down.

"You been sinning?" he asked and took off a bucket hat.

"It's not like you think. I have a boyfriend. I was seeing the doctor on Lester. Momma knows."

He clamped his lips together, his eyes narrowed, and he looked toward the end of the alley. "Got a truck parked at the corner of Laynchark. Walk that direction. Hop in the cab when nobody's looking."

"What's going on back here?" snarled the man from the Regal's lobby. His steps scuffed in gravel as he approached us, hands on his hips.

A younger man followed him, a goofy-looking redhead with a Dobbs hat pushed back on his head and chin full of pimples. "Hell's bells," he said. "Believe you've got some foolin' around outside your hotel by folks refusing to pay our rates." He slid a cigarette from behind one ear and fumbled with a lighter, flicking it on and off. "She one of yours, Mr. Garroway?"

"Ya'all doing it against my back wall?" the older man snapped.

"Out here in the open," the redhead smirked, "in daylight. Swear to God I seen it all now."

My grandfather let go of me, clutched his cap in front of him and stared at the ground. "Naw sir, boss," he said, shifting the hat from hand to hand. "We'll go our way."

"You'll go when I tell you," Garroway said. "You looking for work?" he asked me.

I knew what he was asking and my insides burned with shame and indignation braided up my back. "None of your business what I'm doing here."

" 'Cause if you is," Garroway went on, "that's inside, not out here in the street like dogs, Missy."

"We ain't that," my grandfather said. "I work for the Miss's pa, had to come pick her up from the doc. She got all turned around on these alley streets."

I stood petrified against the wall. My grandfather caught my eye as if to say, go along with his story and we'll be okay. His large presence, even as he humbled himself, reassured me.

The two men stepped toward us, trouble on their faces, the redhead ready to pick a fight and bouncing on the balls of his feet like a boxer. "Reckon I know rutting when I see it," he snickered. "Your beds ain't that expensive, Mr. Garroway."

"That ain't true," I said, anger overtaking my shame. "I accidentally come out the back way." I pointed to the Lester Avenue building. "Didn't know where I was. My momma never let me come on this street. That's how come I didn't know."

I swallowed hard as tears brimmed in my eyes. I already had a Fear Angel on my tail and didn't need a haunt, too. "There ain't nothing good I can do for this child in Notown."

"You think about judgment day when that baby comes to you as a young man or a young woman. What'll you say when he looks you in the eye and knows his momma snuffed out his life? That baby's got survivor blood, too. It'll fight for its life. More'n you know."

"I got to put everything the way it was and get a second chance."

He exhaled and bit his bottom lip. With one hand he pushed back his straight graying hair. "Nobody's throwing stones here. All of us live life as best we can." He paused. "I was as wild a young man as any. Been to Marcescent Street many a time. Green's the only color them girls care about. It was when Marcescent Street came to me that my life changed." His Adam's apple bobbed up and down and he sniffed, his bottom lip protruding. "Girl named Alonsa Sue . . . come up to the coal camp where I worked, handed me this little dark-haired baby. Skin white enough, hair straight, but I could see it in her, and Alonsa Sue did, too."

"You mean Momma?" I turned to him, shocked. "Why didn't she ever say?"

"Would you tell your child?"

I stared ahead at the road whipping under the truck. No, I wouldn't. It'd be something I'd hide my whole life. My mother was a Marcescent Street baby. And what happened to them was they spent their lives trying to hide what they were. So Momma wasn't pushing me

147

toward Marcescent Street but toward a respectable boy with a good family so my children could have it better than she'd had.

"What little boy did this to you?"

I swallowed hard. My grandfather pulled off the side of the road beside a row of mailboxes. "Connor Herne," I said. "But it's my fault, not his."

"Herne," he repeated, eyes narrowing as if he was remembering the family in Notown. "Go on home now. Things have a way of turning out."

I opened the truck's door, slid out and held to the window. The least I owed my grandfather was a thank you. His sturdy features defined a man who could endure. I recognized Momma's full lips, gray eyes and high cheekbones, and except for the eye color, they were mine, too.

"Tell your momma," he said before I spoke, "I'm moving in with a church woman lives in Pruden. This is her truck she lets me use. I won't need meat no more." He nodded, leaned over and pulled the door closed. "Don't know when I'll be seeing you'ins again."

"I'll tell her," I said.

Running around the front, I stood beside the mailboxes and he pulled back on the road, gravel sputtering as he gunned the gas. "Thank you," I shouted, unsure if he heard me. I watched until he turned toward Divergence, then rested my back against the mailbox post. Now whatever I did, even if it was going back to Marcescent Street, it would be my decision and mine to live with. He was right about one thing: there were worst things than a Notown baby.

Afternoon heat curled up off the ground and crickets chirped in the high weeds. I took off my jacket and cushioned it behind my back. No cars. Quiet. Up the hillside, the houses resembled sentries guarding a mountain kingdom. Farther on, Divergence looked peaceful. Two neighborhoods like old buzzards leaning back-to-back to steady themselves.

My grandfather's words touched me deep down, just as much as his putting himself between those two men and me. Except for my Daddy, I'd never expected anybody to protect me that way. I put a hand on my stomach. Somebody in there would need my protection. I'd have to figure out a way to deal with the stares and whispers. I reckon I wouldn't be the first Notown girl to suffer that. My forbearers had come through worse, as had my momma, and who was I to think I was owed a charmed life? I'd live these days as best I could and everybody else would have to figure out how to deal with it. I knew now that no matter what happened, this baby was going to live.

I opened our mailbox and pulled out an envelope addressed to me. My newfound strength dissolved. The ends of each letter curled into tiny familiar whirls of cursive writing as if an artist had drawn my name rather than written it. The paper trembled in my hands. Here it was. My first letter from Uncle Luther.

21

I planted the daffodil buds with trembling fingers. Every snap of a branch and murmur in the breeze made me jittery. I was sure Uncle Luther was out there, watching, waiting for the moment to demand his due. Be the easy thing to point to that patch of ground and let him set out digging her up, but part of me didn't like that he thought he owned that woman. How different was that from Pug thinking he could do anything he wanted to me all those years ago? I might not be in control of a lot of my life, but this one piece of information was mine to keep.

Within a few weeks hardy green tips sprouted from the ground like someone had scattered emeralds. At least she finally had some pretty flowers. I hoped that the rest of her body had been taken care of and not thrown in some potter's grave for poor folk. As I passed the patch of ground on the way to the outhouse I saw Veda Huston out by the creek, her hands palms down toward the ground. She'd been here several months ago and told Daddy where to dig for the new outhouse so our well water stayed clean. Veda could douse, locate lost items, and read the stars. Some folks claimed she could see the future but from what I'd noticed she had good common sense. Veda looked up at me, an odd cock to one eyebrow, and asked, "What'cha holding?" She pointed to the paper in my hands.

"Letter," I said, "only place I can get any privacy is..." I pointed to the outhouse and went inside. I'd kept Uncle Luther's letter in my bra to avoid anybody finding it. After Daddy got out of jail all those years ago Momma had been ready to leave him. Only his promises that his brother would never cross our doorway again kept them together. I opened the blue-lined paper, its edges stained from my fingers. Strips of sunlight filtered through the wood slates and my eyes adjusted in the dim box as my nose grew accustomed to the smell. I had the words memorized but read them again and again.

> *My brother's child, Be out on probation soon. Coming to collect what you been holding for me. Remember what you owe me for protection in the dark of night. An unpaid debt is a lifelong bond just as love is a cutthroat business.*

The last five words made me shiver. Tucking the letter back in my bra, I wanted to believe Uncle Luther was family and would never hurt me but the veins in my neck pulsed like a warning. If only Connor had taken me away from all this. We might have had a nice apartment near his college where Uncle Luther would never find me. Maybe there was a secretarial school down there, too. I could have . . . Well, no use dreaming.

When I stepped outside Veda was holding her doodlebug over the patch of daffodils. "What you doing?" I asked. She strolled toward me, one hand on her ample hips and the y-shaped doodlebug extended with the other. Her dousing instrument was a hickory switch but sometimes she used two wire clothes hangers shaped like antennas.

"Occasionally I run across an Indian burial ground and once or twice come upon some Confederate or Union remains."

"You found something like that up here?" I kept my face expressionless but my eyes darted toward the daffodils.

"Don't know what I'm sensing." She nodded at the end of the doodlebug and it quivered. "It's like something's here . . . dead but not dead. Felt it vibrating when I placed your new outhouse. Bothered me since."

"Reckon lots of restless spirits roam these hills." My neck sweated and my shirt stuck to my back as the sun beat hotly behind me.

Veda looked around and shook her head. "Maybe I'm losing my touch."

"Could be all the city water lines coming this way."

She chuckled and patted her thighs. "Be no use for me much longer."

"Everybody will still want to know their future," I said, moving toward a crest where it was easy to stand and away from the site of our old outhouse.

"Ah, you tell people their futures and they won't live their present."

Her words could have been rocks thrown at me. I swallowed and looked away. Since Dr. Huber had confirmed my condition I lived for my future at the expense of the present. Momma and Preacher Hicks wanted me to stay at a church house up North then give the baby up for adoption. He'd find a good Christian family and Momma promised she'd find a way to send me to secretarial school. I think she felt awful, like she'd done as bad by her second daughter as she had the first, but I couldn't blame her. Who's to say I wouldn't have done the same thing anyway. Sissy and Holly said, keep the child and wait for Connor to come around. My Daddy . . . my Daddy didn't know yet and how would I ever tell him? My survivor blood, if I really had any, would have to lead me to my destiny as it happened. "Can't say the road in front of me looks all that good."

Veda studied my face and said, "Life has a way of living itself whether we want to partake or not."

She had a point but I wasn't sure an answer. "Never thought I'd come to this."

"You planted some flowers there." She focused on the seedling daffodils. "Just like you're planted here, Randi Jo, and some part of you always will be."

"Least it's fertile," I joked.

She turned sharply and stared at my stomach. "Uh-huh." Her perplexed expression gelled into understanding, and she looked up at me and said in a flat monotone, "He's coming for you."

Goosebumps spread up my arms and I put a hand to my throat. Did she mean Uncle Luther? Maybe I was the thing that was *dead but not dead*. Visions of Bette Moss's skull with its strands of red hair in a mushy, reeking sack clotted my thoughts. If I didn't give Luther what he wanted, he might take his fury out on me. I could be a head in a sack. "Is he far down the road?" I asked, holding my breath.

"Lots of different roads. His is full of vision."

"And mine . . . what's on my road?"

Holding a hand to her stomach, Veda cocked an ear to the ground as if she listened to the earth itself. "He got touched by the dark mother. He sees the horror." A gray Oldsmobile turned off Laynchark and drove up the hill. It could only make it as far as the Cooley house and parked in the road. I wiped sweat from my upper lip, holding my breath as much from Veda's words as anticipating who was in the car. I had no idea what she meant, but it couldn't be good.

Connor's father got out on the driver's side. Connor exited through the passenger door and headed toward me. His daddy ambled up the hill and sat on our porch swing. My father came out and sat with Mr. Herne. My lungs heaved in panic. Veda touched my back and that was about all that kept me standing.

"Morning, Miss Huston," Connor said, coming forward but staying downhill of me.

"Hello, son," Veda replied and meandered off toward the creek.

Connor shielded his eyes as he looked up at me, his blondish hair silvery in the sun. It took all my strength not to run from him. Part of me was embarrassed because of what I'd cost him, and another part was scared down to my toes wondering what he'd do. Yet what was being born in me took nourishment from the earth as if my feet were roots. I was as much here as any tree on this mountain, and whoever passed my way would have to deal with me as such, not dismiss me like a child. If Connor was going to call me names and tell me I was unwelcome in his life, then I'd dig my feet in this ground where I was raised and he'd not move me from it. Today, no Fear Angel would wrap her wings around me.

"Pop told me a story on the way here," Connor said. "'Bout a little girl bringing in her hair barrettes to trade for food for her family." He looked directly into my eyes, one hand on his hip. "Not a lot of kids'd give up their treasurers to feed their family. Not a lot of kids can see that far ahead in life. Pop thinks highly of that little girl."

"Connor, what's this have to do with my belly?"

"I quit school. Gonna work in Pop's store and transfer to Kingsley University next semester." He swallowed and looked away as if watching his Duke education slide off the hill like greasy ducks. "So, if we're gonna do this, we'll have to live at my house until I'm out of school."

I remembered how he'd walked away when I told him about the baby. "I have to think about this."

"You don't want to marry me?"

"I don't want to be anywhere I'm not wanted."

"This is about more than you and me, Randi Jo." He

tucked his thumbs in his pockets. "Everybody'll know soon enough. My sister says she doesn't want any little Herne bastards walking around this town."

I picked up a rock and threw it at him. It caught him on the shoulder and he jumped back a ways in case I had another one. "I'll tell you what it's about. It's about you and me and what we done." I stepped down so I was even with him. "Who do you think you were touching? You think a little hometown piece on the side is all I am? Do you know why I gave myself to you? You have the least idea what this baby means to me?" I shoved him on his chest but he stood firm. "And your sister . . . I'll tell you what she can go kiss."

Connor looked like he was holding his breath and his eyebrows arched as he watched me pace in front of him. He patted his hands against the air to calm me down. "First time I saw you, I threw a rock. Reckon it's fitting you throw one at me now." He looked toward the ground and scuffed a foot on a tangle of dandelion weeds. "I need you to understand, it won't be easy. My Ma and Sis feel like they do, but that's not why I came here."

"Why then?"

"Something my Pop said." He looked out toward the range of mountains as if hearing a story that had changed his life. "There's many ways for a man to survive. But a little baby, my baby . . . When he or she grows up, it'll look me in the eye and what will I have to say about how I acted right now? That baby has my blood, it's me and mine, and we're survivors. Just like you, Randi Jo. People want lots of things, big dreams, nice bow-tied answers, but life don't always serve it up that way."

I sniffed and wiped my eyes. Hearing another version of my grandfather's words made my chest tremble and I figured he and Connor's father must have spoken.

In the distance, Mr. Herne shook hands with my father, walked toward his car and leaned on the hood, watching us. I knew what that meant. Daddy had said I had to make my own decision. As much as I wanted to run to him, pride held me back. "One more question," I told Connor. "What about Rory? You always gonna be thinking about what might have been with her?"

His expression cramped as if the college girl was his second painful loss. "Look at it this way . . . if I was with Rory, I'd always be thinking about my child . . . and his mother."

"Let me think." I went over to the creek beside Veda. She glanced at me with a look of having heard the conversation. I reached down and let the cool water run over my fingers. "Veda, you think I might have a chance?"

She swayed like the tender limbs of a willow. "Life is all about what you make it, child, there ain't really a blessed one or a cursed one."

"What do you see for this road, Veda?"

She peeked at Connor and clasped her hands in front of her. "Keep faith with it and it's as good as any."

I took a deep breath and turned around. "Will you tell my Momma?"

"I will, honey."

I ambled toward Connor, Uncle Luther's letter scratching my skin. I took my husband-to-be's hand and we continued toward his father's car. Sitting in the back seat with them in front, none of us spoke. When we turned onto the main road it hit me that I was leaving Notown. I smiled and knew it was good that neither Connor nor Pop Herne could see that my face could hardly hold my grin. No more sharing a room with anyone other than my husband. No more outdoor toilet or smelly pee-pot under the bed in the middle of winter. No more scrimping for food money. No more walking up the hill or telling people I came from Notown. I was going to live in Contrary, in a big apartment above a grocery store that had more food than I could ever eat. It didn't matter that I'd live in the back room. Maybe it was an odd thing that I'd not miss the place I grew up, but my spirit felt like it was escaping a dungeon. I was flying up into the sun where there'd never be another dark day. Notown was now my history, a place I'd never have to own up to again. When no one was looking, I ripped Uncle Luther's letter into strips and threw them out the window.

22

For as long as I'd known Connor, I never saw as honest a smile from him as when he looked down at the face of his daughter. In the last year I'd come to know his smiles. One was his wake-up smile when he realized that somebody was looking at him, another when he was pleased with something I'd done, and one when he was only tolerating me.

Pop Herne had a more sincere smile, like it sprang from deep within him when something made him happy. Mom Herne and Tempy never smiled. Their faces were frozen in frowns same as a block of ice cream. The year had had its ups and downs but once the cold weather hit, the Herne's indoor toilet made up for everything else.

I was another bother to them when I went into labor during Mom Herne's forty-second birthday party. Her and Tempy's eyes rolled as if I'd done this on purpose to be the center of attention, but the baby was weeks

159

overdue. After fourteen hours of contractions the doctor said he'd have to cut me open 'cause I was too little to give birth. I wanted to holler at him for not figuring this out hours ago. They drugged me up and then I didn't care what happened. My foggy memories were a good thing 'cause I'll bet the story went around about how I ruined Wallis Herne's party.

The baby's blood count was low so she needed a transfusion. Some people said maybe she had leukemia and might die. Tempy fussed that all I ate was junk but Momma backed her down, saying she had fed me as best she could, and whose house had I been living in for the last seven months anyway? They had to fight without me cause the medicine they pumped into me made the world a daydream.

Two days later I was still sore as could be, but I sat up and the nurse helped me with bottle feeding since I was on medication and couldn't breastfeed. After the transfusion her little cheeks had pinked up like strawberries and she was feisty, screaming as the nurse walked her down the hall to me. Once she was in my arms, she stopped crying.

Momma peeked in the doorway to see if I was awake. She'd given birth to her own child several weeks earlier. Her eyes narrowed and I couldn't read her expression. She tiptoed closer to peer down at the baby. "You ain't got no feeling for her yet, do you?"

My throat choked and my body felt like some dark force was dumping a bucket of emotion into my head. I hadn't thought it, hadn't said it, but like an arrow shot through my heart, Momma had homed in on what this year had come to. I looked out the window. "Well, she got me out of Notown."

I half thought Momma might smack me, but her face softened and she sat on the edge of the bed. "Now's the time you're gonna have to work. Soon as you're better, don't you deny your husband nothing, no matter how your feel."

"Momma, that's the last thing on my mind." I turned away, not wanting to even think about it. "I got this child and that's all I need."

She cocked an eyebrow, same way she used to when one of us kids was in trouble. "Let me tell you about men, Randi Jo. If you don't own them through and through, they'll turn on you like a rabid dog. Your father loves me down to my bones. Right through my blood. And that's the kind of love you need to make a marriage last. What you got ain't that kind of marriage, so you best start thinking how you're going to hang on to it. Don't think to pin everything on this little girl."

A thought of Rory swam through my mind but I couldn't let Momma know. She opened her purse and pulled out a handful of letters. "Want to tell me what this is about?" Momma's pointed tone could've cracked the wall. "If trouble's coming, best I know."

Uncle Luther's curly writing formed sharp spears aimed at me. "Trouble been here, Momma, and I don't know what to do about it." I reached out and took her hand like I was a little girl trembling in the dark. I could handle a husband but I wasn't sure how I'd deal with a man who'd cut off a woman's head.

"Why's he writing to you?" Momma's eyes flashed like a grease fire, her lips pressed tightly.

"I don't know."

Behind her Holly rolled in a beautiful white wicker bassinette. "It's a party!" Holly yelled and Sissy and Lynn followed holding smaller packages.

"We were more practical," Sissy said as Lynn handed me a bundle of movie magazines and set a gift-wrapped package on the other bed. "Diapers."

My friends huddled around with Holly holding the baby, cooing at my little girl, and baby-talked her. The child screamed with an opera singer's lungs. With the focus off of us Momma tucked Luther's letters into her purse, but continued to stare at me.

"Wonderful presents," I said, taking in Holly's fur coat and coiffured hair, teased and piled high on her head. Marriage had been good to Holly. She lived in a big mansion in Contrary's Indian Hills. In contrast, Lynn held her own baby bundled in a stained wrap that looked like it had never known hot water. Rusty had recently gotten hired on as a policeman in Contrary, but wasn't paid enough to live there so they scrimped by on beans, boiled creek water, and Rusty's winnings at the Saturday night cockfights.

Sissy and Herman had settled into a home beside the gas station. She never talked about children but seemed happy for all of us. I guess you could say they had one of those marriages Momma talked about . . . where the two people loved each other to the bone.

The nurse glanced in and everybody thought now was the time to leave. I figured it was more to escape the wailing baby but once I held her, she quieted down. My visitors straggled out. Momma stopped in the doorway and gave me a look that said I better be on top of my world. I had to hope some kindly Valkyrie would guide Uncle Luther's path away from me. And if not . . . my hands curled into fists. He could destroy my world.

Within the hour Mom Herne and Tempy marched through the door. Tempy, her brown hair pulled back in a bun at the top of her head, was in a bad mood. "We've got a church dinner to go to so we'll only be here a little while," she huffed, then took the baby from me like it was on her list of things to do. The little girl let out a shriek that could shatter glass.

Connor and Pop Herne arrived, both holding bundles of mums. "I'll take my little girl," Connor called out to his sister.

"It's a wonder she don't need another transfusion," I said, "the way she's been passed around today."

Connor took the baby over to his father. "See how good she is." The baby kept crying.

"We have to start calling her something other than little girl," Tempy said.

"Matilda's a nice name," Mrs. Herne said. "We can call her Tillie."

"For a dog," I blurted. The reins of my mouth had loosened and before I knew it, I was a runaway horse.

"That's my mother's name," Mrs. Herne snapped.

"I was thinking Connie, after Connor." I looked at him, expecting support.

"People'll think she's named after Connie Deems," Tempy said, "that preacher's wife that ran off with the deacon."

"No, it's after Connor. That's plain enough."

163

Both Mrs. Herne and Tempy glared, half-surprised that I was talking back to them after barely holding my own in a conversation for the last seven months. Truth be told, they scared me to death. But this baby was mine. I ought to at least be able to name her.

"Connor's his own man and his son should be named after him," Wallis said, "not a girl."

"How about Bathsheba?" I asked.

"I will not have my grandchild named after a biblical adulterer."

"That's my sister's middle name," I said through gritted teeth.

"How about Constance," Tempy offered, half-conciliatory.

"Lord, no," Connor piped up. "That was the second grade teacher that 'bout beat me to death for telling her some day we'd go to the moon. Insisting only Jesus Christ could make that trip."

Mr. Herne laughed and seemed amused. "Some day we'll get to outer space, son. Until then, how about Selena, after the moon?"

Mrs. Herne dismissed it with a wave of her hand. "Too sassy, Pop. Everybody will think the child's daft. It's settled then. Matilda."

I glanced over at one of the movie magazines Lynn and Sissy had brought. Tallulah Bankhead was on the cover, shaking a finger at the photographer. "Tallulah," I announced. "I'm going to name my daughter Tallulah. It's not after anybody. She'll not owe one person a thing in this lifetime. It was me that carried her, me that got cut open and by God, I'm going to call my daughter Tallulah."

Wallis and Tempy's expressions could have melted butter. They mirrored each other by raising a pointed finger, but thank God, Connor jumped in before either of them could speak. "She'll be my little Lulah-bell." He whirled around singing, "Lulah-bell, Lulah-bell, who do you love, Lulah-bell, Lulah-bell, why don't you tell?" Then he put his cheek next to hers and whispered, "Daddy loves you."

She yowled, belting like the world better pay attention. I expected Wallis to say, *See, the child doesn't like the name, either*, but no one said a word now that Connor had approved the name. "Give her to me," I said, reaching out again.

This time he listened and I laid her against my chest where she quieted down. Everybody in the room did as well, amazed that a plaintive wail could be stilled by my touch. I thought she must be listening to my heartbeat and I held fast, afraid to disturb her.

"Got a surprise," Pop Herne said, patting his hands against the air. He stepped up beside his wife. "Tenants of the Notown house are moving in the spring." He looked back and forth between Connor and me. "Mom and I want to give the place to you."

Connor gasped and Tempy allowed herself a tight-lipped smile, trying to pretend she was happy for us even if her parents had just demonstrated the financial rewards that marriage could bring. Well, Tempy, old girl, I was equally as distressed. My belly hurt, my baby screamed non-stop the minute I let go of her, I'd lived my whole life trying to escape Notown, and here I was being sent back, tail between my legs. All I could do was let out a half-hissy giggle.

"See how glad she is, Pop," Connor said.

Wallis clapped her hands and I figured she was happy as plum pie to get me out of the back room that used to be her sewing space. I could have just spit. Connor, big smile on his face, leaned on the edge of the bed and held my hand until everybody left. "Our own house," he said as if he couldn't believe it.

"It doesn't have a bathroom, Connor," I said, my eyes about to spill tears.

"City water'll be there by summer, I'll build us an indoor bathroom." His grin froze like he was getting irritated with me for not being more grateful. "I'll get Rusty and Herman to help, won't take no time at all."

"Yeah, Rusty, he ain't even got his own. They still piss in the creek."

"Doesn't have," Connor corrected me, "he doesn't have his own." He didn't say it in a mean way but it irked me all the more. "Might as well get her used to talking like educated people," he said with one of his goofy grins that made me want to smack him. "Pop and I have to take Mom and Tempy to the church, but we'll stop by later tonight."

I let out a sigh and looked down at the baby, soundly sleeping. I handed him Tallulah. "Put her in the bassinette and pray she don't cry, I've got to get some sleep." I turned my head sideways and closed my eyes. When I opened them several seconds later, he was gone. The baby, mercifully asleep.

෴

When I recalled what had happened this afternoon, I giggled at my brazenness and regretted my coldness. Momma was right. I needed to be better to Connor. This baby was about him and me, and maybe with a house to ourselves, we could rekindle the spiciness. Maybe within a few years I could talk him into moving back to Contrary.

I slept again and when I opened my eyes hours later, the window was dark and reflected the room. The nurses had said it was the darkest day of the year. I couldn't even make out the mountains in the distance. The reflected room looked like a jail cell, only the mums breaking the straight angles of the furniture. I drifted off again into an uneasy rest.

A deep breath startled me. A figure stood in the doorway, backlit by the green hue from the hall. Connor must have returned. I closed my eyes again and listened to the soft padding of footsteps across the room. I debated whether or not to sit up and talk to him, then opened my eyes. The reflection in the window showed him holding the baby. She wasn't crying.

Now that didn't feel right. I blinked, focusing my eyes. Connor's back was toward me, his hair curling over the back of his collar, but Connor's hair wasn't that long. Spiral ringlets bounced like springs from a fountain pen. I remembered a blue eye staring at me through a hole in the door. Luther!

I shot up out of the bed. "Give her to me," I said.

He spun around like an imp I'd imagined hiding in the woods, clinging to the Fear Angel's feet. Surely she was flapping her wings in this room now as Luther gently rocked my child. His eyelids flipped up, an eggplant color like a bruise.

My belly screamed, the stitches busted, and liquid dripped down my leg. My blood. I still held out my arms but was ready to pounce on him like a wildcat. "Luther, I'm ain't telling you again. Put down my little girl or–"

"Then give me what's mine," he interrupted. His body moved like a snake curving around a tree and when he spoke rotted teeth showed between his lips. The years of prison showed on his face . . . a scar embedded in one eyebrow, pasty skin and two black fingernails. His deeply creviced forehead spread unnaturally large, bald at his temples with a lock of white blond hair curled in the middle.

"All I want's my little girl," he whispered. His voice broke on the last words, lips pressed into a frown.

"Put her in the crib," I said softly. "Do that and I'll tell you."

He gave the baby a squeeze and I let out a soft cry. His free hand petted Tallulah's head and cupped her scalp. "L'il darling, L'il darling, will you be mine," he sang gently.

"Enough, Uncle Luther. You promised."

He laid her in the bassinette and his stench wafted over me. I anchored myself in front of the crib, hands wide so he'd not get at her again.

"Where is she?" he asked. "My Bette?"

The nurse passed the door. I had no choice. "The baby!" I howled.

"What's going on?" she demanded and flipped on the light switch. In the brightness Luther looked like a wild man.

The nurse screamed for all she was worth. I jumped full-bodied on Uncle Luther and we crashed to the floor. Nurses, doctors and finally security guards came running. They took Luther away and I kept telling everybody that if we didn't leave the hospital that night, I was suing them all. Soon the doctor patched me up and agreed I could go home.

The nurse tried to take a bawling Tallulah from my arms, complaining that's why babies should always stay in the nursery.

"Let me just quiet her down," I said, holding her firm against me like she was part of my own body. She was Connor and she was Notown and she was an angel. She was my world and I'd never let a thing bad touch her. I guess you could say I took to her, and as she smacked her lips and cried no more. I think she took to me too. By the time Connor returned, I calmed down and acted like nothing had happened. He was so happy that we were going home that he didn't ask any questions and the hospital staff was just as happy to put it out of their minds as well.

❦

By summertime I was back in Notown, rocking a squalling baby on the front porch and watching the cars drive by. Now and then somebody I knew waved. Notown had a particular smell in summer, a suffocating greenness that lingered like burnt food. I imagined it must be the way miners felt when they got trapped underground, surrounded by black rock that made

169

fortunes for some people but broke the backs of others. I knew that Notown would break my back and all I thought about was how to convince Connor to get us out of here. I'd have to lead him gently, make him think it was his big idea. He always talked about how exploring outer space would eventually be a cooperative effort for the greater good. So I aimed to be his cooperative wife and think of this family's future.

It had been a year of convincing people to embrace ideas they didn't like. The September before Tallulah was born, those students in Arkansas had been brave enough to walk into that white school. There were squawks-and-hawks as Daddy used to say when people yelled about things that didn't make much difference. The schools in Crimson County integrated as well with less fanfare. The Negro teachers lost their jobs, except for the principal, who was put on as the high school janitor. Divergence must have hated what happened to their educated people who'd given their lives to youngsters, but they maintained a silent dignity. Notown, on the other hand, had never spawned a teacher so I doubted anybody around here even noticed. Seemed that the greater good always had its victims.

I felt that keeping Bette's burial place to myself was my heroic gesture, even though it had put my daughter in danger. Uncle Luther lost his parole and went back to the penitentiary to serve out his time. I learned then that his last name was Ballard, not Gaylor, and with Momma's help the Hernes never learned he was related to me or about what had happened in the hospital. She had some kind of contact at city hall, but she wouldn't tell me who it was. Luther's reappearance caused a lot trouble between Momma and Daddy and I felt bad, but I'd learned that she had a way of knowing the right thing to do. If I had to live in Notown, I hoped some of her smarts rubbed off on me.

23

That Day . . . June 30, 1987

Again Randi Jo slaps the bound man across the jaw. He winces, then exhales with a deep throaty chuckle. "Don't hurt a'tall," he mouths through the tape. "Come on, honey, give me some more." He looks her directly in the eyes, challenging her like a pack dog.

She sits on the edge of the bed, wanting to kick him in the face. There's nothing she can do to hurt him. Her only satisfaction would be in killing him, and she needs to toughen up to do that . . . to do it and be able to live with it. She has to steel herself to take a life, to justify it. She isn't sure why . . . he wouldn't be the first man she's killed.

There had been more dead bodies in her life than fingers on a hand. Some she'd loved, one she'd feared, and others . . . she didn't even know. He would be the only one where love and hate, passion and disgust, fear and loathing had ruled her. He'd be the only one she would enjoy killing.

She tugs at a piece of duct tape over his mouth, then rips it off, knowing how that stings. "Hurt?"

"I'm the one who tried to help you," he pleads. "You were just a white-trash piece of ass to every man you knew 'til I came along."

His words burn through Randi Jo like a match held to wax. A cardinal lands on the windowsill, looking in at them like a witness. She watches it.

"I taught you things–how to whistle . . . how to hold your own in a fight. Nobody messed with you when you were with me."

The cardinal pecks at the window frame and then flies away. She follows its flight into the pines above the house. The mysterious woods, her refuge from the world where dark things hid, the place she ran where she could cry out her deepest hurt and no one would see.

A deep breath. She remembers the day she met him. For her, he had been an escape. Her world had fallen apart and there was no one to pick her up. She hadn't even been able to help herself. "So you're saying we can try again?"

"Why not?" His eyebrows rise, his gaze like a hungry lion's. "First you don't succeed and all that."

"What about first you call the sheriff, admit everything you've done and pay your dues to society and to me, then we'll sit down and have a real good talk about the future?"

"Sure, R.J., you go call the law."

173

She chuckles, drops to her knees and mocks him. "Like I'd trust the spite that comes out of your mouth."

He jerks in his chair, wrenches one hand free and catches hold of her hair. "I swear to God, Randi Jo, you are still the stupidest bitch this side of tarnation!"

"Let go!" She pushes against him, pounding her small fists on his chest but with no effect.

"Untie this other hand or I'll put your nose in the back of your head." He tries to leverage his leg so he can knee her in the face.

He jerks again and again. Randi Jo watches the strain on the ropes, hoping they hold. She grips his free hand against her head to keep him from pulling out her hair. Then in the room behind them, a scrape of wood against the floor as the front door opens then closes. They stare at each other, frozen in expectation. Waiting. Footsteps move through the house where they wait. Whoever enters the room will be life or death for one of them. A white sheet across the door shivers as a hand touches it. Randi Jo holds her breath. "Here," she calls out finally. "I'm back here! I need help!"

A black man's head ducks under the sheet. He stands upright, his frame filling the doorway and almost touching the ceiling. Skin, an inky blue, eyes like lumps of coal. He looks at Randi Jo, then at the man in the chair, who has ceased struggling against the ropes. The grip on her hair loosens and she feels his fingers relax. The shocked expression on his face melts into fear.

Randi Jo kicks his shin and yanks her hair from his grasp. "Don't have such a smart mouth now, do you?"

24

When I was twenty-nine . . .

Sweeping. Half hypnotized with each swoosh of the scraggy broom. Seemed that half my life was lived sweeping . . . my Momma's house, my house, and the Hernes' giant stockroom in back of their store. Here I was long since married and the mother of a ten-year-old, but still stuck in Notown, and that didn't make me feel like I'd advanced much in life. Wished I could sweep the cobwebs out my mind, but then I'd have to admit I wasn't much more than the swish of a broom.

Today, my sweep was at Herne's Grocery. Connor's pop paid me ten dollars a week to spread sawdust on that storage space floor and then clean it up. Connor was pretty good about letting me keep the spending money while he took care of all the household costs. He taught math and physics at Crimson County High School and in the summer worked as a camp counselor for the First Baptist. I don't go to church unless I have to. Too many reminders of how life is supposed to be lived. I didn't need to feel worse than I already did about all the things I'd done.

Dustpans of sawdust and dirt got tossed outside in an alley behind the store. The upstairs apartment's back porch hung out over the alley and I stood under it to unwrap a Moon Pie I'd sneaked from a box in the storeroom. It didn't feel like stealing. If somebody was at my house, and hungry, I wouldn't mind them taking a banana off the table, so I told myself all this food was family food and they couldn't grudge me a Moon Pie.

Rusty zipped down the alley in his police car, then slowed to wave as he passed. I nodded back, thinking he was acting like such a big shot in that cruiser. He and Lynn still barely had a pot to piss in, but he was a tough one. Couple years back, two old boys from Coalfire tried to rob the First National Bank. Rusty blocked their getaway car with his and waited outside smoking a cigarette until they came running out. He tripped the first one, who went spiraling to the sidewalk, and punched the second one so hard he broke his nose on the first blow.

Just as the marshmallow pastry met my lips I heard somebody talking up on the porch above. I looked up and saw two pairs of legs hanging over the banister and Tempy peering down at me. She was with someone but focused on the Moon Pie raised to my mouth, ready to devour. Crap. My mind rolled out all the excuses I could use . . . found it damaged so what's the harm, bought it at a store in Notown and brung it with me. Crap.

Then I saw my way out, and my lips must have formed the cruelest little snicker 'cause Tempy's eyes shimmered with the panic of having been caught. She was holding Iona Stark's hand. Their special relationship was whispered about in town. Some people just called them old maids, and others giggled behind their backs.

"Hello, Iona," I called out.

The Stark woman looked down at me as she jerked her hand from Tempy's. Her expression was as distressed as her girlfriend's.

"Surprised I haven't seen you out here before," I said with some glee as I bit into the Moon Pie, the graham crackers and marshmallows sticking to my teeth. "I come out here every week to have myself a little break." Tempy and I locked eyes. She knew that I knew, and I knew that she knew. Okay, I thought, we'll keep each other's little secret, girls, but you better not tell mine.

I gobbled half my pie, saving the rest for when I'd finished work. I put Mr. Moon back in the plastic covering and hid it between some toilet paper boxes in back, then took a little rest on the steps up to the apartment above the store in a place where they couldn't see me.

Mom Herne's scratchy voice came from inside the stockroom. "You missed under the shelf ledge."

I jumped up, swishing the broom back and forth on the steps so she wouldn't know I'd been resting. "It's this broom, Mrs. Herne," I said, meeting her at the back door. "It's plumb worn to a nub. If you let me use–"

"It's the stockroom broom, still got a year on it." Wallis Herne pointed at the narrow base ledge of the

177

shelving against the wall. She followed me all the way down the row, making little *uh-huh* sounds every time a piece of sawdust was jarred loose. "And get behind that door, too," she snapped.

I wanted so bad to talk back to her but I bit my tongue. As I swept behind the door, an old rifle slid against the wall and landed in the corner. I picked it up by the barrel.

"Careful with that!" Mrs. Herne swiped the gun from me and adjusted it at an angle against the wall so it wouldn't fall again. "Got the sense of a dustball," she hissed under her breath.

Then I went back to sweeping, nothing but sweeping.

ↄ

Sweeping. My kitchen now. A beef rump roasted in the oven. I should have been happy that I had some kind of meat every night. Sometimes I thought back to the time me and my brothers and sisters devoured our Friday protein like we were in a dogfight. Every pinch, smack and punch seemed like an amusing memory now that we'd grown up. The older boys all married Notown girls, except for Pug, who lived with one whose name I didn't even remember. Gene, Casper and Melvin worked in the mines with Daddy. The younger boy, Hector, joined the army along with Ernie Cooley and was sent straight to what they called in letters the *boonies of Vietnam*. Mrs. Cooley and Momma spent their time worrying and comforting each other, especially with all the news reports about the Tet Offensive in late January.

I figured it was better they were over there fighting the Vietnamese 'cause here they'd just be fighting each other. Some things about Notown never changed.

My broom nudged into a corner behind the stove. Sweeping in a better kitchen than I'd grown up in didn't make me feel all that much better. Everybody's life moved on but mine. Patsy and Rhoda won scholarships to a nursing school in Knoxville, and Cane was in high school. Momma hoped the war ended soon 'cause there was talk of a government draft and she sure didn't want her youngest son sent to fight. For my other brother, Butch, she still took care of him like he was a little baby even though he was fifteen and had only grown to the size of a large toddler. The youngest, Collette, was in the same grade as my Tallulah and both girls got a kick out of telling everyone they were aunt and niece.

In the living room, Connor dozed on the couch while waiting for the six o'clock news. Beside him Tallulah did math homework on a tray. I'd stopped sweeping and watched them like they were a calendar picture, one of those folksy Norman Rockwell ones that the hardware store gave out every year at Christmas.

My husband and daughter had never known the kind of hunger that drove you to do almost anything for food. They saw suffering on the evening news when Vietnamese children ran from bombs exploding their houses, but they didn't understand it. The hard times they'd experienced had been no more than inconveniences. Tallulah had a streak of rebel. Last year she mounted a campaign at the Notown school to get the first grader's room painted, and raised the money by going to every store in Quinntown and Contrary asking for donations. When she got that self-righteous determination in her eyes part of me wanted to smack her, yet when she stood up against something wrong, I was proud enough to bust.

I set the table, prepared the salad and filled glasses with ice. Tallulah liked the cup with the Cinderella picture, a fairytale she never outgrew. I could see why. Her own hair was blond as that of a fairy princess. She had her Daddy's amber eyes and his wide smile. Not much in the way to show that she also belonged to me, but she was a pretty girl and had more friends than I ever did.

I motioned for her to come in to the table, then gently shook Connor's arm.

"It's in the ground," he said, startled awake, "burning up."

I ignored his words. Another one of his dreams. "Dinner's ready." Sometimes he talked in his sleep, saying things like, *World's about to explode.* On nights when he talked scary, I put my fingers in my ears and squeezed my eyes tight until the Valkyries took me into a deep blue sleep.

Connor yawned and got up without saying anything.

At the table Tallulah set her salad aside and heaped her plate with peas. "Eat your salad first," I said. "I'm not throwing half of it away because the lettuce is wilted."

"Aunt Tempy says salad is to be eaten last. It's the European way."

"I don't care what Aunt Tempy says."

"But I have to practice for the church dinner when I'm presented to the congregation as a candidate for baptism. I'll look like a know-nothing eating my salad first."

"You think I'm a know-nothing?"

"Don't want to have to hear fussing at home," Connor interrupted, "I have smart-alecky teenagers all day long who can't divide a positive integer by a negative if their lives depended on it."

Tallulah smiled at her father and salted her peas. Connor ate the salad and that was good 'cause I might have run him through with the butter knife if he'd put it aside. He looked into the living room at the TV set, listening to Huntley and Brinkley talk about the Civil Rights Act that President Johnson was set to sign.

Ten years ago at Copperhead Fields all our friends had argued about civil rights that we barely understood. I graduated from high school, got married, moved in with my in-laws, shuffled back to Notown, and settled into domestic boredom. Those black kids who walked into that white high school in Arkansas had only taken the first step. Now they were getting their very own law and nobody could ever ban them from a school again. I wondered if that law would make them feel as equal as the words said.

Connor tapped Tallulah on the shoulder and asked, "Finish that science paper on Einstein?"

She nodded and followed his gaze to the TV set. "Almost done. Will you check my spelling?"

"Remember me to tell you about Einstein's dream of riding on a moonbeam." Connor's eyes sparkled and his face was animated with life. I seldom saw that expression anymore. He described riding on that moonbeam as if he was sitting behind Albert Einstein himself. I wondered if that was what he dreamed about.

Reckon that's as close to outer space as he'd ever get. In a lot of ways his life ended up being more of a disappointment than mine but for some reason all I felt was jealous that her father was checking her spelling and not me.

Tallulah dug a fork into her salad and bit into a chunk of lettuce. A few pieces had wilted and she pushed them aside when she thought I wasn't looking. "Aunt Tempy says the salad is meant to cleanse the palate."

I let out a laugh. "Yeah, Tempy needs to have her palate cleaned."

"Randi Jo," Connor said sternly.

Connor sat erect and patted his daughter's shoulder. "Tempy's trying to make sure Tallulah gets in with the right people. She'll be in high school in a few years."

"Right people," I said. "You should have thought of that before you moved us to Notown." I got up and left the room, changing the channel to Walter Cronkite, and plopping on the couch where they couldn't see me. I liked him better anyway.

"Call me if they announce anything about the Saturn Five rocket, Randi Jo," Connor called out like I was his appointment secretary. I mouthed the words in sassy fashion. This talk of being accepted into Contrary society was a big joke. Didn't Connor realize he married a Notown girl? Sometimes I thought he didn't even see me. All I amounted to was being this appendage to their important lives. My daughter was nothing like me. She belonged to them . . . the Herne's. I was still a nobody from Notown. No law would ever make me better than Notown . . .

I sat up. Something was wrong with Walter Cronkite. His face had changed as he paused just the way he did when he announced the assassination of President Kennedy. I shook myself and listened to the news about Martin Luther King. "Connor," I called out.

My husband was already up and on his way, probably thinking there was something on about the Saturn Five rocket. Connor lowered himself on the couch beside me as we listened to a report of Dr. King having been shot.

"Who is he, Daddy?" Tallulah asked.

"A brilliant man," Connor answered, leaning forward toward the set and rubbing his hands on his forehead.

"Smart as Mr. Einstein?"

"In a different way."

I went to the kitchen, got my broom, and started sweeping. Connor and Tallulah stayed in front of the TV. Guess there was no law to help Dr. King, I thought, and swept over the same areas as before, not knowing what to do. A while later, an audible sigh came from the living room. "They've killed him," Connor said.

Late into the night car horns blasted into the air from Divergence . . . they rang out like bagpipes all the way down Notown Road. The folks living there wouldn't riot or cause the kinds of trouble that happened in the big cities, but they blew their horns all night long. I didn't mind it. It was like they were hollering out to heaven, "Good-bye, Dr. King, and good-night."

25

Today I had the car so could cart home groceries. After dropping Connor and Tallulah off at school, I swung by Holly's house. If she was free, maybe we could go out to Pinkie's Drive-in and talk like we used to. I so seldom saw my old girlfriends anymore. Seemed like our lives had drawn new circles that seldom intersected.

The driveway gate to the Carmack estate was locked so I parked on the street and walked the stone path through magnolia trees and patches of tiger lilies. A fountain in the side yard spurted water that plopped back to earth in sharp throbs. Stone paths led through bricked-off sections filled with every kind of flower I could imagine. I started to go around back toward the kitchen but movement through the living room window drew me in.

Voices rattled the windowpanes and dented the calm garden. The few peaceful minutes I'd just spent here made me want to turn away from the ugly tones I heard. Through the window, I saw Holly gesturing wildly. Willie stood like an oak tree, hands on his hips. I couldn't make out the words, but his manner was fierce. Holly's face scrunched, her lips quivered and twisted spitefully. Her husband's expression was stone, as if he didn't care, but I knew he did, if only in his hate. Holly threw a vase that shattered against a wall. That seemed to be all Willie could stand and he marched forward, backhanding her on his final step. She flew out of sight.

I leaned against a maple tree, hidden in case they looked outside. I couldn't bear to watch anymore and felt like throwing up. Sometimes I wished Connor cared enough to fight with me . . . until I saw a scene like this. Sometimes I hated myself for not being happy with what I had. Things could've been a lot worse. I'd never tell Holly what I saw, but even if I did mention it she would shrug it off as though vicious fighting was just part of marriage, the way some people considered robbing a bank just another job opportunity.

I got into the car and drove, circling past the fancy houses of Edgewood and Indian Hills, then took the back road to Quinntown where I stopped at Curley's Café to order a hotdog and a coke like I used to in high school. I walked along the main street, window-shopping, and even ventured down Marcescent Street. Nobody noticed me. I was an adult woman now and could walk where I wanted.

I had chosen Quinntown 'cause I wouldn't run into a Herne. I got a soft ice cream cone at Frog's corner store and sat on the Lester Street bridge to eat it. The Regal

Hotel still stood, though its green paint was more worn and flaked off on the alley side. Questionable women still went in and out. Most towns in Crimson County were voted dry, so there was no liquor to be found and all the slot machines had been removed. If you wanted that kind of action you had to know somebody and get into a back room that the bootleggers maintained like luxury suites. The Regal woman knew where to find those who had such needs, 'cause at regular intervals they came back with staggering men in tow.

Dr. Huber exited his office building on Lester Street. With an intent look on his face he crossed the street, carrying his doctor's bag. His hair was gray now and he walked with a slight stoop. He passed me but didn't recognize me, and I didn't call out to him. Did he sometimes wonder whatever happened to me? Probably not. I doubted that he thought of Randi Jo Gaylor from Notown for a second after I left his office. I couldn't blame him. There were other people to help. I was just another invisible person he passed on his way to where he was going. My little excursion away from home was supposed to make me feel better but my mood kept sinking.

Again I drove, trying to feel cheerful. Simon and Garfunkle sang "The Sound of Silence" on the radio and it made me sad. Windows down, wind blowing my hair, I wanted to re-live the high school life, when I'd always dreamed of a bright future out in the wide world. I parked at Copperhead Fields now re-named Stark Park and Recreation Area. It was a school day so I had the swings to myself. I considered going to Sissy's but wasn't sure I had the energy. Hardly ever saw Lynn anymore and when I did, we had nothing to talk about. She lay on the couch all day, watching soap operas and reading *True Detective* when she had the money to buy a magazine. The world passed her by even more than me. Poor Lynn weighed almost three hundred pounds now and it hurt to see her.

A police car slowed as it passed the park, made a U-turn and pulled into the parking lot. Rusty waved, stopped beside my car, then got out and came over to sit in the swing next to me.

"This is starting to be our Thursday thing," he said.

A bit defensively I explained, "I come here 'cause I got the car and it's the only day I can get out of the house without having to be somewhere."

It was quiet between us. Sun was warm for April. We had talked like this every Thursday for the last couple months, and I appreciated someone who understood Notown and worked in Contrary as I did. Connor thought people were people, wherever they were. I knew they were different. Contrary folk considered themselves far better than us. Rusty knew that, too. He protected their homes, broke up fights, kept the riff-raff from Quinntown and Notown from getting too comfortable on their streets, and had 'em back home in their own neighborhoods before nightfall. Two-faced as an Indian nickel, he'd said in one of our conversations.

"How do you manage on just one day of freedom?" Rusty asked.

"I smile and grit my teeth," I said, mimicking a circus clown.

"Too much wear on the wisdom teeth," he chuckled. "Need all the wisdom I can get."

I laughed with him and filled my cheeks with air. He poked a finger on each side to deflate them and we laughed again. "I started to go by and get Lynn today. Thought she might like to go get a bit to eat."

He rolled his eyes and shuddered. "She doesn't need any more food."

"Rusty, you oughten talk about her like that. She's bored stiff in that house with three kids. If I didn't get the car once a week, I'd be fat as her, too."

He laughed and slapped his knee as if he couldn't imagine me that size. His police radio went on. He sprinted to the cruiser, said something into the speaker, then turned to me. "Fire over on the canal bank, gotta go."

"Connor's probably said worse about me," I hollered after him.

"Then Connor's a fool." He rounded the car but paused without getting in.

There was an instant between us, a frozen moment. I should have gone over and smacked Rusty, told him not to speak about my husband that way. Should have got up and walked off. But I didn't. I didn't say anything.

Our eyes locked and he knew the moment, too. He knew what I should have done, what his wife would have done for him, but I sat there mum. "See you next Thursday."

"Got two dollars you can loan me? Ought to get gas before Connor sees the tank's near empty." I didn't expect Rusty to give me money. Didn't know why I'd asked. Maybe just wanted to see if I could get it from him.

He pulled a wallet from his back pocket. "You won't tell Connor, will you?"

"Why would I tell?"

"He wouldn't like me giving you money."

"What he don't know won't hurt him."

Rusty held out the bills, holding to them and making me tug them from his grasp. "Be our secret then."

"Got lots of those," I said, rolling the bills into a straw and sliding them down the front of my shirt into my bra. He grinned, his gaze traveling the length of my body. On the swing I pushed off the ground, my feet aiming at the sun and my head resting on the wind. Closing my eyes, I imagined flying with the Valkyries in a dark sky among millions of stars. When I slowed and came to a stop, the sun was hot. Sweat dripped down my neck. A cardinal flew past and landed on the slide. Spring felt good and free, at least on my Thursdays. I looked over at the parking lot. Rusty was gone. To go fight his fire.

༄

After dropping the groceries at home, I picked Tallulah up from school and we waited in the high school parking lot for Connor to get off work. I hoped to talk him into going to Pinkie's Drive-In for dinner 'cause I didn't feel like cooking. Tallulah leaned over the seat and fooled with the radio, finally settling on The Who singing "I Can See for Miles." She had a neon pink headband tied around her forehead and knew I was staring at it in the rear view mirror.

"Your father'll make you take that off."

She wrinkled her nose. "Bet he won't," she sassed back.

I rolled my eyes and pressed my lips into a smirk, then switched the radio station to one playing The Four Seasons singing "Come on, Marianne."

She moaned, "I've been killed by sugar-laced music, give some of that ole time rock-and-roll, a good protest song, a little 'Eve of Destruction'." Again she leaned over, changed the station, and Janis Ian's "Society's Child" came on.

"You're gonna save the world, Tallulah."

She adjusted her headband. "Momma, why are you so mean to Aunt Tempy?"

A flare of resentment shot through me. "How is it you see it that way?"

"She's got a bad time coming up and I wish you'd be nicer to her."

I shook my head. "Okay, I'll suck in your fish hook. What's old Temperance crying about?"

"Iona Stark's getting married."

I laughed, smacking my knee. "Yeah, I bet that is upsetting her."

"The Starks are making Iona marry Wayne Bacon."

"And you're into everybody's business, because…?"

"It's the pits, making her marry somebody she can't stand to be in the same room with."

I closed my eyes. My daughter, the righter of all wrongs, was a product of her decade. "You're not a baby anymore, Tallulah. You can't talk about certain things out loud."

"If more people talked out loud there'd be less social injustice, discrimination, and war. We're two societies in this town, Momma, and I'm going to point it out every time I can."

"You're just now noticing that?" My gaze landed on the gas gauge. Past empty. I'd forgotten to fill up. "We have to run real quick to the gas station."

"There's Daddy." Tallulah pointed.

My heart caught in my throat. I'd used up the gas driving around and had to keep Connor from noticing until I got the car refilled. From the passenger seat he might not look at the gauge. I drove up to the sidewalk, waved and called out, "I'll drive, taking you out to eat, my treat." I flipped off the blasting music.

Connor jumped in and slumped. "Take the headband off, Tallulah,"

"Ahhhh," she huffed but removed it.

"Long day. I tell you, these kids . . . We back talked a teacher in my day and she'd knock you across the room." Connor rubbed his eyes and leaned his head back on the seat.

I pulled out on the road, smiling as if agreeing with every word he said. He and Tallulah chatted about her science homework. If I could get them to sit out on the picnic tables and order, I could say I left something at Holly's and had to get it while they ate.

Connor rubbed his face with both hands and sat up. "What'd you do today?"

I rambled, sweat beading my lip, and I kept looking over to catch his eye so his thoughts wouldn't wander.

"Did you pick up my hawk feathers from Uncle Gene, Momma?" Tallulah asked. "I need them for art class. He said he'd go up in the woods to find some."

The car sputtered to a stop. Connor's eyes went to the gauge. "We're out of gas. How in tarnation?" He looked at me. "Ain't you got sense enough to watch the meter?" He smacked the dashboard.

"I, I watched the meter—" I stuttered.

"I put in half a tank three days ago."

"I don't know what happened."

"You've been loafin' all day and you used up all the gas!"

"I did not," I hollered back. "I get the car only one day a week! You're the one with it the rest of the time!"

"I know what I used!"

"Stop it!" Tallulah yelled from the back seat. "Stop fighting, I can't stand it!" She covered her face with both hands and fell onto the seat sobbing.

I coasted into a parking space on Laynchark. Connor's lips were pressed into a thin line. The only sound, our daughter crying. He opened his door. "I'll walk over to Herman's and get a can of gas."

I leaned my forehead on the steering wheel. Tallulah sniffed, swallowed a few hiccups, then looked around, rubbing her red eyes. The two dollars Rusty had given me burned in my pocket. I pulled them out and told Tallulah, "Here, when we go to town Saturday, buy yourself something." Shyly she took the money. Then, something hit the top of the car with a thud. "What was that?" I asked, startled.

There was the sound of scratching on the roof, then another bounce, and two feathers floated down the windshield and caught on the wipers. "Reckon there's your feathers for the art project," I said.

Tallulah pointed toward the sky. "There, Momma. A hawk. It must have landed on the car." I shielded my eyes and stared up at the wide wingspan of a bird circling too high for me to recognize the type. "Wow, like an angel dropped them from heaven."

I reached out the window for the feathers and handed them to her. She waved the feathers in the air like she was conducting an orchestra. For me nothing good ever came of angels scurrying about, and I wondered what bad thing would happen next.

"Momma," she said, "if you want, I can say you had to drive up the mountain to get these. Daddy will never know."

"Would you do that, honey?" My lower lip trembled, knowing that I was soliciting my daughter to lie. Now Tallulah knew her first family secret and would tell her first fib to protect her mother, and it was my fault.

When Connor returned with the gas he motioned for me to move to the passenger seat, and I did, and he drove off. He made a U-turn and headed for home. I guess I was cooking dinner.

Later that night in bed I lay turned away from Connor. I closed my eyes and tried to imagine riding a moonbeam. I couldn't. That, I decided, was the problem between them and me. He thought about things like exploring space and so did Tallulah. I wasn't part of their connection and didn't understand my husband and daughter any more than they understood me.

Connor moaned and I turned toward him. His lips moved.

"What?" I asked. He shook his head, eyes blinking as he dreamed. I leaned over and put my ear to his lips. "Mountain's on fire," he said.

I shook his arm. He muttered but didn't wake. It wasn't the first time he'd said strange things in his sleep. His dreams flew off to far off places and I figured he must be riding that moonbeam with Mr. Einstein.

"See the seraphs," he said. "They hate us."

His words gave me a shiver. I thought back to Veda Huston talking about a person coming for me who had been touched by a dark mother and saw horror. Who'd have thought it'd be my husband.

26

Sweeping. Pretty mad, too. With the marriage of Iona Stark coming up this weekend Tempy was in a foul mood and had lost her temper three times today over the stupidest stuff. *Sweep by the vegetables. Don't stir up dust sweeping by the vegetables. Don't sweep up that cluster of grapes, we can wash it and sell it.* I swear she's crazy. Mom and Pop Herne placated her with offers to go shopping in Knoxville and a Niagara vacation in the summer. They were crazy, too. Didn't they know people went to Niagara Falls on their honeymoons? That would remind her all the more. Tempy moped around, slinking into every corner and dabbing at her eyes. I wanted to feel sorry for her but she'd been so mean to me that I'd just as soon my sympathies water the flowers.

My back ached from bending over to get the scum and cobwebs from under the bottom of the stockroom shelves. But that's the way Miss Wallis-Queen-of-Contrary wanted it. Out front she was getting ready to

195

take Tempy to lunch at the Essex Hotel. Bragged to me about it earlier. That left only Pop Herne managing the cash register. At the meat counter cream-colored chickens parked in a row looked lined up for a can-can dance. Pop had been trying new ways to compete with Cas Walker's Supermarkets and his *thumpin' good melons* advertised on the Knoxville radios and his own television show. People somehow considered Cas's products better and drove sixty miles to buy from the *ole Coonhunter,* as he called himself. In our backyard Momma used to grab a chicken and sling it around until its neck was wrung off. The headless body flapped in all directions as if it could find its lost head. Soon as it fell, she'd pick it up by the feet, dip it in scalding water, then flop it on the picnic table and commence to feathering and gutting it. Most people walking into our store these days would faint if they ever saw a headless chicken flailing about.

In the stockroom I closed the door and went to put away my broom. About halfway down the aisle the lights shut off. I thought Tempy or Wallis had circled around and come in the back way to try and catch me doing something.

"Hey, I'm still in here," I called out. "Cut it out!"

The light switch was by the door into the store so whoever had put me in the dark was inside too. Boxes were stacked up so I couldn't see into the other aisle, but my gut told me somebody was over there.

"Tempy? Mrs. Herne?" Someone moved in my direction, their fingers lightly caressing the boxes. A streak of alarm shot up my back but I was also angry if somebody was playing a trick on me. The back door was only twenty feet away so I could run out into the alley if I had to.

At the end of the aisle one box jutted out. A hard shove would push it on the other side and trip whoever was over there. I sneaked up and positioned myself. The sound of caressing fingers got closer, near even with me, and I shoved with all my might.

The box flew all the way through, creating a hole. "Now, who is it?" I demanded, but saw only darkness... dust floating in the air, a rank odor of spoiled food, then I spotted grubby fingertips gripping the edge of the shelf and a face like an old Polaroid picture.

Luther!

We both sprinted toward the alley, his heavy boots tramping after me. I hit the door and fell out into bright sunlight, an instant of blindness. He grabbed my hair and we slammed against a trash bin. I screamed but back here nobody would hear me. He slung me around and I threw my hands up to protect myself.

"Ain't gonna hurt you," he said. Dirty blond ringlets hung to his shoulders and his scraggly beard covered any semblance of a face. Only his dark blue eyes pleaded with me and I flashed back to the eye staring at Pug and me. Uncle Luther looked like he'd been in a dungeon rather than a prison. He held me tightly under control. When he spoke his lips twisted each word. "You know what I want... what I come for ... Waited for all this time."

"Why do you want her?" I asked.

He didn't loosen his grip. "Got your Daddy's eyes." His stinking breath flowed over me until I could hardly stand it. "She had her momma's, all misty and black like the newly dug coal."

"Let me go, Uncle Luther. Daddy wouldn't want you hurting me like this."

"I'm family, Randi Jo." His voice softened, a dirty hand slipped up to my cheek, and he slapped me lightly then wound his fingers into my hair. "You should always be on family's side, no matter what."

If I could keep him talking, I figured maybe Mr. Herne would come back to check on me and scare him off. "If you loved her so much, why'd you kill her?"

He bent forward, like the words were an arrow shot through his chest. "I didn't kill her."

"Then who?" My mind reeled. I'd always assumed he'd killed the girl, and while he could be lying, his tone had the sound of believing every word.

"I know who did. And they'll never be brought to justice, so it's up to me to dish out vengeance." He clenched his jaw as if reliving a hateful memory.

"This don't have nothing to do with me. If you loved her, let the poor woman rest in peace. Where she's at now . . . it'll draw attention. It could get Momma and Daddy into trouble. Just remember that you loved her, Uncle Luther. Let her rest in your memory that way."

"Love?" His features shifted comically, like he'd heard a joke. "You only know a shade of that word, skinny little girl. Love is a cutthroat business." He jammed me against the trash bin, one hand on my throat. "Say where she is," he whispered

Looking into his eyes, I realized he was right. Love was a cutthroat business. Luther didn't have the sense to protect my family. With the mess he'd made of his own life, my father could end up in jail again. I had protected Daddy all those years ago and I'd be darned if I would let some love-crazed, vengeance-seeking uncle hurt him now. I realized then where Tallulah got her stubbornness. It wasn't in the Herne's blood or her father's disposition. It was in me.

"She's dust," I said. "I burned her in a fire, spread the ashes to the wind."

He moaned and his other hand gripped my throat, pressing the breath out of me. I clawed at his fingers, sputtered and kicked at him. "I told you what you wanted to know," I gasped.

His stony expression and saucered eyes had lost any comprehension of the world around him. All that was left of him was a look of emptiness that fascinated me. I'd stared at those eyes in a time of greatest despair. Maybe Fear Angel had come to him as well and possessed his soul, or meanness was something he'd had in him all his life. His pupils contained Pug's lust, and Momma's fury when she'd burned Kim's clothes, and my fear when I lied to Connor, and most likely Tempy's desperation as she contemplated life without the person she loved. I tried to speak, flailing my arms, but words were like cotton balls to men like him.

My life was being squeezed out of me. No thought of my daughter or my husband or my family. Dying was seconds passing, was about the person killing me, a man connected to me by blood.

I got a finger under his hands and grunted into his face. He only tightened his hold on my neck, mouthing words I couldn't make out. Tears spilled down his cheeks. From the side I saw a flash of white. Rusty's police car turned into the alley. I yanked on Uncle Luther's hair, causing him to cry out in surprise or pain, but he held me tight until a blow knocked him sideways.

I fell to my knees, wheezing in air, hands on my chest. Rusty kicked Luther in the stomach until he lay motionless on the ground, then knelt down next to me. "You okay?"

I nodded. He helped me up and Uncle Luther moaned and tried to rise. Rusty kicked him again, saying, "You move and you're a dead man." As Rusty leaned me against the trash bin I trembled and couldn't let go of him. All at once Luther jumped up and ran.

Rusty started to bolt after him but I almost fell, and he stayed with me and watched Luther tearing away down the alley. "I'll call the station," Rusty said, "we'll get people out looking for him."

"No," I said. "Let him go."

"Who is he?"

"Some old man, comes around wanting food. I didn't have none to sneak to him today and he got mad."

"Hell of a way to treat somebody who feeds you."

"You scared him. He won't be back again." I shrugged my shoulders to make a joke of it, eyeing Rusty's expression to see if he believed me. "Please don't say anything," I pleaded. "The Hernes'll be mad if they find out."

We watched Luther disappear past the factory field into the Marlybone neighborhood. "Plenty of hiding places up there," I said, "You'll get your shoes all muddy looking for him."

Rusty touched my neck and whistled. "Gonna be bruises." He patted my shoulder and looked me over. "Let me take you to lunch."

"Now that's what I need." I hoped to get his mind off Uncle Luther and glided through the stockroom and into the store. At the end of an aisle Pop was shelving a box of canned peas. He hadn't noticed anything going on.

I called out to him that I was leaving. He trotted over and gave me ten dollars. "For a job well done," he said.

I nodded. If only he knew.

27

I 'bout fainted when Rusty turned his police cruiser down Marcescent Street. "Where in the world are you going?" I stared at him.

"The Majestic Club. Alvey Stark took it over. Changed the name, added a kitchen. Everybody goes there."

"It's still got blacked out windows and I can hear the clipping pool balls and slot machines when I walk past."

"And when do you walk past?" He playfully punched my arm.

I was caught. He parked beside the Lester Street bridge and told the dispatcher that he was having lunch. "Rusty, it's one thing to walk down Marcescent to get somewhere else, but if somebody tells about seeing me in one of these joints, I'll never live it down."

"It's respectable now." He patted my arm. "Besides, they got the best steaks in the county."

Reluctantly I followed him into the new restaurant, afraid of who might be watching me. Of course, nobody was. Truth be known, only my husband and his family would have cared. Rusty was right. It was only lunch. No harm in that.

The air around me cooled a few degrees, a pleasant feeling. Deep burgundy velvet curtains lined the walls and draped around dark paneled booths. A long mahogany bar glistened and glasses made a sharp clicking sound each time someone rested a beer mug. We sat in a booth and Rusty ordered us steaks, medium rare. On the other side of the room Renita Stark lunched with friends, the only female in the family of rowdy brothers who'd ruled the political landscape of Midnight Valley. Unlike anybody else, she wore clothes ordered from New York and Paris. Renita and her friends toasted each other with sherry glasses while her niece, Iona, sat in the middle of them, looking as miserable as a sheep dog on a scorching day.

Rusty asked if I wanted a sherry. I nodded, though I had no idea how it tasted. "Willie and Holly come here all the time," he said, waving at a man headed toward a spiral staircase at the end of the bar.

"I guess if they come here, it must be okay," I said. "But I'm not dressed and my shoes are carrying sawdust."

"If they'll seat a hungry pooch, don't see why you'd be a problem." At Renita's booth I saw a white poodle sleeping under the table, its head resting on his mistress' shoes. "See that staircase in the corner," Rusty whispered, motioning. "Goes up to a private banquet hall where Mayor Stark takes his campaign contributors. Billiards tables. Cigar rooms. Slots and poker set up in the basement. Best I don't know about all that."

We giggled and he patted my hand. "How's the neck?"

"Fine." I hesitated. "Rusty, are you going to tell Connor what happened?"

"Honey, you were attacked. Old man Herne ought to have better security back there. Could have easily been his wife or daughter." Rusty shook his head, disgusted. "They're always more careful when it's one of their own." He shifted, adjusting his belt, the gun at his side cumbersome as he leaned toward me. "I know you don't want to cause trouble, but . . ." He paused as if acknowledging the anxiety on my face. "All right, I won't say anything."

"Thank you." I squeezed his arm. "That's best for everybody."

"Be our secret."

"Those are starting to pile up." I smiled but looked away in case my eyes sparkled. I enjoyed his company. It was comfortable. I could talk to him. Connor stayed in a compartment of my mind that I put aside until he was with me and I'd become his wife again. "Ever bring Lynn here?"

He rolled his eyes. "Don't want to be seen in public with her."

"Now, Rusty. She's still my friend."

"Not really. Sissy and Holly were your friends. Lynn tagged along 'cause nobody else would hang out with her."

I was about to argue because it seemed like what a good friend should do, but at the bar a curly-haired fella with long sideburns caught my attention. One of his boots was jacked up on a brass foot stand and he leaned on his elbows eating a bowl of soup. Another red-haired man sat beside him cutting into a steak. They pointed to a paper placed between them.

"It can't be." I told Rusty I'd be right back, then slid out of the booth and gingerly walked toward the second man, studying him. His hair had been permed and hung in curls around his collar, but he had the same bow-shaped lips and full cheeks. Was my mind playing tricks?

"Bo?" I asked, "Bo Raynes?"

He looked me up and down but there was no recognition. Of course not. I'd been a little girl when he and Kim left town. "Buy you a drink?" he said.

"Don't you know me? Randi Jo Gaylor...where's Kim?"

His expression froze as if he'd traveled far back into the past only half remembered, then he broke into a smile. "Well, I'll be. The little girl I owe a dime. Give me a hug." He slid off the stool and wrapped his arms around me, patting my back like I was still ten years old. "Meet my friend, Simon." The man stayed seated and seemed more interested in the paper than in me.

"Kim?" I asked again.

That same motionless expression. "Be a minute," he said over his shoulder to Simon. I glanced at Rusty, who was eating his steak, and nodded that I was fine. Bo motioned us into a small alcove by the door where mermaids were carved into the wood. He sat on a blue velvet bench but I couldn't join him. My fingers trembled and I held my hands in front of me to calm my nerves.

"I don't know how to tell you this, Randi Jo." He stared at the floor and clasped his hands.

"Kim's dead," I said. The mermaids seemed about to break into tears. I swallowed, steeling myself against hearing what I didn't want to know. "How?"

Bo rubbed his face with both hands. "Car wreck. Same day we left town. Right outside Louisville. It was bad, Randi Jo."

"Tell me."

"She got all smashed up. They took her to the hospital, but wasn't nothing could be done. She was gone by nightfall."

I pressed my hands to my cheeks. My sister had been dead this whole time. She'd never had her baby, never even gotten out of the state. All her dreams of a home and family, of coming back to see us at Christmastime, they'd never happened, never even stood a chance.

"Why didn't you tell us?"

Bo leaned back, unable to look me in the eye. "I should've. Your father was so mad at me. I was hurt myself. By the time I was out of the hospital . . . it just seemed . . ." He didn't finish, and really, it didn't matter.

"Where'd they bury her?"

"Not sure. State took care of it. I couldn't even pay my own medical bills." He opened the collar of this shirt and showed me the end of a long ropey scar across his chest. "See here, forty-five stitches."

I touched his shoulder, trying to feel sorry for him, but didn't know whether to hug him or hit him.

"You don't owe me a dime," I said. "You're paid in full." Someone came into the restaurant, letting in a bright strip of sunlight. I followed it outside and walked over to the bridge. Brown water trickled through swampy cane and the sulfur smell from the artesian well colored the air. All I could think about was wasted life. Kim's wasted life. Bette Moss's wasted life. And my own life wasting away, too, even if I wasn't ready to admit it.

Rusty came out carrying a brown paper bag, my steak, I guessed. He set it at the end of the bridge, put an arm around my shoulders and pressed his lips to my ear. "Who'd have thought Bo Raynes would end up in these parts again? Had to ask him three times before I remembered who he was." The warmth of his body comforted me and he stroked the back of my head. "I'm sorry about Kim."

I pushed back from him, wiped my eyes and pointed down to the creek bank. "Where do you think they buried Bette Moss?"

"Why in the world would you think of her after all these years?"

"Remember when you and Connor and Herman skipped the Labor Day parade to go see the bloody sheets?"

He paused, remembering. "Didn't see much. Just a few brown smears on a patch of weeds."

I blew out a long hard breath, aiming to control myself. Kim's blood had been smeared on something, too. And she was buried out there, somewhere none of us knew. "Since I'll never see Kim's grave, I thought maybe I'd put some flowers on Bette's grave."

"Don't know where she's buried. Can ask around. Probably had family. Everybody does. Most, anyway."

I touched his cheek. His sad expression melted my heart 'cause I knew his sorrow was for my pain. He wished he could bear this grief for me. I understood the bond between us now, a connection between people who hid their hurt. We lived around the actions of others, hoping we didn't get smashed up in the process. Whether it was parents who ordered you out of the house, or those who threw you away when you were just a baby, or like me trying to fit into a flock of strangers, we both longed for a place where we were safe and accepted for being who we were. I wondered if we'd ever find it. I took a deep breath, swallowed and cleared my throat. "I've got to go tell my mother."

"I'll give you a ride."

The journey to Notown, accompanied by police radio static and the whistling of the wind, rested heavily on me as I prepared to do a daughter's most difficult duty... telling my mother that she'd never again look upon the face of her first-born. Rusty turned on a local station on the car radio. "Sunday Will Never Be the Same" played and I sang along, thinking about how Kim was the first Gaylor of this family to die. How easy it had been to lose all her hopes and dreams. Ashes and faded embers.

28

My folk's house was quiet when I got there. Butch slept in the playpen. Daddy was resting in his bed. Nobody else home. At my footsteps, tinny echoes bounced off the walls, making my ears pop. I could near see Kim and me running through the house, tormenting Pug, or he us. When the younger kids came along we washed them and dressed them like they were our dolls. Momma and Daddy were King and Queen to us. We worshipped them and feared them, but most of all we loved them, and a hurt to family was the deepest grief.

It wasn't like Momma to leave, and I had an uncomfortable feeling of abandonment. I sat at the table planning how best to tell them. It's funny I didn't resent their treatment of Kim or the hard times of those early days, but I was filled with strangling claustrophobia. I reminded myself that I had my own home now, and the old days of living on top of each other were over.

The calm in the house seemed unnatural. One or another kid had always been screaming, crying or complaining, and that drew focus away from the squalor of our lives. Momma was no doubt glad to have Collette, the littlest one, born right before Tallulah, in school now. Finally, she could rest a little.

"Malva?" I heard Daddy ask. Butch woke and made his sound, but it wasn't as full-bodied and demanding as usual. He was subdued and curious when I passed his playpen, looking at me through the bars like he knew this was a heartbreaking day.

"Momma ain't here, Daddy," I said, sitting beside him in bed.

He was on his back and tried to sit up. "Need some more." He nodded at a near empty morphine drip hanging above him on a wire clothes hanger.

"You know where she keeps it?"

He pointed toward a chifforobe. I opened a drawer, knowing that the morphine made it easier for him to breathe and let him sleep most of the time. He hadn't worked all year and his breathing had become steadily worse until the doctor told him he couldn't go into a mine again. "I don't see any, Daddy."

"Where's Momma?"

"Not here. Did she go to get more?"

"Must have." He coughed, a deep congested strangle that sucked the strength out of him. "How you doing, Randi Jo?"

I sat on the bed and held his hand. The calloused skin from years of digging coal was rough against my palms. I debated telling him that Uncle Luther was back. I'm sure Daddy loved or felt deep loyalty to his half-brother, but he'd never have let him get away with attacking me. So I stayed quiet. My neck didn't even hurt anymore.

210

"I'm fine. Everybody's fine." I pushed back a lock of hair from his forehead. Lying to him about kilt me but I knew my voice wouldn't hold if I brought up Kim. I could tell Momma, but not Daddy. Maybe in his state we wouldn't have to mention it.

"You bring Tallulah?"

"Naw, she's in school today."

"That one's gonna be the smart one in the family, Randi Jo. She and Collette, both got your Momma in their eyes." I shook off an involuntary shiver. He raised his head to look toward the playpen. "Butch doing okay?"

"He's fine. I'm surprised Momma didn't leave anybody with you."

"Ah, Collette's around here somewhere."

"Well, she ought to be in the house. I'll go holler for her."

"No." He caught my arm with a strength I didn't expect. "Something I want to tell you." I held my breath. "Day I met your Momma, she was watering daffodils growing along her walk. I watched her 'til she got down by the street and asked if I could buy a bunch and she"– he chuckled–"she watered my toes and told me not to speak to her again until I was wearing proper shoes."

"How old were you, Daddy?"

"Ahhh, so long ago, don't remember. She lived in Contrary then, big house on Laynchark."

"Momma lived over there?"

"Something her father arranged. He stayed in Divergence but had to bring food so they'd keep her."

I'd never heard any of this nor had Daddy ever mentioned Divergence. "How did you two court?"

"Going to church was 'bout the only way you could meet girls, kinda the same as when you grew up. She wore her hair in a ponytail with a red bow. I told Luther, 'There's my wife.' He poked me in ribs and said, 'That one won't look twice at a Missouri hick like you.' Had to find a way to impress her. So I won a pie-eating contest."

We both chuckled 'cause he was always skinny as a rail. "Is that what you wanted to tell me, Daddy?"

"Just that." He closed his eyes. His breathing was labored and scratchy. "Tallulah's gonna win that science prize."

"How would you know?" Her project wasn't due for a week and she was competing against high school kids. Connor had said it would be a good experience but he didn't expect her to place.

"Kim told me." Daddy smiled and looked beyond me. "You make sure she goes no matter what happens."

I stared at a bedside picture of him and Momma on our porch, a young Kim behind him, Pug at his side and me in his arms. Back then nobody knew to smile in photos and they looked like they were trying to see inside the camera. Poor Daddy must be in a haze of the past, not knowing his daughter had been gone a long time. "Kim's not here, Daddy." I blinked back tears.

"Sure she is. Standing yonder in the corner."

I whipped around expecting to see my sister even though I knew the truth. My reflection in Momma's vanity mirror stared back. That's who he saw in the corner and though I wasn't as tall as her, in ways, I did favor Kim.

"Kim says Tallulah will be the one to put out the fire."

I wished with every ounce of me that my sister was

212

alive, that she knew my daughter, that I could turn to her for anything, and that she'd be here at this time when our father was so sick. The strength Kim had given me as a child fed my courage each time I was afraid. She'd brought me through to adulthood and in her way had raised me even when she'd hadn't been here. "There ain't nothing on fire, Daddy."

He pointed at his throat. "Reckon I could get a drink?"

"I'll get some water." Butch reached out for me as I passed him and I petted the top of his head. At the sink I broke down, silent sobs rushing from my chest. Butch howled and banged against his pen. I wiped my nose and eyes, willing myself to get it together. Collette trotted up from the garden with a bundle of daffodils. I knew where they came from. "Get in here," I yelled, swatting her on the backside with a washcloth as she sashayed through the back door.

"What was that for?" Defiantly she pushed out her lower lip.

"You're supposed to stay with Daddy."

"I know that. Momma kept me home from school and she took the bus to Contrary to get his medicine."

"I'd have gotten Connor's car and drove her," I said. "When you take care of Daddy that means in the house, not frolicking outside with flowers."

"I wanted to get buttercups to cheer him up. He always liked them, and by the way, you're not my momma and got no right to whip me." Collette sighed with an irritated smirk.

"Well, I'll just let Momma whip you, see how you like that."

Her lips quivered and tears threatened to skip down her cheeks. Butch wailed like something awful was wrong. "See," I said, "you got to be here 'cause anything can happen." I put the daffodils in the glass of water. "Get another cup. Daddy's thirsty."

Butch strained against the bars of his playpen as I passed by. I switched on the radio to distract him and rubbed his head saying, "Shhhh . . ." In the bedroom I placed the glass on the vanity. "Collette picked flowers for you, Daddy. She'll be here in a minute with your water." I turned toward the bed and something about his position caught me off guard. "Daddy?"

He stared at the ceiling, his green eyes smoky and lips slightly parted. I shook his shoulders. The pale silverfish color of his cheeks spread to his forehead. Only the Fear Angel had that same skin color. I half expected her to swoop in and fan her wings around me as I dropped to my knees. But another devil had come to visit us. Death was approaching and holding out his hand.

When Collette entered the room with a mug of water, I looked at her and my face must have told the story because the cup tumbled through the air and shattered on the floor. Butch wailed as if he'd known long before us.

Collette ran to my side and grabbed Daddy's hand. "Daddy, no," she sobbed and buried her face in the covers. Butch's cries mixed with Procol Harum singing "A Whiter Shade of Pale." I rubbed Collette's back and finally went over and picked up Butch. He didn't calm down, seeming to understand what awful thing was happening. I soothed Collette and Butch, unable to look at my father's body, and knew why Uncle Luther wanted Bette's head. I realized just what had vanished from Luther's life. Even though I couldn't put it into words, I knew that Valkyries would never again dance among the stars, gone were the tales of the Warrior-King Jack, the daydreams of what life could be, gone was the man who'd eaten pies and won himself a wife. What safety I had in this world came from him and now the earth would take him and leave us, the less worthy, to carry on.

29

The saddest time of my life was when I told Momma that Kim had died in a car wreck near twenty years past, in a strange town where no one knew her, and that Daddy, her husband and father of their thirteen children, lay in the bedroom behind me, having breathed his last breath less than five minutes ago. Colette held onto my legs like she was afraid to let go. I finally told her to sit with Butch and keep him calm.

Momma stared at the bedroom door, her throat muscles constricting as she swallowed. I touched her arm but she seemed not to feel me. She took small steps toward the room and stood in the doorway, staring at the bed. Under the blankets my father's shrunken body looked like a child's. She just watched him as if the lifetime they had spent together unfolded before her eyes.

"Well," she finally said, her voice soft as a trickle of water. "Reckon I better call the funeral home."

⁓

Sweeping. This damn storeroom never seemed to get clean. Spider webs and grunge, and customers looking for a short cut tracked in every manner of mud and dirt. The Hernes never locked the back door, saying it was a customer service.

Summer came and went. Kids started school again. Yesterday turned into vague slices of memory: The funeral, with people I didn't know shaking my hand, telling me how fine a man my father was. The younger kids knew what was happening but it settled into them like just another event in their day. Us older ones sat stoic, grim faced, dressed in new black clothes we'd never wear again, remembering the old days, the hard days when meat was seldom and dresses were made from flower sacks.

The image of Pug held me to that day. He'd fallen on his knees in front of Daddy's open casket and bawled his eyes out. I'd never seen a man cry like that, and the anguish of his howls filled the room until I had to leave. My brothers' wives were a big help, making food, handling transportation and helping with the housework. They promised they'd be there for Momma. Gene and Melvin had married pretty good women, so I believed them. Casper's wife was a useless airhead and most everybody ignored her as she sat in the corner reading a comic book. The army let Hector out but he had to go back the following Monday. He looked like a man who held in all the world's brokenhearted despair.

217

Whatever the war was doing to him, I hoped he didn't explode from the strain.

Connor served as a pallbearer and Tallulah read a poem. Mr. and Mrs. Herne and Tempy sat quietly in the back. The service ended and at the cemetery we lingered like we had nowhere to go, like we couldn't leave this gravesite where our loved one would be alone. Up on the hill a raggedy man with wild hair hunched like a sentry. I knew it was Uncle Luther, but he didn't come down and I hoped that now he'd leave us alone.

Sweeping kept my mind off all of it. I swept out the summer. I swept into the fall, and now that winter threatened with flurries of snow, I swept through it, too. The Hernes were decent to me, even Wallis and Tempy being nice the last few months, and Mrs. Herne let me pick out a new broom. Pop Herne wasn't so young and maybe they thought about their own loss that would come some day in the future. Putting death out of mind must've been a safety net . . . 'cause it arrived again faster than we ever could have guessed.

I shook out the new broom in the alley, dust mixing with lazy snowflakes, then hung it on the wall and started up front to tell the Hernes goodbye. Through the stockroom door window I made out two men in black masks at the front counter. A short stout one and a taller one waving his arms wildly, brandishing a pistol like he might shoot anyone in his way. My feet stuck to the floor as the men herded Wallis, Tempy and Pop Herne to the far corner. Pop shielded the women, his arms spread out. Something about the wilder man's movements caught me, the snaky cock of his head like it was looking for a branch to rest on. Good Lord, it was Luther.

Nausea cramped my stomach. I turned, half thinking I'd run home out back and pretend I hadn't seen any of this. He'll only rob them, I told myself. It's just money, they made plenty. I covered my mouth so I wouldn't throw up in panic, then remembered the rifle behind the door.

The stout man dug money out of the cash register and pushed it in his pockets while Luther terrorized the three against the wall. Wallis covered Tempy with her body and Pop Herne shielded his wife. Luther had his back to me and yelled something. My hands found the rifle.

I crept up the far aisle out of his sight, but about halfway the stout one would see me so I had to move fast. He jumped over the counter and shook a bag of coins at Luther.

Just leave, I thought. Just leave! Wallis and Tempy huddled on the floor, faced away from the robbers. Mr. Herne confronted them, arms still spread to protect the women.

I came around and pointed the rifle at Luther. He cackled, a hard, vicious laugh, and I saw that the other man also had a pistol. I yelled, "Get out of here now!" The other man locked eyes with me but he didn't raise his gun. My uncle stared at me as if trying to suss out what I'd really do. He should have known me better by now.

Luther pointed his pistol. My gaze followed the aim. He pointed at Wallis. Pop covered her as best he could. A pop. A flash of discharge. My own rifle fired. Speckles of blood wet Luther's shirt. Mr. Herne crashed into Wallis and Tempy. Their screams shattered the illusion of things happening in slow motion and then all movement whipped by faster than I could follow. The stout man looked at me, at his gun, at my rifle, then realizing that Luther was down, he raced out the front door. I ratcheted the rifle again and followed him to the street. He jumped into a green Plymouth and burned rubber down the road.

The commotion made all the nearby merchants come running. Somebody called the police. I was in shock and could barely talk. Mr. Herne was rushed to the hospital along with Wallis and Tempy. Nobody offered to take me and I stood watching all of them. Rusty arrived and asked if I was okay. I nodded but still couldn't talk. Another policeman pulled the black mask off Luther. He'd cut his hair and shaved, hardly looked like he did before. Another officer asked me, "You know him?"

I shook my head, no, no, and no. Rusty stared at me as if some familiar memory played in his head. I pulled him away from Luther and said, "Go get Connor at the high school and take him to the hospital." He nodded, still glancing back and forth from the dead man to me.

The county coroner came and the corpse was loaded up. Some merchants offered to drive me home but I told them I needed to stay and clean up. When they offered to help I made excuses. It was about all I could do not to lose my mind. I'd shot my uncle dead and his blood pooled on the floor in front of me. Once the last person left I locked the door and went down the aisle for bleach and towels. I got a new mop, which would probably make Wallis mad, but I did it anyway.

Mr. Herne's blood stained the tiles and I scrubbed with all the strength in my arms. I'd just about got all the spatter off the shelf of candy bars when the shaking began. It had been there all the time but I couldn't let it out. Now I had to clean up Luther's blood. From that dark puddle of scarlet the evil-faced thing rose up, her wings dripping red and her mouth salivating. She grinned with an insane hiss, gleeful to see me terrified and trembling. I sat on the floor and wrapped my arms around my legs. The mindless motion of sweeping went through my head, only this time I wouldn't be clearing away sawdust and cobwebs . . . but my family's blood.

With stiff fingers I twisted off the top of the bleach and poured it all around. I cleaned up Luther's blood. I cleaned up streams of Mr. Herne's blood that had mixed with it. No difference to the look of good blood and bad.

By the time I finished no one could tell what had happened here. I'd never been in the store alone and the quiet hum of the freezer was like a comforting song. I ate some cookies and drank a pint of chocolate milk. I covered the fruits and vegetables with white cloths, turned off the lights, and locked the back door on my way out. A thin layer of snow covered the ground.

The sky was dark and I wondered if I should go to the hospital or catch the bus home. Where was Tallulah? At home, gone to the hospital, to one of her friend's houses? Either way, she would get taken care of and perhaps that part of life didn't need me right this minute.

221

My mind re-played the scene, the feel of metal on my finger, the other man watching me, Luther laughing, raising his gun. I squeezed the trigger, the recoil, no doubts in my head of the result. Did that make me a murderer as clear as Luther? Really, as ashamed as I was to admit it, all that mattered was Uncle Luther no longer being a threat. I could rest in peace and maybe Bette Moss could, too.

30

Another funeral home. Visitation, casket surrounded by flowers. People were better dressed than at Daddy's funeral but that was expected because the Hernes were merchant class. In a back corner my old evil friend hovered like a banshee, watching everybody as if they were morsels for the picking. I'd not seen a feather of her until that day I cleaned up the blood, and had figured with all the hoopla in the world that she'd be too busy for me–Martin Luther King shot, the riots, Bobby Kennedy killed, the Democratic Convention violence, Richard Nixon elected President. But here she was at Pop's visitation.

Under her, Pug sat in a pew. I kept an eye cocked her way and she winked at me from time to time. Connor moved among the people, shaking hands and talking in whispers while his mother and Tempy sat off to the side of the casket greeting mourners as they slowly passed

Pop to pay their last respects. The funeral home fixed him up real nice. You'd have never known he had been shot, and with his bow tie and Freemason pin on his jacket he looked ready to open his eyes and talk to us.

Connor checked in with his mother from time to time. Wallis never shed a public tear but her eyes were red-rimmed and she frequently gave Tempy a firm glare to keep her emotions in check. Tallulah sat behind her grandmother and embraced her now and then. Wallis had been cold as stone to me and while I tried to think it off to her losing her husband, her avoidance made me worry. The police had told Connor it was a lucky break that I'd been in the back and knew where to find the rifle. Otherwise, the Herne family might all be dead. They stopped short of calling me a hero, and I was glad cause I didn't feel like one. The only luck I felt was the police didn't link Luther to my family.

Ignoring the Fear Angel, I slid into the pew beside Pug. He nodded, cleared his throat, and said, "Come to pay my respects," then scooted toward the end of the pew.

I moved with him, making my brother uncomfortable as I could. "You didn't even come to my high school graduation, or my wedding party, nor did you stop by to see Tallulah after she was born. Now, I've got to ask myself, why would you come to see Pop Herne in a coffin?"

Pug stared at the burl wood of the pew in front of him. "Guess Daddy's funeral is still close. I felt bad."

"Bet you do."

"Who fed you vinegar, Randi Jo?" He gripped the pew with both hands.

"Nice new boots you got there." I tapped his foot with the toe of my shoe. He shoved his hands into his jacket pockets. "New coat, too."

"Man's gotta look good at a funeral."

"This is the visitation, you coming to the funeral, too?" I leaned toward him. He smelled of liquor. "My, you've taken a liking to the Hernes."

He stood up like a shot and looked down at me. "I'll be headed on."

I followed him out the door into the cold air and down the street to his blue Dodge. "What happened to the other car, the green Plymouth?"

He whipped around and for a second I thought he might hit me. I wasn't a hundred percent sure that Pug had been with Uncle Luther, but his reaction now told me what I needed to know.

"Don't have a cow, Randi Jo," he spit.

I dug into him like a bear on a honey hive. "You think I don't recognize your short fat body and chubby cheeks even behind a black mask?"

He looked around quickly. "Listen, stupid. You're in the clear. Momma made sure nobody knew Luther was related to us. Daddy's gone. Luther's dead. Don't be an idiot by saying something you can't prove." He crossed his arms over his chest and coughed, his breath frosting the air. "You won't be living so high if the Hernes find out your kin killed their daddy."

"Think you scare me?" I let out a shrill laugh, hands on my hips. "There're scarier things than you in this world, Pug."

"What do you want?"

225

I smiled and punched a finger into his shoulder. "Pack up. Go to the big city like you always bragged as a kid, join the army, find your summer of love, I don't care." I stepped back on the curb. "You got the Hernes' money. It's more than enough." I pointed to the road "I never want to see the likes of you in this town again."

He leaned on the car trunk like he was trying to think what to say, then looked me in the eye and spit on the ground before turning to go. A light rain made the road reflect with a black sheen and shrouded the streets in a ghostly haze. I watched his car disappear into it, counting my own misty breaths until the Dodge disappeared. When I looked around no fearsome spirit dogged me. And if it had, I'd have kicked its face. For once, it was good to see Pug afraid. So much of my life had been secrets. Pug would be another one, but in a way it was the truth that had freed me from him.

At the funeral home I nodded to neighboring merchants as they left. Connor stood in a semi-dark room, talking to someone I couldn't see, his back toward me. I maneuvered through the crowds and thanked people for coming. As I approached the room I heard weeping.

"It's all her fault." Wallis' voice shivered. "If she hadn't pulled that rifle your father would be alive."

"Now, now." Helplessly Connor patted his mother's shoulders.

I froze, my heart racing. Connor bent toward Wallis and spoke in whispers. Part of me was furious. Her back had been turned toward the gunmen. She didn't know what had happened. Luther would have killed all three of them if I hadn't shot him. That's what the law found, that's what all the merchants believed. Most had come up to me since, telling me how brave I'd been. Why, I could have walked out that back door and done nothing. Connor would have inherited the store and…

What was I thinking? Trying to justify killing a man same as Wallis Herne was rationalizing a situation she couldn't change. Connor looked up and must have seen the hurt in me but he said nothing. His eyes had been sad since this whole thing happened. Now he was unreadable. Did he believe what his mother had told him?

The pastor volunteered to drive Wallis home while Connor and Tempy stayed. I was relieved when Connor came up beside me and looked out the window at a fountain with dancing marble cherubs in the center. "She didn't mean it," he said, inhaling deeply and touching my arm.

I brushed his hand away. "Connor, that was meanest thing Wallis has ever said about me and I've put up with a lot."

"Wait a minute. Her husband just died, don't you have any sympathy?"

"And my Daddy died just a few months ago, think I don't feel bad?"

"That's different. You knew your father would die. I didn't. It's not the same. Murder and natural causes are poles apart. Murder is the worst thing ever."

I rolled my eyes, wondering since when was miner's consumption considered natural? "Maybe you do agree with her," I huffed and slapped my hands against my thighs.

"That's not what I said, but, while we're on it . . . yes, you should be more aware of the consequences of what you do. Say you hadn't picked up that rifle. Say those men just took the cash and ran off. The money'd be gone, but Pop would be alive."

My mouth hung open. "I tell you what would have happened whether you believe it or not. I hadn't shot that man, there'd be three caskets in there instead of one."

I walked before he could reply. He followed me, grabbed my arm and slung me around, his face red and his teeth gritted against his lips. "Never walk away from me when I'm talking."

"Connor?" a voice at the door asked.

Rusty and Lynn stood in the foyer. "Thanks for coming," Connor called out.

"Let know me if there's anything I can do," Rusty said. Lynn nodded, a well-meaning smile.

"There is something," I said. "Can you give me a lift home? I've had about all I can take tonight."

"Sure," Lynn said. "You poor thing, dying's just been all around you these last months."

"It's been around everybody," Rusty said. "I'll tell ya, this year's been the hardest I've known in a long time."

"Come on, honey." Lynn motioned to me.

Rusty and Connor exchanged handshakes and Lynn stood beside me rubbing my arm. My husband didn't object and I looked away to avoid his eyes.

Lynn waddled ahead, taking the short staircase to the sidewalk one step at a time. Rusty and I waited as she caught up to us at the car. Why couldn't she walk a little faster this one time? I had to get out of here. My mind whipped back to that night. Should I have left it alone? Was Pop dead because of me? Luther's gun was aimed at Wallis. Pop moved and took the bullet. Wallis should have been dead and I couldn't help thinking I wished it were so. Killing, it seemed, left its worst wounds among the living.

I looked back at the funeral home. Connor stood on the porch shaking Walt Gentry's hand but stared over his shoulder at me. We still had to get through the funeral. Only one thought came to my mind: *Love is a cutthroat business.*

31

A night's sleep didn't improve my disposition. Connor tossed and turned, mumbling about fire in the earth, and kept me awake most the night. I finally got up early, did a load of wash, and then scrambled eggs for Tallulah as she sat at the kitchen table reading her science book.

"What's meningitis?"

"You'll have to ask your daddy."

Tallulah turned the page and hummed. "An inflammation of the membranes covering the brain."

"If the answer's in the book why ask me?" I emptied eggs onto a plate and added a piece of toast. "Scoot your book over so I can set this down." She positioned it sideways so she could read and eat at the same time.

"Is that what happened to Uncle Butch?"

"I don't know."

"What did the doctor say?"

"The doctors didn't know much back then."

"Seems like–"

"Close the book, Tallulah."

She slammed it shut and my hand came up at the same instance and bopped her in the mouth. She held her jaw, yowling like I'd wrung her neck, and yelled, "Mother!"

"Shut up!" I stood over her and a frustration poured out of my mouth like a spigot I couldn't turn off. "If that's the best face you can put on, go to your room."

She bounced up and darted to the back of the house. I heard the shower. Connor was up. I transferred the clothes from the washer to the dryer and put on water for coffee. He came in a few minutes later dressed in a suit and tie. "You're going to work today?"

"What's Tallulah mad about?" He glanced back toward her bedroom.

"Connor, no one expects you to work the day of your father's funeral. We've got to be at the church at 3:30."

"Gives me plenty of time."

Tallulah came prancing in with her schoolbooks under her arm. "I'm going to school too," she announced and sat next to her father. "It keeps my mind off things." She stared out the window like she didn't want anything to do with me.

She used to be my little girl, running to me for everything, holding onto my legs and following me around for hours on end, telling me I was pretty. As an infant she cried when anyone except me held her. Now, she was one hundred percent daddy's girl.

Connor rubbed her head. "You sure, baby doll?" She nodded.

"Fine," I said. "I'll pick you both up at 2:30."

"I can take the bus to the high school and wait with Daddy," she said, without looking at me. "It'll save you a trip in case you get too busy." She was daring me with a little flip of her eyelashes in my direction, then back to her books. She wolfed down half of the scrambled eggs and ignored the milk. It was all I could do not to reach across the table and smack her again. If I'd sassed my Momma the way my daughter did me, she would have kicked my butt down the hill.

"I'll wait at the car, Daddy-O," Tallulah said. "Want to check my garden experiment, to see if mint grows in winter." She'd won the science prize, just like my own father had said before he passed away. Now all she thought about was proving she could ride on moon-beams.

"Be right there, doll." Connor got up and grabbed the car keys hanging from a nail.

"Don't you want me to drive you? Today's when I go shopping."

"Can't you organize a little better, Randi Jo? I mean, shopping on the day of my father's funeral. What will people think?"

"Well, they'll probably think the same thing seeing you go to–" The front door slammed. "–work." I stared at the door and wanted to throw something through the window. The car started and pulled out of the driveway, passing the house with the two of them in the front seat, staring straight ahead. How the hell was I going to get to the funeral? Connor hadn't said a word about coming back and picking me up. He hadn't listened to Tallulah and when this messed up, it would be my fault. Neither one of them thought an inch past themselves.

I grabbed the broom and started sweeping.

༄

I swept the kitchen, bedrooms and living room. I swept already clean floors and did one room twice. I swept until I threw the broom against the wall and collapsed to my knees, sobbing. All the tension. All the smart words. All the venom coming my direction when all I'd done was try to protect my family . . . both of them. I couldn't help being related to Luther, or that Pop was shot. I couldn't help that coal dust clogged men's lungs or that meningitis made babies like Butch.

When I wheezed in a breath, I heard knocking. Not now, I thought, sucking in air to calm my nerves. I peeked through the chiffon curtain. Rusty stood at attention in his police uniform. At the next tap I opened the door. He must have noticed my red eyes 'cause he squinted and his half-smile closed down.

"Got half a pot of coffee left from breakfast," I said. "Take a seat and I'll get you some."

"Connor gone already?" He followed me into the kitchen.

"Don't ask me why. Still wanted to work today."

"How are you doing?" Rusty raised the coffee cup to his lips and took a long sip.

I waved off the question then poured myself some coffee but didn't drink it. Rusty reached over and took my hand. I realized it was shaking. Silly, I thought. He's only trying to comfort me. I pulled back from his light grasp and pressed my fingers to my temples. "I don't know what's wrong with this world anymore."

"Abraham, Martin, and John," he recited, "and Bobby and Pop Herne and Randy Joseph Gaylor." He smiled his sideways grin. "On the other hand, Elvis got hitched."

A curt laugh burst from my lips. "And don't forget Jackie."

"That Onassis fella." Rusty shook his head. "Good thing he's got money, not much in the looks department."

We chuckled again, avoiding eye contact. "Maybe this weekend you could take Connor hunting. Get his mind off things." I turned on the radio. Peaches and Herb were crooning "For Your Love." Rusty sang along and waited for me to sit, holding my gaze in a long intense stare. "Connor'll probably call you tonight," I said, "to see if there's any word on the other gunman."

To my relief Rusty shrugged, leaned his elbows on the table and shifted toward me. "Luther Ballard had only a few known associates, all no-accounts. Most of 'em scattered, knowing we'd be looking at them." He bit his bottom lip.

"I know you recognized him," I said. "Rusty, please don't tell the Hernes I gave that man food. I feel guilty enough as it is." A small cry escaped my lips. "He must have gotten mad, come back with a gun. It's all my fault. They'd hate me even more if they knew. It'll destroy what little marriage I've got left."

Rusty waved his hand. "I'll never tell them. They don't need to know." He rubbed my shoulder and dabbed a napkin at my cheeks, drying tears I didn't realize had dripped from my eyes. "Ballard did a stretch for armed robbery in the state pen and one of the old timers remembered an attempted kidnapping about ten years ago, but those records got lost in the flood the same year. Other than that, not much to know about him."

"Good. I mean, I'm glad he don't have people around here looking to even the score." I gulped my coffee, sure that Momma'd had something to do with Uncle Luther's records disappearing.

"Any of his gang comes around, my money's on your aim." Rusty chuckled. "This other man . . . I'm guessing he's long gone by now."

I blushed, sensing warmth on my cheeks and a giggle in my belly that I hadn't felt in so very long. We'd long finished our coffee and sat at the table, staring at the gingham pattern and only catching eye contact now and then. "How's Lynn?" I asked.

He bit into a slice of bacon from Tallulah's plate and took a sip of her milk. "Same."

"It'd do Connor good to get out in the woods. He needs a friend to take care of him right now."

"I'd rather take care of you," Rusty said.

A frozen moment. One that had been there before. A connection both of us felt but didn't acknowledge. I didn't dare look up from the tablecloth. His tone had been blunt as if he was surprised the words had come out of his mouth. "I'll get us some more coffee," I said, rising and taking both the cups.

Before I knew it, he rose with me, knocked the dishes from my hand and pushed me against the wall. His arms held mine down, his face close enough for me to smell coffee on his breath. "Rusty, stop."

"Don't think you want me to."

"I do."

"I see how they treat you."

"Stop."

"Like you're their slave, their doormat, their pet hound who jumps to their tunes."

"Every marriage has problems," I mumbled, our lips so close his breath was mine. "Look at yours."

"I try not to."

"You need to go," I managed, the fervor of song between us, knitting our bodies together.

"I'm gonna kiss you."

"No," I murmured as his lips took mine. In my mind I said no, no, no . . . over and over, even as I kissed him back I said the word, knowing this was wrong and betrayal now held me like a vise. He kissed me again, and again and I could not stop. Lost in his world, I forgot my husband, my child and my pain. All I knew was a yearning ache to be touched.

32

He came back too many times. I knew it was wrong. Knew I might be damned to hell, but I did it anyway, lost in a passion I never thought I'd feel again. But there was one thing I didn't know, one careless thought I never let myself have. I never contemplated getting caught.

Several weeks later Rusty and I were in bed a couple hours before I was due at the Herne's Market. I dozed lightly with his face in the crook of my neck. I reached over and grabbed one of his cigarettes, lighting it and blew smoke rings.

The slam of a car door.

I popped upright. "Get dressed."

I ran like a maniac around the room, throwing clothes, picking up anything that looked like it belonged to a man. Who, I thought, who? When I got to the front of the house my heart sank. Tempy. She made it halfway to the porch then saw Rusty's police cruiser parked behind the storage shed so no one would see it from the road. By the time I opened the door all I saw was Tempy's backside as she got into her own car, started it and drove away.

I held my breath, thinking wildly of anything I might say to make this look other than it was. Rusty came in the room, police cap on his head, utility belt full of equipment. He looked prepared to bluster out some official reason for being here. "Who was it?"

"Tempy," I said. "She knows."

It felt like I held my breath for a solid week, waiting for the world to come down on top of me. Maybe Connor's sister had thought better about speaking out. After all, she hadn't seen anything and there could be a dozen reasons why my husband's best friend was in our house when he wasn't home. Of course she probably ran right to Iona and they'd been planning a perfect strategy to get me in the worst trouble of my life. Or she waited in a corner like a spider for my weakest moment.

༄

Connor came home as usual and didn't act any different. His routine stayed the same as he watched the news, read the paper, ate, and fell asleep on the couch. Some nights he left for several hours to tutor students of wealthy families in Contrary and bring in a little extra money. He always helped Tallulah, but she could dance circles around him explaining the difference between a full moon tide and neap tide.

Oddly enough our lives took on a homey sweetness: me sewing on her Girl Scout uniform, consoling her when a crush on a boy didn't work out. Even Connor

238

occasionally gave me that pert grin I hadn't seen for quite a while. How long could this happy family mood last? Or were we finally getting back to normal?

One morning a loud knock on the door woke me. I looked at the clock: Eleven a.m. I'd gone back to sleep after getting Connor and Tallulah out the door and wasn't due at the grocery for two hours. Insistent knocking jiggled the glass in the window. At the front of the house Holly, blond hair teased high and covered by a red scarf, held her hand over her eyes peaking through the sheer curtains.

When I opened the door she regarded me with an aggravated scowl. "Get dressed," she said curtly. "Your whole life depends on this."

I sighed, accustomed to Holly's dramatic entrances, thinking she wanted a new dress and Willie wouldn't give her the money. But I did as she asked and minutes later, still half-asleep and balancing a mug of coffee, I sat in her red sports car as she screeched out of our driveway.

"Slow down," I said.

"My thoughts exactly." She held up a hand like she was testifying.

I could have spit when she turned from Notown Road into Divergence. "Where are you going? They see two white people here and we'll get our tires shot out."

"Stop being a spaz, Randi Jo!"

"Why're you talking to me that way?"

"Only place I ever got my tires shot out was Notown."

She drove out of the Divergence hollow and onto a curvy road that made me nauseous. I held to the dashboard as her car hugged the bends. We ended up on the backside of the mountain in a rough section of hills that I believed must be in Tennessee. "I've got to be at work at two," I told her, "so I can't spend all day driving around." She uh-huhed and ignored me.

Finally she said, "We're here," pulled onto the shoulder of the road and bopped her horn twice. From a log cabin about ten feet back a black man emerged, putting on a jacket as he ran toward us. She opened the door on her side and he squeezed into an undersized backseat, folding himself like a dishtowel in an overstuffed drawer.

Holly reached over and put a finger under my chin to close my gaping mouth. "What have you got us into, Holly?"

She smacked the steering wheel. "Don't you wig out on me, Missy. This is your mess." She turned to the black man and patted his arm. "Dallas Shepard, Randi Jo Gaylor. I mean Herne." Facing forward, she lit a cigarette.

Dimly I recalled her telling me they'd been lovers when she was twelve. He was tall and lean, his hair rounded into an Afro, with blackberry skin and warm brown eyes. "Okay, why am I here?"

Holly shifted to look at Dallas. "You're sure?" she asked.

"Nothing wrong with my peepers." He leaned forward to point at a yellow house hanging on a hillside. Two black children played around a lopsided, melting snowman in the front yard. A woman swept the front porch and occasionally scolded the kids with a wag of her finger. "Shows up a few times a week and stays the

240

night every other Thursday. Runs a midnight auto supply out of the back room."

I still wasn't sure what either of them were talking about but flashed on Thursday nights when Connor left to tutor the Contrary kids. No, couldn't be a connection. "Okay, somebody tell me what's going on?"

"Midnight auto supply," she said. "Stolen auto parts. But that's not what I want you to see."

A Contrary police cruiser pulled into the yellow house's driveway. Rusty didn't bother hiding his squad car the way he did when he came to see me. The kids ran to him, grabbing his legs. He picked up the littlest boy and swung him around. The woman dropped the broom she held and melted into his arms, then the four of them went inside.

I felt like shattered glass spider-webbed out to the edges. Broken, unusable but held together in a beautiful design. That was me, not destroyed but held in a cruel knowledge that life was breaking apart.

Holly motioned at Dallas with her eyes and opened her car door. He returned to his house. I swallowed, feeling like a stupid clown. I'd planned on ending it with Rusty, firm in my mind to be considerate of our families, my friendship with Lynn, but I never expected the pain of him cheating on me. In a way, it was funny. It told me just how much it would hurt for Lynn and Connor to find out about us. "How long have you known?"

"Tempy's dropping hints to everybody you know. Me. Lynn. Everybody at the New Bethany Church." Holly pounded the steering wheel. "Randi Jo, do you know how much trouble you're in?"

241

"How long have you known about this?" I pointed at the yellow house. "How long has that been going on?"

"Well, the oldest looks to be about six, does that tell you something? She's not the first. He's had a string of girlfriends all along. Willie used to laugh about how stupid Lynn was and even lent Rusty his cabin at Norris Lake a couple times."

I steadied myself between the seat and the dashboard. "How could he . . ." Anger surged though me and I felt self-righteous indignation for Lynn and myself. "Treating me like–"

"A Notown girl? Did you hear what I said a minute ago?"

"Tempy," I repeated, but thoughts surged through my mind like slippery minnows. I wanted to vomit. "Has she told Connor?"

"She don't have to, baby. That carp does more with innuendo and half-truth than the Pope does with a Bible."

"Why would anybody believe her? She's got no proof."

"Honey." Holly stared at me. "We're talking about marriage, yours and Rusty's. Don't think any of these girls in town, even your friends, are gonna come down on your side. You've known all your life you're a Notown girl and that's how you'll be judged. Nobody can do anything for you now except your husband. He looks the other way, so will everybody else, but it's all going to depend on him." She leaned her forehead on the steering wheel. "You got your work cut out for you."

Holly started the car and drove back to Notown. I put my head in my hands and cried all the way home.

33

Tempy had been absent from work for two weeks so I hadn't been able to gauge her manner. I had a story all planned out about how Rusty was helping me with a special birthday surprise for Connor. That his birthday was still over a month away was something I'd have to overcome. Looking at the store from across the street, I saw my sister-in-law at the cash register. Casimir O'Brien layered green grapes onto a bed of ice. They'd hired him to help four days a week after Pop was killed. Didn't think to hire me, I thought, resentment filling my belly. He earned eighty dollars a week while I still swept out the storeroom for ten and felt grateful.

I entered through the stockroom. Up front I looked around like nothing was wrong. Tempy read a book called *The Waves* by Virginia Woolf. She glanced up.

243

"Afternoon, Tempy," I said. "Good book?" She kept reading. "Must be fab. I thought of getting Connor a book for his birthday but have come up with a better idea of building him a fireplace. Rusty's helping."

Tempy told Casimir, "When you're done would you be kind enough to sweep up the storeroom?"

He stopped, looked from me to Tempy, then gave her a tentative nod.

"Why'd you want to sweep it twice?" I asked. "Casimir, wait."

"Do as I say, Casimir," she said and moved her book farther along the counter.

I had to act like I'd done nothing wrong even though part of me wanted to chop her down. "This store is half Connor's," I said, "that means it's half mine, too."

She slammed the book closed and crossed her arms. "This store is one hundred percent my mother's. And it'll belong to whomever she decides to leave it to after her death, which will be a long time from now barring more Notown trash coming by to shoot us up. But it sure as hell will never belong to a whore!"

I backed up almost to the doorway and felt the cool outside air streaming in and whipping around my ankles. Somehow, I walked off and caught the bus to Quinntown without realizing I'd left my coat hanging on a nail in the stockroom.

I barely felt the cold when I arrived in the center of town, and paced two blocks, then took the path to the high school and watched cars pull out of the parking lot. Connor would be driving home. Tallulah would be on the bus headed that way, too. It began to rain, a light sprinkle.

At a loss, I went to Sissy's house and knocked, my hands trembled in front of me as I waited. Sissy shuffled forward but paused when she saw me through the window. She looked aside, back at me, then slowly cracked open the door.

"Can I come in?" I asked.

Sissy glanced beyond me to the gas station where her husband washed the windshield of a gray Oldsmobile. "Sorry. Got to get dinner started." One hand went to her bulging tummy. She was six months pregnant with their only child.

I looked down at her stomach then pleaded into her eyes. "Like to bring you some of Tallulah's baby clothes. They're in good shape."

"That's all right. Don't need anything."

"I haven't been in touch the way I should have, Sissy." I gasped and broke into tears. Rain pelted the porch, and I wished it could wash me clean.

Sissy grabbed a handful of tissue and thrust it at me, not making eye contact. "You have to go," she said, biting her bottom lip. "I can't talk to you." She gently shut the door, watching me through the lace curtain. I felt a puff of hope when she re-opened the door, but all she did was hand me one of her raincoats.

I walked until I got control of myself, the coat pulled tightly around my shoulders, shivering as much from fear as the cold and not caring that I got wet. Tempy Herne didn't know a damn thing. I could stick to the birthday present story, say Rusty had stopped by for a cup of coffee. After all, he was Connor's friend. Would Rusty's other girlfriends make us both look like liars? I could be outraged that people scorned me. But Holly was right about the only thing that counted . . . my life now depended on Connor. He could look the other way or he could throw me out.

I thought back on the lies I'd told: lying to Connor about gas in the car, lying to Luther about Bette's head, lying to Rusty about knowing Luther. Those had been necessary and hurt nobody. Yet if I wanted to keep my life, I'd have to concoct the story to beat all.

⁓

TV applause and laughter blared when I opened the door to our house. Connor sat on the couch, hands clasped and staring at the floor rather than watching *Truth or Consequences*. I hurried past saying, "I'll get dinner started. Tempy has Casmir sweeping out the storeroom from now on, so I won't be going back." There was no response. "I want to talk to you about that after dinner." Still he said nothing.

In the kitchen I set about fixing ham sandwiches without even drying off. Tallulah was prancing around in her room singing with a record but nothing came from the living room. I leaned in to ask, "Want some coffee while you're waiting," then I gasped. He was cleaning a rifle, the gun from the storeroom.

His eyes flipped up at me. "Uh-uh." He ran an oily rag around the barrel and pushed it inside with a thin rod.

I felt frozen as if snow iced over my skin. A clap of thunder caused me to jerk. "Where'd you get that?"

"The store." Connor pointed the barrel at the ceiling. "Mom don't want it there. Said for me to take it."

"You got enough hunting guns—"

A blast from the muzzle flashed and I felt like the bullet had gone through me. The acrid smell of gunpowder filled the room. "Connor!" I shouted, unsure if I'd been shot.

He laughed and looked up at the hole in the ceiling. Tallulah came running from her room, asking, "What happened?"

"Hair trigger." Connor waved her off then looked at me as if I were in the crosshairs. "No wonder you killed a man so easy."

"I'll be in the kitchen," I mouthed, barely hearing my voice.

"Open the windows while you're there," he called after me. "I keep smelling cigarette smoke in the bedroom."

I turned around as Tallulah went to her father and examined the hole in the ceiling. They both chuckled, pointing and making jokes about how they'd stop the rain from coming in. I ripped open a bag of chips and put the sandwiches on the table along with sodas and mustard. They continued talking, their voices blending into one sound. Then, I slipped out the back door and ran into the storm.

34

As the weeks passed, a copse of woods high on the ridge above my Momma's house became my secret hiding place. Somebody must've tried to put in a garden but found the slope too steep and gave up. Ferns and tall grass had taken over and I lay on the ground hidden by foliage, wrapped up in my winter coat, scarf and cap. Only my eyes showed and many a day up there I cried them out.

Returning home to a warm coal stove radiating heat, my tears dried and I played with Butch until I tired him out. His constant demands for attention made me forget my troubles. Momma gave me Pug's old room so at least I had some privacy. Much as I cleaned, that room still smelled of rot and boy stink. Night sounds became familiar and in some ways routine. I grew sick of beans until I insisted on doing the cooking. Not that I was great, but after working in the Herne's grocery I knew how to stretch a dollar into a nice meal.

That month I only saw my husband once when he showed up at my mother's house with divorce papers. I watched our navy Buick climbing the hill after it crossed the railroad track. In my thicket of greenery I might have been a rock, a tree stump, or a salamander on my way to the creek. He knocked on the door and spoke with Momma. She crossed her arms, stared at the ground, then pointed up at the ridge. Her sixth sense knew where I was.

I ducked, hoping the ferns would swallow me, but heard his approaching footsteps and an unbearable yearning pulled me upright.

"What are you doing way up here?" He looked around at the unwieldy mishmash of weeds and plants. He didn't seem angry and even smiled at me as he pulled himself up the final slope.

"The view." I waved my arms at the mountain range that was pretty much leafless trees with branches like rips in the sky. If March wanted to burst out in buds, the spring fairies were taking their time about it.

He dropped down beside me and it struck me that we must look funny sitting here with only our heads sticking up above a patch of ferns. I felt awkward, yet seeing him filled my belly with excitement as thrilling as chocolate. "How's Tallulah?" I asked, hungry for information. "I stopped to see her at school but they wouldn't let me on the property. Told me I wasn't the legal guardian." I said the last with a sneer, half hoping he'd start a fight so I could tell him off.

"You're not," he said calmly, almost softly, without a trace of orneriness. He pulled some folded pages from his jacket and opened them up. "Here's divorce papers. I got a pen if you'll sign 'em today."

I took the papers, my fingers closing on them like petrified limbs. "You didn't answer me. How is my daughter?"

He nodded as if to acknowledge the question and stared at a dirt patch between his legs. "Since you left her—"

"I did not leave her." I turned on him. "I wouldn't have left except you were acting all crazy, shooting guns in the house."

"If I was that crazy, why'd you leave your daughter with me?"

"I knew you'd never hurt her." An instant of silence like we'd reached an impasse or maybe we both knew to hold back and not say what we'd regret or maybe both of us wanted something more . . . wanted something back. I opened the papers and read. "What's this?" I shook the pages at him. "You get full custody?"

"How are you gonna support her? Where would you live? Up here with your mother?"

I hated that he was right and didn't respond. "Do I even get visitation?"

"You can call me up, maybe a few times a year, and if I can, I'll arrange to let you see her."

"She's my daughter, too."

Connor closed his eyes as if holding in a temper that wanted to explode. "Don't fight me. You won't win."

"Well, don't that sound just like Wallis and Tempy."

"And leave my family out of it. My mother has been good to you and she didn't cause what happened."

"Connor?" My voice stretched into a plea, wishing he could see the pain I felt, and I wondered if he'd ever been a man I knew. "I can't lose my daughter."

"She doesn't want to see you."

The words cut like a knife, but he knew they would. "Well, she's a child, she doesn't get a vote in the matter."

Connor reached out and with a finger traced the edge of my cheek. "Randi Jo, this is the way it's got to be." He looked away. "I don't know why you did what you did. I was the best husband I knew how to be. Sign the papers and you're free to be with Rusty, if that's what you want."

I leaned my forehead on his shoulder. "It's not what I want. It was never what I wanted."

"You saying Rusty forced you?"

"No, but it wasn't what I wanted. Can you let me–"

His lips touched mine and I kissed him back. Our arms wrapped around each other, embracing all the familiar places. At first my mind screamed, *what are you doing*? Part of me thought I should hold him off, but the softness of his lips, his familiar taste took root in me like a flower pushing through the soil. I opened my eyes and he was looking into mine. We connected and I felt myself give him a little bit of my soul. He took me to the ground. Our bodies moved in mounting swells. I slid off my panties and he was inside me, the joy of it connecting us with the earth itself.

Afterwards, I lay beside him, stroking his chest. The world felt right again. He kissed my forehead. I started to ask when I could move back home when he turned on his side propped on an elbow. "You look a mite tired," I said, pulling a strand of grass from his hair.

"You look like a wood nymph, lying in wait for an unsuspecting hunter."

"Like you," I giggled, then pulled his face to mine so he'd look directly into my eyes. "This, Connor, this is what we are. I love you . . . with everything that's in me. I love you to the bone."

He glanced out at the horizon, a cold, gray, and cloudless sky, then he sat up. "You have to sign the papers. It's the only way Mom will have it after all that's been done."

My heart sank to the ground. He cupped my face in his hands and kissed me again. "We'll let some time pass," he said, continuing to press his lips against my forehead. "Then we'll get married again." He leaned back. "Next time in a church, with the whole town invited."

"I'd be happy doing it right here in these trees with only the hickory nuts for witnesses."

He chuckled and winked. "I think they've witnessed enough." He handed me the pen and pointed at the papers.

"A church wedding," I said, imagining it.

"I promise," he said.

My hand shook as I wrote my name but I had reason to hope. I was signing away the past for a new beginning. A wedding in a church. I'd never had a white gown. We'd gotten married in the clothes we wore that day so long ago. A church and flower girls dropping petals on the path I'd take back to my husband.

I dated the form and handed it to him. "Think Tallulah might want to be a flower girl?"

He stood up, took a deep breath and shoved the papers into his jacket. "We're not getting re-married, Randi Jo." He looked down on me sitting on the ground. "If you believed that, then you're a bigger fool than I thought."

⁓

I never told anybody what happened that day on the hill, except Butch, who seemed to be the only one who understood that I wanted to be held and touched and needed. When my brother raised his arms to me I'd carry him out on the porch where we cuddled in the swing, his head resting between my neck and shoulder as he sucked his thumb. He'd make his sound now and then, wanting me to tell him stories of Jack the Giant Killer, like Daddy had told me. At fifteen Butch was still the size of a small child. Sometimes I took him out into the woods, propped him against a tree, and we'd pretend the whole world was our special kingdom.

Late one night in mid-July I walked over to Notown Road. There was a *For Sale* sign in front of our house. The lights were out so I went up to the door and looked in the window. All the furniture was gone. The oil stove sat unlit. Walls stripped clean where pictures had been pulled down. I checked around back and found Tallulah's science experiment full of weeds. This place had been empty for weeks.

I ran down the road like a crazy woman. My feet

clapped on the asphalt and I lost my shoes. Every time I passed through the glow of a streetlamp I growled at the light. I made it as far as the abandoned house at Gray's Pin and dove through one of the windows, moving from room to room as if looking for a dragon to slay. I landed in the chair my grandfather used to have out on the porch and pulled my feet up, arms wrapped around my legs. I knew She was behind me, my plumed friend, giggling, hissing, flapping her wings with glee.

I gripped the chair, begging for strength. Puffing out air was like giving birth. Breath was all that I could concentrate on. Nothing else mattered. Not my past or present, and the future disappeared in a black hole of my own mind. I sang a little tune I used to sing to Tallulah, a song Momma had sung to me, "Bonny Portmore," high and clear like I was in church. When I stopped the silence wrapped its coat around me. Fear Angel hissed near my ear so I sang again, hoping to scare her away.

But she was here to stay. Every bad thing I'd done in life hung from her wings like Christmas ornaments. All night a single thought haunted me: *I don't know what to do.* I repeated the words over and over until they ran together. *I don't know what to do.*

At last dawn peeked through the loose boards. I wanted to growl again. Instead I rose, following the gleam of sunlight that soon blinded me. Some measure of grace gave strength to my muscles. Outside I stood on the porch and looked at the three roads: Divergence, Notown, Laynchark. Then I hoisted the old chair onto my back and I carried it home. I dragged my grandfather's chair up that hill, into my room, and sat down. I rocked back and forth, staring at worn floorboards. This chair fit me. It held my body when nothing else would. It felt like the only thing in this world that was mine.

35

It hurt me deep and bad how easily Connor walked away from our marriage. Like he never gave it a second thought. Yeah, he'd pulled a fast one on me and maybe I deserved it, but I was more than his wife and the mother of his child. He'd grown up with me, the girl he'd thrown a rock at, somebody who was owed . . . respect. He never called, and when I did he often hung up, finally saying I could call Fridays between seven and eight p.m. Momma still had no phone so I walked down to Wink's Market. He allowed Tallulah twenty minutes to talk to me. At first she didn't say much. I knew she was confused and promised her I'd answer any questions. Sometimes she made an excuse to hang up before our twenty minutes were done, but lately we talked the full amount and more if her father wasn't standing right there. She told me about summer camp, the new friends she'd made, the church she now attended, and how their new house in Contrary had a second story. Once she mentioned a boy and I asked his name but she had to go. Every time I hung up, all I could do was cry.

Mrs. Wink took to feeling sorry for me and she always sent me home with a half gallon of ice cream. Butch and Collette loved Friday nights. Sometimes it felt like the old days when Kim, me, and Pug ran the roost, hollering at Casper, Gene and Melvin, and Patsy and Rhoda forever underfoot, but they always did something silly in that twin way of theirs so we'd break up in laughter. Ice cream nights gave me a warm feeling and kept me from falling apart from missing Tallulah.

I dipped out a spoonful of strawberry and fed it to Butch. He bounced up and down as the taste swirled in his mouth. I was happy to treat the kids still at home, but there was an undercurrent they couldn't feel. I was a drain on Momma's black lung money and had to find work—the only time I was sorry that girls couldn't hire on in the coal mines because it was the one decent paying job around these parts. After weeks of scouring the paper, going door to door seeing if anybody needed housework help, I'd only taken in three dollars for doing Mr. Paulsen's wash.

Rusty's squad car cruised up and down Laynchark Avenue, slowing when it passed our house but he never turned in and for that I was grateful. What could I have said to him or him to me? I heard about awful threats he and Connor had made to each other, and every night I prayed for the sake of our children one would not kill the other. Rusty and Lynn stayed together. She didn't have anywhere else to go.

In late July, Hector got out of the army and I found him one morning curled up on the front porch between the wall and his army duffle bag. He'd put it in front of him like he expected a bomb to explode. When I woke him, he shot up, checking his chest and searching for his weapon.

"It's me." I shook him until the wild panic left his eyes. We sat on the swing and he gripped his hands to keep them from shaking and told about people yelling at him in the airport for being a baby-killer.

"Those protestors think we're bad," he said, "oughta see what Charlie done to his own . . . chopping 'em up, burning old men and women alive, whole villages wiped out. Sometimes I'd dream I come home and every person on the mountainside lay dead in the yard . . ." He glanced at the patch of a dozen houses, then closed his eyes and rubbed his hands over his shaved head.

I swallowed hard, thinking that in a way we'd both been fighting a war that couldn't be won. The Hernes had never wanted me. I'd never been good enough for them and when I finally slipped, they beat me down even further. Hector had lived the real horror, watching life depart this earth in the worst ways at the hands of people who relished pain. Too many people on this earth enjoyed dishing out anguish, and both of us were up here on the hill hiding from them.

After I confessed all that had happened to me Hector asked, "How you doing for money?"

I looked down at a beetle crawling across the porch, embarrassed. "Momma got a black lung settlement from the government 'cause of how Daddy died."

"Got some service money coming." He hesitated. "Reckon I could stay here? Get jumpy at night and if'n I go to Gene, Casper or Melvin's, I might scare their young'ins."

"I'll give you the back room. Collette and me can share her bed." My little sister wouldn't like that but she'd have to make do, same as we did when we were little. It was a terrible thing, us adults putting ourselves on our mother. We both hated it, wished we could find a way out, but every direction we looked there were no jobs, no other solutions. So every morning I went door to door looking for work until my feet were wore out, and soon, Hector followed along after me.

One day Mrs. Cooley told me about a help wanted sign in the window of Leeds Cafe in Contrary. She was in a good mood 'cause her son Ernie was coming home next week and she'd bought a new dress at the Dollar Store to meet him at the airport in Knoxville. After hearing about what happened to Hector, she wanted to make sure Ernie saw friendly faces. Momma loaned me bus fare and another quarter for dinner in case I got hired that day. I waited on the side of the road, pacing back and forth, hoping I'd get there before anybody else got the job. The thought of a paycheck tickled my insides. A job in Contrary also meant I'd be closer to Tallulah.

Finally, I flagged down the bus and headed on over. Connor had moved to a two-story house near Contrary just over the county line. I wondered if he did that because if he ever had to call law enforcement, it wouldn't be Rusty's unit responding. There were lots of kids my daughter's age living nearby and she could walk to school. I couldn't admit wanting to reconcile with Connor but deep inside of me that hope still fluttered around. If I could get a job in Contrary, prove to him I could take care of myself, then maybe he'd respect me again.

It was close to dinnertime when I arrived at Leeds Cafe. Mrs. Bray remembered me from when Pop Herne got shot and commented on how brave I'd been. "This stuff with you and Connor though . . ." She hesitated and looked out the window at Herne's grocery across the street. "I don't need trouble with neighbors."

I thanked her for giving me the chance to explain and said, "There's no hard feeling between us and I'll work for a quarter less than what you're offering."

Mrs. Bray's lips pursed to the side as she thought. "Our evening crowd's beginning to come in."

She gave me a note pad and pen, then sent me to the last booth. "What can I help you with?" I asked, then gasped. Holly and Willie sat on one side of the booth across from Sissy and Hermann. "First day of work," I added, "glad to see friendly faces." But Sissy stared at her menu and the two men stared at each other. Holly was the only one with the gumption to look at me.

"Sausage pizza to go," Holly said.

I wrote it down, pausing to see if they'd be any friendlier. Holly's eyes widened so I took the order to the cook. Not all that long ago, Connor and I might have been with them. Thank goodness Rusty and Lynn were not there. No doubt Connor told all of them his side of things. I'd called Sissy several times since the divorce but never gotten through, and Holly's maid always said she was busy. I never had the courage to call Lynn and apologize.

When I waited on the table near the front window, across the street Casimir rolled in the vegetable carts. I'd have to be careful not to walk that way until I was sure Wallis and Tempy wouldn't cause trouble. In the rear of the café Holly and Sissy got up and went to the ladies bathroom.

"Mrs. Bray," I whispered, "can I run use the facilities?"

"Past the coffee cart, hon, and don't forget to wash your hands."

I followed Sissy and Holly into the customer's bathroom. Holly stood at the mirror, applying pink lipstick. Sissy leaned against the sink, arms crossed over her stomach.

"Reckon the boys are really mad at me," I said.

"After what you did," Sissy said, shooting me a glare, "why would decent people ever trust you?"

I glanced at Holly, expecting her to defend me just a little, but she said nothing. "Sissy, it's complicated–"

"More than a little girl crying her eyes out? I had to calm that poor little thing down when she realized you weren't coming back."

"Oh, God." I covered my mouth. "The Hernes won't let me see Tallulah."

"And Lynn . . . what about her?" Sissy spat out, hands on her hips. "How can any woman trust you?"

"I'd never do anything with Herman or Willie," I pleaded, "You've got to know that."

"Like Lynn knew it."

"Let me explain."

"I'm not interested," Sissy said. "There's no excuse."

"Holly?" I touched her arm.

"I told you this would happen," Holly whispered, looking at her reflection.

It infuriated me the way she stood there in her fancy clothes with her swanky hairdo, sparkling diamonds on every lobe and finger, self-righteousness oozing from her while I knew all along that black man Dallas Shepard was back in town. "I'm not the only one with secrets," I said in a challenging tone.

Holly revolved like a turnstile ballerina on a jewelry box. "Honey, life is secrets, and you were too stupid to protect yours."

That left me wordless. Holly had protected herself too well for me to ever be a threat, and I wouldn't have wanted that anyway. I only wanted their friendship, needed their acceptance. Sissy picked up her purse and left. Holly shrugged at me and followed her. When I came out of the bathroom, the booth was empty.

⁓

Guess my luck at getting that job had been running too good 'cause one night when the Hernes locked up, Wallis crossed the street. That took her past the front window of Leeds Café. She saw me put a plate of meatloaf in front of a customer, but she walked on, then came back to look directly at me as if her eyes were playing tricks on her. I waved and smiled, thinking fast as I could. If she came in, I could offer her a meal on me since she was Tallulah's grandmother. But I ran to the employee's bathroom and waited, hoping she'd go on home.

When I came out, I didn't see her. I walked past every booth twice to make sure she hadn't come in. Mrs. Bray looked back at me so I wiped down a clean table to appear busy.

"Randi Jo, up here," she said in a distant tone.

"What'cha need, Mrs. Bray?" I put on my best employee attitude.

"Honey, I'm so sorry, but it looks like we're not going to need you after all."

"But it's so busy. Every booth filled twice tonight."

She pulled five dollars out of the cash. "It more than covers your four-hour shift." She snapped the register shut and fixed her eyes on the door.

I left with a growing fury that played tug-of-war with surrendering to them. What else could they do to me? I'd lost my husband, my daughter, my friends, my job. And for sure I'd not get other work if they had a say in it. They were running me out of town. Slowly I walked toward the bus stop, hardly noticing when I bumped into a man coming out of the bank. At an open-air market, shiny red apples filled a wood slat basket. My stomach growled. I picked one up and bit into it, the flavor exploding in my mouth.

"You steal my food!" An Italian man rushed out of the market, pointing at me.

"I did not," I said, offended by his tone.

"Police! Police!" He grabbed my arm, waving his other hand and yelling. A policeman came running toward the commotion. Behind me an uproarious laughter slid into a high-pitched cackle and the approaching cop looked that direction. A red-haired man was holding his stomach and pointing at me, laughing so hard I thought he might toss his cookies.

"What's so funny?" the policeman said.

The redhead straightened up. Something about him seemed familiar. He wiped his eyes and shook his head. "I was about to buy an apple," he said, pointing at the rows of ruby reds and the granny smiths, "when this young lady picked up the one I wanted and was headed into the store to pay for it."

His words produced a roar of gestures and expletives from the storeowner that no one could make out. The policeman shushed him with a wave, then nodded at the red-haired man to continue. "All this commotion started and only thing I can think is maybe I ought to buy my produce somewheres else." He started laughing again and wiped his eyes, holding the storeowner's gaze.

The Italian man still gripped my arm and I lay down the half-bitten apple and pulled the five dollars from my pocket. "See," I told the policeman. "I was gonna pay."

The policeman shook his head while the storeowner talked, fast and garbled, eyeing the redhead, then said in broken English, "Eh, people steal. Eh, I see lady eat and think . . ." He spread his hands in apology to the red-haired man and I realized he was afraid of him.

The policeman rolled his eyes, nodded to the carrot-top, and walked on.

Reluctantly I paid for the apple, half feeling I should have gotten it for free. When I came out of the store the laughing man waited on the corner, a camouflage boonie hat tipped back on his head and a grin on his face that was about to bust. "You know," he said, coming up beside me, "I was about to steal one myself."

"Well, I would never do that." I finished the apple and dropped the core in the gutter.

Again he laughed, slapping his knees to keep from falling down. "I'm sorry. That was just the funniest thing I've seen in all my days. Bet you could have whipped 'im if it'd come to that, Miss–?"

I wasn't sure how to answer. With my maiden name? "Herne," I said, leaving off the Mrs. "You a soldier?" I gestured at his cap.

"Simon Tuller," he announced, "I'm a warrior of the world." He had charm all right, not just liveliness that at first had seemed a bit goofy. His smile sent tingles all down my back and his black eyes were two sparkling stars anchored in his pale skin and topped by his bright red hair. "How's 'bout I buy you a steak? After this ordeal it's the least you deserve."

My stomach growled again and the thought of meat made my mouth water. Yeah, a steak dinner was the least I deserved. "Lead on, Soldier Boy."

36

Herman's Hermits sang "There's a Kind of Hush" on the radio of Simon's Mustang convertible. The top was up 'cause it was still cold outside. When the news came on about charges against servicemen for the My Lai massacre, he changed the channel and sang along with The Moody Blues' "Tuesday Afternoon." As he headed toward Quinntown I figured my steak was quickly becoming a hamburger at Pinkie's Drive-in, but he turned onto Marcescent Street and parked on the Lester Street bridge.

"Got to do a little work while I'm here," he said. He pointed at the blacked-out windows of The Majestic Club across the street from the Regal Hotel.

Now I knew who he was. Simon Tuller had sat beside Bo Raynes the day he'd told me that Kim died in a car wreck. Simon was also that awful man who'd scared me so bad when I was a teenager in the Regal's alley, the day my grandfather had put his dignity on the line for me. He'd been a pimpled-faced boy, barely out of his teens back then. Now he was a nice-looking man.

He obviously didn't recognize me and I'd just as soon he didn't. As he opened my door I popped out and said, "I've changed my mind." Pointing toward Laynchark, I stepped away from him. "I'll go catch the bus."

Simon caught me by the shoulders, reassuring and calm. "Nobody turns down a steak," he said like he was singing a song, and put an arm around me.

At first, alarm shot through me as he directed my path, but hesitantly I followed the aroma of sizzling meat. He led me in past the long mahogany bar and the horseshoe-shaped booths. Simon pulled a wad of bills out of his pocket, handed a waiter a twenty, and pointed to a black curtain strung halfway up a staircase. "Two steaks medium rare and gin gimlets."

I preferred my meat well done, but Simon Tuller had a way about him that dripped confidence and I said nothing. Other than champagne at weddings and the occasional glass of wine at Holly's house, I hadn't touched hard liquor since getting sick on it in high school. So, I wasn't too sure about this gin drink and hoped they'd bring a glass of water with the meal.

Upstairs in a private dining area, the walls were lined with deep-seated booths, dark maroon wallpaper, oak paneling, cushioned seats. Burgundy curtains could be closed around the booth but he left ours open, a relief since I hardly knew him. Ours had a window that opened to a view of the Jumpin' Jonas's Mobile Homes and Used Cars advertisement on the side of the Regal.

The paint had recently been touched up and the Js were extra large.

The gimlets came and I watched as he sipped his and said, "Ahhhh."

I tried mine. God, it was awful, but I "Mmmmed" and pretended it was good. After a few sips my tongue was so numb I didn't taste the liquor.

"Best steaks in the state served here," he said, "And best gimlets in the whole wide world."

"You must be a drunkard to know that."

"Well, whoop-de-do and call me ignorant." He whirled a finger around on his cheek.

We were served plates of iceberg lettuce and I recalled Tempy's old claim of salad being served after the main dish. "I'll have my salad last," I said to the waiter. I'd just as soon Simon Tuller knew that I wasn't some hick.

"As you wish, madame." He took it away.

Simon's eyebrows rose. "Fancy-dancy," he said, swishing his fingers back and forth at neck-level, then he leaned in to whisper, "Other than apple thief, what's your profession?"

"I did not steal that apple," I shot back, defensive and arms crossing over my chest.

He started to laugh but recognized I was getting irritated so he sat erect and ran a finger across his lips to indicate zipped. "You look familiar." He cocked his head and studied my features. "But if I'd seen you before I can't figure why I didn't invite you out for a steak back then."

"Well," I said, drawing the word out, "the last time we saw each other you were already eating a steak."

His puzzled expression told me he didn't remember, a good thing 'cause he also wouldn't remember what had happened in the Regal's alley all those years ago. I still wasn't sure he was a decent fella after the mean things he'd said to my grandfather and me, but back then people said those kind of things. My stomach gurgled and I tried not to act desperately hungry.

"You know Bo Raynes." Simon snapped his fingers, then his expression cramped. "Bo told me about your sister. Terrible thing."

I nodded, took a deep swallow of the gimlet, and the steaks came along with another round of drinks. As the meat melted my taste buds, I closed my eyes and lost myself in the sensation of food. I'd had mostly beans the last few weeks and while we still got the Friday meat, it didn't taste as good as this. "I was a waitress," I said, "until about ten minutes before I bit into that apple."

"You quit?"

"Terminated." I let out a laugh. "And if they could, they'd make it a real elimination."

"Now who is *they*?"

"My ex-mother-in-law, with a sister-in-law not far behind." I shook my head as if there was no explaining it. "And guess what, the sister-in-law likes girls."

"I like girls."

"No, I mean she *likes* girls," I said, emphasizing the words.

"Ohhhhh." He pointed a finger at me and tapped my nose.

I finished the gimlet and started another. Before I knew it the steak was gone and I ate the salad to cleanse my pallet. Soon I was pouring out the whole story, my divorce, my powerful former in-laws, how they wouldn't let me see my daughter and had just had me fired. I left out the stuff about Rusty, but realized that my babbling made me more comfortable with Simon.

He sat silently, head cocked, listening. I couldn't remember the last time a man had listened to me. Then our first meeting when I'd been a teenager flashed to mind. He'd been the opposite of heroic: loud, crude, downright mean. But he was acting okay now, respectful and polite. Maybe he'd just been young and silly like me.

"Question." He paused in thought. "Ole Mister Herne have a will?"

"Not that I know of."

Simon leaned back in his chair, a wicked smiled pasted on his mug. "You got 'em," he said, "Your father-in-law died intestate. You know what that means?" I shook my head. "No will, then the estate, meaning that store, has to be divided between all his heirs and their spouses."

"Well, I don't want to go into business with them." I gulped the gin gimlet, making the room seem whirly. Then more than the liquor hit me: *I owned a quarter of that store.*

"You let me work on this. Bet I can get you a tidy sum."

"You a lawyer?"

He pointed over his shoulder at the advertisement. "See that? I'm Jumpin' Jonas's number one salesman."

"Does he really jump?" I broke into a loud cackle.

Simon glanced around to see if anyone was staring,

then he whispered as he rubbed my shoulder, "Jonas Stark is the mayor's uncle. I've been his right-hand man near a decade now and happen to be his second cousin."

"Mayor Stark's got more relatives than a feral cat." I giggled. The room was taking on a distorted haze but I let myself enjoy it and sat there happy as a squirrel in a nut shop. I knew I'd drunk more than I should but finished the gimlet and raised my glass the next time the waiter went by. "Let's toast my tidy sum."

"You need a job, right?" Simon rubbed his chin. "Can you type?"

"Like the wind."

"Then you're hired. Our Coalfire office needs a typist. I got a room you can rent."

Going as far away as Coalfire was something I'd never considered. I straightened up. "I need the job but the room wouldn't be proper."

"My dog lives with me, you'll be safe. And proper. You got nothing to worry about. Mister Jonas Stark, he's a big family man. You'll like them and they will just fall in love with you."

"I don't know," I said, yet the thought of having a family as influential as the Starks on my side would be a good thing. Then the Hernes could never keep Tallulah away from me. If the Starks liked me, I could be in the same society as Holly.

Simon reached over and rubbed my shoulder. "I got a good lawyer. Bet we could even get custody of your daughter." He smiled, straight white teeth, black eyes, and a lock of red hair fell across his forehead. "Come on, we'll go right this minute."

As he paid the bill I thought about what Holly had said . . . that I didn't have the sense to know what to keep quiet about. Well, if life was skeletons and secrets, then my whereabouts for tonight would be the first secret in my new life. I walked out of my old life and started a new one with a man who would ruin me.

37

That Day . . . June 30, 1987

"Simon Tuller," the black man says, pulling the overturned chair upright and letting it bounce.

"Well, if it ain't Dallas Shepard." Simon sneers as if his status in Midnight Valley still gives him power over his captors. "Thought you died in jail."

"Depends on what you mean by died." Dallas sits on the bed next to Randi Jo. "After you and Jonas railroaded me on that dynamite charge, I got used to jail. Read a lot books, relaxed . . . you could've used some time like that to reflect."

"Had plenty time to think," he spits. "Three years. Right, Randi Jo?"

Dallas looks down at his knee then back up at Simon with such hatred that Randi Jo puts a hand on Dallas's shoulder to steady him. "Got my leg cut off, too. But then, that wouldn't've happened if Jonas hadn't come down on it with a baseball bat. You still walking on two." Dallas spit on Simon's left leg.

"Brought it on yourself," Simon argues. "Sticking your nose where it didn't belong."

Dallas chuckles. "Yeah, I was real good at my job." He turns to Randi Jo. "Wanna know why they busted my knee?" She nods, immune to the horrors of violence.

"Washed ole Jonas's Cadillac every single day. That man couldn't drive a car that ain't been washed." Dallas paused, looking at his good knee as the memory bloomed in his mind. "I was taking water to pour in the creek and I sees one of his vans, bright and shiny, the way he liked to send 'em out, but somebody'd smeared mud on the license plate and I'm thinking, here I am with wash water, and I know Jonas likes his vans clean, so I set about cleaning the mud off. Made it glisten like a shooting star."

Simon shakes his head, implying that Dallas's stupidity was to blame for his troubles. "Why didn't you just mind your own business?" He strains against the ropes. "That mud was so state police couldn't make out the plate number. If you'd walked away that day nothing would've happened."

Randi Jo studies Simon. "That's the craziest thing I ever heard, breaking a man's leg 'cause he cleaned a license plate. I mean, the police have faster cars, they'd 've gotten the van anyway."

He looks away. "You know Jonas. Somebody has to be held responsible. Not my fault. The Starks are what they are."

Dallas shoots up off the bed, raises his fist and punches Simon, bloodying his nose. Simon's eyes appeal wildly to Randi Jo. She ignores him. Dallas leans over Simon and screams in his face, "That don't explain what you did to Holly, do it?"

38

When I was thirty-six . . .

Mirror. The overhead bathroom bulb highlighted me in lemon yellow. Nursing my swollen eye with ice wrapped in a washcloth. I hoped it wouldn't bruise because Tallulah's high school graduation was Friday night and I didn't want to show up with purple skin. I could do without Connor's Oh-my-God expression and Wallis and Tempy doing their she-deserves-what-she-got eye rolls. The Hernes weren't even my family anymore but they still got my goat like nobody's business. I adjusted my halter top and pulled on a pair of high-waisted jeans. Didn't have anywhere to go today so no need for makeup.

"Get the damn iodine in here!" Simon hollered from the kitchen.

I took my time and placed the bottle on the table in front of him with a sharp snap. He pulled out a chair and sat, still wiping blood from long scratches on his arm. I'd raked him good, all right. "Reckon that'll teach you to fight with a cat."

"Teach me to get you on a leash before I tame a dog."

I sat next to him and dabbed iodine on his wounds. "Connor invited us to dinner before graduation out of respect."

Simon's cheeks turned bright pink. "He invited you, not me, and that's about as disrespectful as a man can get to another man."

"I am her mother." My tone slid into a plea. He'd come to hate the mention of Connor's name more than I ever did in those days after he left me sitting up on the hillside feeling like a dang fool. Everything I did for the next few years had been to get back at the Hernes, not to hurt them but to show them up. Simon had been as good as his word, getting me a two-thousand dollar settlement to keep from challenging Wallis's ownership of the store. He wanted to go after alimony, too, but I told him I'd done enough to them and they'd done enough to me. How they held that two thousand dollars against me! Yet whenever Simon attacked Connor, I had to stand up for my ex although I didn't know why. Taking up for my first husband had just caused the fight that led to my black eye and Simon's scratched arm. Now, hubby number two got mad if I even thought of Connor and I could swear he always seemed to know. This old fight was starting to drive him crazy and me into the nut house.

Capping the iodine, I leaned back in my chair. "The invitation says *you and a guest*. All invitations say that. Let me call and I'll make sure you're included." The card that lay in pieces scattered on the floor actually didn't say that, but no need for him to know.

"I don't want that buttwipe calling here." Simon ran the fingers of his uninjured arm through his red hair. He was balding at the crown and made up for it by letting the rest grow around his collar in pert curls. "I'll show up whether he likes it or not. Let him try throw me out."

It'd taken forever for Simon to even get a phone for this house 'cause he didn't like me talking to people. He had a fit any time a long-distance call showed up on the bill, so that pretty much confined my life to Coalfire. "I'm short ten dollars for her graduation present," I said.

"What kid needs a fifty-dollar dress?"

I got up to take the iodine to the medicine cabinet and paused in the hallway. "You bragged about Jonas giving you a new car for your graduation. All I want is this one dress. It looks just like one Julie Christie wore in *Shampoo*."

"Don't even think I'll let you go," he hollered. "Drive forty miles there and back. Not like the little brat even thinks of you as her mother. You did up and leave her."

I threw the iodine bottle at him. It hit the wall beside his head but didn't break. He lunged at me and I scooted a chair between us, sprinted down the hall, and locked myself in the bathroom. He fisted the door and called me a dirty name. The phone rang. I exhaled, resting. It might be satisfying to scratch the hell out his other arm, but I wasn't showing up for my daughter's graduation with two black eyes. In the mirror, my face had an impish quality. Simon called it my know-nothing look and it irritated him, but that was okay because he bothered the hell out of me too.

I cracked open the door. His back was toward me as he whispered into the phone. I ducked down the hall into the bedroom so I could hear. Couldn't make out words but I recognized his high-pitched sweet talk. That fool. The only sex he could get, he'd have to pay for.

Simon hung up and yelled toward the bathroom. "Going down to the store 'n get some smokes." The screen door slammed into the frame and the house rang with an aggravating quiet.

I paced back and forth in the kitchen, the tone of voice he'd used on the phone call pissing me off more by the minute. The corner store was the local hangout for Coalfire's teenagers and the owner sold marijuana under the counter. I stepped into my shoes and headed out.

By the time I got there, Simon had his big butt sticking in the air as he leaned on the car door of a white convertible talking to a blond-haired woman. She smoked a cigarette and gave him a drag, fixing on his eyes like she wanted to eat him up. He glanced to the side and saw me with a look of startled recognition. I could imagine the depraved wiggles in his brain bouncing around. He gave the blond a little air kiss.

The cat in me came out and I pounced, grabbed a handful of her bleached hair and punched her in the face. The lit cigarette went flying across the passenger seat to land on the white upholstery. She screamed, hands flying, the steering wheel blocking her as she tried unsuccessfully to defend herself. She managed to get the car in reverse, and I was left with a fistful of platinum hair as her white convertible spit gravel all the way down the road.

Simon had moved to the bench in front of the store and was drinking an RC Cola. "Guess you whipped her ass," he said, chuckling between sips. He sauntered toward me. I was ready to get knocked down but he put an arm around me and we walked up the road toward home.

"Pork chops for dinner," I said.

"Want a drink of pop?" He held out the RC Cola and I took a swallow.

When we got to our house the phone was ringing. He took it off the hook and led me to the bedroom. That's how things were with us: fighting mean and making up sweet. It wasn't a good way to live but I'd gotten stuck on it.

39

Jumpin' Jonas' Mobile Homes and Used Cars had adopted a bullfrog in a red cowboy hat jumping over a row of automobiles as its mascot. The new giant billboard was painted on the side of the electric building, and other signs were up and down the interstate all the way to Lexington. The car lot was within walking distance of our house, a good thing for me since every day Simon drove our car the six blocks to work. There were times I found it hard to believe we'd been married seven long years. No white gown, no flower girl and not even a church wedding, just a quick stand up at the courthouse so us living together in Coalfire wouldn't cause any upset with Jonas Stark. He didn't like people living in sin, especially his relatives.

Over the years Simon's laziness had given him a potbelly but I still looked pretty darn good. I took in typing for Jonas Stark, the daddy of Evander, Buddy Jr., and Alvey, the mayor of Quinntown. Alvey and his Uncle Floyd ran Contrary when I was a kid, and now Buddy Jr. was mayor of Contrary. The patriarch Jonas also had a bunch of nephews and cousins that peppered Crimson County like crab grass. Seemed the family got their start in Coalfire in this little used car lot close to the freeway. It was home to Jonas so he never moved to Contrary with his sons. Years ago people had said that by the end of the century the Starks would own the whole state, and I guessed they were working up to it.

Coalfire was a mean place, even by Notown standards. Every single person here looked to steal something, and believing a word that came out of their mouths meant you might as well paint *Fool* across your forehead. I got used to it. But nobody but nobody stole from Jonas Stark. One time a couple ole boys got drunk and took one of his cars off the lot for a spin up the mountain. Jonas had them rounded up along with their momma. He broke that woman's knees in front of her sons, leaving her in a heap on the ground. Never touched the boys. Just said at them, "Any woman who'd give birth to two malfeasants don't deserve legs to walk." I guarantee if anybody else ever thought about hoodwinking Jonas, they put it out of mind.

At the outskirts of Coalfire was a shantytown called Spit. Nobody decent went there and only the foolish ever walked out that way. Full of drug addicts, drunks and criminals. Need something stolen or a house set afire for insurance money, get somebody from Spit to do it for you. Jonas and Simon must've had their hands dirty from some of that, but I didn't want to know about it.

Mr. Stark always treated me decent. He even let me take the typewriter home. I used to work in the office but Simon got jealous when a couple customers asked who the cute girl was. He never could stand competition. So from home I typed letters to customers and businessmen, state senators and sometimes even the Governor of Kentucky. My style was perfect and Mr. Stark liked how I added a little flair to his sentences now and then. Today I worked on an insurance claim over a fender bender he had last year, a petition to a judge on behalf of a cousin who Jonas felt got railroaded on an arson charge, and a contract with a Knoxville auto parts dealer. He signed everything, then I gave the copies to his secretary for mailing.

Zelda Gambrel had the job that was supposed to be mine years ago when I came over here with Simon. She didn't type and for the longest time I couldn't figure out why she got hired. Finally Simon said she was Jonas's girlfriend. He was about thirty years older but as I sat in the waiting room and watched Zelda change the polish on her nails from red to pink, I could believe it. She wasn't what you'd call beautiful, mousy brown hair that she backcombed about an inch from her head, and a little on the chubby side, but she babied Jonas and he ate it up until his cheeks flushed. It made me sick to even think about them in a bedroom.

A familiar voice came from Jonas's office and since Zelda was busy with her nails, I got a cup of water from the cooler so I could stand next to the door and listen. Out the front window I saw Simon talking up a Chrysler Toronado to a gray-haired man. People from the cities came to trade in their old cars, especially if they'd been in a wreck and wanted to hide it from the law. They drove out with a new model and the old ones got fixed and re-sold or chopped up for parts.

In the office I heard a man ask Jonas, "How much longer?" It was Willie Carmack's voice, and I peered in the door. He seemed irritated, checking his watch. I didn't know of any business between the Starks and the Carmacks but figured that rich people talked all the time.

"The Chicago contractor is in Contrary now," Jonas replied. "Your old friend'll show him the ropes."

I glanced back at Zelda starting on her other hand, concentrating so the polish didn't smear. Outside Simon waved his arms around a Grand Prix like it was Noah's Ark. I dipped behind the Coke machine to peer into the other side of the office.

Jonas was on his knees in front of the safe and Willie stood watching him. The safe popped open and Jonas reached in for an envelope. Farther back both sides of the safe were stacked with money. I felt my eyes bug out. He closed the safe and they turned toward the office door. I went back to my chair.

Willie left without acknowledging me and maybe he didn't even realize who I was. I didn't keep in touch with anybody other than Momma and my Christmas and birthday phone calls to Tallulah. I was allowed an extra call because of graduation so I knew she wanted a white dress. It irritated Simon that I was spending money on her but I didn't let anybody know 'cause I wanted Connor and all the Hernes to think I was doing just fine married to a Stark relation.

"Got my papers there," Jonas called out and motioned me into his office. He landed in his green leather chair with a wheeze, his girth about to spill over the sides. A plaster frog on his desk wore a red cowboy hat, and a real cowboy hat hung on a coat hook behind him. I handed him the letters and he read them over and passed each one back after signing. My eyes kept straying to the safe behind his desk. All that money. Lord, it must be a million dollars!

"Good job as usual, Randi Jo." He reached into a drawer and pulled out some handwritten pages. "Think you can get these done by tomorrow night and bring 'em over to the house?"

"Sure can," I said without looking at them.

"I gotta take 'em on a trip this weekend." He waddled around the desk and handed the papers to me. "If you can't make out my handwriting, give me a call. Be up 'til about midnight."

"I never have trouble with your writing, Mr. Stark."

He chuckled and his belly shook. "You're a good girl, Randi Jo. That Simon better be good to you."

"That's what I tell him." I smiled and moved to the door. "Mr. Stark," I added, turning back. "Think I might get this week's pay today? My daughter is graduating high school and I'm buying her this white dress she has her heart set on."

"How 'bout that? High school." He reached in his pocket and handed me a ten-dollar bill.

I thanked him again and left. Funny he always said things like *Simon better be good to you*. Hadn't he seen my bruised eye? Or the dozens of bruises I'd had through the years? Yet he never mentioned them, never said anything to Simon. Just gave me my ten dollars a week and patted me on the head like a good dog. I knew what I had to do to get paid. With Simon it was different, being related to Jonas somehow, but I doubted he was a second cousin like he'd told me all those years ago. Probably more like an illegitimate child of the upstairs maid. They sent him out to do the dirty work, picking up a truckload of hot car parts or collecting the weekly take from the gambling joints in the back of the Stark restaurants. He did it all, just like a trained seal. He talked a big game to people who didn't know any better but he was as insecure around the Starks as a chick in a snake den.

Outside Simon leaned on the trunk of a Cordoba. "Sell your car?" I asked.

"Damn, no." Simon spit on the ground. "Ship to China's already sailed, sweetness." He pointed at a cream-colored Winnebago. "I sell me a few of those, momma, and I'm buying me a new suit."

"How 'bout a new dress for me?"

"One you're wearing is fine."

"I wear this dress every single day."

"And it smells it too, like pickled pigs feet. Why don't you wash it from time to time?"

I walked away as he snickered like he was tickled with himself and then he called out after me, "Don't get hyper. I'm kidding." I didn't care. Let him think I was mad.

At the end of the lot stood the dank garage where they chopped up cars. Guess there was one person working there that was from home, but I didn't really know him: Dallas Shepard was washing Mr. Stark's

Cadillac. I nodded as I passed. He never acted like we were acquainted and our eyes only met briefly. Other than my grandfather, I couldn't recall ever talking to a black person except for Dallas, and I couldn't rightly remember if I'd actually spoken words to him. I suspected Holly had something to do with him getting a job here, and having just seen Willie it seemed even more likely. So often I wished I could talk to her. Sometimes when I argued with Simon I even pretended to be her. It gave me enough backbone to stand up to my husband and hit him a few knocks on the noggin. As always with Simon and me, we fought, mouthed off to each other, and then made crazy love like we were holding on to the only thing that kept us from drowning. We didn't have anything in this world but each other and still our passion mixed with hate. Maybe I needed that, and maybe that's why things never worked with Connor and me.

Dallas knelt and soaped a headlight. Even though a sentence never passed between us, every week the nod we exchanged became a connection, almost like saying hello to Holly.

I wound on through a row of stores and came to Kempler's Bar and Grill. Inside I looked for the waitress who'd gotten me the white dress. I'd explained to her which Contrary store had it and she'd managed to steal exactly the right size. The bar reeked of liquor and I waved a hand in front of my nose. She saw me and brought the dress over.

Peeling off the money I'd saved for weeks now, I paid half-price for that beautiful dress, pure white, princess neckline, gathered skirt, lace edging the sleeves and hem. It hung in a plastic bag and the waitress had thrown in a mood ring since she'd heard about my daughter's graduation. I tried on the ring and got a pink color, not my favorite. Never mind, Tallulah would be so surprised. She'd look like an angel in this dress and I could hardly wait until tomorrow.

40

Stayed up until two a.m. to get the bulk of Mr. Stark's typing finished. Few hours later, after getting Simon's breakfast, I fell asleep longer than I'd intended even though I needed to re-do two letters. One to a banker for a loan to buy an interest in a Carmack mine; no doubt the reason for Willie's visit. The other was a thank you to the Secretary of the Interior for inviting Jonas on a big game hunting trip. The third I'd typed perfectly asking the governor to pardon one of Jonas's cousins convicted of murder years ago and citing old age as the reason. Mr. Stark got pardons for most his relatives that ended up in the joint, but he'd had a hard time with this one because Simon said the killing had been so vicious.

I already had on my dress and makeup for the graduation, and Tallulah's white gown hung in a dress bag with a big red bow tied around the hanger. I kept the mood ring on so I wouldn't forget it. It was still pink but the minute the screen door slammed and Simon came in cussing, the ring turned brown.

"That blamed Jonas Stark." He plopped down at the kitchen table and peeled a banana.

He came home every day after his cocktail at the Jolly Roger so I didn't pay much attention and finished the last letter. "Connor used to come home complaining about the teenagers, and you come home complaining about the boss. What is it with men, can't seem to have a day without griping?" I knew that would irritate him and smiled to myself.

"Blamed Connor. I don't want hear about him. Why do you even think of blamed Connor anymore? You're not even his wife, and all I have to hear about is Connor, Connor, Connor."

"I just meant there are ways you're alike."

"I ain't nothing like blamed Connor. I ought to knock your head off for saying that."

I yawned and pulled the paper out of the typewriter. Just the envelopes now and I'd be done. "Well, I'll stop talking about him if you'll get dressed so we can leave in the next half hour. I want to get there early and give Tallulah her dress. Maybe she'll change and wear it under her graduation gown."

"I needed five dollars out of that pay, you didn't spend it all?"

"I told you I needed my typing money for Tallulah's present. How many times did I say that?" I was getting mad. Sometimes Simon had Pug's stubbornness. If I'd been big enough I would've kicked both their asses. "I laid out your clothes on the bed."

"Don't I get nothing to eat?"

"We'll stop at Pinkie's on the way." I struggled to stay calm but my teeth were starting to clench. He was going to be trouble all night long. I could feel it. I wasn't even bothering with the graduation dinner Connor was giving Tallulah at the Contrary Steak House 'cause I knew he'd act like this.

A police car's whirling lights reflected on our wall, and a cruiser pulled up out front. "You didn't rob a bank, did you?" Simon asked, tapping his fingers on the table.

A state trooper and a man in a black suit came up to the house and knocked. I glanced at Simon, who'd gone paler than birch bark, then I opened the door. "Afternoon," I said, holding open the screen door for them to come in.

Officer Finley Colson took off his cap. "Here to see your husband, Ma'am." I'd seen Colson stopping speeders along the road and he once gave me a warning instead of a ticket for going too fast. Simon had plopped in the corner of the couch after turning on the TV. Crap, I thought, what's he done?

Colson stepped toward the couch. "Mind if we talk, Mr. Tuller?"

Simon looked up like he hadn't realized anyone had walked through the door. He interlaced his fingers in front of him. "Not a'tall. What can I do for you gentlemen?"

"This is Howard Redmond from the FBI," Colson said. The man in the black suit flipped open a wallet, showing a badge and ID.

That sent a shiver through me. State troopers weren't like small town police, owned by whomever was in office at the time. Even the Starks couldn't buy them off and a couple times troopers had taken over cases from the locals if the state believed justice wasn't being done. That was about the only time a Stark ended up in the joint.

Simon rested his hands on his thighs, stared at Colson, glanced at the other man and said, "I ain't been nowhere near Richmond today."

"How would you know something happened in Richmond?" Colson asked.

"Heard about it at work. You talked to Dallas Shepard? He's the one drives that route. Picks up newspapers and distributes them around the county. If he does anything other than that, I wouldn't know about it, and Jonas would have no way of finding out. Jonas just wants his advertisement papers delivered."

"What?" I couldn't keep my mouth shut hearing such a bold-faced lie. "Dallas Shepard washes the cars. He doesn't drive Jonas's trucks."

The officer seemed to consider, looking at the floor.

"Shut up, stupid." Simon spread his hands in a what's-the-use gesture. "My wife ain't got the sense of a ham sandwich." He leaned over and flicked my ear.

"And you're bold as brass, Simon." If the police hadn't been there he'd have knocked me into the wall, and still might later on tonight, but while I could I was going to get my oar in. "Officer, I have some papers to deliver. You mind if I leave?"

"If you know anything, Ma'am—"

"My wife sits on her ass in the house all day, Finley. She don't know a fly from a mosquito."

"They're both flies, ignoramus," I looked hard at him.

"Where have you been today, ma'am?" Trooper Colson asked.

"I've been here typing," I said, determined to point out that I was working and not sitting on my backside. Trooper Colson nodded me toward the door.

I left, disgusted that my husband was trying to get Dallas in trouble. Probably one of Jonas's trucks with stolen goods got stopped and the driver ran. I bet Simon was sent to pick him up. His red hair would've shown up like a carrot in a garden patch, so of course they came looking for him. Poor Dallas. A black man's word in Coalfire stood for nothing. At least in Contrary or Quinntown they could get a defense lawyer. Even somebody from Divergence stood a better chance than here. I hoped these state people and the FBI had sense. As I walked to Mr. Stark's house I knew that the lies were about to start. If the real driver was a Stark relation . . . Dallas was looking at being railroaded.

41

I knocked on the Starks' screen door and Jonas's sister, Renita, called out from the living room, "He's upstairs on the phone, come on in." She waved me in, tucked her feet up on a flowered couch and sipped a soda through a straw.

"Got typed letters he needs tonight," I said. I'd never been any further than the foyer and getting a better look at their big house was a treat. It wasn't as new or fancy as Holly's but had the spaciousness of a home that had been here a long time. Black and white tintypes of ancestors who had flooded the area in the late 1880s hung on the walls, along with knickknacks, a sheriff's badge, a needlepoint alphabet sampler, and a chipped bowie knife with large lettering at the bottom explaining that the tip had been left in the belly of a Chickasaw warrior. The Starks were the kind of people who sat on their money. They owned dozens of businesses in

Coalfire, Contrary and Quinntown, but lived like the rest of us, never flaunting their wealth. One or another of them had been in Crimson County politics for as long as I could remember. Their ordinariness always won them votes–that and a drink of whiskey or ten dollars slipped into your palm.

"Have a seat." Renita pointed at a suede recliner. "Was about to have some Coke. Pour you some, too?"

"Just a little." I took a goblet from a burled-wood cabinet against the wall. "Driving to Contrary tonight. My daughter's graduating high school, and I don't want to have to stop and find a toilet." I bit my tongue, feeling uncouth, but Renita just filled my glass half way from an open bottle and didn't act at all like I'd said anything wrong.

"Bet you're real proud of your baby." She smiled sweetly but glanced aside and her eyes had a sad scrunch to them.

"I am," I said, watching her expression. She'd slurred her words and I realized she was drinking more than Coke. "Wish I could see her more often, but life is what it is."

She nodded, her smile now wistful, and gestured at a row of pictures on a credenza beside the fireplace. "That's my daughter in the middle. All boys, the others, a Stark curse." She toasted the air with her glass of cola.

I went over to look at the young woman with pale eyes. Renita followed me and picked up the black-and-white photograph, which seemed odd with all the ones around it in color. She had smooth skin and a long swan's neck. Her hair curled back from her face in soft waves just like Renita's except her mother's hair was a darker steel gray. "I didn't know you had a daughter. Where's she now?"

Renita dismissed the question with a wave of her hand. "Oh honey, she's dead."

"I'm so sorry. Didn't mean to bring up hurtful memories."

"Naw. No more than what I think of every morning when I open my eyes."

"What was her name?"

"Bette."

Every muscle in my body clenched. I pretended to listen as Renita explained taking the name from Bette Davis but everyone pronounced it without the *e*. Curiosity gnawed at me. Could it be the same person? "My older sister, Kim, knew some of the Starks but I don't remember her mentioning a Bette."

"My married name was Moss back then. Bette grew up in France so Kim probably didn't know her."

"That's a far piece."

"Left after her daddy died in a shootout at the courthouse that my cousin Fitz got him into." She shrugged as if to say, *Heaven help us*, then leaned close to me. "But I'll tell you a little secret." She gulped her cola. "Johnny Moss wasn't her real daddy." She sighed and put her hand on her heart. "I'd fallen head over heels and down the road in love with a traveling piano player named Luther Ballard and . . ."

She continued telling me about Uncle Luther. How he'd flirted by putting her name into "Peg o' My Heart." How they'd sneaked around out of sight of all her brothers, who would have shot Luther if they'd known she was dating another man behind Johnny's back. She spoke like a young woman in love, her little joke on a family that still kept her on a short leash. Taking a vodka bottle, Renita went back to the couch and motioned for me to sit beside her. My tongue tasted pasty as she described a man I didn't recognize. What in the world had happened to Uncle Luther to change him?

"Whenever I got scared he'd always tell me, *Live for today 'cause love is a cutthroat business.*" She closed her eyes and smiled as she stretched out the word *love.* "Then Jonas got the bright idea of marrying me off to some Knoxville fool to help him get a Tennessee liquor license. Thank God that husband dropped dead of an aneurism on our wedding night." She coughed, a congested smoker's hack. "Two more husbands and here I am a Stark again. I'll be damned if I'll ever wed another man."

"I understand." The vodka had loosened her tongue perhaps more than she'd intended. "I had a bunch of brothers, too." She gave me a little conspiratorial wink, but if one of my brothers had done me the way they done her, I'd have shot them in their sleep. In a lot of ways she was worse off than I'd ever been, even with all the Stark money.

Jonas stomped down the steps cussing for all he was worth. I froze, suddenly afraid of him, afraid of the knowledge I'd just gained, even if he had no way of realizing what I knew. He might see it in my eyes. Renita stared at her Coke straw.

"By all fools in hell!" He stomped past us and went out onto the porch, continuing his tirade. The living room walls filled with the reflections of police lights. I heard car doors slam and men's voices making demands.

"Sure you don't want a refill, honey?" Renita asked, then poured Coke for me and added a little vodka. Outside the voices got louder. Jonas yelled that he was madder than a swatted hornet. I stepped over to the window. Two policemen held Dallas Shepard between them and leaned him on the hood of the patrol car. Simon stood off to the side, staring at the ground while Jonas berated him. The cops were Coalfire police. No sign of the state trooper or the FBI. Jonas stomped around Dallas, screaming in his face and shaking his fist.

I stayed behind the curtain but couldn't pull myself away. "I'm so sorry about Bette, Miss Stark," I said, "I kinda recall what happened when I was a little girl, but it's a fuzzy memory."

Renita sighed. "It was news more over here than in Quinntown, I guess. I was so out of my mind I couldn't keep up with it all and if Jonas did one good thing for me in his life, it was to keep all that quiet. We thought we'd have a better chance of catching him that way."

Dallas screamed as Jonas brought a baseball bat down on one of his knees. I jerked and covered my mouth with both hands. Renita sat comfortably on the couch, acting like nothing was wrong. "Catching him?" I asked, not wanting to hear what she said next.

"The killer. Oh, I didn't say . . . my daughter was murdered."

"I don't know how anybody gets over something like that."

She started to speak, then caught herself as Dallas's painful yells vibrated the room. "Well, somehow you just do."

"You know who done it?"

Her eyebrows rose and she propped a hand to cradle one side of her face. From outside, another painful shout slid into sobbing, pleading protests of innocence. "I'll tell you one thing," Renita said calmly. "I'd do anything, and I mean anything to bring her home . . . all of her . . . I'd have her buried right beside me. Only then could I have an easy rest." She exhaled a slow sigh as Dallas collapsed to the ground. I closed my eyes as the cops threw him into the back of the squad car. "You can't rest in peace if you can't rest whole . . ."

The police car started up and I couldn't turn to look at Renita grieving and reliving the loss of her daughter. The front door slammed and Jonas marched in with the baseball bat over one shoulder, then he leaned it in the corner of the hallway. "You got my letters?"

"I do." I kept my face as passive as his sister's. She sucked the last of her Coke and I handed Jonas the folder and envelopes.

"Randi Jo's daughter is graduating high school," Renita said. "Let's send a little something along for her. It's not every day that–"

"Why sure." He pulled out his wallet and gave me a twenty-dollar bill.

"It's not necessary," I said, "but she'll sure enjoy it and I'll make certain she sends you a thank-you note."

"Don't be cheap, Jonas," his sister said. "It's high school, after all."

He shot her an irritated glance and pulled out a fifty. "High school. Why didn't you tell me?"

I hesitantly took the bill, giving the twenty back as Renita grinned at her brother. "I'll be going," I said softly.

Renita waved 'bye and Jonas showed me to the door. Outside I tiptoed down the porch steps, carefully avoiding blood spots and a couple of teeth scattered on the ground. I hoped they'd taken Dallas to the police station rather than dumping him out on the mountain to die. Two blocks away I started shaking. I'd been wrong about so many things in life. Bette Moss was not a floozy from Marcescent Street. She might have gotten killed on a canal bank in the bad part of town, but I doubted that she'd ever worked the hotel. She had been beautiful and innocent, Uncle Luther's daughter and kin to me by distant blood. As much as I might have wanted to, I could never tell Renita where her daughter's head was buried. My Momma still lived there, and I didn't trust the Stark's craziness.

ᴄ⁓

When I got home Simon was nowhere to be found. The car was gone and all the lights were out. "Damn, damn, damn," I said, walking through the house.

He'd done his worst to get Dallas Shepard in trouble and now he was going to ruin this special night. But I was not going to miss Tallulah's graduation even if I had to hitchhike. The fifty dollars in my pocket meant I could call a cab.

300

Simon had left a suitcase pulled half out of the closet like he'd been looking for something to wear. I shoved it back in with my foot but the suitcase caught. I snatched it up and threw it across the room. Something on the closet floor moved. A board had jiggled loose.

I got a flashlight and shined it on the floor. A red color shone between the cracks. Pulling on the board, half a dozen of them slid sideways, revealing a hole under the closet. I picked up a red stick then slowly replaced it. Dynamite.

What had that fool done? We'd been sleeping on explosives for God knows how long. We could've been blown up in the night.

Pressing my fingers into my temples, I tried to think. Ole man Stark would do more than break Simon's knees if he found out my husband had done something and blamed Dallas. Betrayal was something no Stark put up with. Except maybe Renita, but she looked like she would weep over none of her brothers' graves.

A vehicle pulled up outside and I jumped to my feet. "Thank God," I said, thinking of Simon, and grabbing Tallulah's dress.

Out on the porch, I stopped cold. Instead of Simon's car a Winnebago took up half the street, hastily parked and leaning sideways because the right wheels were off the road. Simon got out of the driver's side and slammed the door. He ran to another door in the middle of the Winnebago, opened it, and I saw a little red-haired girl. He spoke to her then turned to me.

"I don't know what you got going on," I called out, "but I've got to get to graduation." He came toward me and I held out the dress for him to hang up in the back. "Who is she?" I pointed at the little girl.

Simon stood in front of me with sweat beading on his forehead. The child had red hair just like his and I thought, niece, cousin, but I knew. I knew. My husband had gone and had a child with another woman.

Still no words from him, and I didn't see it coming, and can't remember the blow, but it must have been his fist. All I recalled later was blood from my nose spattering the ground as he flipped me over his shoulder, a fuzzy memory of the white dress lying in the dirt, the mood ring dropping from my finger . . . black.

42

Opened my eyes. It was dark. I was moving. In a car? No, the big hunkering house on wheels. I lay on a bed. My head pounded with the worst pain I'd ever felt. Car headlights flipped past the window like an old movie arcade. I tried to sit up but nausea filled my stomach. I looked over at a table. A little girl sat there. "Tallulah?" I asked.

My voice was weak and shaky. The child didn't speak. Her big eyes stared from under bangs cut straight across her forehead and made her look like one of those paintings of children with enlarged pupils. Her lips formed a sad frown and she held a rag doll in one arm. I realized that she was not my daughter.

I pressed one hand to my head and the other to my chest, struggling to soothe the pain and nausea. It didn't help. I turned on my side and saw a man asleep on the floor. He wore a black coat. As I looked at him he faded

303

in and out. His eyes were open, mouth ajar. He should wake up, I thought. Get up off the floor. There was blood around his nostrils.

Blood had also caked on my cheek. I flicked some of it off, then I lost all sense of time to the dark.

e⁊

When I woke again the house wasn't moving. It was still dark. Outside I heard Simon talking to someone. I pushed up on my elbows and my head pounded. The room swam around me. The side door opened and the little girl came in carrying a bag of potato chips, candy bars, and a Coke. She sat at the table with her doll propped in the other chair. She emptied the chips into two bowls and put one in front of the doll. Then she noticed me, came over without a word, and put a candy bar in my hand. I tried to speak, ask her name, but my words were scrambled and she ran out the door.

Seconds later Simon was at my side. He put a hand on my head and pushed me back down. "Rest R.J.," he said. "You've got a concussion." He fetched a glass of water from the sink. I heard the click of pills in a bottle and he poked two into my mouth. "Swallow. You'll feel better."

"What's it?" I mumbled.

He might have said sleeping pills. Soon the Winnebago's motor started. We were on the road again and before long I was asleep.

The passing of time became a long blur but I was aware that Simon came several times to put more pills in my mouth. Was I really that sick? Why didn't he take me to the hospital? Where in the world were we driving? I still had to get to the graduation.

As drowsiness again overtook me, a sliver of reality sank in: I missed Tallulah's graduation. What would my daughter think? The promises, the dress, the special dinner . . . Tears dripped down my cheeks and my nose was so swollen I could hardly breathe. Sleep, deep dreamless sleep was my only escape.

The next time I woke I could sit up. I pulled open the window shade and thought I must be dreaming. The Winnebago was parked, and cashew-colored sand stretched as far as I could see. The brightness hurt my eyes. I squinted and saw mountains of some kind on the horizon, but they didn't look like Kentucky mountains. There was no dead man on the floor.

Slowly I slung my legs over the side of the bed and stood, holding on to the furniture. I heard nobody, nothing. When I swung open the door sunlight flooded in, so bright I shielded my eyes again. Outside, Simon and the little girl sat at a picnic table eating sandwiches.

He caught sight of me, jumped up and came over. "Slow now," he said, "slow." He put an arm around me and led me to his side of the table. About ten feet away the dead man lay on his back. His head was covered with a canvas bag. The air was hotter than a sizzling frying pan and the corpse smelled awful.

"We got baloney sandwiches," Simon said. "You feel like food?"

"I feel like him." I pointed at the dead man.

The little girl sat quietly eating and gave me a curious look. "This is Wendy," Simon said. "Say hello, honey. This is Randi Jo and she's your new momma."

I glanced at Simon but knew better than to say anything. The little girl mouthed a wordless, *Hello.* "Where are we?" I asked.

"The forty-ninth state."

"This ain't Alaska."

"Arizona, foolish. Didn't you graduate high school?"

Nauseous but even feeling like I was dying he could still piss me off. "Arizona's number forty-eight."

"Don't be a know-it-all." Simon smacked my arm and hints of his mean self sparked in his eyes. He set a candy bar in front of me. "Divide that up between the two of you. I'll be back in a minute."

He went over to the dead man and dragged him about twenty feet further to where a shovel was stuck in the sand, and started digging.

At the table Wendy pointed at the candy bar. "Okay," I said, and let her have it all, hoping it didn't make her sick. I managed to get down half a baloney sandwich and the Coke calmed my stomach enough so I could stay upright.

Whatever road we'd pulled off of was deserted. In the next hour only one car approached from the distance. Simon stopped digging as it passed. We must've looked like the average family pulled over at a rest stop for a picnic 'cause the car didn't slow down and the passengers didn't look at us.

By the time Simon finished burying the man it was late afternoon and the sun had sunk low in the sky. The worst heat of the day was over. Simon walked toward us and called my name. When I looked over he motioned for me to join him. I panicked. Was he going to kill me? I glanced at the road, thinking I might run, but there were no cars and in my shape he'd catch me for sure.

I looked back at him, trying to judge how mean he looked. One hand on his hip and the other holding onto the shovel, his posture told me that I was looking at a man who was afraid.

"Hurry up," he yelled, "I don't have all day." He raised the shovel overhead and threw it as far as he could. Relief spread through me. I walked toward him and he said, "Sorry about all this." He rubbed his damp forehead. His skin was red from standing in the sun and his clothes stank of sweat.

"What's going on, Simon?"

He took a breath and coughed. "So much has happened."

"Who's that man?"

He parted his lips as if to speak and gestured toward the grave, then lowered his hand. "I'm not sure."

"We travel with a dead man all the way to Arizona and you don't know who he is?"

He wiped his eyes and pressed his fingers on both sides of his nose. "Holly's dead, too."

Stunned, I started to repeat her name. "You didn't bury her out here, did you?"

"Naw . . ." The word slurred from his mouth and I realized he was inhaling shivery breaths, trying to control his trembling muscles.

"You're crying? How can you cry? Why are we out here in the middle of nowhere? Take me home! I missed my baby's graduation. And my friend is dead." Crying myself now. Starting to bawl.

He cocked his fist at me and I raised my arms to protect my face. Then he only made a *grrrr* sound and dropped to his knees. "I'm sorry, Randi Jo. I'm sorry. You have to help me. You have to." He wrapped his arms around my legs and held on tightly.

Behind the mountains the sun was setting, making the sky all manner of pink, scarlet, and purple. He sobbed into my lap, barely getting out a story I could make no sense of. The Starks, of course, their trouble he'd gotten mixed up in, and now this dead man buried in the desert under the Arizona sun. I couldn't tell what had happened to Holly but it sounded like her car had been blown up. Dynamite? Right now I couldn't even think about that possibility.

"Help me," Simon pleaded. "We can live out here. Raise my daughter. Her momma was no'a'count, whipped on her, barely fed her. Bitch died in a car wreck last week. All that past is gone. None of it good. You know that. None of it good for you, neither. We'll have a fresh start, a new life."

He had the most pitiful look on his face. I thought of how Tallulah must've felt abandoned when I left all those years ago. Now I was faced with sticking by Simon or running from him the first good chance I got. And abandoning the little girl as well. How could I explain?

Letting go of me, Simon stretched out on the sand and inhaled deep breaths. I went to the picnic table and sat across from Wendy. "How old are you?" I asked.

She held out five fingers. "My momma's dead," she said in a sweet monotone.

My nose filled with congestion and I picked up a napkin to wipe my eyes. "You're very pretty," I told her, and for the first time a timid smile appeared. I recalled Tallulah at age five: more energy than any ten kids and she didn't cling to her father or me. Didn't need us, maybe a testament to how we raised her, confident and strong. Then it came to me that right here and now was the daughter I hadn't been allowed to raise. A girl who had no mother. I was away from everything and everybody I knew. I didn't want a new start. I'd gotten used to my life with all its mistakes. Part of me would give anything to have it back . . . my daughter and my first husband and even my frustrating relatives. But I'd lost that life and there was no need to cry about it.

I looked at Simon lying on the sand staring up at the sunset. "We better get on the road," I hollered, "before it's too dark to drive."

He got to his knees, then rose and walked toward us, hands on his hips.

43

I never got used to the heat. In the summertime, breathing Arizona air was like inhaling fire. We settled in a trailer park called The Phoenix, living in that too-small Winnebago. One thing I kept to myself: the fifty dollars Jonas Stark had given me that last day back home. Simon never found it tucked in my dirty clothes after we drove out of the desert. I hid that bill well and good.

When it was so hot I couldn't breathe I took Wendy to the library and we spent our day reading books. The thought of Simon back at the Winnebago sweating his ass off was an amusing comfort to me. I asked the librarian if she might be able to get a *Crimson County Sun* and she said she'd check into it, but it never showed up on the shelf and I didn't want to draw attention to myself so I never asked again.

The little girl was studious, not rambunctious and full of life like Tallulah. Always sad and I figured something awful must have happened to her. I felt sorry for Wendy and that kept me from feeling sorry for myself. In late afternoon, when the weather cooled, we played on the swing set of a Catholic school that was closed for the summer. I saw nuns walking about inside, and sometimes they looked out at us, but so far no one told us to go away.

Simon couldn't get work and it made him all the more foul. He disappeared sometimes and came home with enough cash to get us through the next month. Other times he made collect calls from the payphone near the manager's office, then headed off to the Western Union. Then he'd return with cash so I figured the Starks were sending him enough to get by. I hated all of them for what they'd done. Me living so far away from my daughter . . . and Connor. Much as I sometimes hated my ex-husband I hated myself more for losing a life that hadn't been so bad after all.

Days passed, became months. I could tell something was wrong between Simon and the Starks. Each time he got a letter from them, he'd drink until he passed out. I'd check on the money in his pocket and it was less and less until finally it was ten dollars. Part of me thought, how fitting.

Wendy and I lived our lives as best we could. I grew to love her like my own daughter, and while she was always shy, she seemed to take to me too. She loved riding the merry-go-round at the school. When I'd launched her into a spin she held on with one arm and let the other fly to the sky, her red hair floating behind her in the breeze. It gave me such pleasure to see that. It seemed like the one time when we were both free. "Time to go home, honey."

She ran to me and took my hand. It made me smile with the true joy of being a mother. She still didn't speak much, only a few words now and then.

When we got back to the trailer park Simon paced in the small concrete front yard. A heavyset bald man sat in our lawn chair, and I smelled beer. I tried to catch Simon's eye to see if I should come in or walk past.

He stopped pacing and ran out to meet me. "Go stand by that cactus, Wendy," he told her. "I have to talk to your momma." He pulled me out of the man's hearing range and grabbed hold of my arm.

His grip hurt and I twisted out of it. "Is there trouble?"

Simon shot me a half-grin that stayed on his face longer than usual. "Naw. Naw . . ." His lips twisted into a fractured smile. "Only the money kind."

"Who's that?" I nodded at the man.

"Listen, Randi Jo." Simon put an arm around me and turned me toward the man. "Starks ain't gonna send money regular. They got big problems in Midnight Valley and got to keep a low profile."

"Good for them," I said, meaning just the opposite.

"That's my friend, Dempsey." He gestured. In response the bald man in the lawn chair raised a hand with a half-smile. "You know I love you, R.J."

"I know," I said even though I didn't believe it and it made me nervous the way Simon kept repeating my name. What Simon and I had was not love. It was a sick kind of passion that neither of us could let go of. "What's this all about?"

"You know." He nodded toward Dempsey. Simon's so-called friend stood up, hands in his pockets, and rocked back and forth on his heels with the same stupid half-smile on his face.

"No, I don't." Half of me did know, but my mind flipped away from the awful thought.

"He'll give us thirty dollars."

"He'll give *you* thirty dollars." I panicked, jerking away from him. "Tell him to leave, Simon."

"I don't know why you won't do this for us. You did it with a black man on the wall of the Regal Hotel." He laughed, pointing at me. "Thought I didn't remember from all those years ago, didn't ye?"

"I did not."

"I saw it. I know what I saw. Heard the lie you told. You're just like me, R.J., so don't get on no high horse, thinking there are some things you won't do. You'll do anything to survive and so will I."

"That man was my grandfather!"

"I . . ." Simon's features froze like he was posing for a picture, taking in what he'd heard. He laughed and slapped his knees, bending over like he'd heard the funniest punch line in the world. "Your granddaddy is black?" He hooted like some big joke had been pulled on him then whirled around and backhanded me.

I flew, falling, and blood dripped from my nose. He was down on me faster than a wrestler, his fist aimed at my face. "You broke my nose!"

"Got to learn to listen better, darlin'," he said in a singsong tone. "And if you can't listen, then just do what I say. Better it hurt a little now than a lot later."

Dempsey rushed up beside him. "No way, Simon. I don't need none of this."

Simon got up and patted Dempsey on the back, and led him back to the lawn chair.

I was ready to run. Wendy still stood by the cactus. Her expression had returned to the blank-eyed, staring little girl I'd seen when we first met. Her little mind wouldn't let in reality and what had been a smile a few minutes earlier had reverted back to that lonely, sad frown. "Honey," I said.

Simon sauntered back to me and knelt down. He took a pill bottle out of his shirt pocket and opened it. Grabbing me by the hair, he forced a pill into my mouth. "There," he said. "That'll make it not so bad. Now you know what to do."

He jerked me to my feet and shoved me toward the trailer. "Come on, Wendy," he told his daughter. "They're building a swimming pool on the far side, let's go watch 'em dig." They marched away, him pulling Wendy along, her small legs skipping to keep up. She looked back at me as she tried to keep pace with her father.

Someone touched my shoulder and I jumped. Dempsey stood beside me. His goofy grin was gone and his expression genuinely concerned. "I don't have to," he said. "Simon said it was okay. I thought . . ."

I covered my face with both hands, let out a laugh, and wiped my bloody nose on the hem of my tee shirt.

"It's okay, Dempsey. It's okay." I limped back to the trailer with Dempsey, thinking of how afraid I'd been as a young girl of ending up in this very situation. Here I was, and I wasn't scared. Seemed like this was where I'd been destined to be all my life.

44

I took more and more of those pills as the days passed. No idea what they were, but Simon was right when he'd said I just wouldn't care about anything, and while I was under their control, I didn't. Looking over the shoulder of whatever man was on top of me, I could stare the Fear Angel right in the eye without even a flinch. She didn't like it, hovering over me and settling in the corner of the trailer like a bat hanging on a rafter. I'd crack a smile at the corner of my mouth like I finally had her on the run, but she watched carefully, studying me like I was her school project. She'd be up to something soon.

At first I thought maybe this life was what Fear Angel'd had in store for me all these years, then I realized she was not happy with the situation. Her plan was grander. When I was in the trailer by myself I often sat across from her and stared into her eyes trying to jar myself to a greater reality, but I couldn't even be afraid anymore. I couldn't imagine a worse way to live, but Fear Angel wanted more. She preferred to gargle on a wallowing pain that I might bring on myself, not something imposed by Simon. Still, I figured Fear Angel had won, 'cause there was no way I could despise myself more.

None of the women in the trailer park talked to me. Mrs. Gordon even spat when I walked past her yard. Couldn't say I blamed her. Her husband was at our place every payday. I didn't know how much Simon got for me anymore. People out here weren't much different from the folks in Notown, so it couldn't be much.

Wendy and I still liked to go to the playground at the Catholic school but classes were in session and we had to wait until the kids were gone. When Simon didn't have me scheduled, we went to the library. She read the same book almost every time, about a mother bear who'd lost her cub and discovered that a lost little girl was following her. By the end of the book the human mother, who had found the bear cub, met up with the mamma bear, and each child was returned to its rightful home. I read romances. I guess I'd gotten that from Momma. I felt sure she must be worried sick about me. Might even feared I was dead. If it had happened to Kim, it could happen to me.

Sometimes I checked out a book and took it to the playground to read while Wendy played. Getting lost in stories of other people's lives was my greatest escape. If I couldn't escape in real life then I made the most of it in my mind. Late at the night I thought about running away, disappearing so Simon would never find me . . . but I couldn't leave Wendy, and that poor child's mind would not stand any more upset. So I stayed here, reading my books, earning the money, none of which I saw, and I guess for the time being we were safe from whatever had happened back in Kentucky.

As the months passed what pain I felt faded into an acceptance of this being my life. One day I struck up an acquaintance that turned into an unlikely friendship. A nun who looked about my age was tending rose bushes around the door that led to the sisters' quarters. To my surprise Sister Mary Thelma came over and introduced herself to me. She wore her hair covered and a simple kind of long dress. I'd never known much about nuns. She was polite and over the next week we chatted in a pleasant way, mostly about Wendy or the weather or other such harmless topics.

These conversations made me blossom even though I had a terrible fear that my new friend would discover the truth about me. Yet we got along easily during the half hour or so when Sister Mary Thelma came out to tend the roses.

One afternoon Wendy enthusiastically dug in to help plant a rose bush. Before I noticed she had gotten her arms dirty to the elbows. "Good heavens," I said, starting to scold her.

Sister Mary Thelma just smiled. "Come in and wash," she told Wendy, and led us toward the school.

Inside, the building was cool. The rooms were wide and neatly arranged with chairs and tables, a narrow hallway led past schoolrooms prettier than any I'd ever known. We started across a white marble floor, so shiny it looked like ice. Then, I saw an Angel. She reached almost to the ceiling, formed of marble as white as the full moon. Her wings were spread, ready to take flight. Her hands reached out, palms up, as if you might run to her and be embraced. Her face, tilted slightly, looked down with eyes that followed me.

"Ohhhh," I exclaimed and dropped to my knees.

"I fell to my knees the first day I saw her, too," Sister Mary Thelma said.

"Wendy, child," I said, looking at her arms and then back at Sister Mary Thelma. "We're bad dirty to be in here."

"We're all naked before our Blessed Mother. She would never judge us if we only do our best."

It was the kindest reply I'd heard in years. I looked up into the Angel's face. In her posture and expression she was everything opposite of the Fear Angel. I didn't believe in the same way Sister Mary Thelma did, but I knew I was in the presence of a holy spirit.

The next half hour passed in a sweet dream. We washed Wendy's arms in a clean bathroom sink and dried her with a white towel. Then Sister Mary Thelma tipped a bottle of scented water onto a washcloth to wipe all our hands. I put mine to my nose and smelled fresh flowers. Wendy also sniffed her fingers, smiling with delight.

"Lavender," the nun said. "We make it ourselves and sell it to support the school."

The idea of scented water reminded me that another world existed, one I'd forgotten about, where people were decent and lived respectable lives. "If I had the money, I'd use lavender water everyday."

"I think we can spare a bottle."

Sister Mary Thelma sent us on our way with not only that nice gift, but I now had a vision of what an angel really was.

ᛉ

When we got home Simon sat in front of the TV drinking a gin gimlet. The news anchor reported that Teamster President Jimmy Hoffa was missing. Possible criminal involvement was suspected. That made me wonder about the dead man buried beyond the picnic table all those months ago. I wondered if anybody was missing him.

Simon saw me watching him and asked irritably, "What?" then he sipped his drink and ignored me. He'd gone out and wasted money on a crystal goblet so he could have his gimlet just like back home.

I didn't have to worry about Wendy saying anything about a corpse in a black suit. She never mentioned the past, not even the previous day or what had happened to her that morning. She stayed in her moment in present time, cause to her that's all there was and ever would be.

"You smell good," Simon said. "Not your usual sauerkraut."

I imagined cracking the bottle of lavender on his head. "Don't use it on pigs," I murmured to myself.

"What?"

"Nothing."

Simon rolled his eyes like I was a waste of his time. He didn't touch me anymore, not to hurt or to comfort me. I was his cash cow and better not to be bruised. "Wendy and me are going to a movie tonight," he said and nodded toward the bedroom.

I knew what that meant. All my clean feeling of the afternoon was gone in a second. "We need to get Wendy in school," I said. "Somebody's going to get suspicious."

"No," he growled.

"She's a good reader but she needs a teacher."

"Like Connor." He stretched out the name in singsong sassiness. "When we met, you hated ole buttwipe. He dumped you on the side of the road like a bag of trash and still that's all you ever think of . . . Connor."

"Yeah, 'cause you treat me so well," I mouthed sarcastically.

"Shut up, you stinking, ignorant rube!" He threw the goblet, missing my head by inches, and it shattered. I saw that desire in his eyes to strangle me, but he held back. He needed the money. "You teach her," he demanded. "You got past eight grade, didn't you? That's as far as they let black people go, ain't it?"

"Simon, you're being mean. This is about her, not me."

"School means records. People asking questions."

"What questions? You said her mother was dead. You said you were her guardian."

"Come on, Wendy." He turned to her. "*Jaws* is on at the Roxie."

"She'll have nightmares," I protested.

He looked down at his broken glass. "Clean that up, 'cause you have to buy me a new one."

The door slammed. I hid the bottle of lavender water under the sink. If Wendy's mother was dead, I wondered, then why wouldn't Simon want to put her in school? It didn't make a whole lot of sense. He wasn't all that attached to her and seemed to me he'd want the girl out of sight for most of the day.

In a few minutes, Mr. Gordon knocked on the door. He held out a rose, his nervous manner always a little amusing. I sent him to the bed and went to the closet-sized bathroom. In the tight space between the shower and toilet, I took a pill and closed my eyes and waited for it to take effect. Even in the drug haze I kept thinking: Did Simon steal that child? Could Wendy's mother be alive?

Fear Angel's face came onto the mirror and stared me straight on as if daring me to shatter the glass. To my surprise, I wasn't afraid of her anymore. I hated her. She was there, always would be perhaps, yet today my chains had been loosened. Today I'd witnessed a white vision that could obliterate her.

My fancy thoughts seemed silly and wishful. In truth I had best deal with life like it was. Stepping out of the bathroom, I paused at the tiny kitchen for a drink of water to make sure the pill went all the way down. Behind the cups on the cabinet shelf the fifty dollars Jonas Stark had given me a long time ago was still hidden. I drank, shut the cabinet door, and then crawled up on the bed.

45

Sister Mary Thelma often sat with me as she faithfully tended the rose bushes. Keeping them alive in this hot air was no easy job. Today she was excited because a woman named Elizabeth Seton had been canonized as the first American saint. She continued on about some day going to see the Vatican. Realizing she'd been babbling, she looked up at me. "What places do you want to see?" I looked away and didn't answer, asking her to tell me more about the saints. Sister didn't know much about me and was careful in how she inquired about my past. She knew my name but not what I did in the trailer park. "Your little Wendy goes to the public school?" she asked, changing the subject.

A reply stuck in my throat and I wondered what would happen if I lied to a nun. I stared at a spot on the ground between my feet waiting for words. Thankfully, she seemed to sense my discomfort and instead noted it was going to be an unusually hot Christmas.

I agreed, chatting in an ordinary way, but my thoughts tangled in the mess of lies and deceit that had held me captive since we'd fled Kentucky. It had been flat out crazy to run away with a dead body and a child who wouldn't speak. What was going on in the rest of the world was even worse. Saigon had fallen after fifty thousand American lives were wasted, including Ernie Cooley. My brother Hector had been lucky even if his hands couldn't stop shaking and he woke up every hour in a nightmare of blood. A crazy hippy had tried to shoot President Ford, and Patty Hearst, a girl with more money than I'd ever see, was arrested for robbing a bank. What kind of sense did any of that make? The one thing I had to know the truth about hung between Simon and me like rotting meat. Wendy's mother. Had he stolen that child?

"Sister," I said softly, "some day when it's not too much trouble, might I see that Angel again?"

When I looked at her I realized she'd been studying me, and I knew that I must be a mystery to her . . . a strange woman with no past and a little girl who played alone.

Sister Mary Thelma stood and gestured toward an arched entrance. I glanced at Wendy. "She'll be fine," Sister Mary Thelma said, and waved at another nun watering rose bushes to watch out for her.

Again we went through a large oak door. The air cooled as I entered. The white marble floor gleaming down the hallway looked like a milky sea. The Angel's majestic presence flowed into the hall like a river of hope whose current carried me to her feet. I'd been afraid of seeing her a second time, worried that she would not be as loving, would look more like a piece of art than the commanding spirit that filled the room.

At the full sight of her, again my breath fled. Her outstretched hands were a beacon calling me to redemption. Her soft features followed me with no judgment, only a whisper that promised *within these walls you are safe, my child*. The large wings set to take flight to heaven told me that she knew those pathways well.

I sat on a marble bench and silently asked Angel what I needed to do. Sister Mary Thelma stood at a distance. When I motioned to her, she came over and sat beside me.

Words tumbled out of my mouth like I'd turned on a spigot. I didn't tell Sister Mary Thelma everything. I left out the dead body that had traveled with us from Kentucky, the dynamite in the closet that had probably killed Holly, and the fact that I now spent my time as a prostitute. There was only one important thing she needed to know: Wendy. I described my suspicions and worries about her, then asked, "Do you think you could find out if the girl's mother is alive?"

For a moment Sister Mary Thelma was thoughtful, digesting my complicated story. "From the information you've given me," she said, "I'm sure I can locate some family. My brother is an attorney. He knows how to do these things."

I said goodbye to Angel, thinking it was for the last time. Soon my life could well take a dangerous turn because I'd be messing with Simon in the worst way. I told Angel that I was sorry for the bad things I'd done–the lies and hurts I'd caused, the mistakes I'd made–and promised like never before to do the best I could for the little girl.

∾

Back at the trailer Simon was pacing like an unfed lion. He had a letter in hand that he kept reading over and over. I took Wendy inside to wash her up and put her in pajamas. She settled on top of her bed and read a book she'd gotten from the library earlier.

Outside, I heard Simon flop down into a lawn chair. I stepped over to the door and asked, "What's the matter?"

"Buddy Stark's an idiot, that's what."

I went out and sat beside him. Letting Simon rant was usually the best way I could get information. He talked up a storm when he was mad, hardly aware of what he was saying. "Jonas," he declared, "should've strangled little Buddy the minute he come out of the womb for all the mess he's caused."

"His kin always got him out of trouble," I remarked.

"Not this time. Herman Cahill has them all by the short hairs. Nobody's walking away from this. Who'd thought a dufus like Cahill could've done it?"

Herman, I thought, Sissy's husband.

Simon raged on about Jonas and Buddy, and how the Feds had sent in a man undercover, who'd gotten more than a few Starks, including Simon, admitting to crimes on tape. So Jonas had killed him. Killed an FBI agent. They could never let the body be found. Put out a lie that he'd run off and left his wife for a local girl. Quickly I pieced together the story of why we'd run. But I hadn't run. I'd been taken against my will, kidnapped, and maybe little Wendy, too.

Trying to be casual I said, "If they're all in trouble and get put in jail, maybe we can go back home."

"Naw," he cawed. "We can never go back there. Feds'll grill me about the FBI agent's death. We end up in FBI custody and the Starks'll think I turned. We'd end up buried where we'd never be found."

I smirked. "You'd end up dead. Jonas likes my typing too well." I'd figured out at this point that the man we'd buried in the desert was the FBI agent investigating the Starks, but I still didn't know how Holly figured into the whole story.

He threw the letter to the ground and leaned forward. "Damn it, they owe me." I leaned down and cautiously picked it up, reading as fast as I could about how Buddy was turning state's evidence against Willie Carmack, who had Jonas hire a Chicago hitman to kill his wife. The law was pressuring Jonas to give up the man who'd supplied the dynamite. It said for everyone involved to run and disappear 'cause Buddy was naming names.

Simon clinched his fist and closed his eyes as if imagining giving a beating to those who'd wronged him. "How could they do this to me, after all I did for them?"

It was good to see Simon Tuller with his tail between his legs. His important friends had deserted him, wouldn't even claim him as kin, and him now scared as a rabbit running from two different packs of dogs.

At the last instant he turned away, made a growling sound, then stood tall, rubbed his hands over his head and looked out at the sunset. "We need to go."

"But our front tires are worn to a nub."

"Guess you'll have to buy a new set," he hollered. "One of them gives up where we are, we'll have the law on us."

Now that did alarm me. Would Sister Mary Thelma have time to find out about Wendy's mother? If we moved from the state all trace of us would be lost. I might never find out. I thought about the FBI agent killed and buried in some soil where he'd never be found. I thought about Holly. I thought about Bette Moss, wondering if she'd called out for her mother before she died. But those people were dead and there was nothing I could do to make things right. Maybe I couldn't help Wendy, either. Maybe we'd all end up murdered. Maybe that's what my entire life had been leading toward.

46

Sister Mary Thelma didn't show up on the playground for the next two days. Each time I waited until almost dark. By the end of the second day worry ate into me. What if there was nothing she could do? Or she'd decided I wasn't worth it? I couldn't blame her. She lived a good and useful life and I did not.

Wednesday afternoon while I entertained a customer, Simon took Wendy to watch the swimming pool being filled with water. It wasn't scheduled to open until Friday at noon and we'd probably be gone by then. My customer was a Mexican who had helped build the pool. He'd just left when there was a knock on the door. I thought the man had forgotten something.

When I opened the door I saw Sister Mary Thelma, a shock. She had a bland expression but determination in her eyes. She glanced past me into the trailer and said, "I've come asking for donations for the church."

"It's okay," I told her, "I'm alone." I invited her in but was afraid of her seeing the rumpled bed. "How did you find me?"

"I figured you had to live within a few blocks of the school, and not many people named Randi Jo in Arizona." She looked back as if expecting that someone might have followed her, then she stepped inside. "Your neighbors don't think very highly of you."

My face heated and I figured my cheeks were bright red. "Sister," I said with sudden anxiety. "This is too dangerous. I shouldn't have gotten you involved."

She held out a piece of yellow paper. I read it quickly, a description of Wendy on it: Red hair, three feet tall, freckles across her nose, age, weight, last seen on her school playground carrying her rag doll. "Wendy's last name is Brewster," Sister Mary Thelma said. "She was given her step-father's name . . . her mother never married Simon. She's alive."

"There's a phone number on this paper. Do they know she's out here?"

Sister Mary Thelma took hold of my hands. "I wanted to talk to you first." She hesitated and pulled me closer to her. "Can you get away from this man, Randi Jo?"

A bleak resignation filled me. "I'm afraid."

"He'll be arrested. He may implicate you."

"He'd kill me if I tried to leave." I sucked in air, ready to die if I had to. "Can't you take Wendy now? I'll hold him off 'til you can get her away."

She shook her head. "This is going to take some time. Two days at least to get her family out here. Call the FBI. The local police . . . they could take the side of the father."

"Yeah, I know that story." All at once the enormity of what I'd done filled me with regret. I should never have believed Simon. Should have gotten Wendy and myself out of here as fast as possible, no matter what I'd had to do. Sister turned aside as if to think.

Outside, Simon crashed into our yard, cussing and kicking a lawn chair that sailed into our neighbor's yard. I flinched in terror.

"I'm not afraid," Sister Mary Thelma said, clasping my hand and touching my cheek. "I'm not afraid." The iron in her voice was like a rod in my backbone.

I nodded, hardly breathing. "Okay, I'm not afraid, either."

"Bring Wendy to the playground on Friday as usual. I'll be ready." She leaned over and picked up a Raggedy Ann doll just as Simon snatched open the door.

He blinked as if unable to believe he was seeing a nun in our trailer. Sister Mary Thelma kept her expression impassive until she saw Wendy holding Simon's hand. The two of them came inside and he held onto her with a look of anticipating trouble. "What's this?" he asked.

"There's the little red-haired girl," Sister Mary Thelma said, smiling at her. "The child left her doll on our playground and I wanted to return it before the school day tomorrow." Her flat smile stayed in place and didn't give away that she knew she was speaking to a criminal.

"How'd you know where we lived?" he asked.

"One of the students she plays with knew where Wendy lived. I guess she told her." Sister stood erect, an intimidating figure Simon dared not question. She handed Wendy the doll and patted her on the head. "Good day to you."

331

Simon watched her go, scratching his head. "Wendy," he fussed. "Don't tell people where we live." He looked at me. "And don't go to that playground again." He went outside and looked around but I didn't think he had any idea what he was looking for. For my part, I knew I'd have to act as normal as possible if I was going to pull this off. "You need to schedule some more appointments for me if we're going to have enough to pay off the tires," I said, part of me dying as I spoke.

Simon got the lawn chair out of the neighbor's yard and settled down in it, whistling while I made some sandwiches. I had to figure out how to keep him from leaving early and get Wendy and me to Sister Mary Thelma.

e⌇

On Friday, Simon was up at the crack of dawn. He sat at the kitchen table studying a map of the West Coast, hands still dirty from putting on the new tires. As I moved around restocking our shelves with canned food, he mouthed the names of states and towns, following a route with his finger. "California, Los Angeles, Eureka, Oregon, Portland, Seattle." He glanced over at me to complain, "Can't you move a little faster?"

I had been going as slow as possible. Anything to waste time. When you carried your house around on wheels there wasn't much to pack but you had to be ready for the road. "I need to stock up on toilet paper," I said. "Store doesn't open until ten."

"Told you do that yesterday."

"You had me scheduled for six appointments. I barely got showered, much less went to the store."

"You're a idiot, Randi Jo."

I had words in my head for him, too, but kept my mouth shut and prayed for time. After dawdling as much as I dared, I called Wendy to breakfast and set Simon's food off to the side of his map. She came to the table wearing her bathing suit although nobody had suggested she put it on. Simon didn't notice but it gave me an idea. Today was Sister Mary Thelma's deadline to put everything together, all the complicated legal and practical work of contacting the little girl's mother. But would things be ready by noon as she'd told me? How many hours did I have?

When we'd finished breakfast I went about cleaning up, making the bed, and took a shower. Simon and Wendy left for a walk while I had what I hoped would be my last Arizona appointment with Mr. Gordon. He came promptly and finished up quickly, as he always did, then I went to the grocery store.

Simon and Wendy were back when I returned with the toilet paper and food. I tossed them candy bars and put the canned goods on the shelf. While the candy kept both of them busy I carefully pocketed the fifty-dollar bill hidden all these months behind the cups. I also had what was left of Mr. Gordon's money.

Turning to Simon, I asked in a casual tone, "Why don't we let Wendy go swim before we leave?"

"No time," he said. "I want to be on the road by noon."

"The pool doesn't open until noon. This is the first day. Poor little thing watched it built, filled with water, and knows every kid in this place will be there, and now she doesn't even get to swim in it."

"Please, Daddy." Wendy so seldom spoke that her sweet, soft voice couldn't be ignored.

Simon looked down at her and petted her head. "Twenty minutes, no longer."

I watched the clock and made Simon a drink, crushing one of the pills and putting it in the gin. Within the hour he was asleep. I sat at the table and willed time to move faster. Wendy played with her Raggedy Ann and coloring book. Simon turned on his side and snored. He woke up once and checked the time: eleven-fifteen.

"You want another drink?" I asked.

"Naw." He yawned, crossing his arms over his chest and closing his eyes. I knew that pill wouldn't last forever.

Finally it was ten 'til noon. "Come on, Wendy," I said.

She put her shift over her swimsuit and excitedly slipped on her flip-flops. I grabbed her Raggedy Ann doll as we left, closing the door as silently as I could.

As we stepped out into the yard Simon opened the door. "Twenty minutes," he called out. "I'm gonna go get gas. Pick you up at the pool."

I shuddered all the way down to my toes. We walked in the direction of the pool, the opposite of the way I needed to go. If we went to the pool it would take me almost fifteen minutes to circle back to the Catholic school.

The Winnebago drove past us and Simon tooted the horn. I knew that the gas station he'd go to was two blocks past the playground. If I didn't hurry and get there, after the tank was full he'd drive right past us on the road and see that we hadn't gone to the pool.

Soon as Simon turned toward the gas station, I leaned down to Wendy and said, "We have to go see Sister Mary Thelma first." She didn't ask why. She never did. It was sad, a child who always did as she was told.

I straightened up and walked fast, pulling her along, half dragging her. About five minutes later we came to a row of hedges in front of the houses that bordered the school. I stopped at the end of the row and peered into the playground.

Beyond it, in front of the arched oak door, a blond-haired woman paced. Sister Mary Thelma stood behind her, hands clasped in front of her. The sight of them thrilled me. We had a chance and I said a silent prayer to Angel for protection.

I knelt beside Wendy and cupped her cheeks in my hands. "Honey," I said. "I want you to learn to talk, not just a word now and then, but really talk. Learn to sing and holler. Learn to argue with your mother and your brother and sisters. You need to know you are strong to come through all of this, and don't ever doubt what you know inside yourself is the truth."

"But my momma is dead," she said, her face placid.

"No, she's not."

She stared at me in confusion. "My momma . . ."

"I know what your daddy told you but I found out different." Gently I took hold of Wendy's shoulders, turned her toward the playground and pointed at the woman. "See, there's your momma. Beside Sister Mary Thelma."

Wendy stared, blinked and looked back at me, still confused, but I knew she was ready to believe me. She looked again at the blond-haired woman and took a few steps. "Momma," she whispered. Then she broke into a run. "Momma! Momma! Momma!" she cried out as she ran, the Raggedy Ann doll clutched to her chest.

The woman dropped to one knee and held out her arms wide.

"Wendy!" Simon's voice came from the end of the block but it split the hot air like a spear of fire. To my horror he climbed down from the Winnebago, leaving the door open, the radio blasting "Bohemian Rhapsody." He sprinted toward the playground and in seconds he was closer to Wendy than she was to her mother. He could scoop her up and throw her into the Winnebago.

Her little legs kept running toward her mother. Simon made a beeline for Wendy. My mind exploded into a mass of shattered pain and I broke into a run, aiming myself at Simon. I crashed into him and we both fell onto the grass. He shoved me aside and leaped to his feet. I looked up and saw only the tail end of Sister Mary Thelma's habit as she slammed the arched door.

Simon banged his fists on the door, yelling. Policemen were on him faster than I'd thought possible. They threw him face down on the ground and cuffed his hands behind his back. He glared in my direction. Even from a distance I felt more hatred in his eyes than I'd ever seen before. I pushed myself up off the ground, not waiting around to watch his arrest. For the third time in my life, I ran.

47

With sudden wariness Simon looks away from Dallas and stares at the floor between his feet. "I didn't even know Holly Carmack," he protests, but can't hide the fear in his voice. "She was Randi Jo's friend, not mine." Dallas lets out a grunt of disdain.

"That make her easier to kill?" Randi Jo asks as natural as she might take a lunch order.

"I had nothing to do with it," Simon insists.

"Then why the dynamite in our closet? And why'd you try to frame Dallas for buying it outside the law?"

Simon raises his head and eyes Dallas. "Because you were there," he says, sounding deflated. "Because you'd messed up washing that license plate and it cost Jonas. Because somebody had to go to jail for it."

337

"And it sure as hell wasn't gonna be no Stark," Dallas sneers. He steps over to the window, disgust wrinkling his forehead.

"Hey," Simon calls out. "Wasn't me that killed Holly. They had a man on the payroll who'd worked with explosives."

"All you did is buy it for them." Dallas puts a fist to his mouth as though holding in fury eating at his insides.

"Somebody would have, if not me. I didn't know what they were doing. I was in Coalfire most the day. Ask Randi Jo, she'll tell you."

Randi Jo joins Dallas at the window and looks out at a landscape she knows intimately. Crickets chirp cheerful songs and in the high weeds near the creek katydids sing like a school chorus. She smiles ruefully to herself; the two of them damaged people standing side by side, perhaps trying to take joy in the smallest creatures and wondering what fate had brought them to this harsh destiny. She touches his back and then strokes his shoulder to comfort him . . . but there is no real consolation she can offer for the terrible events that had scarred his life.

"Wait for me in the van," she says.

"You sure you can do it?" he asks quietly. "We can't go back."

"Don't want to," she assures him.

She walks Dallas outside, studying the hillside to see if anyone is watching him drive the van down the hill. Dinnertime. Everybody inside, probably eating beans. One thing that hasn't changed.

Below she sees Dallas turn the van west to park behind the abandoned house at the curve of Grey's Pin and wait until she's done with what needs doing. Calm and efficient, she picks up a metal canister and pours gas at the back door, making a trail out to a patch of daffodils growing near the outhouse.

A few minutes later Randi Jo returns to the room where Simon continues struggling. He's intent on loosening the ropes but they are too strong, and along with the chain he's held tightly in place. For the first time in her life he is completely under her control.

"Here we are," he says, still playing on charm, trying to coax a smile from her. "What now?"

"Judgment Day." Randi Jo goes around behind him, clamps a hand under his chin, pulls his head back and plants a kiss on his forehead. "Goodbye, Simon. Good trip to you. Tell the Devil hello."

"You ain't going to do this, Randi Jo," he said. "You know you can't. Not to me. You can't kill me."

Randi Jo walks around him and stares into his black eyes. "Tell me something, Simon. Why'd you take Wendy? Why'd you take me? You could've left the state without involving either of us. You hadn't had us, you'd probably got away free and clear."

He leaned forward, features softening as he strained against the ropes. "Cause you're all I got. Jonas talks a big game on kinfolk, but I'm the family dog and don't I know it. You were always on my side, Randi Jo. No matter how bad it got. Wendy was my blood and that bitch of a mother of hers didn't even tell me about her. Found out when I went to pick up one of Jonas's drivers. There she was, my little girl living twenty miles from me and I didn't know." He paused, bit his lip and let out a shivery breath. "I finally understood how you felt about Tallulah. I finally saw how it could all come together, us and Wendy. Least that's how it felt then. All the trouble started. Jonas begged me to get rid of that body and stay low, said he'd take care of me and I couldn't leave without her . . . and I couldn't leave without you." He looks up into her eyes. "Can you kill me now? Knowing what you know."

48

When I was forty-seven . . .

I drifted from town to town. Never staying long enough in any one place where there was even a slight chance that Simon or the Starks would find me. Not that I was important enough for them to hunt down, but I knew how men like them carried grudges. Resentment could keep them going for years, could inspire them more than any striving for something good. In my nightmares I saw that killing look Simon shot me as he lay spread-eagled on the ground, the police cuffing his hands behind his back. He might not go out of his way to track me down, but if he got a lucky break and my whereabouts fell into his lap, I could expect to exit this earth in a most painful manner.

Mostly I stuck to small towns–Benson, Arizona; Ely, Nevada; Arcata, California. After a while I didn't pay any

341

attention to what state I was in. Went to a couple cities, wandered the streets, picked up work as a waitress, typist, even hauled trash for a movie studio in California. But I didn't like cities. Living in them I realized that there was more than one Fear Angel wandering this earth. Mine was attached to me, appearing when I needed courage, spitting at my weaknesses and waiting for my failure. Yet all kinds of Fear Angels showed themselves in the cities, unashamed and haughty as spoilt felines. They lurked behind the haunted eyes of hungry children standing in lines at homeless shelters. They tormented girls working street corners, trying desperately to catch the attention of men in passing cars, and they hovered over drunks and addicts passed out in filthy alleys. Fear Angels even followed well-dressed folks, men and women who hurried along sidewalks, their expressions tense with self-importance. No one got in the way as these terrible creatures did the Devil's work. Soon I came to hate cities. I never wanted to see that much pain again and stuck to small towns where tyrants could be recognized by vote-for-me smiles, and good people made safe havens among them.

Earning honest money was the nicest surprise of my life. I made thirty-five thousand dollars on my best year and couldn't believe I used to do the same kind of work for ten dollars. About a year after I ran from Simon I called Wink's Market. It was a long wait while they sent a young'un running up the hill to get Momma. And more waiting 'til she got there, me putting coins in the phone box to keep the connection going, but the cost didn't matter. Hearing her voice again was like lapping up soft ice cream. I wanted to cry and sing at the same time.

Momma confirmed that Holly had been killed when her car blew up. The law investigated but no one was ever charged. Momma scoffed at that and didn't have to say anything more. It was clear Willie Carmack would never serve a day in jail, and his money and influence had bought him that freedom.

"And what about Simon?" I asked. "He get any time a'tall after they caught him in Arizona?"

Momma hesitated and in my mind I saw her lips pressed tight and her eyes rolling. "Three years for kidnapping. Wasn't longer 'cause he's the little girl's daddy."

I exhaled and leaned my head against the glass wall of the phone booth. "Wendy is safe?"

"With her momma, and they're a well-to-do family, live in New Jersey now, so he'll never get near her again."

I heard hesitation in my mother's voice. There was still something she wasn't saying. A train whistled in the background and I pictured the rusted black and maroon cars loaded with coal shifting back and forth as they chugged around the hill and disappeared into mountain mist. Momma paused and the phone operator asked for another forty-five cents. After I slid in the coins Momma sighed, then said, "I don't think you can come back here, Randi Jo. It was a big story about Simon and his daughter. The law'll hold you just as responsible."

"I know, Momma." I couldn't bear to say good-bye, just *I'll talk to you later*, and I hung up without asking about Tallulah or Connor. I realized then that Momma hadn't been holding something back. She'd been waiting for me to ask about my family, and my daughter. I grabbed the phone but sank to my knees, clutching the receiver as if it were a lifeline, and bawled my eyes out. My daughter had been without me for so long. For her I didn't even exist. Better she forget about me all together.

∽

As the years passed, I only once saw people I'd known in my previous life. I was working as a typist for an insurance agent in a beach town outside of Fort Walton, Florida. On weekends I went to the shore and walked for miles with my bare feet sinking into perfect white sand and warm Gulf waters. Last Sunday in September. As I approached a fishing pier two women coming toward me caught my attention, particularly one whose hair was pulled back in a bun on the crown of her head. Only one woman I'd ever known had never outgrown that topknot: Tempy Herne. There she was, and the thin woman with her must be Iona Stark . . . now Iona Bacon.

I studied them as they approached, pulling age off their features and figures, and recognized the solitary couple that everyone had talked about in whispers. The sun was in their eyes and I lowered my head, pulling my slouch hat low to hide my face.

A gangly girl of about twelve ran past them along the beach and threw sand up into the air. I turned to follow them at a distance. The girl circled the women, running into the surf and kicking up water. Iona scolded her for getting their pedal pushers wet. I figured the girl must be Iona's daughter. Tempy had always loved Tallulah like her own and I wondered if my daughter was with them. The possibility suddenly obsessed me. I hoped . . . I prayed . . .

They approached a low-rise hotel with individual cabins and dropped onto lawn chairs facing the beach. I sat on the sand some distance away to wait for someone else to join them. No one did. After an hour I had to ask myself what I'd been thinking. My daughter was no longer a teenager. She could be anywhere in the world now.

The sun set and I went home, resolved to never come back here. I blamed myself for not being with Tallulah until guilt overwhelmed me and a fitful sleep filled with nightmares replaced the regret. But the next day I found myself meandering down the beach, thinking I'd cut up to the road at the next path, yet I kept going until I reached the cabins.

The women sat outside, read magazines and books, threw beach balls with the girl, and laughed like a happy family. I followed them all day, to miniature golf, to a clothing shop where they purchased swimsuits and tee shirts with *Fort Walton Beach* in curly script. I watched as they ate fish and chips, stood in the background as they lay in the sun and swabbed themselves with tanning oil. I returned every day after work and my mind ran off to all sorts of hopeful places, still believing Tallulah could show up.

At times when the girl ran off down the shoreline or hugged the waves on an inflatable raft, the two women moved closer. They never touched and what words they spoke seemed to be said into each other's eyes. There was a purity about it all. After a while I knew I was watching as clear, clean and true a love as there was in this world, and I was envious. For over ten years no man had come close to me, not physically and never emotionally. Some had tried and if it was a co-worker, I chose to move on.

The next Saturday, the girl took her raft back to the rental store. They were leaving and it made me sad, however spiteful my relationship with Tempy had been in the past. I was homesick but knew it was foolish to feel that way 'cause surely no one would welcome me back.

At a beach concession stand Tempy pulled out a wad of bills to pay for food, then sat with Iona at a picnic table to eat hotdogs while shooing away seagulls and pelicans. The girl had gone back to the cabin, maybe for a nap, or to pack. I got up to leave. I'd intruded on their space long enough even it they hadn't known it, and my daughter wasn't coming.

I looked back once, thinking it was my silly way of saying good-bye to the past. The two women took their sodas and walked onto a fishing pier. A man staggering from the main road followed them. With a stab of alarm I recognized Byrd Tagget, a local tough who hung around soliciting money from tourists when he wasn't drunk and starting fights. A big lout, his unshaven, scarred face and muscular arms spelled trouble. He'd been in jail more than he'd been out and locals avoided him. Tempy's purse was slung over her shoulder. Byrd eyed it.

The two women strolled on toward a boarded-up fishing shack at the end of the pier. That's where he'll do it, I thought. Waves crashing on the shore would cover up any cries for help. Off-season, so not many people were around.

I followed him onto the pier, keeping my distance. The breeze kicked up a harsh whiff of bait. Fishermen drifted from one fishing pole to the next, checking the lines, but no one was near enough to help. I picked up a piece of driftwood lying on a bench and continued on toward the end of the pier.

Tempy and Iona disappeared behind the shed. Byrd increased his pace. I went around the opposite side and flattened myself against the wall. Shouting erupted from behind the shack. Ice and soda cups clattered down onto the wooden pilings.

Peering out, Byrd pushed both women against the railing, screaming threats and waving his arms. Tempy and Iona clung to each other.

I came up behind Byrd, anchored my foot on the slat of the pier and swung the wood like a baseball bat. I caught Byrd on the side of the head, knocking him to his knees. "Run!" I shouted to the women.

Iona bolted. Tempy stood frozen with shock, then pointed a trembling finger, "I know you!"

Before either of us could react, Iona rushed back, grabbed Tempy's arm and dragged her away. Byrd stayed down like someone used to having the police right behind him. They'd be arriving soon enough with Iona yelling for help all the way back to the beach.

I climbed up on the pier railing and jumped into the water. It was shallow enough that I touched bottom and I pushed off with all my might. Swimming parallel to the shore, I came up on the beach a hundred yards away. Police lights flashed at the pier entrance. I hurried to my apartment, packed up, and was gone that night.

49

Seasons came and went, holidays, birthdays. I marked them on my calendar and had a cupcake with a candle every year to celebrate Tallulah's birthday. Silently I wished her the best life, and imagined her telling me that she understood what I had done. Then I'd open my eyes to an empty room with not even a picture of her.

The only happiness I had was making phone calls to Momma, who now had a phone thanks to the black lung settlement the government had given her. In time, I learned that Tallulah had gone to college and graduated *summa cum laude*—which meant highest honors in Latin and made me bust with pride—and then she took a job at the *Crimson County Sun* even though she'd been offered one at *The Washington Post*.

Connor still taught high school and had never re-married. If he dated, Momma didn't tell me and I didn't want to know. Being without him all these years I'd come to realize how clear, true and fragile our love had been: We'd been children playing at being adults. If he could know me now, he'd never again have reason to doubt my fidelity. But I'd made my bed and now had to sleep in it.

Finally I got up the nerve to ask Momma in detail about Simon. He'd be out of jail by now, I figured, and I knew I best keep his whereabouts on my radar. "Back working for the Starks," Momma replied in a flat tone. "He came up here wanting to know where you were living. Said he was sorry for everything and wanted to tell you so. I told him I'd believe that when pigs piss Pepsi," she hissed. "He called a couple times, trying to make nice, asked if I'd heard from you, but I just acted like I'd lost my hearing."

Often on the phone I had to speak loudly to her. Just as often she'd drift into long silences, and then be unsure who I was. Sometimes she'd hang up, other times she thought I was a bill collector or a librarian complaining about overdue books. Age trickled more and more into her voice. The next time I called no one answered. I waited a month before calling again. Still, no answer. I called again and again but finally got only a recording: the phone had been disconnected. I knew what that meant.

༄

My longest stay was in the small North Carolina town of Boone. I worked as a typist for a medical clinic in the day and took over the evening housekeeping duties when their elderly janitor retired. The boss didn't mind me doing both 'cause it cost him less. I saved enough money to buy a used Ford and took drives deep into the Smoky Mountains. On some days I realized that I'd found a measure of peace. Fear Angel hadn't been around for quite some time. Yet my life was still marked by the past, the good and the bad, and by the people I continued to love even if they weren't aware of it.

I allowed myself the luxury of a subscription to *The Crimson County Sun*. My landlord let me use her name and address, and using a postal order to pay for it, I maintained my anonymity. Reading articles written by Tallulah was a thrill. Some were feisty and challenging, while others were nostalgic reminders for readers to appreciate and take care of the natural beauty that surrounded them. Her editorials often blasted decisions made by local politicians. Reading those, I'd laugh out loud. Nobody was going to run her show.

The papers usually arrived in a bundle on Fridays, and I spent Saturday morning sitting in the sun, enjoying a cup of coffee and catching up on folks back home. The Midnight Valley political machine was the mess it had always been. Now it seemed about to blow up . . . again. I was glad not to be there. People in Notown rarely mattered in those fights but often were the ones who paid for them.

One morning I saw Connor's name and sat upright. He had formed a committee to investigate why so many pockets of cancer and birth defects had cropped up in Crimson County. After federal officials found massive pollution in one of the creeks, townspeople pointed at the mining industry. The big companies mounted scare campaigns claiming that protests would lead to lost jobs. In the meantime, people kept dying and babies were born deformed. Connor was quoted as saying, *Public servants have lined their own pockets at the expense of public health.* A rush of pride filled me. The next sentence made me freeze. *My own daughter lies in a hospital, dying of a sickness she shouldn't have. She's only twenty-eight years old and she's dying.*

I got up, knocking my coffee cup off the table. It shattered, not fazing me. In my gut I knew one fact and nothing else mattered: I was going home.

∽

There had never been a proper lock on my parents' front door. At night a chair was propped against it, and if ever they left, some stranger coming in would have found precious little to steal. The porch swing had broken and dirt daubers were busy building a nest on the underside. I turned the doorknob, pushed, and the door scraped open.

"Hello," I called out. No answer.

An empty living room. Odd. Momma had bought all new furniture when she'd gotten her black lung settlement. The bedroom was empty, too. A sheet still hung between it and the next room. I pulled it back. My old bed was still there, a pink chenille bedspread crumpled on a bare mattress along with two rumpled pillows. I flipped up the spread, straightening it until the bed looked made. Pug's filthy decaying mattress was shoved in a corner, the stuffing protruding from a rip. The back room was empty except for my grandfather's chair. That old weathered wood plucked at my heart and I sat down as I used to, pulled up my legs and anchored my knees. Still sturdy as ever, it held me like the arms of the grandfather I'd never appreciated.

The adjacent kitchen had an electric stove and piped-in water, and the back porch had been converted to a toilet and bathtub. The porcelain was pink. I grinned, thinking how the boys must have hated that color. A note was taped to the door:

> *Bros & Sisters, if you stop by I'm in*
> *county working off those thirty days for being*
> *drunk. Don't do anything to the house until*
> *I'm out. The lawyer says he can get me a*
> *year's grace cause I'm a Vietnam vet. Hector.*

I couldn't help but laugh. Apparently Hector lived here. The rest of the furniture had probably been divided up rather than stolen. Yet the place was falling apart: peeling paint, rotted floorboards, insects swooping around. Where was the rest of my family? Thirteen children and I didn't know where eleven of them lived. I had no home anymore. The thought of Butch brought tears to my eyes. Everybody else could take care of themselves, but Butch, still little and helpless . . . what had happened to him?

I walked down to the road and crossed over to Grey's Pin. My grandfather's house had fallen to ruins. I entered through a back door, passed a rusted-out sink full of burnt wood where someone had started a fire; a ragged bedroom curtain and a rusted metal headboard leaned against the wall. I had never known his name. In a way, I didn't even know my own or who I was other than a scared girl haunted by Fear Angel. The ghosts here and in my parent's house were unbearable. Their presence pleaded for recognition they would never get . . . loving their memory was all I could do.

As I walked toward my car, memories called after me to come back and relive them again and again. But then I'd lose what little substance held me together. I swallowed a trembling emotion and willed myself not to feel it. I didn't need a place to stay tonight. I would see my daughter at the hospital, pay my respects to my parents' graves, and leave for good.

50

I wasn't prepared for what I saw: a skeletal frame supporting a head with hardly any hair. Her condition was beyond words. Stepping through plastic curtains around her bed, I wanted to fall to my knees. Nothing about my baby was recognizable. Her cheeks were hollowed as if someone had scooped them out with a spoon. Two IVs hung over her head delivering blood and a clear liquid.

"Tallulah," I said, knowing she probably didn't hear me.

Her lips parted. She took a breath, her chest rose and her eyes cracked open. "What are you doing here?" she mumbled.

"I live on the wind, Baby."

"Am I still alive?" She let out a tiny laugh, then winced. "It hurts."

With that she seemed to fall asleep. I held her thin hand, lacing her fingers through mine and I closed my eyes. Tallulah moaned, her eyebrows drawing together in pain and every muscle in my body tightened. She was going to die and there was nothing I could do about it. I looked out the window at a ring of dark mountains that made Midnight Valley seem like a prison. "Why have I lived?" I asked, looking up into the sky. "Not to see my daughter die . . ."

"I know why," she whispered. I turned to her. Her eyes wandered the room as if in a haze. "Your life," she murmured.

She drifted into those strange lands where sickness took you, and I stroked her forehead. "Just rest, Tallulah. No need to think about me."

"Your life has been about surviving it." She stared out the window at the mountains and each breath took all her strength. Briefly she slept, then opened her eyes and asked, "Are you really here?"

"No, Baby. I'm a dream." I had missed most of her life. She was taller than me but had the same slim, delicate hands, and her hazel eyes had a little bit of the Gaylor green. I wish I could see her as a young healthy woman. She must have been magnificent. All my life I'd made deals, promised what I might not deliver, but I never negotiated harder with the Unseen Presence as right then in that room: *Give my child a spark of spirit to thrive in a dying body.*

I leaned down to Tallulah and whispered a tale Daddy used to tell me when I was afraid. "I have a good friend named Jack. Couldn't have a better friend in all the world. Jack's killed a giant, fooled a king, kissed an ornery princess, defeated an army all by hisself, and lived to share the tale. But I tell you, there was this one time Jack bit off more than he could chew. Him and me had been out gathering ginseng to sell at the market. Thought we'd take the money and build us a tree house. But that night Jack got in a fight with the Devil, and I didn't think I'd ever see him again." I continued telling it in Daddy's voice. Tallulah's breathing became regular and her eyes moved in a dream. I held her hand and kissed her forehead. "Jack's been a friend of my family for as long as I been around and he was kicking up dust a good hundred years before that. Ain't nothing he can't do. So, Baby, if you want, he'll be your friend, too. He'll help you every way he knows how. He'll even fight the Devil for you if you need it."

One of the machines let out a loud monotone. I flinched in alarm. From the hall came a pattering of footsteps. A medical team rushed in, rolling machines ahead of them. I put a hand over my mouth. *Oh, my God, she's dying.*

A nurse pushed me from the room. I huddled in a waiting area across the hall and stood watch. A woman doctor ran in and grabbed paddles connected to a machine and pressed them to Tallulah's chest. Her body jerked up off the bed as if she'd been electrocuted. It happened again and again. A white-haired man hurried into the room. Connor, I realized. Once more the woman doctor shocked her heart, and this time the flat tone reverted to regular beeps.

The awful tension in the room deflated like a pierced balloon. The nurses left. An intern started to push the machine out but the doctor had him position it beside the bed and leave it. I started to go over and talk to Connor when the doctor went to him and put her arms around his neck. They leaned on each other, their eyes closing in relief. When they stepped apart I recognized Rory. Older by twenty-odd years, but not all that changed.

I wiped my nose and held my hand over my mouth to keep from crying out. This woman whose life I'd stolen all those years ago had just saved my daughter's life. Tallulah took an audible breath then stretched and put one arm over her forehead.

Rory and Connor were glued to the bedside. I knew then. I knew. That familiar gesture was exactly what Tallulah had done every single morning of her childhood. She'd arch her back like a cat, hum herself awake and throw an arm over her eyes like daylight was an imposition she had to get prepared for. A good sign. The sign of a fighter. I silently thanked whatever angel had watched over her.

"Momma was here," she said to Rory and Connor.

Connor glowed, the same smile I'd seen on his face the night she was born. "You're dreaming, honey." He kissed her hand and petted her forehead.

"Did Momma know anybody named Jack?"

Connor looked perplexed. "Don't think so," he replied.

"Well," Tallulah stretched and stifled a yawn. "He's one mean cuss 'cause I dreamed him and me fought the Devil."

It was time for me to go. I was the outsider here. My daughter couldn't be in better care and there was nothing I could do but weep if she died and hide if she lived.

As I passed the front desk a nurse stared at me. It was the focused look of trying to identify someone. At the elevator I glanced back at her. She was still watching me and had picked up the telephone. No need to imagine the worst, I told myself, and yet I did: being detained by the law, being found by men I feared.

As the elevator doors closed the nurse spoke into the receiver and continued to study me as if memorizing the features of one long dead.

51

Walking quickly, I headed down the few blocks of Quinntown, where the smells of sulfur mixed with car exhaust. A gaggle of teenage girls passed me, mirror images of Holly, Lynn, Sissy and me in younger days. Farther on I kept up my pace, not so fast as to attract attention.

I got a drink from the artesian well pipe at the bridge and looked down into the muddy canal. A new concrete path ran along the edge and benches had been installed every hundred feet or so. Tulips and pansies now bordered the swampy pit where Bette Moss had lost her life.

On Marcescent Street the old Regal leaned to one side. A man came out, paused to light a cigarette, and walked on. I walked on as well and knew that I'd finally outgrown my fear of Marcescent Street. I'd lived through worse. Part of me ached to dawdle in places with happier memories but I couldn't risk running into Simon. My only remaining task was to visit my parents' graves. For that I needed flowers. Gilmore's Floral Shop had been on the corner but I stopped like a trained dog when I looked ahead. On its front window was my name . . . Gaylor . . . Gaylor's Florist.

In the window display amid vases of daffodils and parsley colored ferns lay a pick ax, carbide miner's cap, shovel, and lunch bucket. Daddy's tools, I realized. A framed note explained the history of the tools, which next year would be on display at the Smithsonian Museum in Washington DC. Signed Greg and Serena Gaylor.

I opened the door and breathed in the fresh honeyed aromas of flowers. A blond woman in back nodded that she'd be right up after helping another customer. As I moved among the plants and arrangements, a wooden gate at the side of the room rattled. A skinny arm poked through the slat and waved as if trying to get my attention. I saw a wheelchair and then the fuzzy head of the person seated in it. "Butch!" I whispered.

I went to him and he made his *Aaaaa* sound and reached for me. I gathered him up in my arms, holding him so tight he squeaked. He'd grown into a boy but I could still get him onto my lap like I used to. His good arm stayed wrapped around my shoulders and his head rested gently in the crook of my neck. He knew me. Even after all these years, he knew my touch, my smell.

The woman showed her customer to the door and then came over and said, "I'm sorry Butch bothered you."

"I have a way with kids."

"He usually doesn't care for strangers." The woman moved the wheelchair to one side and placed her hands on her hips. "My goodness, look how he takes to you."

"Is he yours?" I asked, trying to suss out how she was connected to us.

"Butch is my husband's younger brother. He lives with us."

"Knew some Gaylors back when I lived here, the older ones."

She nodded her head. "I didn't know them but they all had a rough time of it. Eldest, Kim, died a long time ago, and a boy, Pug, died years back in a fight. Sad . . ." Serena paused and then rubbed her hands together. "So what did you need today?"

Still holding Butch, I followed her and looked around as if still shopping, but wanted to squeeze information from her. "Flowers for my parents' graves. A few bunches of daffodils, since you have so many."

"They're my husband's favorite." Serena pulled a bunch from a bucket of water. "He watched his sister plant a patch of daffodils out behind their house. After she left, he commenced to taking care of them. Guess that's how he got the green thumb 'cause he grows 'em in our hothouse year round." She folded pink sheets of tissue and laid the flowers on them. I rocked Butch, smiling at the thought of Gregory tending my daffodils.

"Where 'bouts are your folks buried?" she asked.

I didn't answer her and pretended Butch had my attention. But one thing I'd wanted to confirm. "Rest of the Gaylors, they doing well?"

She described successful nursing careers of Patsy and Rhoda and mentioned Gene, Melvin and Casper would soon retire from the mines. All had large families that to me sounded like the way we'd grown up, although now times were better. Cane worked at an architectural firm in Knoxville.

"The youngest, Colette," Serena nodded as she spoke, "works for a senator in Washington DC. Uses the experiences of her family to prepare his speeches on the importance of equal education." Serena tied a gold ribbon around the flowers.

"I think he's fallen asleep." I nodded at Butch. "Or playing opossum," I whispered to him. He popped open his eyes with a wide, teasing smile.

Serena chuckled. "He does that to us, too."

"Greg around?"

"Gone to the hospital to see his niece. Poor little thing. I don't know if you keep up with the local news but some of our ground water ended up poisoned and she might not make it. So sad, she was about to get married."

Married. My heart fluttered and I soared back to memories of her as an infant sleeping on my chest.

"Now her mother's the one we don't know anything about," Selena continued. "Sad, she and Hector both. She disappeared, got in with a bad bunch and we think they might've killed her. And Hector . . . well, after he got back from the Vietnam . . . he just couldn't fit in. Still lives in the old home place but it's about to slide off the hill and the county's making us tear it down."

I carried Butch to the wheelchair and gently placed him in it. "Good of you to take him in," I told her.

As I stepped away Butch made his unhappy sound and it broke my heart. "Can't stay, baby," I whispered.

"Why don't you leave your name. I'm sure my husband would like to know you stopped by."

I simply nodded, laid down money as I picked up the flowers and made my way to the door, but I knew what Butch would do next. By the time I got outside, he was screaming. Serena would have her hands full. I hoped he'd think I'd been a dream and could go back to his happy life and forget me.

Eyes closed, I leaned against the building and willed away tears. I ached to stay, but like tearing myself away from Tallulah, I could not be part of his world again. They were better off without me. That was the simple truth.

⟡

I knew that going to the graveyard would be hard but it was the last thing my insides called me to do. It might have been safer to leave the minute I'd seen that nurse on the phone. I rationalized Crimson County was home to thirty thousand people and I was just a stranger passing among them. Yet the image of the nurse's stare and how quickly she'd picked up the phone burned in my brain. Experience had taught me not to disregard a hunch.

I found Holly's grave on the way up to my parents'. The stone was small, hardly big enough for her name. How she'd come to this place was a story I'd never know for certain. I lay down some daffodils where her head would be, kissed my fingers and pressed them to the earth. Holly might have pointed out my mistakes but she'd stood by me as much as our world had allowed.

Up the hill Daddy's smooth ash-colored tombstone reflected the sun. Next to his headstone was another, copper-colored. I dropped to the ground between them. Under Momma's name was *Daughter of Silas*. I spoke my grandfather's name aloud. I'd never known it. The world had made Momma so ashamed of her past and I understood the reason she'd hidden it. Thoughts of all my people . . . Momma, Silas, Daddy, Kim, Uncle Luther . . . filled me to overflowing. We were like worker ants on this earth just hoping not to get pounded. Like my daughter said, my life had been about surviving it.

But there were only so many days you could cheat the Devil. Jack the warrior, Jack the devil killer, and Jack the wise man had always gotten away with it, but I was no Jack. I wasn't nearly smart enough to be a folk hero.

A familiar singsong voice cut the air behind me. "What'cha doing, R.J.?" I didn't look back, couldn't even turn around. Up the hill I saw a barbed wire fence and wondered if I was limber enough to jump over it.

"Didn't think I'd forget about you, now, did'cha?" Simon asked.

52

I sprinted toward the fence, jumped over gravestones and scattered flower arrangements behind me. Simon tripped on them but caught up, grabbed my hair and slung me backwards. I held onto a tombstone as if its owner could rise up and help me.

My husband chuckled in a low tone that sent terror into my bones. Three men were with him. I didn't know them but they had that swaggering Stark look. Simon's half-cocked grin matched his *Miami Vice* strut in a white jacket and periwinkle tee shirt. His red hair was long and pulled back in a ponytail. With a glance at the men behind him he said, "She's yours, boys. When you're done, get rid of it."

He walked away, never saying another word to me. The three men triangled around me. I scoured the ground for a weapon, a stick, a rock . . . nothing. A skinny man touched me on the shoulder and I jerked away. A

366

full-bearded man stamped his feet and gargled a laugh. "Hey!" I hollered, staring around. Somebody had to hear me.

The third man grabbed me around the waist and took me to the ground. I screamed even louder but fat stubby fingers wrapped around my mouth. I bit and got socked in the jaw. Someone has to come, I thought wildly.

The skinny one kicked me in the face and my teeth came loose, some filling my mouth. I shut out the raging pain as they argued about who'd go first, who'd get my car, where'd be the best place to dump my body.

Again I hollered through the pain and blood, a choked yell demanding someone help me. Nobody appeared. Well, no person anyway. The only figure I saw was Fear Angel. She hunched on top a tombstone, radiating hatred and howling into the wind, *Suffer, my child, for that is thy mission.*

✑

When the men were through I got hit over the head with a board they'd pulled off the fence. Then they threw me into the back of a van and we drove for a long time. My snarling, detached Fear Angel rode with me the whole way, her yellow raptor's eyes following my final route and tapping her foot as she waited for the end. I hated the thought of leaving the world with her holding my hand. I wished I looked better and that my hair wasn't so matted. Funny that my tresses concerned me at such a moment.

The men gathered at the back door and talked about

where to throw me. "Got to finish her off first," one said. Their harsh voices changed to an excitable babble edged with panic.

Fear Angel stirred and leaned closer. In all the years I'd known her, I realized that her power didn't come from leading people astray, but delighting in the disasters they brought upon themselves. Face to face with me on the greasy floor of the van, she hissed, *"Do you want to live?"*

I didn't. I'd had enough. But she must have seen some spark in my eyes and in a gargling whisper she said, *"Play dead."* She lay on top of me, her tainted spirit slipping into mine, her bluish skin, twisted neck, foul stench meshing with my muscles. My body surged with an electric charge and I passed out.

Minutes later I sensed a vague image, almost as if I were floating above: the rear door of the van opened. They dragged me out and I hit the ground with a thud. A dirt road. A few houses. Music. At a window someone pulled back a curtain to watch. Each man took a turn spitting on me, then all three stomped my chest. Fear Angel held me firm

"Ain't nothing left of her," one man said. They spat again for good measure.

One of them dragged me up by the collar to look into my eyes. "She's history," he said.

The van drove away and all I knew was the cold, welcoming feel of the earth. I didn't feel alive and wasn't sure if I was dead. The person behind the window kept looking out. Voices came from a tavern in back of me.

Loud music and rowdy yelling like someone winning a card game. Dimly I realized where I was . . . in that barely named place called Spit. Best place to leave a dead body so no one would investigate. The men had to prove to Simon I was dead, so best for the corpse to be found in Spit. The law would say I'd brought the killing on myself. Local police'd ask each other where I'd been all these years, probably living with some ex-con from Spit. Doing the ugly things people did here. Stealing and drinking, fighting, drugs, and worse. Low types from Spit ended up dead for no reason at all. I would be just another one.

Hands turned me over. Maybe somebody who'd help. A man. He pulled my jeans pockets inside out and felt me up and down to see if I had any hidden treasure. Sorry, buddy. Not today.

Drunken muttering as he scurried away, then a man and woman guzzling from a bottle came closer. She slowed to stare into my face. "Hey, you drunk?" She cackled hysterically and the man pulled her along, but she came back and nudged me with her foot. "Here's another swig for you." She poured tequila on my face, bent backwards howling a molasses laugh, then trotted after the man.

The curtain across the window of the shack swung down. The door scraped open. A pair of boots walked my direction, someone who favored his right side and dragged his left leg. *God, God, God,* I prayed, *let me die before he gets here.*

He went down one knee, the other leg splaying out to the side. I looked up into his face. Dark, dark skin. My granddaddy? Come to save me again? This man had skin like blackberries, eyes like hard raisins. Not my grandfather. He lifted my head and pushed hair back from my face.

"Lemme die," I murmured, then I lost the world around me and slipped into a blue inkiness.

53

In and out of a haze. Doctors and nurses moving around me, taking blood and replacing saline bags. I saw Daddy, Momma, Kim, Connor, and Dr. Huber. Later I realized that most those people were dead. But Connor was alive. For sure he had stood at the foot of the bed, his expression horrified, talking to Dr. Huber. I didn't want him or the doctor to know what had happened. When I could talk, I'd lie. Tell 'em I got hit by a car. Just let me go. Just let me out of here so I can go hide again.

My arm was in a cast and I felt thick wide bandages around my chest. A nurse stood over me and said, "Don't try to open your mouth, it's wired shut." When she went out I touched my face with my other hand. My head felt twice its normal size. Stitches all over my scalp, some of my hair shaved. I couldn't see out of my left eye and wondered if it was even there. Why hadn't I just died?

◌

Several days later my mind cleared but my entire body throbbed. Dr. Huber regularly checked on me, even calling me by my given name. I couldn't answer but communicated with eye blinks and it was a comfort to see him. Getting pain medicine was the only time I didn't hurt.

I wondered if the police had Simon and the three men. Probably not, I figured, if the law even knew about them. But by now other people knew about me, and Simon might well come in here to finish me off. When I tried to tell Dr. Huber he didn't understand. When I tried to write a note it looked like a scribbled mess. I tried saying the name over and over . . . Simon, Simon, Simon. Dr. Huber called for more pain medication. The lull was inviting, but my mind worked feverishly. With my good arm, I reached out to the bedside table and pulled a lamp toward me. Getting the cord wrapped around my wrist, I tugged until it teetered on the edge. I tried to stay alert but the medicine took me to darkness.

Sometime later I awoke to my worst nightmare. By now I had a better grip on reality and this was no dream: Simon stood at the foot of the bed. He watched me like I was sack of spoilt potatoes he could no longer sell. Here it comes, I thought. He's going to blow my brains out.

In his singsong voice he said, "I swear, R.J., you have got to have nine lives." He tapped the bedrail with a diamond ring on his pinkie. It looked like my grandfather's ring but I doubted that was possible. I breathed hard through my wired jaw, unable to get air through my broken nose.

Simon rounded the bed and came up beside me. "Let me fluff your pillow," he whispered and pulled one from behind my back. I moaned loudly, trying to get somebody's attention. "They don't do so good," he said, holding onto the pillow with both hands. "You want something done, got to do it yourself." He raised the pillow. His expression was cool and satanic, a man ready to suffocate a helpless woman. My life might be over but by God, somebody was going to see him leave this room. With all my might, I jerked the lamp cord bringing a crash of shattering glass. It stunned Simon for a second, but was it enough?

A nurse ran into the room, saw Simon with the pillow and screamed. Dr. Huber hurried in behind her. "You will leave now, Mr. Tuller," he said.

"See you got my wife here." Simon plumped the pillow as if to remove suspicion. "She's been missing a long time so you have my thanks for taking care of her."

"Get out."

"She's my wife," Simon said in a mocking tone, his expression hurt. "You can't order me out."

Dr. Huber raised a pistol and pointed it at Simon. "Yes, I can."

For a moment Simon stared at the gun, mouth pressed into a frown, debating with himself.

"Security!" the nurse called out into the hallway.

A uniformed hospital guard stepped into the room. His pistol was already in hand and he pointed it at Simon.

"Okay," he said, dropping the pillow. "I'll leave." Fast as a snake he shot his hands to each side of my head and growled into my ear, "Tell about me, R. J., and I'll do your daughter the same!"

The guard seized hold of Simon and forced him from the room. I tried to scream, tried to tell them, but all I could manage was a howling sob, thinking I might be the cause of such horror to my baby. Simon was the evilest man I could imagine, hurting a poor girl that lay in a bed dying. Then, I thought . . . *laying in a bed dying . . . just like me.*

Dr. Huber worked to calm me down. Shortly after, two policemen came in and stood at the foot of the bed looking at me like I was already dead. One of them was Rusty, his expression the same as Connor's, part pained and part astonished, as if I was a reanimated corpse. They asked me questions I couldn't answer. I gasped and cried then closed my eyes. If I named Simon, my daughter would suffer the same horror as me. I bit my tongue and stayed silent. Dr. Huber phoned for more medication.

"Nothing I can do if she don't shake her head yes or no," the other policeman said.

"You know who did this," Dr. Huber protested in frustration.

"Knowing ain't proving. She's going have to stand in a court of law and point the finger and it don't look to me like she cares." The officer scratched his head with a pen. "Sometimes this kind of thing happens between a man and wife. We stay out of it."

Angrily Dr. Huber gestured in my direction. "Does this look like a willing participant? She's terrified. Are you so much in the Starks' debt that you'll look past attempted murder?"

The policeman slapped his notebook shut and slid the pen into his shirt pocket. "When she's ready to talk, give us a call." Rusty never said a word. He paused at the door and looked back at me. His lips parted and his eyes seemed sad, but I don't think it was for me.

"It's okay, Randi Jo," Dr. Huber said, and made another phone call. When he hung up he came over to my bed. "I'm moving you to a clinic up north. A friend of mine runs it. You'll be checked in under a false name. Their ambulance will come down today, and I'll stay by your side until it does." He pulled the pistol from the back of his pants and checked the cylinder.

My daughter, I tried to say, *my daughter* . . . but he couldn't make out the words and then the medicine kicked in and the world went black.

54

Several months passed before all the wires were removed from my jaw. My broken arm and several ribs mended but back injuries made it difficult for me to walk. On the first day I looked in a mirror again, I saw a face that didn't seem like mine. They'd shaved my head to stitch up all the cuts and my hair was now a quarter inch of fuzzy gray.

"It'll be stiff for a while," Dr. Levine said, pointing at my jaw. "Before long you won't notice."

"Feels fine," I said, but the Fs flapped over my lips. I could hardly pronounce words without my teeth. Embarrassed, I put a hand to my mouth.

"We'll fit you for dentures soon," she said, seeing how it affected me. "Nice new smile."

"Doctor, I don't know how I'm gonna pay."

She wrote on a chart and waved off my concern. "It's taken care of. You concentrate on recovery."

I wondered how it could be *taken care of*. This had to be an expensive clinic with its manicured gardens and private rooms. I recalled thinking that Connor had come in the room to see me when I was in Dr. Huber's clinic, but he didn't have this much money. Maybe I'd never know who my benefactor was but I would be grateful for the rest of my life.

It took me a long time to learn to walk without pain and my fingers never worked as well as they had before. I was healing physically but nightmares haunted me. I'd wake up trembling like a frozen rabbit, curled in the corner of my bed, shivering like I was naked in a snowstorm. I couldn't stop shaking. I'd see myself at that cemetery, how I almost got away, the faces of those men punching and kicking me, and Simon laughing, saying this was gonna happen to Tallulah. I couldn't stop crying. And I was powerless to stop Simon if he got the mind to do what he'd planned. I hadn't told on him, but depending on his good graces was not something I couldn't trust.

Dr. Huber came to see me the following spring. We sat in a garden out back of the clinic. It'd been almost a year since I'd seen him and I knew that he had saved my life. "You look great," he said.

"I feel like an old carpet that's been beaten clean." The image tickled me and I giggled. We chatted like old friends about his Communist days of handing out free food to people he'd had to convince to take it, and the time a little boy brought back lima beans and asked to trade for candy.

Notown

As we spoke he pulled papers from an envelope and handed them to me. "Here's a driver's license, social security card, and two credit cards with fifteen hundred dollars pre-paid." He pointed at the name. "I used Tallulah Banks. Thought it might make you feel closer to your daughter."

"This kind of stuff illegal?"

"Hell, yes, it's illegal," he spouted, "but you know how I feel about the government."

We laughed out loud and I had to stop 'cause my jaw hurt. I looked at the papers, my finger tracing the name Tallulah. Slowly I said, "I haven't asked 'cause I didn't think I was strong enough to hear the answer." I clenched my teeth and felt the tip of my nose burn. "Is my daughter okay? Is she alive?"

He took my hand, patted it. "She's fine. Fully recovered. Her wedding's been rescheduled."

I exhaled a long breath, wallowing in joy that felt like Christmas and my birthday put together. "That's all I need to know."

"Starks are in a load of trouble. Simon will get caught up in it."

I winced and held up my hands as if to push the thought away. "They've been in trouble since the day they set foot in that valley but they're still standing when a lot of us are in the ground." My hands had clenched to fists. "Simon, too. Nobody can make him pay for the things he's done or what he might still do."

"Lot of people are worn out by the corruption. This time, I think they have a chance." Dr. Huber bit his bottom lip and looked aside. "I want you to think about

378

telling the state police what happened to you. With your story and a number of others, I believe we can bring the Starks down and put Simon in prison where he belongs."

I smiled, thinking of Dr. Huber as the idealistic young man who'd handed out food to cure the evils of the world. He believed he could fight Midnight Valley politics, but I knew better. What hadn't changed in over a hundred years would continue as always. "I'll think on it," I said politely.

Dr. Huber leaned over to give me a farewell hug. I hoped he knew that I'd do my best to make my life worth his saving it. "Whatever you decide," he said, "make sure you can live with it." He touched my nose and kissed me on the forehead.

After he left I sat watching a bee land on a patch of daffodils growing in a terracotta pot. The Starks filled my mind to bursting. And Simon. Even if I was never heard from again, my daughter would never be safe. My mind could never rest easy. Nobody was capable of taking down the Starks or breaking through the impenetrable wall of solidarity that their men had created decades ago. They were the absolute rulers of the roost, princes of their kingdom. They were a unified force.

Except . . . it occurred to me . . . except for one. There was one Stark who might be a weak link. I ran my fingers over a scar on my chin and considered this.

෴

I came to the garden every day and thought about a plan. I played out scenes in my mind as if fashioning situations from one of Momma's soap operas. I brought out all the people I knew and made them come alive in my imagination and asked their advice: Kim, Momma and Daddy, Connor, Mr. Herne. Even Tempy, Wallis and Pug supplied some sneaky ideas. I used my tremors and nightmares to bolster the plan. After I cleaned it up into a single vision, I went over all the details until they were committed to memory.

Finally late at night I wrote out everything I knew about the Gaylor family's history. There wasn't much about Daddy's background but I put in all my experiences with his brother Luther. I hoped somebody would learn the real story about a traveling musician who fell in love with a rich girl and had a child with her who ended up murdered. I described my grandfather Silas and how he'd saved me one day beside the Regal Hotel, and saved our whole family from starving by giving us an ancestor's ring. I recounted the story Momma had told about the slave woman whose blood ran in our veins, buried in a ditch after a life of misery, and her son who'd stolen the ring handed down to Silas. I wrote down everything I remembered about the Gaylors.

I signed the last page, *A family friend,* and added, *who thought the Gaylors might like to know.*

I folded the papers and put them in an envelope to save for when the time was right. Then I called the nurse and told her my back was bothering me and asked for pain pills. Whenever a different nurse came on duty I asked again for pills until I had collected more than two dozen. Finally it was time to go.

55

In mid-afternoon the Greyhound bus stopped at the outskirts of Coalfire. Pulling a baseball cap low on my forehead and adjusting an oversized jacket, I got off the bus and walked the quarter mile into Spit. Carried a duffle bag, and inside that some others made of canvas along with a sheaf of folded pages. Two blocks of dilapidated buildings with jagged wood sidewalks bordering a muddy road looked like an Old West town bypassed by progress. A foul odor permeated the air: garbage thrown into a creek and sewer pipes hanging out over the water. Spit had the reputation of being rough, the kind of place where respectable folks didn't go. What the residents had in common was being drunk, drugged up, or lost souls unable to tolerate reality. I didn't mind reality. By now I could put life's gratifications and consequences in a place where they didn't matter. Only one conviction swirled inside of me . . . finishing my last chore. I'd complete it or die trying.

I listened for music and followed the sound of it to the end of the block. The Wabash Tavern blared Madonna singing "Live To Tell." I didn't see anybody in the interior darkness, but from the cartons of empty bottles stacked against the outside wall it looked like a 24/7 kind of place. I paused on the sidewalk to engage my memory. Yeah, the middle of this street was where I'd been left that night. Kitty-corner stood a gray plank shack. Dingy curtains were closed and a heap of slag piled against one wall looked as if it steadied the hovel from falling over. Has to be, I thought, that's the house.

The street was deserted except for a man passed out face down, and a coral-haired woman sitting motionless with her head between her knees. I stepped up onto the shack's concrete porch and knocked on the door.

It was near three p.m. so I wasn't worried about interrupting dinner. I wasn't worried about anything a'tall. Putting my ear to the door, I heard someone moving around. I tapped again. The knob turned and the door opened a crack. A charcoal eye stared at me through the gap. I stared back without speaking. Best let the shock of seeing me wear off.

A black man edged open the door until his face showed. He looked beyond me, his expression wary. Silver tinted hair at his temples. Shirtless, with a faded maroon robe pulled around him, he held on to both the door and the wall. I glanced down at the dirt floor. He stood on one leg, the stump of the other jutting below the robe.

"You know who I am," I said, stepping closer.

Dallas Shepard studied my features and his haunted eyes revealed painful thoughts as if he was cursed by memories he didn't want to revive. But a nod from him told me I had a chance.

"You know what we need to do," I said.

He looked at the floor, probably trying to decide if I'd lost my mind, but I knew we'd been to the same hell. And I saw a spark of justice denied in his eyes, just as he must have seen it in mine. What had to be done was something neither of us could do by ourselves. Alone, we were weak, but together . . . together we had a chance. He opened the door and let me in.

౿

Anybody who had grown up in Divergence and lived in Spit understood that Mr. Death was a party companion that stamped your ticket any number of times throughout the day. Every morning waking up alive was another day to dance to Ole Spite's tune.

There wasn't a place for Dallas and me to sit so we stood facing each other. He listened without interruption as I explained what I intended to do, knowing that if I succeeded I would even the score for both of us. If I failed . . . well, it wouldn't much matter. He only questioned my resolve.

"People find Jesus," he said. "Think they ought to confess, cleanse their souls and take their punishment." He hesitated and looked at the floor. "I need to know you can make peace with your God."

"Holly used to say we're in a world where there's them and there's us, and in the us part there's enough snakes so you need keep a sharp hoe always ready." Under the baseball cap I ran my fingers across my scalp, feeling the ropy scars. "They're all vipers looking to protect their den . . . the Starks, the Carmacks, Simon . . . they killed Holly just as much as the person who rigged dynamite in her car. God ain't got a dog in this fight."

I glanced around the two-room shack, a mattress and box springs shoved in the corner, and a musty-smelling corduroy chair with a prosthetic leg lying across it. A coal stove in the other room looked to be his only source of heat.

I pulled a folded piece of newspaper from my pocket, opened it and showed him. "My daughter's getting married tonight. Family'll all be at the wedding." I looked up at Dallas, holding his gaze. "Now is the perfect time."

He stared at the picture of Tallulah. Lips pressed together, hands clasped. "You sure?"

I pointed at the story underneath the photo. "It says here there's a big charity benefit at the hospital beforehand, giving thanks to all the people who helped save her life. The Hernes and the Gaylors will be there. Everything goes right, there's some icing for this cake."

"This goes wrong, what happened to you'll be done twice over."

Pulling off the baseball cap, I exposed my scalp. "I don't blame the men who attacked me. Didn't know their names but their faces were Simon's, their fists were Simon's. I do know who left me for dead out there in that street. Simon. I do know who supplied the dynamite that blew up Holly's car . . . Simon." The name choked in my throat and I crossed my arms over my stomach. "I admit, if it was just me I'd run away again and hide in a patch darker than Spit where he'd never find me. But he'll always be there . . . in the shadows of my daughter's life, and that's why I won't feel a ping of guilt. That's why I won't make a mistake. My daughter's safety is worth anything I could suffer."

I stepped over to a scratched-up bureau where Dallas had cut out Holly's high school picture and pinned it to the wall. Her young face, so fearless, eyes determined to win over the world. "Did you know Holly was in trouble?" I asked.

"Lord, no. I'd've moved heaven and earth to stop it, had I an inkling."

"Wonder what she did to them?"

Dallas looked away with a sagging expression like a crust falling off a burnt pie. "She stood up to them." His mouth trembled. "A Notown girl standing up to a rich husband who thought he was better than her. That's for killing." For several minutes, he couldn't speak. Finally he said, "She laid trapped in that car for two hours 'fore they could get her out. She knew her legs was gone, knew she wouldn't live and they said . . . people was there told me she sang a church song, *Deep Down In My Heart*. Used to sing it to her when we were little, sitting out in the woods learning what it was to be a boy and a girl . . . just that . . . a boy and a girl. Starks had me packing up TV sets from a store they'd robbed in Lexington. I accidentally saw a dead man, same day Jonas broke my knee. I didn't get to go to her, didn't get to tell her . . . People said . . . she sang that song until her voice was just a whisper on the wind." His breath caught in his throat. He stared ahead without seeing me, voice barely audible, and sang:

> *"Lord, you know I love everybody,*
> *Deep down in my heart,*
> *Lord, you know I love my brother*
> *Deep down in my heart*
> *Lord, you know I love my sister*
> *Deep down in my heart*
> *Lord, you know I love everybody*
> *Deep down in my heart."*

He covered his eyes with his palms, his mouth grimaced in hard emotions from so deep within him it pained me.

I pressed my hand to the back of his head and embraced him. He sobbed on my shoulder. "She knew you loved her, baby. She knew."

He looked up at me, tears shining on his skin. "What do you want me to do?"

56

Simon was a creature of habit, most of them bad. Even years later he still took his liquor at the Jolly Roger tavern on the edge of Coalfire. Fridays and Saturdays he splurged on better bars in Contrary and Quinntown . . . where we'd met all those years ago . . . him coming over to pick up the cut on the slot machines in the backrooms of the Marcescent Street gin joints. That's why he'd had a pocketful of cash that night. I chided myself, remembering how naive I'd been to be impressed by him. He hadn't been socializing, just collecting Stark money. I was equally sure that each time he returned to the Jumpin' Jonas's dealership with cash, he skimmed a little off the top and left the rest at the office door. No doubt the whole of Midnight Valley knew about that bag of money sitting inside in plain view, but nobody dared steal from Jonas. Enough busted heads and graves in this valley proved that it never paid to cross a Stark.

Dallas and I walked over to Coalfire. He kept several yards behind me, and no one paid us any mind. By the time we got there the late afternoon sun shone bright in our eyes. He pointed out Simon's blue van in the dirt parking lot of the Jolly Roger. I pulled my baseball cap low around my eyes and unzipped the oversized jacket. It was warm and I wouldn't be able to get away with wearing the jacket inside for very long without attracting attention. Dallas would come into the tavern a few minutes later and sit in the booth by the door.

My fingers trembled as I took a seat at the bar. It was next to the hatch door where the waitress retrieved the drinks. I ordered a beer and quietly looked around. If any part of my plan could go wrong, it would happen here. My every move had to be right. I dipped my head over the mug, scanning the booths that lined the wall all the way back to an alcove with the word *Toilet* handwritten atop it in red paint.

Simon's carrot top head inched above the back booth. He was talking to a bald man who faced me. Didn't know him, so little chance of being recognized. I waited. Out the window Dallas sat on a bench and eyed me inside.

The bald man's glass was empty, which meant they had to re-order soon. A moment later he motioned to the bartender, who poured a glass of whiskey and a gin gimlet. I turned toward the window and nodded for Dallas to come in. From my pocket I took out a small envelope with half the saved pain pills, now crushed to a power.

The bartender set the drinks on a tray next to me and called out to the waitress who was busy taking Dallas's order. I had my chance . . . but did Simon still drink gin gimlets? What if he now drank whiskey? I watched the waitress in the mirror behind the bar, willing Dallas to keep her occupied. If I put only a portion of powder in each drink it wouldn't be enough to knock Simon out. I had to play my card and dismissed my doubt. Swift as a lizard I slipped the crushed pills into the gin and stirred it with my finger.

The waitress picked up the tray and took it to the back booth. Unnoticed, I tipped my beer into the sink and left.

Soon Dallas followed me out with a pint of bourbon he'd purchased. We sat behind a copse of beech trees by the parking lot where we could watch the blue van. To anybody looking our way, we were just two pals sharing a drink. We waited. And waited. Simon'd had time to drink another gimlet, maybe two. I hadn't counted on him getting drunk. He could hold his liquor all right, but with drugs on top of gin I doubted he could stay conscious.

"If Simon passes out in there," I told Dallas, "it'll wreck everything. I'm going back in. He sees me, he'll follow me out."

Dallas grabbed my arm. "Too dangerous. He'll come out fighting and with more than just hisself."

"Can't stand the thought of him getting away."

"Look!" Dallas said in a harsh whisper.

Simon swaggered out. In one hand he clasped a brown paper bag against his chest, probably full of cash. He stopped at the front of his van and cranked his head to the side. Clutching his stomach, he cleared his throat and inhaled before bending over and throwing up. Then he stood straight and shook himself like wet dog.

In panic I realized that the pain pills weren't going to put him to sleep like they had me, they'd only made him sick. He was going to get into the van and drive away. "I need something," I said.

"What?" Dallas asked warily.

"Something to hit him with."

"That won't work." He held onto my shoulder.

I reached up and put all my weight on a tree branch until it broke then handed it to Dallas. "I'll draw him over. Stand ready."

"This'll make a scratch on him." He stared in disbelief at the branch.

Before he could argue I lurched from behind the beech trees like a drunk, holding the pint and fell against the car next to Simon's van, keeping my back to him.

"Who's 'at," Simon called out.

"Sorry, Mister," I said in a low voice. "Just taking a pee."

"Not on my van!" he yelled, coming around. I watched his reflection in the car windows and heard his queasy panting. I turned to face him. His eyes narrowed. Sweat dripped down his cheeks. Slowly he placed the bag of money on top of the van.

"Sonnuvabitch," he muttered.

Hard as I could I threw the pint of bourbon at his head. He knocked it away. Each step toward me I heard the slap of his hand across my face. I moved back, and pulled a second envelope of the crushed pills from a pocket and emptied it into my palm. Step by step I drew him toward the beech trees.

"You're supposed to be dead." He looked up at the sky and cussed. "By God, this minute, I'm gonna see it done."

"Seems like you'd learnt I don't go down easy."

"Shhhh," he shushed. "Don't want anybody inside to hear what I'm about to do to you."

He leaped at me. I flung the pulverized pills into his face. His hands flew to his eyes and he fell on one knee. I picked up the bourbon bottle and slammed it into his head. He cussed, reaching for me. From behind the trees Dallas hopped out one-legged, leaned on the nearest car and clobbered Simon under the chin with his fake leg. Simon lurched backward. Again Dallas swung the leg like a pro, catching him on the side of his noggin. Simon fell forward, cussing. Dallas hit him again on the back of the head and he was out.

In astonishment I stared at Dallas. He stood there in his boxer shorts. With an irritated glance toward the trees, he sent me to retrieve his pants. While he put them on and reattached his leg, I turned Simon over, searched his pocket and found the van keys.

We loaded him in the back, tied him up and taped his mouth. Dallas yanked the diamond ring off Simon's pinky finger and tossed it to me. I searched the remaining keys and found two with JJ scratched on them in tiny letters.

Grabbing the bag of money from atop the van, I ground the ignition and we headed to Jumpin' Jonas' Mobile Homes and Used Cars.

The keys got us inside the dealership. Dallas and I moved frantically, he filling the back of the van with topped-off gas canisters while I broke into Jonas' office. Not much had changed over the years. Pictures of his children lined the wall, photos of his brothers, cousins, one of Alvey's many mayoral inaugurations, an old black and white of a young Jonas and his father at a moonshine still.

When Dallas peered into the office I raised a cloth behind me and revealed the safe. "How you gonna get in?" he asked.

"And now for the icing on the cake." I sat down at Jonas's oversized desk and flipped through a Rolodex. "A Stark is gonna help me." I picked up the phone and punched in numbers. "The one Stark who could give a crap about all this." The phone rang and I closed my eyes, concentrating.

A woman's voice said, "Evening."

"Renita Stark?" I deepened my own voice and forced my breath forward to sound like a best friend.

"Hell, yes," she replied. "Who's this?"

"Jonas around?"

"Out back at the bar-be-que."

"Good, leave him out there."

"Who is this?"

"There's something you and I can do for each other, Renita."

She laughed. "Honey, nobody can do anything to me

that ain't already been done twice over."

"It's about your daughter. Bette Moss."

There was a pause and the sound of breathing. "Go on," she said.

"I can tell you where to find the rest of her."

Another pause, another breath. "I don't know who you are, but you're asking for a beat down like you've never known."

"I've known more than a few of those, Renita." Now it was my turn to wait.

"Okay. I'm listening," she said.

"This is a one-time-only chance. When I hang up, you'll never hear my voice again. You give me the information I want, and I'll tell you where to find Bette. If you don't tell me the truth, you'll die knowing your little girl lies in the ground in pieces."

Quiet. Only breathing. But she didn't hang up. "Reckon you want money. How much?"

"We both have something the other wants."

She chuckled, her voice deep from years of smoking. "If you know me, you know I don't take kindly to forced quid pro quo."

"I don't even know what that is. But you, more than anybody else in this world, knows the stinking cauldron of love. You know how it fills you up, how it takes you into the blazing sun and then drops you into the guts of the earth and eats you alive 'til all that's left is a black bile that won't leave your belly."

"What do you want?"

"Combination of the safe in Jonas's office."

"You know Jonas and his boys could be there in two minutes flat. You ever seen a person's head bashed in with a baseball bat?"

I swallowed hard. She wasn't going to tell me. "Got to go," I said.

"Wait!"

I breathed into the phone, biting my lower lip, not sure what to do. "Renita?" I said loudly, ready to hang up.

"You tell me first."

I heaved out a breath I'd been holding in and pressed my lips to the phone. "Tonight, an hour after the sun sets, there's going to be a fire in Notown. Start at the edge of the ashes and walk sixty feet back, off to the side you'll see a patch of daffodils weeds. Dig down. Six feet at least. You'll find her."

"How do I know you're telling me the truth?"

"Because love is a cutthroat business."

A gasp. She expelled a congested cough and then cleared her throat. "That safe works on the ages of Jonas's favorite children. Fourteen, Thirty-two, Forty-six."

As she said the numbers I mouthed them to Dallas, and hung up the phone. He turned the dial on the safe. The door opened with a creak. Quickly he pulled stacks of money off the shelves and stuffed them into my duffle bag.

Just as quickly I wiped down the phone, the desk, anywhere we'd touched, then dropped Simon's diamond pinkie ring between the safe and the wall. When Jonas found his safe raided, he'd think Simon was responsible. Yet the truth could be better: If the ring was indeed my ancestor's, then once again it had come to the aid of a Gaylor.

❦

As I drove, Dallas divided the money. He put his half in a backpack and stuffed it behind his seat. I took the beltline road over to Notown. "You'll have to ditch this van," I said.

"I'll leave it in a big city and set it afire. Be no fingerprints, license plate, nothing to find. I'll disappear after that."

"I'd like to ask where you'll go, but better you don't tell me."

"Got a place in mind. Summer's warm, winter's warmer, everybody's browned skinned and nobody's ever heard of a Stark."

"You're about to break out in song." We both laughed off what we knew were nervous fears about what came next.

I pulled in behind Wink's grocery and looked up the hill. The Gaylor house hadn't been torn down yet, so I figured Hector must've gotten a year's grace for being a veteran. I walked up the hill and checked the house, empty . . . thankfully. I'd guessed right that everybody, including Hector, would be at the charity benefit and wedding. I waved at Dallas and he reached the house a minute later and parked on the far side so no one could see the van. Simon was woozy but not conscious enough to put up a fight. We got him into the house and tied to the chair. Dallas found a chain in the van and we wrapped that around Simon as well.

"There's something I need you to do," I told Dallas.

"You been right about everything so far, I won't argue now."

From my duffle bag I counted out ten thousand dollars for myself. I put that aside, took out my pages of family history that I'd written out and two flat canvas folders. I unzipped the folders and divided the rest of my half of the money between them. With a felt pen I addressed one folder to my brother, Hector, care of Greg and Selena Gaylor. Selena could pass on the history to all the Gaylors, and maybe Collette could use it to do some good for other Notown folks. I hoped Hector would get himself a fresh start, a new house up on the hill, or a spell at a hospital where they could help him finally heal. But whatever he decided, I had to let it go. He had to make his decision and live with it, just like I had to live with mine. The other folder I addressed to Butch. He would always need a safety net.

I gave both folders to Dallas. "Might be a day or two 'fore I can mail these," he said, "but you know I'm good for it."

"I know. Some things between us don't need saying." I handed him the keys to the van. Together we brought the gasoline canisters inside, then he drove off to take up his final post at Gray's Pin.

57

"Reckon there's nothing else to say." Randi Jo keeps her voice soft, no trace of accusation. Simon's eyes water and she avoids looking at his face.

"I know you, Randi Jo. You can't do this." He bends his head farther back, trying to see her standing behind him, trying to stare into her eyes. "This is outright murder and you ain't got that in you."

"You got it in you, don't you, Simon?" She walks away and pulls Pug's mattress across the door and soaks it in gasoline. Drenches the bed she'd once slept on. Pulls off the blanket and drapes it around Simon's shoulders.

"You don't want to do this, honey. Look at me! You gonna burn me to death?" His voice breaks on the last word.

398

"Uh-huh." Randi Jo steps over the mattress, picks up another canister and splashes the bathroom, the back porch, the kitchen, uses a third canister on the living room and her parents' room. With about half a can left, she returns to Simon. "I'm glad this house is still here. I'm glad it's me that takes it down." Memories rush through her of fights, laughter, terror—everything that had happened to make her the right one to reduce the house to ashes.

"I'm sorry, Randi Jo." His words quiver. "I'm apologizing to you. I should never have done any of those things. You didn't deserve them. I'll confess, I'll tell the law everything. There's lots you don't know. Things the Starks did. Things I got caught up in. Hadn't been for that, none of it would have happened to you."

"This ain't about what you did to me, Simon." She runs her fingers through his hair. "No need to say how sorry you are. I already know. You made a promise to me when I was laying on that hospital bed, my jaw held together by wire." Gasoline fumes rise from the floor, filling the room. She coughs and pulls the blanket tighter around his neck. "You will never threaten my daughter again."

"You know me, Randi Jo," he howls. "I'd never've done that! Remember our early days? We can have that again. I can be a different man. What about everything I gave you?"

Randi Jo kneels down and kisses the back of the chair. "I hate leaving you, Chair, but I can't take you with me. Could've left you with my family, but . . . I'm the only one who knows your true worth."

"Listen to you. Talking to a chair, a blamed chair. You need help, baby. I'll get it for you. You know I'll take care of you."

She stands up and empties the last of the gas onto Simon's head. He coughs and sputters and squeezes his eyes shut. "Yes," she says, "better that it all goes down to ash. It's been a good house, has worked hard for all of us . . . and now it can take its final rest after doing me this one last favor." She circles Simon, looks out her daydream portal for the last time, and closes the window. "It can take you to Hell."

"Randi Jo," he screams, "I'm begging you!" His pleas deteriorate into sobs and then crazy laughter as she steps into Uncle Luther's old room and closes the door. She flicks the lighter and lights a cigarette, inhales a puff then chucks it through the eyehole. Flame whooshes and shoots across the room.

"You idiot," Simon hollers, "ha, ha, ha, ha, ha, you can't get out! You'll burn, too!"

Randi Jo watches him through the eyehole. The blanket catches fire and he squirms and screams but the chain holds him firm. The stink of his burning flesh gags her but she keeps watching, witness to this task she has to finish. Smoke chokes her. Flames engulf him and consume the floor. Finally, she turns, lifts up the floorboards and drops into the space under the house. Kicking out the baseboard door, she races outside into fresh air just as a crimson sun drops behind the mountains.

58

Now . . . June 30, 1987

Dallas sees me coming across the railroad track and starts the van. I jump in the passenger seat and roll down the window to look up at the house. The far side has a wall of smoke streaming up into the dark sky. So far no one's running toward the fire. Nobody's noticed it yet. The path to the daffodil patch fizzles out, leaving a perfect trail of breadcrumbs for Renita. A few flowers bloomed out of the season as if they were a promise now fulfilled. Renita will have no problem finding them. A burst of red flame explodes from the roof. My fingers and hands tremble. I look down, unable to watch any longer, and my whole body shakes.

"Gonna be okay?" Dallas asks.

"This is the happiest day of my life." I control the shaking and nod at the road. "Better get me to the bus station. My Greyhound leaves in forty minutes."

We drive on through to Quinntown and I say silent good-byes to the stores, the fountain at the artesian well, even to Marcescent Street and the green whorehouse that leans to one side. The road curves around to the clean streets of Contrary, and I say farewell to those places, too.

As we approach a traffic light I dig into my duffel bag for the Sno Ball I'd gotten earlier at Wink's Market. My fingers locate the packet and I tear into it. I start to bite into the cream cake when a streak of white shoots up in front of the van. For a second my mind flashes on the wing of an angel.

Dallas hits the brakes, squealing to a stop as the yellow light changes to red.

In the crosswalk an auburn-haired girl whirls to face us, hands to her cheeks, but smiling wide. "Sorrrrry!" she exclaims with a wave. She and four other fancy dressed young women are struggling to get control of a large sheet of white material. Quickly they move to the traffic island in the middle of the street. At their center I see that one woman surrounded by all that white material is holding onto an unruly veil. She looks over her shoulder and I see her face. Tallulah. My daughter in her wedding gown.

The light changes and Dallas drives on.

"Pull over," I say.

"What?"

"Pull over."

He steers the van into a parking space and lets the motor idle. I climb over the seat to the back window, wipe dust off the glass with my sleeve, and look out at the group of bridesmaids. Tallulah turns and calls out, "I love you, Daddy."

My gaze follows hers across the street where Connor stands, dressed in a tuxedo, his white hair combed back, glasses high on his nose. Beside him Rory wears a pale blue dress, her black hair curved into a French twist. Connor pats the air and his lips formed the words, "Watch for cars."

It's the happiest day of their lives. I see the joy on their faces as I press the creamy Sno Ball to my lips, biting into it and letting the sugar fill my senses. Tallulah and her bridesmaids hurry ahead, a flock of beautiful swans floating up the steps of the First Baptist Church. Connor and Rory follow them.

"Let's go," I tell Dallas.

There's nothing more to say, nothing more to think about, not one thing left to do. I have finished my list. Simon's death is my wedding gift to the people I love most.

Minutes later Dallas stops at the Greyhound bus station. A fire engine roars past us in the opposite direction. I take his hand and we stare at each other for a long time. We both know the real snake responsible for Holly's murder is still on the loose, but someone else will have to hoe his head. Randi Jo Gaylor and Dallas Shepard have done what they could.

"You done good by Holly," I say. "Let it rest there. Enjoy what's left of your life."

He nods and our eyes meet in a bond I don't want to let go of, but I step out and close the door.

In the station bathroom I throw away the gassy-smelling jacket and put on a new summer jumper and flip-flops. I dump the baseball cap and let my thin gray hair show itself to the world. In the mirror my face reflects peacefully, and in a lot of ways I think I look like Momma. The announcer calls my bus.

Shouldering my duffel bag, I go to the boarding area, get on, and stretch out in the backseat of the half-empty bus. A boy in front of me is strumming a guitar and singing about love not being a victory march.

"What's that song?" I ask.

"It's called 'Halleluiah'," he replies. "By Leonard Cohen. He's a god."

"Ah, not much experience with gods," I say as he continues playing. "Little bit with angels."

I lean back in my seat and close my eyes, listening to him sing and thinking I'll never see this place again. It's real this time. I remember all the times I ran . . . from home . . . from Connor . . . from Simon . . . but this time I'm not really running from anything. There's nothing left here that I have any claim on, nothing I need to take care of. Momma and Daddy are at rest. My brothers and sisters are as well taken care of as they can be. Kim is with the good earth, even if I don't know where she is, and Pug is gone. Connor has Rory. Tallulah is getting married.

So much of Notown holds my secrets, just like it held my mother's, my father's . . . and I'm sure a whole lot of other people's. For now, this knowledge stays with me and with the land that will not give up the tale. Maybe I'll go to my grave without ever speaking about it, or maybe there will come a day of sunshine when I can tell my truth out loud and everybody I know will rise up and be unafraid of the lives we've lived, be forgiven for what we've done and shout to the world, *Halleluiah, halleluiah!*

As the bus pulls away from the station I look out the back window and see Fear Angel tumbling in the dirt. I'm not even surprised. Maybe I'll always be running from her, but as long as I stay ahead, I'll be all right. She might be behind me for the rest of my life, but now I face a road where a bright, shining Angel opens her arms to me and announces purely and simply, *Halleluiah, halleluiah,* just like the boy in front of me is singing.

I keep my eyes on her confident face, her powerful stance, and it hits me like a dash of cold water that she and Fear Angel are indeed one and the same. I might see her fearful side again, but that will always be in the distance. The next time I'm truly afraid, I'll be ready to leave this world and will only be anxious because of the unknown. I'll thank her for the opportunities she gave me. I'll know that every hurt and every tear was a true initiation of my soul, making it possible to honorably claim the events of my life. I'll acknowledge her as a true friend even if at times it didn't seem so, then I'll close my eyes and imagine the face of my daughter and know that I've done one good deed.

The End

Author's Note

Gratefully, today there are many more resources available for victims of domestic abuse and missing children than there were in Randi Jo's day. Below are a few of those.

Rape, Abuse & Incest National Network (RAINN). The nation's largest anti-sexual assault organization. 1-800-656 HOPE. http://www.rainn.org/

National Council on Child Abuse & Family Violence. 1-202-429-6695. http://www.nccafv.org/

National Coalition Against Domestic Violence. 1-303-839-1852. http://www.ncadv.org/

National Network to End Domestic Violence. http://www.nnedv.org/

National Domestic Violence Hotline. 1-800-799-7233; TTY: 1-800-787-3224

National Center for Missing & Exploited Children. 1-703-274-3900.

Hotline: 1-800-THE-LOST (1-800-843-5678). http://www.missingkids.com/

When making holiday purchases or charity donations, keep in mind the following organizations or your local woman's shelter:

http://thistlefarms.org/
http://www.ncadv.org/products/Products_61.html
http://www.whowomen.com/index.html
http://worldcrafts.org/artisans.asp

Also available
from BearCat Press
Book Two: The Midnight Valley Quartet

The Hunter of Hertha
By Tess Collins

1

August 1948

Connor Herne ran the uneven ground of Beans Fork Hollow. Out of breath, he pushed himself up the hill, protecting a sack under his arm, and hopped rocks across a snaky creek. At the peak of the next ridge, he looked west toward the setting sun to judge how much light he had, then speeding up his pace, he jumped onto a dirt road and trotted toward a giant beech tree beside a stone bridge. Choir practice hummed from a Baptist Church on the far side. Connor ran around the beech tree and looked up at a red-lettered sign reading *Renegades Hide Out. No Girls Allowed.*

"Rusty, you up there?"

A freckled face peered down at him from a tree house twenty feet above. "Hurry up." Rusty Haskew motioned with a hand.

Connor anchored his feet onto square boards nailed into the tree and held the brown bag with his teeth as he climbed.

"Got it?" Rusty asked as Connor fell onto the floor.

Connor spit out the bag at Rusty's feet. "Got yours?"

The auburn-haired boy fell on the sack and pulled out buttered biscuits that he stuffed in his mouth. Rusty nodded toward a tattered magazine.

Connor took the coverless journal to the door and held it toward the setting sun. He flipped though the pages until he found it. "Ugh," he said, looking up at Rusty. "They cut her in two."

"Told you," he said with a jaw full of pork. "Look how they sliced her mouth."

"Whooooh," Connor traced the black-haired woman's mouth, cut up each side like a clown. He glanced over at Rusty. "You get enough?"

Rusty nodded as he bit into the second biscuit and a piece of pork. "Sure your Mom ain't noticed?"

"Naw, she just reckons I eat a lot." He turned the page and looked at a half-page photo of a dark-haired woman, smiling, a small cross on a dark cord around her neck, white flowers behind each ear. "The Black Dahlia," he read. He turned back to the picture of the woman's body, staring at the gap of open flesh that split her into two pieces, and he swallowed hard. "Who in the world would think to do such a thing?"

"A monster," Rusty said.

"Can you get this back without the other boys noticing?"

Rusty waved his hands. "Detective magazine's ours. I ain't afraid of them."

Connor's eyes widened at his friend. He had to be the bravest or the craziest boy in the world. Living in an orphan house with boys twice his size, he regularly stole from them; their dirty magazines, their hidden candy, sometimes even their clothes. He'd shown up at the tree house with a black eye more than once, but his stories told of how he'd given more than he got. Connor brought him food because he was always hungry, and sometimes when they swam in Big Creek his ribs showed under his skin.

"Herman seen this?" Connor asked.

"He's on watch out." Rusty nodded and slowly punched his fist into his other hand. "Tonight Little Preacher Boy gets his."

"Without mercy," Connor laughed, rubbing his belly at the thought of what they had planned for their nemesis, a ten-year-old, self-righteous shortie that went door-to-door spreading his version of the word of God that had nothing to do with anything Connor had ever read in the Bible. More like whatever Preacher Boy wanted, people better do or he'd denounce them from the pulpit. One time he embarrassed Connor's parents into going to Wednesday night, Sunday morning and Sunday evening services. Connor had thought he was going to fall over and die if he had to listen to one more hell-fire sermon from the white-shoed tyke. People came from all over the county to hear the Little Preacher Boy, who didn't have his own ministry but hired himself out as a non-denominational evangelist, and was currently leading a revival at the church across the bridge. Connor thought that little as he was, Bryson Pomeroy was still a punk worth whipping.

The trill of a whippoorwill caused both boys to head down the ladder. Next to the tree trunk stood the third renegade, Herman Cahill. He took off his glasses and pointed toward the bridge. "He's yonder down the road."

The boys hid on sloping support braces of the stone bridge and waited. Dusk washed out the outlines of trees but the glow from the church gave enough light for the boys to watch their plan play out. And here he strutted, ten-year-old Master Pomeroy, dressed in his checkered suit with striped tie and his signature white shoes. Flattened against the rails, the boys raised their heads as he passed. Bryson slipped and waved his arms to keep from falling. An afternoon thunderstorm had made the bridge all the more slippery. He slid again and let out a shrill "Shit!"

The boys stifled their laughter. "More'n he knows," Herman whispered.

A third step took Bryson to one knee. "Holy damnation!" he yelled, sliding in dog poop that the boys had collected for the last two days. He let out a string of cuss words. The boys giggled, unable to control themselves any longer. Bryson scraped his white shoes on the bridge rail, but they were hopelessly mired. "I see you heathens," he yelled at them, "you're going to burn in hell with Satan and his minions, and I'll be there on the Day of Judgment to testify against you!"

The boys hopped the creek, holding up middle fingers toward Little Preacher Boy, who continued to cuss them. Downstream, they climbed onto a castle-shaped rock protruding in the middle of the water. Herman flicked on his USALite Mickey Mouse flashlight as they fell to their backs, holding their sides from hard laughter. "Reckon he went to pray for our salvation," Connor joked.

"He didn't get a good 'nuf look at our faces." Herman smacked his own cheeks. "God won't know who he's talking about."

"Anyways, the Lord don't listen to people who cuss worse than a drunk soldier," Rusty chortled.

"But we have to figure a way," Connor sat up and emphasized each word, "to get rid of him for good." He cocked an ear upstream. "What's that?"

The boys listened. Sounds of the early night faded into a gentle roar. They looked at each other, alarm overtaking their features. "Water from the mines!" Herman yelled.

The boys jumped rock to rock to get on high ground. Herman held the flashlight while Connor grabbed onto wild honeysuckle vines, pulled himself up the creek bank, then turned and offered a hand. Behind them Rusty slipped into ankle-deep water. "Come on!" Connor yelled, and Rusty again started up the slope. The roar upstream grew louder as Connor and Herman stretched out their hands toward their friend, who had frozen in place.

"Yonder it is!" Herman yelled, pointing at a wall of water barreling toward them.

The wave hit Rusty, sweeping him from their sight. Connor and Herman stared at their empty hands. "Come on," Connor said and began running. "We'll catch him at Big Creek."

The two friends sprinted through the dark. Herman lit a path through backyards, gardens of cornstalks, and both boys jumped a beehive as they raced through the woods lining the creek bank. Out of breath, they'd beat the flood to Big Creek, a large tributary where Little Creek emptied. Huffing for air, Connor looked upstream where the bank of water would emerge. He turned in a circle, looking for something to hold on to. "There!" he said and jumped on a low hanging branch of a young birch tree. "Hold it down, Herman. After I catch Rusty, let loose."

Herman anchored the flashlight between two rocks and pointed it upstream, then put his weight on the tree limb as Connor crawled out over the water. The rush of wind over the water grew stronger. "It'll get you too," Herman yelled.

"Yonder he is!" Connor pointed upstream at a bobbing head and flailing arms. He circled his legs into the branches. "Get me down low!"

Herman leaned on the branch with all his strength. The crest of the water hit Connor and he struggled to hold on while reaching out into the flood. He snagged Rusty by the hair and one shoulder, holding him tight. Herman released the branch and it sprang upward, taking the boys out of the waves.

Rusty coughed and wheezed as Connor held him. Slowly they made their way along the branch to dry ground. The boys collapsed on the shoreline, Rusty spitting water and Herman patting his back. "Damn coal mines," Rusty said, his shoulders trembling from exertion. "Their dams break every hard rain and everything floods."

"I thought you two were goners," Herman said.

"Take more'en mine water to get shed of me." Rusty shot out his middle finger at the flooded stream. "I swear, one day I'm gonna break a window in a mine owner's house."

"I'll help," Connor agreed.

"Me, too." Herman shook a fist.

"Think we lost our big rock?" Herman wondered.

The boys sat quietly, watching smaller stones tumble into Big Creek. In a few seconds, their castle rock-hiding place crashed into the larger stream.

While Connor and Rusty dipped themselves naked in a far pool to clean off coal slurry, upstream two men inspected the break in the coal mine's holding pond. They were unconcerned that their flood had claimed a dog, three chickens, half a dozen gardens, swamped the backyards of every creek-side home, and washed away a boy. It didn't matter that the poison in the coal ash would stunt the growth of every tree whose buried roots now withered, or that the toxic sludge would contaminate the well water of all the homes in the hollow. There was no concern that the fish were dead. It'd been an accident, after all, an act of God. The men couldn't be held responsible . . . that is, if anyone found out, if anyone could prove it was their fault. People didn't know what to do when these things happened, people didn't know whom to call or even if there was anyone to call, and the men . . . they liked it that way. Acts of God always worked in their favor.

Rusty's clothes were mud-caked, and Herman snuck into the backyard of a nearby house and stole a pair of overalls off the clothesline. They hung loose on Rusty, but they were good enough. Connor's clothes were more splashed than covered and he figured he could blame it on playing in the creek beside his house. "Gotta get home before the folks notice I'm not in my room," he said.

Herman shined his flashlight as far as Beans Fork where he turned off. They made their secret handshake and promised to meet at the tree house the following day. House lights lit a path down Notown Road. When they came upon the orphan house, Rusty motioned for Connor to give him a lift. Connor fell to all fours underneath an open window and Rusty stood on his back to get inside.

A screen door slammed. The wooden porch creaked with heavy footsteps. The boys held in place. Rusty's fingertips dug into the window ledge, toes balanced on Connor's back. "What in tarnation!" a high-pitched voiced yelled.

Both boys crumbled to the ground. Whirling around the side of the house, Judge Rounder swung a razor strop through the air. He caught Rusty by the arm and thrashed him. Rusty trotted a circle around the guardian of the orphan house, but was unable to get free of the grip. Connor sprinted away. At the main road, he turned and watched as Judge Rounder beat Rusty to the ground, then jerked him inside. When the door slammed, all went silent.

Connor stared, teeth clenched, perched on the balls of his feet as if ready to pounce. In his mind, he could see himself beating the tar out of Judge Rounder. But Mr. Rounder was a respected jurist who took in boys for the good of the community. Connor hated him for the bruises he saw on his friend. Beatings and an empty belly were hardly worth the bed Rusty got, and Connor wished Rusty could move in with him, but Mom had already said no. Sadly, he left, knowing there was nothing he could do, but as he walked, he calculated . . . first, Preacher Boy; second, the mines; and then Judge Rounder.

Connor continued up Notown Road and cut through his neighbor's backyard to jump the fence over to his house. He didn't need a lift to the open window. Earlier, he'd left a ladder against the wall. As he dropped into his room, his father sat on the bed, arms folded. "Thought I saw a bear," Connor said. "Went to check it out."

Pop pointed at the dirt on his shoes. "No fibbin', young man." He handed Connor a set of pajamas. "Mom finds you sneaking out and we will never hear the end of it. Now, where were you?"

"With Rusty and Herman," he said and looked at the floor.

His father sighed and glanced at the ceiling. "You've got the rest of summer to play, but promise me you'll be home before dark."

"Promise, Pop," he said, and crossed his fingers behind his back.

"Okay, get in your pjs," he said. "I told Mom I'd make sure you said your prayers."

Later on, lying in bed, looking out the window at the moon, Connor mused on the difference between his and Rusty's life. He was lucky to have a father who never hit him and a mother who only occasionally hollered. Could have done without the bossy sister, he thought and closed his eyes. But he didn't sleep easily. His rage at Judge Rounder overtook any annoyance he felt toward Bryson Pomeroy or some nameless mine owner and merged with images of the murdered Black Dahlia. Ghosts of the monster who tore her up hid in the shadows of his dreams. He jerked awake more than once as the dead woman clawed to be part of his landscape, to live behind his closed eyes.

The story continues in . . .
The Hunter of Hertha
By Tess Collins

Portrait by Bill Sturdivant

About the Author

A coal miner's granddaughter, Tess Collins was born and raised in a crater. Yes, really, a crater formed by the impact of an asteroid millions of years ago where her hometown of Middlesboro, Kentucky, was eventually built. Tess spent much of her childhood in a one room Carnegie Library reading around the room. She started at *Sally and the Bear* and ended with *War and Peace*, at which time she thought, "I want to do this."

She is the author of *THE LAW OF REVENGE, THE LAW OF THE DEAD, THE LAW OF BETRAYAL,* and *HELEN OF TROY.* Her non-fiction book, *HOW THEATER MANAGERS MANAGE,* is published by Rowman and Littlefield's Scarecrow Press. Ms. Collins received a B.A. from the University of Kentucky and a Ph.D. from The Union Institute and University.

Visit her website at www.tesscollins.com/

CPSIA information can be obtained
at www.ICGtesting.com
Printed in the USA
LVHW090441061221
705390LV00004B/320